THE A.

ACADEMY

BOOK ONE:

DARK ORIGINS

ANTHONY KALLAS

ACKNOWLEDGMENTS

I do not have a long list of acknowledgements unlike other authors. But it is only fair to thank the folks that made my dream of becoming a published author a reality.

First and foremost is Anthony C. Kallas…my Dad. He has been my guiding force in the literary world for my entire life. Emulating him from the earliest age, typing horrible little one-page stories on his typewriter (and eventually breaking it), watching him read every day as a child and then sharing the joy of reading with him in my adulthood has been a blessing. Thanks for everything Pop. This book wouldn't have been possible without you.

Tim Schulte, editor par excellence and owner of *Variance Author Services.* Your guidance and knowledge are second to none. Thank you for your patience and understanding. I am looking forward to collaborating on the rest of this trilogy and many more stories after that.

My son, Anthony C. Kallas III. My first Beta reader and my right-hand man. Thank you, Buddy. You rock! You helped make this dream come true. I am so proud of you.

To my mom, Sue Kallas, for always buying me the books that I loved, supporting my youthful nerd needs with comic books and Star Wars toys and forever being there when I needed her for anything and everything in life. There has never been a better mother.

To my best friend, Shawn Penny, Thanks for always believing in me and pushing me to be my best year after year. I can never repay the years of dedication Paizon.

To Timothy Walker and Terry Miles…Loyalty is the world's most underrated gift. Thank you for all the years of coffee, conversation, friendship and discussion.

Brian Compton, Rhys Bovie, Shawn Rogers, my brother Tim, Colby Penny, Caeleb Kallas and every other person that has sat and gamed with me, helping me to build up my imagination over thousands of hours of RPGs…You're a helluva crew!

And lastly, to my tenth-grade English teacher (Mr. Clark) who stood me up in front of the entire class (Shawn Penny was there) and told them all that I would never amount to anything because I was an athlete…How does it feel to eat your words?

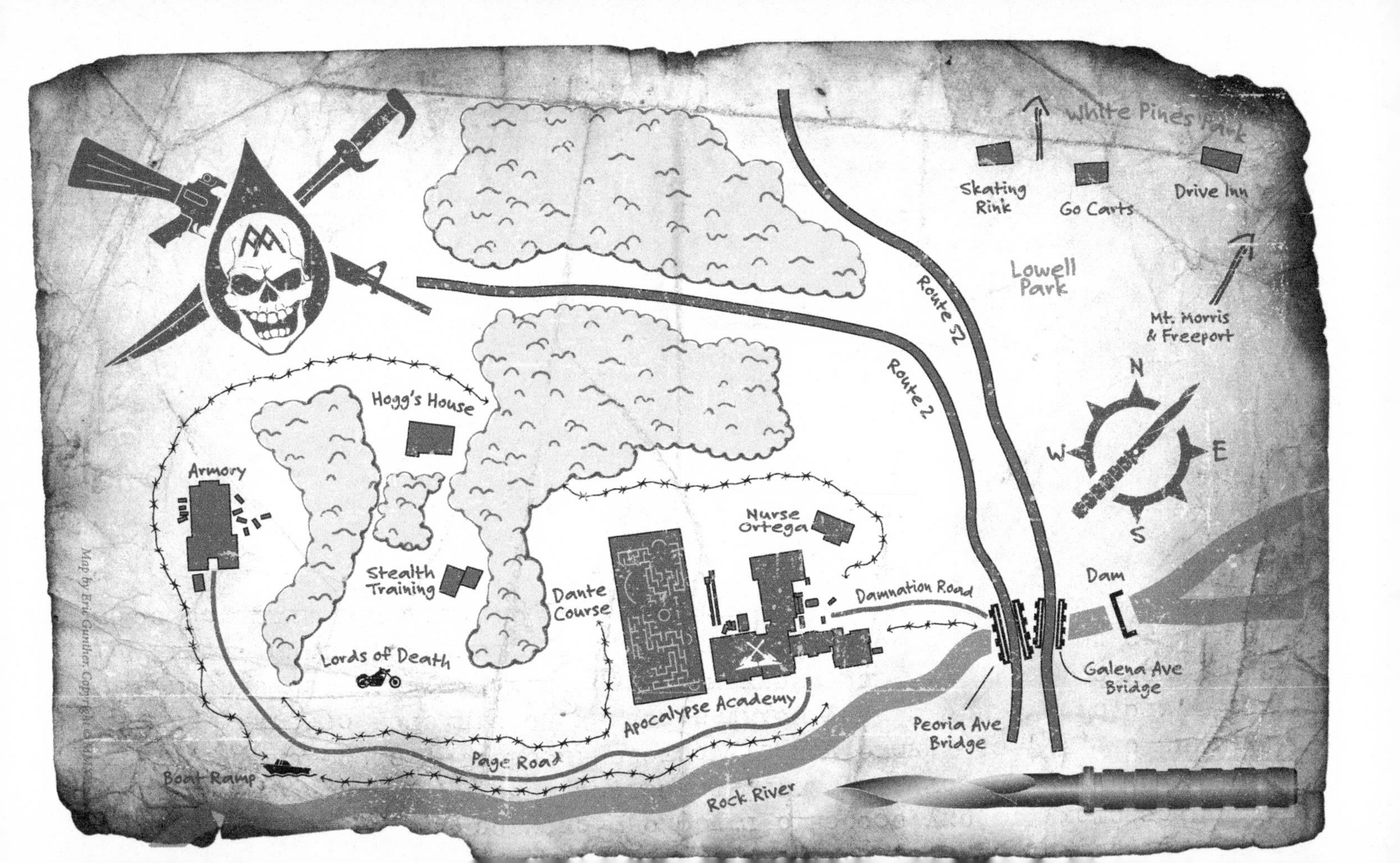
White Pines Park
Skating Rink
Go Carts
Drive Inn
Lowell Park
Mt. Morris & Freeport
N
W
E
S
Route 52
Route 2
Hogg's House
Armory
Nurse Ortega
Stealth Training
Dante Course
Damnation Road
Dam
Lords of Death
Apocalypse Academy
Galena Ave Bridge
Peoria Ave Bridge
Page Road
Boat Ramp
Rock River

The Apocalypse Academy

Book One: Dark Origins

Anthony Kallas

Prologue One

Ancient Sparta, 480 B.C

King Leonidas of Sparta silently sat, brooding over the scarred and blood-soaked battlefield, remembering the final words of the Pythia, Oracle of Delphi and High Priestess of Apollo, whom he had visited just days ago in her prophetic chambers at Delphi. There amid the vapors and the ancient columns she had foretold of a bloody fate for all of Sparta; especially for Leonidas and his warriors, who were destined to seek passage into the domain of Hades, God of the Underworld after the upcoming battle. A destiny that predicted not only his death as leader of the phalanx as well as the deaths of the three hundred Spartan warriors that would accompany him as his personal bodyguard to the pass of Thermopylae to stand against the invading forces of the Persian army. He had chosen to ignore the national festival of Carneia in favor of facing the Persians while the land could be scouted, prepared and best used to his tactical advantage. He was certain that the Gods would understand his lack of revelry in exchange for the thousands of Persian souls that he intended to offer them as tribute while he protected Greece from invasion. Once again, the Oracle's words came to his memory.

For you, inhabitants of wide-wayed Sparta,

Either your great and glorious city must be wasted by Persian men,

Or if not that, then the bound of Lacedaemon must mourn a dead king, from Heracles' line.

The might of bulls or lions will not restrain him with opposing strength; for he has the might of Zeus.

I declare that he will not be restrained until he utterly tears apart one of these.

But his prognosticated death was not what had him troubled. It was the greatest honor of a Spartan warrior to die in battle defending his homeland and he had long since set the thoughts of death aside as he entered battle. In fact, in his coin pouch, as did every Spartan warrior's, always contained at least two golden drachmas as payment to Charon, the skeletal ferryman of the river Styx for their passage when their destined time had come, and their mortal lives would end. War did not provide the courtesy of scheduling death ahead of time, so King Leonidas had seen to the distribution of the golden coins personally; to every man in his retinue before they ever left Sparta proper. What had truly troubled him had been the witch's final whispered words that had been for his ears alone, unheard by the many priests in attendance that he thought about as he descended from the high mountain in Delphi. It had been a warning that had instructed him to select only men with living Spartan sons to march to protect the pass at Thermopylae against the Persians. Those men were destined to die, yet their scions would one day save the world from the shadow of the abyss. Failure to follow the instructions would certainly result in not only death for his men, but inevitably spell apocalyptic doom for the future world that would one day need the deadly efficiency of Spartan warriors to defend it.

Upon returning to Sparta, he had been emotionally distraught over his meeting with the mystical woman. Selecting three hundred Spartan warriors based not upon their skills with shield, sword or bow but upon their ability to procreate male children had been unnerving enough. Leonidas had done as the Oracle had instructed despite the instructions forcing him to leave several superior warriors and sub-commanders behind. It had been extremely difficult to leave some of his most skilled veterans behind, especially those valiant and brutal warriors that had suffered injuries in battle to their manhood; preventing them from ever siring children but had instead resulted in the unforeseen good fortune of bestowing an almost bestial savageness to the men upon the battlefield.

But that had been only half of the instructions whispered on the wind from the opium laden Oracle as he had descended hand over hand, down Mount Parnassus.

Waiting for nightfall, he stood alone upon the balcony of his home with his wife. There he told his queen; Gorgo that the mystic had further instructed him to spirit those same children far from Sparta and scatter them by land and sea to the four winds, leaving no two Spartan children within one hundred leagues of any other Spartan. By doing this the Spartan bloodline would not die beneath the oppressing boots of the Persian War King as one day they would be needed to rise again as warriors to defend the world from an evil to which the likes of the Persians would pale in comparison. But how could they attain the fighting spirit of a Spartan warrior if they were denied the strict training at the agoge? Would they prosper or die as just another human, never knowing the glorious brotherhood of a Spartan phalanx entering the jaws of combat?

He felt guilty sending sons of Sparta away from their homeland, depriving them of their right to achieve glory, yet the Oracle was rarely wrong. So, he had entrusted his wife, the queen mother to send the sons of Sparta onto random paths through land and sea. Their destinations were hidden, so that their location could never be betrayed by any living being, even under the duress of torture. With regards to the need for education and training such as they would have received beginning at the age of six at the Agoge; Queen Gorgo convinced her husband to allow the children, some of which were infants, to be guided only by a single retired Spartan Warrior. These men were given knowledge of the full prophecy and instructed to train the children in both the Spartan ways as well as the ways of whatever new homeland they found in order to be best prepared for whatever maleficent evil the world would one day face. Despite knowing that the order was essentially an exile for life, all three hundred warriors donned their armor, took up spear, sword and shield and complied without complaint; eager for a last chance to serve the magnificence that was their homeland. To attain the glory that was Sparta's legacy. Whatever the evil was, a Spartan would stand ready.

A heavy pouch of gold taken directly from the coffers of King Leonidas, as well as a full set of Hoplite armor, a short sword, a spear and a dagger were all issued to the veterans prior to commencing their journeys. These weapons were of the finest quality and were to be used by the guardian but given over to the child when the time was right, and the youth had been adequately trained. In addition, educational materials ranging from books on mathematics to philosophy were crated up and sent along to ensure that the child would become intelligent in whichever corner of the world Zeus saw fit to place them.

Lastly, Queen Gorgo had told him that she had ordered goats to be sacrificed at the temples of Zeus, Hera, Apollo, Poseidon and Hades to seek the favor of the gods for the children's travels. Satisfied that he had met the visions of the Oracle to the best of his ability, Leonidas had donned his best armor, sharpened his spear to a razor's point, hefted his shield and led his entourage out of Sparta for what he knew would be the final time. There had been no fanfare. No tearful goodbyes. No emotional baggage…only a nod of resolution as he led his men into history.

Prologue Two

Xerxes Damned

Xerxes dangled from cold wrought iron manacles, his wrists bloody, as he hung above a boiling pit of human fat, down within the bowels of Hell. A palm-sized skeletal, white beetle stood precariously upon his cheekbone, balancing on emaciated flesh and sallow skin before plunging its inch-long mandibles into the side of his nose and burrowing its five-inch-long body into his skull. The once King knew what was to come from this torment. The beetle would nest deep in his skull and lay eggs. The eggs would then hatch, allowing the miniature creatures to freely feast on the soft flesh of his sinus cavity and brain before finally burrowing throughout his body, following the veins and arteries like game paths to the fresher and meatier portions of his body. There they would feast, until upon some unheard demonic signal they would surge outward, burrowing through all obstacles to reach the open air in a continual spray of bloody mist and chunks of innards. Then, the unholy insects would dive freely from his body only to be incinerated in the boiling lake of melted fat below.

But always one would remain. One beetle would stay balanced upon the curvature of his body, to begin the cycle again. Each day at dawn, his flesh regenerated to a semblance of its former muscular god-like stature. Then, each night, he continually suffered a curse of the damned, being eaten alive by the scarabs and scourged with the iron shod whips of the lesser demons that served as his jailers within this layer of Hell. He had prayed so many times for true death that he was certain that there was no god above to hear his pleas, and so he suffered each reoccurring mutilation stoically, learning to relish the pain as a harbinger of the coming dawn and the renewal of his flesh that it would bring.

When death had first claimed the Emperor of All that He Surveyed in 465 BC, it had come from the Commander of his own Imperial Guard or Hazarapat, the Commander of Thousands, with the assistance of one of Xerxes' favored eunuchs and a rebellion within the very immortals that he so coveted as his personal guard. Before his death he had sent many millions of enemies to their deaths and had earned an especially renowned place in the incalculable depths of the abyss due to the cruel and calculating manner in which he had slaughtered numerous thousands of Greek Hoplites and Spartans in his attempts to cross the Hellespont

and capture the then city-state of Athens. Feeling death's cold touch upon the blade of Artabanus's sword as it entered his belly; the once mighty King of Kings had sworn to rise again from the very bowels of Hell to resume his rightful rulership of the world. Grasping the sash of Artabanus, the mighty king fell to the floor, dragging the bearded military man with him. Golden coins spilled forth from the Commander's pouch, spinning and rolling upon the marble floors of Xerxes palace. Greek Drachmas…and the Emperor knew why he had been betrayed. Greed had guided the sword deep into his belly, and so to would greed force the betrayers to serve him long after death.

Calling forth the blackest magic of the Persian Empire, Xerxes cupped a handful of his own blood as it spilled from his torn intestines. With a strength born of purpose, he forced the sword's metal blade deeper into his own abdomen until he could reach his attacker where he smeared the foul-smelling bowel blood across the former Commander of the Imperial Guard's face. Strength fading, he cursed the man and his Imperial Guards to servitude beyond death for their betrayal and murder. Then, he used his dying breath to cast his soul from his body before it could be captured by the Hell Spawn and dragged into the nether realms for eternity. As his spirit soared away, Xerxes last sight was of his once faithful Nubian eunuch Aspamitres as he delivered a death blow to the now vacated corpse with his thick bladed scimitar. Xerxes watched in horror as his head was sheared from his body and rolled upon the marble floor of the throne room, bleeding upon his favorite rug.

Seeking vengeance upon the cowards that betrayed him, the dead king thrust his ethereal spirit through the mystical veils of time and space as fast as the soul could be projected until he located the Persian court sorcerer Merodak. The king and Merodak had discussed a plethora of scenarios regarding his demise over the years, from old age to treachery and even murder. In each scenario, the king and sorcerer had agreed to rebind his soul to his slain body upon the blood consecrated black alter of both Angra Mainyu, the Persian god of dark evil and the demonic entity known only as Dev, a ruthless and immoral god of war. Through the blessings and granted powers of these dark Gods, Xerxes would rise again to wreak merciless slaughter upon those that had betrayed him. Merodak had done as he had been bidden. Securing the dead king's corporeal body from where it had been cast deep inside of a charnel pit, he rescued it from the ripping beaks of the sand vultures despite receiving several grievous wounds of his own in the process. Placing the body upon the altar, Merodak began to chant ancient words of power and scribing sigils of resurrection and vengeance upon the ground in the blood of a dozen slain infants, the sorcerer began drawing forth the magic of the ley lines that bound the mortal and immortal worlds together. Xerxes could see the slashed flesh of his body mending before his sight. Though in this ethereal state he could not produce a tear, he knew that he would have been emotionally moved at the dedication and devotion of his loyal court mystic at a time when so many others had turned on him. He would ensure that the man was rewarded with a king's ransom when the job was complete.

As the ceremony came to a close, Merodak used an obsidian dagger to slit the throat of the lone sacrificial virgin girl over the altar, therefore consecrating the enchantment to the gods. It was only in that final moment, as his mended body and spirit rejoined upon the altar and he first opened his mortal eyes that Xerxes realized that he had been betrayed yet again. The blood-black sigils began to glow with an unholy blue light. As the symbols glowed before his newly repaired eyes, he saw that the markings had not been consecrated to Angra Mainyu and Dev as he had instructed. But instead, his soul had been bound to Dahaka, the eternal Lord of death and deceit. As the oily black substance boiled into the room and began to take up the frightening visage of the Death God, Xerxes turned to Merodak, fire and bloodlust filling his reformed eyes.

"I shall not go to the underworld alone sorcerer." The rejuvenated king spat at the mystic through gritted teeth. "I do not know why you have betrayed me, but for that dishonor I curse you to serve me for all of eternity in Hell!"

Before the sorcerer could utter a single word of magic in defense, Xerxes snaked out with one massive hand and lightning fast snatched up the obsidian dagger from where it sat upon the alter still covered in sacrificial blood and rammed the knife upwards under the mage's chin. The blade penetrated flesh, bone and brain skewering the sorcerer. Holding the body aloft long enough to ensure that the light of life faded from his eyes, Xerxes cast the traitor to the ground, then began to stomp his golden sandal repeatedly upon the man's skull until the bone shattered as if made of an eggshell and splashed brain and blood throughout the chamber. There would be no resurrection of that body. Perhaps the mystic would be reborn as a camel or goat. Wiping his sandal upon the robes of the mage, the King of Kings calmly turned and faced the God of Death.

Prepared for the agony that was certain to come, Xerxes nodded only once to the Death God's black visage. The creature exposed five razor sharp talons from beneath its cavernous robes held at the end of long, sinewy arms, and thrust his clawed hand deep into Xerxes' chest. Strangely there was little pain. The king felt his flesh rip as the talons dug deeper into his rib cage. He ground his teeth against the clawed fingers as they tore through muscle and bone, seeking the beating warmth of his newly reformed heart. As the Death God wrapped his cold fingers around his life-giving organ, Xerxes uttered not a sound. As a ripping

sound reached his ears, followed by an acute but short-lived pain in his chest. The last thing that he experienced as his body died for the second time in just as many days was a thudding sound that reached his ears signifying that his corpse had fallen to the floor.

That had been an eternity ago and without the rise and fall of the sun to mark time; it was irrelevant to guess at how long he had been a captive anyway. Time held no measure in Hell, except in the refreshing of the spiritual body so that the demons could begin their tortures all over again. A trio of hook-faced lesser demons stopped before him, looking at the pathetic human with such contempt that their presence began to annoy him. Slowly they unraveled their wicked metal barbed whips and began to crack them in the air beside him. He had seen this attempt at intimidation so many times that their actions had begun to bore him. Spitting a wad of phlegm upon the closest creature, he called out to them with a taunt of his own.

"Come beasts. Get on with your duties. The sooner you complete them, the sooner I will sleep and dream of my freedom as I did with the others that came before you. Your lack of creativity bores me."

The comments enraged the demons, driving them into a fury-soaked rage that flayed his skin and broke his bones with each stinging bite of the lash. Blood poured from his torn flesh and the broken bones canted his limbs into odd angles, but still, he did not lose consciousness. Perhaps he had been wrong and these three, particular demons *were* more skilled than their predecessors.

Dahaka, the Demon God of Death, appeared next to Xerxes dangling, broken body. One of the God's three enormous dragon-like heads leaned forward and reached out a forked tongue, lapping up the blood from one of Xerxes' open wounds across his chest. The creature's acidic saliva hissed as it touched the once king's chest, burning him wickedly. Little trails of white smoke drifted upward from the now cauterized wounds. Short black horned spikes and crimson scales covered the visages of the heads to either side, while the head in the middle proudly wore thick, massive ebony horns jutting upward from its red brow like twin spears of curved death. Hugely muscled arms bore the creature along over apelike legs as it moved, and a segmented scorpion's tail of gigantic proportions wove like a cobra over the Demon Lords' shoulder while venomous creatures draped the rest of his body.

Reaching out with an enormous claw the size of a chariot wheel, the god grasped Xerxes' chin and yanked his head upward, forcing the King of Kings to look directly into the beast's volcanic red eye. Blood trickled from where the demon's claw sank into the man's cheek and Xerxes wondered if just maybe the massive god had skewered the scarab that had entered his face in roughly the same area as the claw. Reaching its second hand upward until the points of its claws barely penetrated the flesh of Xerxes' upper chest, the Demon Lord slowly drew the talons downward slicing thin ribbons of flesh that rippled in the humidity of the boiling fat below. Xerxes' organs threatened to spill from beneath his skin, but the cuts had been so precise that the intestines merely bulged outward in a gray-white bubble rather than dump into the lake below. Again, he had been denied death in a horribly cruel fashion.

The Demon God spoke, its voice a low, menacing growl that reverberated throughout the cavernous abyss surrounding them causing micro-flares of splashed molten fat to jut upward with each syllable.

"I have heard your pleas." The God of Death stated in a voice of Hell thunder. "I have the power to grant you death. Do you seek death?" Dahaka the Death Demon placed a taloned claw against Xerxes' navel, his claw barely penetrating the tortured man's abdomen with a smoky hiss.

"Yes…" Xerxes begged through clenched teeth as he fought to keep from passing out with each new pain. "Kill…me!"

The Demon God laughed. It was a rumbling sound of long promised death. Lava fat bubbled and jumped in the molten lake below Xerxes. "If I grant you this mortal death that you so desire, will you swear fealty to me with your *immortal* soul?"

"Yes…"

"You will serve me for all eternity as my Hellborn General of the undead and in return I will offer you destructive vengeance unparalleled in both written and oral history upon the humans who embarrassed you through defeat. Into your army I will commission one hundred demons to fill the rotten mortal shells of your long-deceased Immortals. Furthermore, I shall deliver unto you the means of returning the dead to shambling, ravenous un-life. The apothecaries of the modern world seek to penetrate the mystical veil between mortality and the blackness of the eternal void. By using their modern magic and sorcery, I have taught these same apothecaries how to breach the veil. Their feeble minds have manufactured a machine of war that they have named the Hadron Collider. By searching for the mysteries of the Gods they have unwittingly delivered mankind's downfall right into your hands by creating the very portal that shall allow you to release my hellborn virus into their world. There it will germinate in their very midst, causing the dead to rise as your servants. Your rule shall know no equal. Humanity shall fall before you, whether it is from the plague of undeath or the return of your blade into the world.

The fool humans will seek to contain their discovery behind words and false safeties when in truth they are cultivating their own self-perpetuating doom through their very hubris. Only when my hellborn virus escapes its containment and the walking dead have scourged the earth clean of humanity will my bloodlust be satiated. Only when the last scions of ancient Sparta fall, and I have conquered all that there is to conquer upon the domain of man; shall I grant you the finality of immortal death and eternal peace. Do you willingly and knowingly consign your soul to be bound under my spell by these terms, in a manner that is unbreakable by word, action or deed in your name or by others?"

"Yes…" Xerxes again replied. He did not know what a Hadron Collider was, but he was willing to accept almost any deal to escape his tortures. "I accept you, Dahaka; Demon Lord of Death and deceit as my one and only lord and master. I serve your will as general of the forces of Hell and will take honor and pride in delivering the destruction of the Spartans to your throne room, for their souls to be feasted upon at your pleasure. Grant me death and the ability to rise again alongside the Immortals in your name so that I may slake the very fires of perdition with their blood."

"Good…" The Demon God twirled an enormous claw deeper into Xerxes' intestines, gently tugging a few inches of the man's innards through the savaged rib cage. Blood ran freely down the creature's cracked nail and across his scaled hand; dripping in small rivulets of crimson rain that sizzled upon striking the lake of melted fat. The Demon's snakelike tongue flicked out, lapping at the falling blood. Savoring the taste of the man's soul contained within each drop. "Prepare yourself mortal. This will not be pleasant I assure you." The Demon God said with a wicked grin that flashed three-foot-long teeth in front of Xerxes' face so close that the doomed man-king could see his own reflection upon the enamel of the enormous fangs.

Before the tortured man could react or reconsider his chosen path of fate, the Demon sank the clawed fingers of both hands deep into the lacerations that had shredded the man's chest. Gore and steaming organs fountained outward as the sternum and rib cage of the King of Persia was torn asunder with such savagery that the watching lesser demons quailed at the sight. Exposing the beating heart of its prisoner, the Demon God reared back its massive jaws and plunged his yellowed teeth into Xerxes' chest cavity. Clamping its teeth together, the Demon worried its head side to side like a great crimson shark, tearing the organ free of its protective muscles and gulping the bloody prize down its throat. Xerxes screamed forth all his remaining air in one mighty shout of mortal fear and abject terror. Drawing itself up to its full height, the beast then rammed the razor-sharp talons of its right hand deep into its own chest. Wrapping its fingers around its own heart, the Demon used its claws to surgically slice a chunk of its own heart free, bisecting the crimson and black organ. The creature then rammed the still warm organ into Xerxes' chest. Slivers of black, wormlike ichor immediately snaked out of the demon heart, binding muscle and restructuring arteries to allow blood to again begin beating throughout the Xerxes' body. Muscles sewed themselves together, and bones re-knitted, enclosing the man's now demon cursed heart once again with a whole rib cage. New pink flesh covered the orifice, leaving only pale purple scars where the demon had torn into the man.

Xerxes could only dangle limply from his chains while the Demon God's ichor rebuilt his body. When at last, he could raise his head from where it lay upon his own chest, he only had a microsecond to acknowledge the clawed finger that poked through his eye socket and plucked out his right eye like a grape. White hot pain blossomed within his skull as the orb popped loose, hanging from a bloody chord, tearing free of the optical nerve with a slight ripping sound. The demon then clawed at its own yellow and red slitted eye from its socket and rammed the replacement into Xerxes' head. Flesh bulged and the oversized orb shattered Xerxes' facial bones as it was unceremoniously forced into place by Dahaka's all-powerful hand. The king could only thrash weekly as the black ichor ebbed out of the demonic eye and wheedled its way along the optical path, burrowing deep into his brain. Xerxes could feel the Demon God's malevolence as the ichor driven tentacles bore through his brain, revealing his every thought to his new master.

Motioning to the barbed tail lesser demons that stood nearby, scourge whips forgotten, Dahaka indicated that they should hold the man firmly, preventing him from moving or escaping. Severing the chains with a single claw, the God of Death allowed Xerxes to fall into the lesser demons' arms as they drew him to the cliff side, and away from the charnel pit of melted fat. Hanging limply between the two Hell spawn, the man did not have the will to resist as the lesser demon on his right reached up a clawed hand to his hair and violently jerked his head backward. Dahaka slashed one of his mighty claws across his own wrist, opening the darkly pulsing demonic vein and allowing blackish-green ichor to drip poisonously upon the ground where it sizzled into the dirt and gore of Hell's floor. Reaching up with its undamaged claw, the demon lord pried the human's jaws apart, holding them open as wide as the socket would expand with its thumb claw. Carefully it placed its damaged wrist above the man's open mouth, allowing its demon blood to run freely into Xerxes's mouth and directly down his throat. Thick, black smoke roiled out of the man-king's esophagus and gullet as the poisonous ichor burned through the walls of his intestines and corrupted his blood fully. No sound escaped Xerxes' lips as the lesser barbed demons finally let his unconscious, smoldering body fall into the yellow, sulfurous slime.

"Sleep now and recover your strength my vassal. When you rise, you shall know that you have become a part of me. You have become an extension of my hatred and desire for the destruction of the human perversity that inhabits the mortal world. The mortals and their Spartans shall not stand before our wrath for we are Legion. The dead shall walk and serve in my name and you shall rule over them all, as my General. May the mortal world be wary. Our coming foretells of the Apocalypse!"

Prelude: Z Night – A Night of Terror

Madness and horror orchestrated a veritable symphony, as the world spun out of control in a torrent of terror filled with sights and sounds. Strobing bursts of light illuminated the chaos, pulsating of red and blue, as emergency vehicles screamed through the night and the city's public servants attempted to restore order to the bloody and dying urban environment. Amber lights intersected across buildings and reflected along the black asphalt of the street as a tow truck careened into a power pole destroying the power converter as it fell to the ground. Brilliant white sparks and jagged blue-white electrical discharges arced through the night sky in a simulation nearing a Fourth of July fireworks display, as power converters were ripped from their moorings.

On the roadway to Sparta, Wisconsin, as it had been in every metropolitan area throughout the world following the implosion and the subsequent abyssal rift created by the Hadron Collider; chaos caused by the rise of the undead ensued. Beyond the emergency vehicles, people of all ages flooded into the streets of suburbia adding to the confusion that was Z night. Police officers in blue nylon, firefighters in yellow rubber suits and ambulance drivers in white jumpsuits ran from person to person attempting to aid the injured. Soldiers clothed in olive green waved weapons of various calibers attempting to intimidate and command the panicked civilians into a semblance of order within the small Wisconsin town. Intermingled within the crowds; freshly risen Z's drooled bloody ropes of infected saliva as they tried to chew upon the nearest fresh meat that ran by, like escaped hounds chasing a car on the highway.

The sense of sound was distorted by the continuous sharp reports of innumerable handguns and rifles discharging. America was known for its civilian armaments. Occasionally the deeper bass report of a shotgun, a weapon prominently used for hunting in the Midwest, punctuated the pop-pop-pop of smaller caliber weapons. Crackling electricity and wailing sirens flooded the night, from the emergency vehicles that raced from one critical call to the next.

The stampeding footfalls of those people lucky enough to initially avoid the terror that had invaded their small town in the dark of night fell in irregular patterns. Like rabbits before the hunter's gun, the people could not decide whether to run or to hide. Order had disrupted into chaos as the living were running in fear for their lives, chased by packs of virus infected living dead. The survivors crushed against the barricades of police and soldiers who sought to prevent the infection from spreading beyond the town proper. Wooden posts and boards shattered as screams of pain and terror overrode the electronically magnified commands for order screamed by commanders into the patrol car and military public address systems. Above the din, the undead moaned in unison and all pretenses of command and control were lost.

Over the din, a commanding voice bellowed to his men, issuing an order that had not been issued from an American against an American in more than two hundred years.

"Shoot anyone bleeding! We can't let the pandemic spread! Fire…fire…fire!"

And as disciplined soldiers do; they followed orders. Automatic weapons opened fire into the charging crowd. The wounded fell as the bullets tore into and through their bodies. Blood splattered in crimson arcs and drenched those persons running nearest to those that were shot. Unable to discriminate between the wounded and blood splattered, the order became indiscriminate and the selective fire became a fully automatic massacre. Bodies fell by the hundreds and the unidentified commander wept for he knew that he had just secured his place in history's infamy. Raising his military issued sidearm to his own temple, the Captain pulled the trigger without a single word to his men, blowing his brains out and dropping his body among the legion of corpses that littered the roadway.

As the last bullet was discharged and the night fell silent, a single Sergeant surveyed his dead Captain, kicked his corpse as a coward and barked commands to the soldiers who stood around him.

"Alpha, Bravo and Charlie teams sweep the houses. These pukes won't be dead for long and we don't have the ammunition to keep them down permanently! We know the virus will reanimate anyone with a brain in a very short amount of time so let's move people. Any survivors are to be mustered back here in fifteen mikes! Remember that the children on the list are our priority mission. Extract them first. All other survivors are secondary. Be careful and do not take any chances. If they are bitten…shoot them in the head and cross them off the list. You can't save 'em. If they are clean but resist or refuse to come back to the rally point for extraction out of this shit storm, let them go. Make sure they know that they are on their fucking own. We won't be coming back here again to save their sorry asses. We've lost enough Americans today."

The teams spread out as they had been trained to do through hours upon hours of intensive Special Operations training. Not just normal Spec Ops type stuff like blowing things up and rappelling from buildings. These soldiers had been specifically trained to deal with a biological or chemical attack exactly like the one they were currently experiencing. The only difference was that they had not expected the attack to occur on American soil. But when you had an idiot for a President that allowed thousands of unvetted refugees from third world countries into the United States, what could they have really expected. The sergeant accompanied the first team as it peeled off into the suburb on the left while the other two teams kept moving ahead, deeper into the town. A call from his point man brought him to the front on the double.

"Sarge! Need you up front most Riki-tik! You ain't gonna believe this shit!"

Reaching the open doorway of a two-story brownstone, the NCO looked to his point man who stood just inside the foyer, looking upward. The soldier said nothing but nodded his head. Looking up, the sergeant saw the sight that epitomized the chaos of Z night within his mind. High above the soldiers, standing at the apex of the homes' curled white banister, a muscular, dark haired teenage boy stood quietly surveying the carnage and hell that the undead pandemic had brought to his quiet little corner of the world. Bodies lay battered, broken and sprawled in various positions at the boy's feet, upon the stairs and down the hallway behind him.

From one hand dangled a slick black plastic chord, carefully wrapped around his wrist and fingers. At the end of the chord, a gore covered iron twisted and swung slowly; blood and brain matter slowly dripping onto the plush white carpet below it. In his other hand the boy gripped a wooden baseball bat that had once belonged to a homerun hitter at legendary Wrigley field, but was most recently used to shatter the skulls of infected strangers, friends and loved ones. Crimson splattered gore marked the placement of each homerun swing along the bat's smooth wooden barrel and the direction of each swing had been painted along the wallpaper in bloody arcs. A hollow look haunted the youth's eyes as if his very soul had been pulled from his body. The teen did not even acknowledge the soldiers entering his home; he just stared out into the night through the open windows.

Not wanting to frighten the boy further, the sergeant issued orders to contain the teenager using hand signals. Moving with the sure footedness of dozens of combat missions, the soldiers quickly scaled the blood-soaked stairwell. As the sergeant mounted the stairs, a door burst open and a woman wearing a pink bathrobe burst through, knocking the boy to the floor. Baseball bat and iron flew in opposite directions as the teenager grappled with the "Z". Holding the creature up from his body by the neck, his free hand scrambled about madly for anything that could be used to fend off the infected woman. Leaping over the dead corpses on the stairs, the sergeant struggled to help the boy. He got onto the landing just as the valiant teenager grasped a butcher knife from the blood-slick floor and shoved it into the terry cloth wearing woman's mouth. The blade slid in effortlessly and the "Z" began to spasm and twitch, instantly releasing the teenager before collapsing on top of him. Grasping the robe with both hands, the Sergeant heaved the undead creature up off the boy and over the balcony railing, eyes frantically searching the boy for bite marks. Gently he picked up the teenager by both arms, guiding him to his feet. The teen offered no resistance. The boy wobbled; his eyes glazed and staring off into the distance in an unfocused daze. Kevlar coated gloves gently but firmly eased the impromptu weapon from the boy's rigid fingers and cast it aside to clatter against the floor. Still the boy showed no reaction.

"Was he bitten?" a muffled female voice asked from within the confines of her chemical protective suit.

"Too early to tell with all of this blood and shit all over him." The sergeant replied. "I don't see any obvious punctures or bite marks on his exposed skin, but it's tough to say until he is hosed off and run through the standard decontamination protocol."

"Agreed." The female voice said.

"Corporal. Tranq' his ass and put him in 'cuffs and leg irons. I want full level five restraints. The last thing we want is for a fresh Z to turn in the middle of transport to the Academy and eating the face off some goddamn newbie." The Sergeant ordered.

The corporal hesitated.

"Ummm Sarge?" the junior NCO asked "If we can't be sure that a person is uninfected, orders are to terminate the subject with extreme prejudice. No exceptions."

"I know what the fuck orders say corporal!" the sergeant growled menacingly, annunciating each syllable carefully. "That order came from a chicken-shit officer who pissed his pants at the first sight of combat, then ate a bullet because he was ashamed of being a pussy. I'm in command now. That boy will be fine. Do as I ordered with him, or you will find your ass humping it back to the Academy through Z's galore and then you will find your fucking ass on latrine duty for the next month! You care to argue orders anymore boy?"

"Roger that Sarge! Jeez, I was just trying to help!"

"Good. Now move your ass and assist Ortega in securing the boy's restraints before I shove my boot so far up your ass that you will start burping shoe polish!"

Click, click, click went the hand and leg cuffs as they were secured around the boy's wrists and ankles. A thin but sturdy chain connected the cuffs together behind the boy's back. A sharp sting followed at the boy's elbow as the hooded female shoved a needle through flesh and vein. The initial stick was followed almost immediately by a sensation of warm numbness as the tranquilizer flooded the boy's system.

Involuntarily, the boy's eyes closed, and his breathing became slow and deep. Two soldiers slowly lowered the teen onto a green canvas litter. The teenager was completely unaware of the plastic oxygen mask that was strapped firmly over his nose and mouth.

Without another word, the Special Operations team moved as one back out of the house. The litter carrying the teenager was kept at the center of the formation to provide maximum protection for the boy in case the undead attacked. Beside the youth, the sergeant walked silently, his M-4 held at the ready. Unbeknownst to the sleeping boy, the surviving senior military advisor in charge of the operation known as "Project Orphan" looked down at him with a critical eye. The boy was a scrapper that was for certain. To have gone through what he did in that home alone was enough to make even seasoned military men go bat-shit crazy. He'd seen it plenty of times before in the Middle East, Somalia and other war-torn countries. He silently hoped that the boy's youth would provide enough mental resilience to the horrors that he had seen during the nights since Z day. If not, the boy could psychologically end up like a Z for the rest of his life. Mindless and blank.

Lifting his chemical mask up over the bridge of his nose, the sergeant spit an enormous gout of black tobacco juice out through his pursed lips, and then resealed the mask tightly around his face. His mind still puzzled over the boy. His hopes silently intermingled with his fears for the boys' wellbeing. He didn't want the boy to become a Z; in mind or in physical reality after knowing everything that the teen had already endured.

"No" the sergeant said aloud to no one in particular as he considered the possible outcomes of the child's fate. "If it comes down to that, I'll shoot him myself. I owe his father at least that much."

The brawny NCO watched silently as the litter was slid into the back of the olive drab five-ton military truck. Grasping the metal handle on the truck's rear gate wall, the sergeant swung himself up into the bed. Ensuring that his team was all aboard, he slammed the metal gate shut. Standing up, he surveyed the small town. Buildings burned in several places and smoke hazed the land and sky like a perverse fog. Through the gray air, waves of undead figures first shambled; then ran full speed for the military vehicle.

"Fuck!" the sergeant yelled as he slapped the side of the truck hard with three sharp raps. "Ortega, we got Z's on our six! Neighborhood sweep is compromised! Get us the fuck out of here or we are dead meat!"

The NCO and two other soldiers quickly shouldered weapons and selectively fired on the undead. Several leading bodies tumbled to the ground in a splay of arms and legs. The soldiers did not know if any of their shots were kills, but a dozen bodies rolled end over end into the onrushing horde. The resulting tumble of bodies, as the unthinking corpses tripped over each other, bought the team time to get the large truck moving in a grinding of gears. The agonized moans of the undead filled the air as the truck rumbled safely away.

Leaning his helmeted head against the truck's sidewall, the sergeant pulled the chemical mask free and tossed it on the bed. He hated wearing the fucking thing. Just as the truck reached full speed, the heavy canvas wall pulled aside and Ortega, the teams' resident nurse, silently pulled herself into the truck's bed.

"Good fuckin' way to get shot Ortega." The sergeant stated noncommittally, spitting a mouthful of chewing tobacco juice onto the metal bed of the truck. "What if the guys thought you were a Z?"

The nurse just shrugged and mumbled something about men and a lack of self-control that the NCO missed over the roar of the truck's massive diesel engine. Dropping down next to the sergeant, she silently studied him for a minute before speaking. She noted that the sergeant sat nonchalantly against the wall of the truck, with his M-4 resting lightly across his lap. She couldn't help but notice that the barrel of the weapon never strayed from where it was pointed at the teenage boy on the litter, nor did the big man's finger stray from where it rested just above the trigger. He looked very tired.

Nodding her head at the boy, she spoke just loud enough for the sergeant to hear over the trucks' noise.

"I heard he put up a helluva fight." She said, "I thought I would take a look at him while we were driving to see if he was injured if that's ok with you?"

The sergeant just shrugged. "Be my guest but be careful. We don't know if he's gonna turn yet. Who's driving?"

"Surfer."

"That's just fucking great. Wonder if the drive away from the Z city will rank up there with his Great White shark story? Probably be a million-man Z march when he's done."

Ortega smiled. She had heard the story of Surfer riding the ultimate wave and jumping the gaping jaws of a Great White shark on his surfboard at least ten times since she had joined the team. Each time the wave grew in height and the shark grew in length. At the last telling, the beast was at least twenty-five feet long.

"Probably." She agreed. Looking back at the boy she spoke aloud. "Why'd you take the risk for him Hogg? The Colonel's gonna shit kittens when he hears you went against his orders."

"He was on the list. Besides, the boy had twenty-six confirmed "Z" KIAs and the pacification of his own father, mother and three siblings. Kid is tough as nails and deserved the chance. Besides, he will probably make a good team leader if he survives this."

The nurse gently lifted the sleeping boys' eyelids and shone her penlight into the eyes.

"His pupils are dilated. Probably from the tranquilizers."

Pulling her stethoscope out of her thigh cargo pocket, she placed the end against the boy's chest, mindful to avoid the dried gore.

"His breathing is shallow and labored. Did he suffer a head trauma?"

Sergeant Hogg shrugged his broad shoulders. "Unknown" was all he said.

"He's in shock and his body is shutting down. I need him at the facility stat if we are going to save him. I don't have the equipment out here to care for him properly!" Immediately she began hooking electrodes to the boy's chest.

Hogg turned and pounded on the truck wall with a clenched fist.

"Surfer! Where the hell are we? How much time until we arrive at the Academy?"

The California native replied in his native slang.

"Dudes and dudette; we are now passing Burger World on your right. Oh man, if you look closely you will note that the Z over there looks a lot like George Bush! Next stop, Apocalypse Academy in three mikes! I seriously have the munchies for a Burger World Mega-Burger deluxe! Whoo-hoo! Man, those things were great."

"Put the hammer down Surfer! Major medical issue back here! The boy's in shock!"

"Copy that Bro! We are shittin' and gittin'!"

Ortega's yell brought Hogg's mind back to the boy. The sergeant's eyes darted from the boy to Ortega's heart monitor. The green line was bouncing faster and faster as the constant beeping filled the bed of the military truck.

"Oh, shit Hogg! Help me! I'm losing him!"

Then the boy's monitor changed tones as the spiking green line fell flat across the screen and the incessant beeping became a single solid tone.

Chapter 1:
Entrance Day:
Week 1 Day 1

He looked slowly around the sterile classroom where a couple dozen fellow teenagers had been gathered. All walks of life seemed to be represented within the assembled boys and girls. Black, Asian, Caucasian, Hispanic and various intra-shading of the races had all been similarly attired in one-piece navy-blue jumpsuits and black combat boots by an unknown benefactor. There was no delineation between male and female beyond the obvious physical distinctions. Noting the white, hospital style wristband on the arms of several of the teens, the boy looked down at his own wrist. There he found a similar identifying band securely attached. Turning the band slightly he noted a single word printed in large, dark print. It read **SPARTAN**. Remembering a trip to the hospital after breaking his wrist during a football game, the teen found it interesting that the band contained no other identifying information such as his Social Security number, blood type or even a doctor's name.

The band itself had been cinched snugly yet comfortably on his wrist. He tugged on the band experimentally, but the plastic seemed to be far stronger than it initially appeared, resisting his efforts to tear it off his arm. Holding his arm up towards the lighted ceiling of the room, he gave the band a closer inspection. Laced within the plastic were visible microcircuits and what appeared to be metal filaments woven between each board. That explained why the band did not break when he pulled upon it. What the microcircuits were for, he could only guess. Anyway, the band was not coming off without some sort of tool to cut it free.

At sixteen years of age, the boy was one of the older children in the room. Most appeared to be somewhere between his age and twelve although ages were hard to distinguish other than by best guess. Especially on the girls. Boys at least had facial hair to provide some idea of their maturity. Girls were anyone's' guess. They could look fifteen or twenty-five depending on makeup, physical development and maturity.

Personalities seemed to be just as diverse as the ages of the teenagers themselves. Some children sat quietly, lost in the haunted corridors of their own thoughts and memories. Perhaps they were remembering lost family members and friends or the tragedies that had surely befallen each of them since Z night. Others happily gabbed and gossiped freely with their neighbors seated in the parallel rows beside them as if they did not have a care in the world and had known the people seated next to them for their whole lives.

In the front of the room, near a large oaken desk flanked by an enormous whiteboard, sat a small knot of girls talking and giggling freely amongst themselves. Their eyes cast randomly across the room and when a new target of conversation was acquired, they would huddle back together and speak back and forth in hushed whispers and hidden smiles. The grouped looked almost conspiratorial in the way they evaluated the room and its various members.

To Spartan's left, a black male teenager sat quietly all alone, slowly flexing his biceps which threatened to split the sleeves of his navy jumpsuit. Obviously, the boy had been an athlete before coming to wherever they were now. Either that or he had the genetics of the Incredible Hulk because he was massive in stature. Spartan noticed the thick chords of muscle starting at the boy's bull like neck, across bowling ball like shoulders that tapered down his back at a forty-five-degree angle to his waist, creating a perfect "V". As Spartan watched, he noted that the teen idly rotated and squeezed a worn leather baseball in his huge hand. His hand seemed to locate the seams blindly and effortlessly on the baseball, casually swapping the grip from a fastball to a sinker to a curveball without ever having to look down.

To the rear of the room, a group of teenage boys seemed to be contenting themselves by verbally tormenting a chubby, younger Asian or possible Middle Eastern youth. The target of the abuse sat stoically looking straight ahead and attempting to ignore the bullies. The boy, whom Spartan decided was a very tan Asian youth, flinched as a rubber band snapped and released a folded paper hornet into the air. The V-shaped folded paper plowed through the boy's black bowl cut hair and struck him firmly on the side of the head with a resounding thunk that Spartan heard from across the room. This elicited great guffaws of laughter from the bully boys seated behind him. The Asian boy to his credit, never cried out in pain. He merely reached up a single hand and rubbed the spot on his scalp that had been stung.

Adjusting his round lensed glasses more firmly upon the bridge of his nose, the boy glared straight ahead at empty space, completely ignoring the bullies behind him. Though he was stoic, Spartan could see the tears that had welled up in the chubby lad's eyes as he quietly stood up and walked to the boy's restroom at the rear of the classroom.

Spartan continued to watch, knowing what was coming. Eager to hide his anguish by leaving the room, the boy had unknowingly made himself an easier target, hidden behind closed doors. Several moments passed as the toughs in the rear of the class whispered and laughed amongst themselves. Watching high fives and fist bumps being exchanged, Spartan gritted his teeth. He truly hated bullies. Then three of the boys, led by a rat faced, blond haired thug rose as one and entered the restroom behind their chosen victim.

"It's none of my business." Spartan thought to himself as he slowly turned back around at his table, facing the front of the room once again. He slowly began to drum his fingers on the tabletop to keep his mind off whatever maliciousness was occurring in the restroom. The classroom itself seemed to be the recipient of an electrical charge as the gathered teens silently anticipated the assault that was sure to come behind the tiled walls of the restroom. This was nothing new. Spartan had seen the same behavior in public schools since he was a child. There were always bullies. Wolves that preyed on the sheep of the social pecking orders.

Sure enough, moments later the heavy-set Asian boy could be heard pleading with the group of bullies to leave him alone. This was immediately followed by the sound of flesh repeatedly striking flesh and then cries of pain. Spartan clenched his jaw so hard that it began to ache.

"Ignore it…ignore it…" he thought to himself. *"It's none of your business."*

Glancing up, Spartan chanced to catch the soft brown eyes of one of the young ladies from the classes "giggle group" at the front of the room. Silently she pleaded with him to act. Spartan could tell by the mortified look on her pretty tan face that she wanted him to intervene on the Asian boy's behalf. Casting her eyes from Spartan to the restroom and back again, she silently mouthed "Help him" as the sounds of physical abuse continued to resonate behind the closed door. Spartan knew he was hooked. He had never been good at turning down a female's request under the best of circumstances. If there was a chance to earn points with a pretty girl by thumping a few bullies along the way, even better.

"Damn" he muttered as he placed his palms flat on the table, took a deep breath and stood up. This was probably going to end badly. *"What the hell"* he thought to himself. *"You only live once."* Besides, his own personal code of honor would not allow him to ignore the assault on a defenseless boy, even if the beautiful girl hadn't batted her long eyelashes at him. Looking towards the restroom door, he winced as a crashing sound echoed behind the door. Something, probably a trashcan, had been thrown, kicked or overturned loudly.

Steeling his jaw, he cracked his neck from side to side as he had done so many times during football warm-ups. Spartan adjusted his jumpsuit, pulled up the sleeves over his forearms and began to purposefully walk towards the restroom. Boys and girls alike quickly pulled their chairs out of Spartan's path. An aura of malice surrounded the teen. Someone was about to get hurt and those seated in his path did not want to be an accidental casualty or become collateral damage, but they did want to be close enough to witness the carnage firsthand. It was a strange paradigm that had its roots in every school.

A huge, heavy hand fell onto Spartan's shoulder. The hand was the size of a catcher's mitt. Looking back and up, Spartan saw the grinning brown face of the beefy baseball player grinning ear to ear, looking down at him from at least six inches above.

"Yo dawg, in Chi-town hoods we had punks like that. Granny always said the best way to git rid of them was to whup their tails so bad that they never want no more! I'm thinkin' that this is a good time to follow Granny's advice. What say we go whup some candy-ass?"

Spartan suspected that the bullies were about to truly understand the meaning of the phrase "Play ball!" probably at the expense of their teeth and bones.

"Yeah" Spartan replied, returning the grin. "Welcome to the Major Leagues." As he walked forward and shoved open the restroom door.

The three bullies at the rear of the group stood with their backs to the now open door, watching and cheering as unseen events unfolded beyond Spartan's line of sight inside the enclosed stall before them. Laughter was accompanied by the splash of water and a distinct gurgling sound of air being forced out underwater. Looking past the boys, Spartan saw the blond leader of the pack holding the Asian boy's face down into the toilet bowl, his fingers firmly wrapped through the Asian boy's bowl cut black hair. The Asian boy was struggling to keep his face out of the water, but his punches were muted by the angle that his head was being held downward. The boy's struggles became weaker as his oxygen bubbled out, as did his attempts to ward off the physical attack.

Anger filled Spartan's eyes like a red cape dropping before an enraged bull. His brain seethed with the desperate urge to pound the living shit out of these boys who seemed to be taking so much pleasure in hurting an innocent kid. The world had literally gone to Hell with the living dead stalking the Earth, and there was still an innate need to dish out pain from a group of these schoolyard bullies.

Crossing the tiled floor quickly, he lashed out with his booted foot, catching the first boy he came to squarely in the testicles from behind. The boy, thin by all standards, squealed in agony as he was lifted from the floor by the toe of Spartan's steel toed boot before falling off to one side of the stall. Spartan paid him no further thought other than to idly remember giving his field goal kicker a hard time during practice and that he would apologize if he ever saw him again. A good kick was invaluable.

As the skinny boy curled up in agony, his mouth seized into an "O" and his hands clenching his damaged genitalia, the fat boy next to him turned to see what the disturbance was. Spartan brought a smashing hammer fist down across the bridge of the tub of lards' nose. The resounding crunch of devastated cartilage was followed in rapid succession by an explosion of blood, snot and tears as Tubby's nose flattened under Spartan's fist. Grabbing the boy by his now bloody shirt, Spartan flung him backward into the baseball players' waiting arms. Spartan just had time to register the boy as he was spun upside down and slung into the mirrors above the sinks. Glass shattered and the resulting plop of heavy meat upon the tiled floor told Spartan that Fat Boy was out of the fight.

The third boy, a middle-sized youth, darted past Spartan wanting no part of either of the two warriors standing before him. Spartan let him go, trusting the giant to bring the pain to the boy. Instead, he focused his eyes upon the leader of the pack. His eyes burned with a silent fury. Facing the blond boy, Spartan spoke through gritted teeth.

"I will ask you only once. Let…him…go!" he snarled.

To the bully's credit he actually laughed aloud, a wide smile crossing his face as he released the boy's hair.
"Sure…sure…Just havin' a bit of fun with the boy. That's all. A lark to blow off a bit of steam ya know? It was all in good fun. Really. No permanent harm done."

The Asian boy fell to the side of the toilet, gasping for air. Spartan looked down at the wet teenager and was almost gutted across the abdomen as the blond-haired boy slashed a hidden knife through the air in front of him. Backing quickly, Spartan took up a defensive fighting stance. He knew how to fight someone with a knife thanks to years of Aikido lessons that his parents had insisted upon. Gauging the blond boy's technique, he knew that this was no amateur. Slowly the knife wove through the air forming figure eight patterns. Spartan never let his gaze waver from the blade. As his Sensei had said, it was much better to receive an offhand punch to the head or body than an unprotected slice from a knife.

The two teens circled each other, both looking for an opening to strike. Spartan caught sight of the youth's white plastic wristband before him. It read "**CUTTER**".

"Figures." Spartan thought.

The boy feinted to the left, slashing with his knife, and then threw a stiff jab with his right hand. Spartan's forearm shot upward in a practiced block. Relying upon his years of training, Spartan snapped a front kick to the boy's hip driving him backward. In and out the two teenagers circled, throwing punches and kicks. Slashing outward, Cutter scored a hit on Spartan's forearm, creating a thin, bloody line.

"First blood mate!" he sneered.

Rage filled Spartan's mind. Furiously he began to rain punches and kicks towards Cutter's head, abdomen and legs. The blond-haired boy managed to block many of the blows, however several found their mark splitting the teens lip and marring the boy's face with a black eye. Seeing an opening,

Spartan drove a kick full force into Cutter's stomach. The force of the kick drove the air from the boy's stomach, launching his legs from beneath him and causing Cutter to collapse onto his knees losing his knife and gasping for breath. Spartan kicked the fallen knife off towards the stalls.

"Not so funny when you're the one that can't breathe is it Cutter?" he asked the fallen gang leader.

Hearing an ongoing struggle behind him, Spartan turned to see that his gigantic comrade had grabbed the boy that had attempted to flee in a full nelson and was swinging him back and forth like a rag doll, cutting off his air supply. A huge smile beamed on the giants' face which reminded Spartan of a dog he had known once, as he played with its favorite toy. The imprisoned teens' lips were turning blue and his eyes bugged out of his pock-marked face as he flailed his feet and kicked wildly. One kick caught the metal trash can and spilled its contents across the floor. Desperate for air, the teen lashed his booted foot backward, narrowly missing the giant's unprotected groin and striking him on the inner thigh.

The giant's smile vanished in a snap as a thundercloud of anger crossed the powerhouse's face and his mind registered what the boy in his arms had just tried to do to him.

"Shouldn't have done that bitch. Now you gotta pay!"

The massive hands clenched tighter and Spartan saw the giant's torso and back muscles flex. Spinning the helpless teen through the air by his pinned arms, the powerful baseball player slammed the bully's face downward into the sink basin. Porcelain cracked and Spartan thought the boy's face probably did too. The once flailing feet now dangled limply as the athlete released the lock and let the unconscious boy slump to the ground in a heap.

Looking back down where the leader of the pack of bullies still kneeled, bleeding upon the ground, Spartan snarled an order at the teen.

"Get out!" Was all he said, malice and further threats of violence evident in his voice. Cutter would leave or he and his gigantic new friend would make him regret it.

"Sure" the boy said standing up in front of Spartan until the two boys were almost nose to nose "But this isn't over by a long shot!" he sneered.

"Whatever…" Spartan said looking at the forms of the prone bullies lying about the room, and the giant idly tossing a baseball up and down in one hand as he leaned against the wall. "It looks pretty over to me."

"You heard the man Dawg…start steppin'." The giant added with a grin.

Cutter turned and took a step towards the door. Spartan allowed the teen to walk off, even though every instinct was telling him to finish the fight. He needed to see to the Asian boy and make sure he was alright. Turning, he reached out a hand to help the smaller boy to his feet and out of the stall.

"You ok kid?" Spartan asked.

The boy nodded, water dripping from his forehead and chin.

"Yeah… a little humiliated but ok." He said quietly. Turning he spit on the floor away from Spartan. Reaching down beside the toilet, he picked up his glasses from where they had fallen and wiped the lenses on the bottom of his jumpsuit. Adjusting the glasses on the bridge of his nose, the boy turned an angry look towards Cutter and his fallen goon squad. Rage filled his chubby face and he yelled his disgust at Cutter. As the boy ranted his voice steadily rose in pitch.

"A freakin' swirly? Really?" He yelled "The world is filled with the undead that want to eat our guts for breakfast and you A-holes want to take the time to push my head down into a freakin' toilet? You're freakin' pathetic! I…watch out!"

The Asian boys' warning came a fraction of a second too late, spinning defensively; Spartan barely had time to dodge the knife blade that slashed for his eye. A flash of silver drew a bloody line beneath Spartan's eye across his cheekbone. Burning pain registered in his brain as he realized that he had been cut. Clasping a hand to his slashed face, he peered up through watering eyes at Cutter.

"I told you, this ain't over!" Cutter said and turned, sprinting towards the door.

The athlete launched his baseball at the fleeing teen, but Cutter either saw or sensed the ball as it flew towards him through the air. Ducking and twisting, the boy avoided the sphere and it crashed harmlessly into the wall beside his head. There was no hesitation as the blond leader of the thugs lurched out of the door and out of sight.

Spartan walked over to the paper towel dispenser, stepping over the prone bodies of the three unconscious teenagers on the blue tile floor. Grabbing a handful of paper towels, he wet them in the one sink left functioning and looked up to observe the wound in a shard of broken mirror that still hung from the wall. The cut was about three inches in length and ran directly across his cheekbone beneath his right eye. Cutter had definitely been intending to blind him. Satisfied that the cut wasn't too deep, he held pressure to the wound until the bleeding slowed and finally stopped.

Looking up he saw the big baseball player looking over his shoulder with an ear-splitting grin. The athlete clapped him on the back hard enough to rattle Spartan's teeth.

"Shit Dawg…You gone and got yo'self a war wound! Chicks dig that kinda stuff. Makes you all heroic and shit. I saw ol' girl lookin' all wide eyed at ya! You're the man!" he said laughing aloud and holding up a ham sized fist for a fist-bump. "Name's Benjamin Franklin Jackson. My friends call me Freak. Which coincidentally is wha' my wrist bracelet says too." He said displaying the white plastic band for Spartan to see.

Sure enough, the bracelet read "**FREAK**" in big, bold lettering. The name seemed to suit the giant.

Spartan held up his own wristband. "Spartan." He said, "Don't know how I got the name and to be honest…I don't remember my real name or much else really beyond a few days ago. Thanks for the help." He said, nodding at the boys still out cold on the floor.

"Shit Dawg, ain't nothin' but a thing." Freak replied with a smile. "Was like bein' back in Chi-town."

The smaller Asian boy shuffled over to Freak and Spartan. Spartan handed him a handful of paper towels.

"Thank you both. Those turds have been on my butt since St. Louis. I tried to ignore them. You see what I got for my troubles."

The boy paused as he wiped the last of the toilet water out of his hair and ears.

"Lee...Billy Lee" the boy finally said using a ridiculous James Bond accent that immediately cracked up Spartan and Freak. Then he held out his hand to both boys.

"Band says my name is **"TECHNO"**. He said displaying his wristband. "I really hope that's because of my computer proficiencies rather than the music. Techno music sucks! Country is the only way to go! I really do appreciate you guys' help. I really owe you one. That was getting so out of hand."

After a quick handshake, the three teens headed for the restroom door, pausing only once for Techno to deliver a vicious kick to the fat bully that was beginning to stir on the ground. The boy doubled back over in pain and moaned pitifully. The whimpering groan that escaped the boy's lips was not that different than the moans of the walking dead. Perhaps they were in perpetual pain too.

Walking back to their individual seats, Spartan met the gaze of the brown eyed girl that he had intervened at the behest of, at the front of the classroom. Her smile immediately stole the sting from the knife slash Cutter had given him beneath his eye. Spartan smirked and nodded once in the girls' direction when he saw her silently mouth "Thank you" and throw him a wink.

Looking back over his shoulder, Spartan saw that the fat kid and the skinny, weasel faced kid had returned to their seats. The third boy that Freak had face planted into the sink was lying with his head propped on his forearms, no doubt posed there by Cutter to avoid notice by whoever was in charge of this place. Cutter glared at Spartan so hard that he imagined the leader of the bullies was mentally finishing the job with his knife. Spartan smiled and flipped the boy the bird with his middle finger. Fuck him.

He had been here less than one full day and already he had made friends, made enemies, impressed a girl and wound up in a fight needing stitches. He wasn't exactly sure why but this seemed to be right in what he expected to be the normal course of actions in his life. If not perfect, then it was at least a good start or at least as good as he could expect in this screwed up, dead world.

A single white door opened at the front of the classroom, adjacent to the right side of the white board. A deep, growling voice that rumbled like a thunderstorm boomed from beyond the doorway.

"Attention! On your feet maggots! Officer on deck!"

From the tone of the voice, this wasn't an optional request, so everyone stood up except for one boy at the rear of the classroom who lay face down on his forearms: apparently blissfully asleep.

Chapter 2

The Offer

Four men wearing matching gray, white and black urban camouflage uniforms and wearing round, brown drill sergeant hats marched in unison to the front of the classroom. Simultaneously the men, obviously military from their precise movements, executed a perfectly timed left-face maneuver and upon command from the man in front snapped into a classic parade-rest stance. Each man stood with his feet slightly wider than his shoulders and his arms crooked at a forty-five-degree angle behind his back with his eyes focused straight ahead. They all looked mean enough to chew up a steel girder and then spit out ten penny nails onto the ground in disgust.

On a silent command that was understood by no one except the four men, one man snapped to the position of attention and took two strides forward to stand before the class. The man's jaw appeared to have been carved from a solid block of granite with a single divot chiseled in the center of his chin. Blue eyes glared out from under the brim of his hat as he silently surveyed the teenagers standing in front of him. When he spoke, there was a severity in his voice that clearly articulated the menace within the man.

"All right sweethearts; be seated before your candy-asses fall down and you cry for your mamas."

The man gave the teenagers a moment to complete the scuffing of chairs as the boys and girls sat back down.

"My name is Sergeant Hogg." The man paused long enough to see if anyone was foolish enough to titter or smirk at his name. Seeing no one with an obvious death wish, he continued.

"You are currently in an experimental military facility located within the heartland of America. Your families and friends are dead. That's the plain and simple fact so runnin' on home to your mamas and daddies is no longer an option. All of you were selected on "Z" night for a very specific reason. Each of you survived alone. Some by strength, some by stealth and some by fear as you fled in terror. The reality is this: you've all been selected to participate in Project Orphan. You were all selected for this reason. So, let me repeat this just to make certain that it is sinkin' into those little noggins: everyone you know is dead. Anyone that fought with their families and had survivors was left to succeed or fail on their own. We cannot babysit the world.

My job is simple. I am here; supported by this cadre of finely tuned military men to offer you all a single, non-complicated choice. Choose to stay here and learn what we must teach you. Which is, how to survive in this fucked up and hostile world full of dead fucking things that want to eat your fucking pancreas, or..." He paused for dramatic effect.

"...sign your own death warrant by turning your back on Project Orphan and walking out of the front gates of this facility. I should add that currently there are several dozen, free roaming undead, wandering around out there so your ability to become a wandering feast for the walking corpses shouldn't take too long. No pressure. We don't really care who lives or dies. We get paid the same either way."

The brawny drill sergeant paused to allow the weight of his grim words to sink into each teenager. Mutterings and tears began to fall. The man allowed them to continue for several seconds before he brought everyone's attention back to himself with a commanded "As you were!"

"For those of you that choose to stay and learn what it takes to thrive in this new Hell on earth; these fine soldiers will teach you all that you can possibly need to survive and potentially even thrive, both as part of a team or even as an individual. What you do with that knowledge afterward will be up to each of you individually. Some of you may choose to stay here at the Academy and others of you will opt to journey out into the world on your own or in groups. In the interests of complete disclosure, it is only fair that I warn those of you that wish to stay, that you may wish that you had taken the quick, easy death under the teeth of the Zs in the long run, because staying..."

The man slowly let his eyes roam across the faces of the teenagers seated before him. When he reached the last boy at the back of the room, he continued.

"...staying means that you will be forced to watch new friends die. Staying means that you may be forced to pacify someone that you have come to care for. Staying also means that you may even be forced to ask a friend to pacify you if you become infected."

"So, in the spirit of diplomacy as is the way in the good ol' United States of America, I am going to give each and every one of you two whole minutes to decide what your future will be. Those of you who decide that a well-structured, paramilitary life is not for them; get up from your tables and stand at the rear of the classroom. Rest assured there will be absolutely no hard feelings attached to your decision. After all, Z's gotta eat something too. If they are chasing any of you, that's one less chasing any of us."

The man looked down at an olive drab colored military watch. Waiting for a precise moment he spoke again to the assembled teenagers.

"Alright... Its 19:28 hours maggots. You got two minutes to make your decision starting...now!"

Spartan had no decision to make. He couldn't remember his past nor if he even had any family outside of the walls of this academy. A random decision to leave would be pointless. Looking around the room, he was surprised to see how easily he could read the decisions on the other teenagers just by looking at their expressions.

Freak, seemed calm and collected as he sat in his chair, manipulating a baseball in his huge hand. Spartan was glad to see he was staying. The teen seemed to be of a like mindedness which could easily end up in a friendship between the two of them.

Scanning the rest of the room, Spartan evaluated the people sitting around him. The formerly rambunctious gaggle of girls at the front of the classroom now seemed almost dysfunctional. Girls cried, wrung their hands in terror, pulled their own hair or in the case of one young blond, fidgeted repeatedly. A distant memory remembered the phrase *"nervous as a whore in church."* He couldn't remember whom he had heard the comment from, but it seemed to fit. The brown-eyed girl turned slightly in her seat and caught his eye. After ensuring that the burly drill sergeant was not looking at her, she silently mouthed "Staying?" to him. He quickly gave a single nod of his head and was rewarded with his second smile of the day from the young lady.

Turning a bit more, Spartan sighted the Asian boy; Techno was also fidgeting in his seat. It was plainly evident that the boy was nervous as hell about his decision but was probably far more scared of being alone outside of the Academy walls. Two large paperclips were being unbent and then intertwined absently by the boy, forming a single ring of woven metal. He didn't appear to be going anywhere. For some reason, Spartan was glad. He was a likeable enough boy, though completely the antithesis of the giant Freak.

"Thirty second pukes. Make a decision or we will make one for you!" Sergeant Hogg instructed loudly.

Spartan used the last few seconds to look back at Cutter and his cohorts. The entire group sat silent, almost as if they were moping after the beat down that they took from Spartan and Freak. *"Serves them right for bullying kids weaker than themselves."* He thought to himself. Cutter glared at Spartan, meeting his eyes. There was definite hatred there. Spartan knew he would have to keep an eye on that one.

Another axiom popped into his mind from an unknown source in his past. *"Once an enemy; always an enemy."*

Letting his eyes roam over the rest of Cutter's crew, he had a hard time suppressing a smile. The three boys that had been in the restroom with Cutter looked like swollen, doughy lumps of bruised, purple flesh. All of them appeared to be struggling to sit upright and the fat boy that had suffered the broken nose as a result of Spartan's punch was continuously prodding the damaged proboscis as if trying to determine the extent of the damage.

"Time!" The drill sergeant roared. "Any of you pansified sissy-fuck crybabies wanna leave, get your asses up and to the back of the classroom right now!"

Nobody moved.

"Out-fucking-standing! Good for all of you. The first step in survival is being willing to make a choice and then livin' with the consequences of that decision. By deciding to stay here at the Academy, you have chosen to try to live."

The drill sergeant held up his right wrist, displaying the name bracelet wrapped there.

"For those of you that are completely oblivious, you have all been assigned a new name. In this new world, your old name is dead. True names require personalities and individualism. There is no place for an individual here. Real names imply relationships. There is no place for relationships here. Relationships will get you killed. Real names imply giving a shit about the past. It's dead and fuckin' over with sweethearts…deal with it! From here on out, you will answer only to the name on your wristband or the title of cadet. You will be a cadet until such time as you graduate, or you die. Anyone using their old name will answer directly to me and I will have your ass for lunch on a biscuit; is that clear cadets?"

"Yes, drill sergeant!" the entire class yelled in unison.

"Check the bracelet on your wrist. When Sergeant Boomer calls your name…" Sergeant Hogg said indicating the only black drill sergeant "…he will direct you to a team and a drill sergeant. Line up behind that drill sergeant when called and keep your mouths shut.

Sergeant Hogg snapped back to attention and took two steps backward, relinquishing the floor to Sergeant Boomer. The drill sergeant paralleled his counterparts' movements in reverse, taking command of the class. When he spoke, it was a voice like cotton covered steel that clearly could be both soft and powerful.

"Echo team: Cutter, Savage, Orc, Skull and Lotus Jane! You will be assigned to Drill sergeant Havok!" A dark haired, hawk-nosed man stepped forward. His eyes were dark holes in his head and appeared to look directly into the Cadets' souls. Spartan immediately felt a dislike for the man. He just radiated menace.

"Delta team: Gator, Stiletto, Knight, Jive and Deacon! You are assigned to Drill sergeant Surfer!" he said, indicating the bleach blond drill sergeant at the end of the line. The drill sergeant smiled and gave each of his new team members a hang ten hand sign as they approached. Clearly, he was much more relaxed than the other drill sergeants.

"Charlie team: Cowboy, Princess, Popcorn, Vulture and Rooster! You are assigned to Sergeant Stone!" A caucasian male sergeant stepped forward. His arms looked like they would split the seams of his uniform and body fat seemed to be non-existent on the bulging man.

"Bravo team: Dragon, Medusa, Lightning, Pig and Meatball! You are assigned to me!"

"And finally, Alpha team: Spartan, Freak, Dancer, Deadeye and Techno! You are assigned to Sergeant Hogg!"

Dread filled Spartan's stomach. Sergeant Hogg seemed less than likable in the best-case scenario and a consummate hard ass in the worst. The only upside to the selection was that two of the cadets that he had already begun to establish friendships with were on his team and by some quirk of fate, so was the brown-eyed girl he now knew was named Dancer. Walking forward, he was quickly joined by Freak and Techno. A dark eyed, lithe teen came next. The boy moved with quiet dignity and bearing, his head held high. Unlike the rest of the assembled cadets, the boy's boots did not make any noise as he walked. It was almost as if he was barely even touching the ground. Lastly came Dancer, her brown ponytail swishing from side to side as she walked. Where the boy, Deadeye, moved with an almost regal bearing, Dancer moved with dignity and grace that befitted her name. Every step was measured and deliberately calculated to accentuate her movements. Spartan had a difficult time peeling his eyes from the girl, as did several other male cadets. The continued speech from Sergeant Boomer finally broke Spartan's trance.

"Together your five squads will form Zero Company. Your individual drill sergeants will see to your individual needs, hygiene supplies and equipment issues from here on out. You are to take any issues, of any type, directly to your drill sergeants only. Failure to stay within the chain of command will have severe repercussions. Do I make myself clear cadets?" he yelled.

"Yes, drill sergeant!" the squads replied as a whole.

"Then your first briefing as the inaugural class of the Apocalypse Academy will be at 21:00 hours this evening with the Company Commander. Do not be late. Any questions?"

Sergeant Boomer looked around the room at the cadets. Seeing no questions, he addressed the drill sergeants.

"Drill sergeants take charge of your troops! Release them for chow, proper haircuts and equipment issue! Dismissed!"

Chapter 3
Commandant's Briefing

The remainder of the afternoon passed in a blur of issued items, fast marching from the barracks to the Quartermaster, to the chow hall and back again. The massive castle-like structure of the Apocalypse Academy towered over the grounds along the riverfront. Formerly a high school, the Academy sported more than fifty rooms, a gymnasium, a library, as well as a chow hall and athletic equipment rooms that now served as the quartermaster areas. The Academy seemed to issue everything from socks and underwear, to gun cleaning kits to each and every student. Every item was stowed within a full-sized military rucksack and was toted along on the cadet's backs as they moved from place to place. Questions were whispered as to why they would need certain items at various times. All of which were answered succinctly by their drill sergeants with basic catch phrases and occasionally they were followed up with rather creative expletive's. Spartan's personal favorite had come from Sergeant Hogg when asked by Techno why he had to wear briefs instead of boxer shorts. Sergeant Hogg had turned so crimson that Spartan was certain that the man was about to have an aneurism when he bellowed his reply.

"You think there is something special about your crotch fat boy? My Great Granddad wore briefs during the Big One. My Grandfather wore briefs in World War II and in Korea. My father wore briefs during Vietnam and Afghanistan, and I have worn briefs every single day of my military life including "Z" night when someone was kind enough to drop your sorry ass on our doorstep like a turd-bomb that had been lit on fire; but you think you should be treated special and be allowed to wear boxer shorts? My grandpa used to say that anyone who wore boxer shorts just wanted easy access to diddle themselves anytime they wanted to! Is that your issue boy? You one of them, hide in a corner and jerk it until you scream teenagers? Maybe peek a little out the curtains at a pretty girl? You do like girls don't you boy?"

Techno looked so confused that he sputtered when he answered. "N…n…n…no drill sergeant. I mean yes drill sergeant. I mean…"

"Well, if that's the case then you must be a PT God, right? Everybody knows that pretty girls like their men in shape. Do you think you're a PT God Cadet Techno? Judging by the fine shape of your physique you must do PT at least three times a day! Hell, I think you're such a stud, if my sister wasn't a goddamn Z, I would invite you over to my house and let you get a little strange in the middle of this here apocalypse."

Spartan's smile faded as Sergeant Hogg turned his wrath onto the other cadets of Alpha Team.

"Cadet Techno is a physical training God. Out of the respect for his dedication to physical fitness we will no longer walk anywhere. When Alpha Team is on the deck for any reason, they will double-time to their destination."

A look of horror spread across Techno's face. It was painfully obvious that any sort of exercise was pretty much a rarity for the boy.

"And…" the drill sergeant continued "Since you so obviously think that you're better than four generations of the Hogg family, and since I obviously do not want to fail you as your drill sergeant, we will begin our new physical fitness program together immediately. Well, you little fat, whiny, snot nosed, Twinkie eating, sack of human waste …" Sergeant Hogg said, again turning his malice on Techno. "You will lead your Team for the remainder of the day. Every hundred meters of movement, you will stop the formation, select push-ups, crunches or mountain climbers and perform twenty repetitions. You will have one minute to complete these exercises. If you fail to complete these exercises due to fatigue, I will personally walk your asses down to the gates and boot you straight out into the Z's as this academy's first failures! Do you all understand me?"

"Yes, drill sergeant!" the cadets of Alpha Team all screamed in unison.

"We will just see about that. Move out cadets!"

Whereas the other four drill sergeants seemed to delight in the torment and mind games that they placed upon their assigned teams, Sergeant Hogg was a master of misery. Every type of descriptive, non-complementary insult that could be imagined was lavished upon Alpha Team. For the entire day, the members of Alpha Team "beat their faces" doing push-ups, "busted gut" doing crunches or "broke their backs" performing mountain climbers. The new boy, a dark-skinned youth glared daggers at Techno as he performed every exercise. The teen never said a word, but his expression said that Techno had a bad day coming on the horizon. To his credit the teen humped his gear without a word of complaint, but his endurance began to clearly wain as the day wore on.

Spartan managed to hold his own with the drill sergeant. He matched the man set for set and paralleled his every step. Silently he was thankful to his old football coach for insisting on endurance training.

Dancer, the pretty, brown-eyed girl and Techno were clearly miserable. Individually they staggered and fell so often that the palms of their hands were skinned from the impacts as they hit the ground.

Where Dancer appeared on the exterior to be a girly-girl, there was obviously a hidden strength to the young lady. Silently, exhausted and fatigued, she plodded on. Never once stopping or showing a willingness to quit. Although she was on the verge of collapse. Spartan thought that her toughness only added to her beauty.

Techno on the other hand had sweated so much that his jumpsuit was stained a completely darker shade of blue than the rest of the cadets. Rivulets of sweat poured down the boy's face and dripped freely into the dirt below. His head bounced side to side with each step and he kept his eyes tightly closed. Spartan knew the end was near for the chubby boy. He had seen many athletes fall out on the football field.

This kid had every sign that he would be eating dirt very soon. Glancing around to see if Sergeant Hogg was looking, he caught Freak's eye. The giant was sweating like everyone else but seemed like he could run for at least another full day without tiring. The teen was in such phenomenal shape it was scary. Nodding at Dancer and Techno, he silently communicated his intent. Understanding registered on the giant's face and he nodded his agreement with Spartan's plan.

Sprinting forward, Spartan fell into step with Dancer while Freak adjusted his long stride to match Techno's. Spartan paralleled the girl's double time march and reached out a hand silently lifting a portion of the weight from Dancer's rucksack from her tired back. The relief was immediate and obvious. Although the girl could not speak for risk of fatigue stealing her breath, her walnut eyes beamed their gratitude. Quietly, under his breath, Spartan whispered words of encouragement to the girl. He was certain that Sergeant Hogg had heard him; however, the drill sergeant said nothing.

Disaster came as Freak attempted to lift Techno's rucksack. The Asian boy's legs wobbled and buckled, spilling him face first into the pea gravel beneath them. Sergeant Hogg allowed the formation to run on for an additional twenty yards before finally calling a halt. While the cadets in formation gulped air, Spartan was amazed to see Freak strap Techno's rucksack across his chest and sprint back to the formation leaving the fallen boy in the rock and dirt. His strength was astounding.

Instructing the other cadets to remain at of Parade Rest, the drill sergeant spun around and marched purposefully back to where the boy lay face down in the gravel. A small leaf swirled in the autumn breeze, ricocheting off the chubby boy's ear before whirling away. Sergeant Hogg reached down and grabbed a handful of Techno's straight hair. Pulling the boy's head up off the ground, he used the handhold and the toe of his combat boot to unceremoniously roll him onto his back.

"You gonna die on me boy?" He asked in a withering tone, just loud enough for Techno to hear him above the dry leaves that scraped by in the wind.

"I…don't…know…. drill…sergeant. It…hurts!" Techno replied.

"If you're gonna die, then be Goddamn quick about it…" he said, reaching behind his back and pulling a shining steel spike out of the quick release strap on his drill sergeants' belt. Holding the spike directly before the boy's eyes he continued "…that way I can pacify your sorry ass and get back to the business of training these fine people over here that want to keep on livin'." He said nodding towards where the rest of Alpha Team stood awaiting further instructions.

Glancing upward at the sound of metal being drawn from a scabbard, Techno's eyes widened in abject horror as he looked at his own reflection in the shiny body of the foot-long, twisted metal pacification tool. He did not know what being pacified entailed, but he imagined that it had a whole lot to do with the business end of the spike glaring in the sergeant's meaty hand.

His adrenaline surged and Techno struggled back to his feet. Wobbling unsteadily, and stumbling back towards the formation of cadets, he fell back into his place in line, tears running freely down his pudgy cheeks. Whatever words had passed between the drill sergeant and Techno, seemed to have galvanized the teen toward hidden reserves of energy.

The drill sergeant jogged back over to the formation and resumed his place at the team's left-hand side. The cadets were mentally gearing up for the return to double-time when the drill sergeant rounded on all of them.

"Freak!" he screamed at the top of his lungs. "Get fuckin' front and center right goddamn now, you ignorant, steroid using, pile of donkey scrotum sweat!"

Taking a single step back from the team, Freak spun on his toe and heel smartly, executed a perfect right face while still carrying both rucksacks and sprinted to the drill sergeant double time. Stopping smartly, he stood stock still at the position of attention. Spartan was surprised to see that the Sergeant's face was a crimson mask of rage; his lips snarled as if he wanted to bite the cadet's face off as he stood in front of him. What the hell was this all about? More mind games?

"What the fuck did you think you were doing numb nuts, grabbing that man's gear like that? Your actions made that cadet fall. If you had been surrounded by the un-fucking-dead, that man would be fuckin' dead right now! You take a man's gear you might as well sentence him to death! Do you understand me Private?!!" The drill sergeant screamed as he circled the athlete like a shark. "Do you all under-fucking-stand that?!"

"Yes, drill sergeant!" The cadets all screamed. Hoggs' round brown hat bobbed forward with each syllable, repeatedly hitting the big black teen in the bridge of the nose with the brim as he continued the rant.

"You leave a man to die like that, broken and tired, and you're gonna take his gear, then you better have the common decency to stick around because you owe that troop a final soldier's courtesy: a clean death. A pacification of their immortal soul that is achieved by twisting a spike directly into their brain therefore preventing reanimation." The drill sergeant sucked in another huge lungful of air before continuing his tirade.

"Fail to do this and the cocksucker that was your buddy is going to rise back up, chew out your throat, tear out your guts and leave you calling for your fucking mama as you bleed out and then slowly become a puss-bag yourself."

"But today cadet… today is your lucky day. Instead of either of you dying… you have gained a battle-buddy. Where you go, he goes. If he dies from a "Z" bite, then it will be 'cause you failed as his backup. If he dies, you will personally pacify him."

The D.I. known as Hoggs' face was so red, swollen with veins that he himself barely looked human. His eyes glared into Freak's daring defiance, or even for the big man to blink.

"Am I perfectly fuckin' clear soldier?!"

"Crystal, drill sergeant!" Freak replied.

"Well, that's just fucking lovely sweetheart…now get your buddy and get the fuck back in line. Assholes and elbows; let's go … move it!!!!"

Freak spun still carrying the dual rucksacks and sprinted to Techno's side. Never pausing for conversation or agreement, the gigantic athlete scooped up his partner in a fireman's carry over the two rucksacks and ran back to the formation.

"Mental note," Spartan thought. *"That dude is retardedly strong; no wonder he is called Freak."*

Four hours later, directly at 2100 hours, the teams were all seated wearily back in the briefing room. Everyone looked exhausted, even haggard as they reclined in various positions in chairs or face down on the white plastic tables. No one seemed to be immune to the physical and mental abuse of their first full day as cadets at the Apocalypse Academy.

The door at the front of the classroom flung open and the drill sergeant known as Havok strode into the room barking a command at the top of his voice as the Commandant of the Apocalypse Academy followed closely on his NCO's heels.

"Officer on deck!"

The cadets leapt to their feet, having learned this lesson earlier in the day, hands closed on the outer seams of their pant legs, eyes straight ahead. No one spoke.

The man was wearing a full set of United States Army dress greens with a pair of shining silver eagles adorning the epaulets on each side of his shoulders. A silver rifle on a blue background and a silver laurel hung at the top of his left breast above more than twenty-five assorted ribbons of various colors. Below the ribbons, atop the pocket sat three silver badges. The first was a silver parachute over a set of wings; the second was a helicopter also bearing wings and the third was some sort of a cross which bore the word expert beneath it. From his right shoulder hung a light blue braided rope, and on his right breast pocket sat a single black and white nameplate which read "Slade". On his collar sat a pair of crossed sabers on a circular gold field. Patches had been stitched carefully to his left and right shoulders. On the left shoulder sat a red, white and blue patch bearing crossed swords, the emblem of the 10th Mountain Division. On his right shoulder was a yellow and black combat patch bearing a black horse head and a black diagonal line across the yellow field. The man's uniform was impeccable all the way down to the glossed shine of his shoes.

Spartan noticed that the man's eyes were cobalt blue as he executed a left face maneuver and faced the cadets directly, yet silently. The Colonel's gaze travelled slowly over each of the teenagers assembled in the room at the long white conference tables, boring into each of them as if evaluating their minds and souls. It was difficult to meet the man's stern gaze. Standing stiffly, with a scowl pulling his eyebrows down, the man's face seemed to be carved of granite. Salt and pepper black hair was closely cropped into a perfect flat top, before slowly fading into silver at the man's temples. Although shorter in stature than any of the drill sergeants, the man held a powerful aura about him that made him appear much larger as he looked out over the cadets, commanding respect and attention.

"Be seated." He said simply and the cadets fell as one into their collective seats. No one dared speak and the tension within the room seemed almost palpable as the teenage warriors-to-be awaited their Commanding Officer's first words. When the commander finally spoke, his low strong voice rumbled like thunder across the conference room.

"My name is Colonel Phineas Armbruster Slade. I have served twenty-two years in the United States Army and I am formerly of the 5th Special Forces Group assigned to Fort Bragg, North Carolina. I am the Commandant of the facility in which you currently find yourself. The building in which you now sit is known colloquially as The Apocalypse Academy or sometimes just the Academy or the double "A". I stand before you now to establish the rules of conduct during your stay here and to help you understand the mission statement by which this Academy was created. By looking over this group I can tell that one of the primary rules of the Apocalypse Academy has already been broken. There will be no fighting among cadets. If you do, you will be immediately expelled with no chance for reinstatement. For those of you that are a bit slower on the uptake, that means you will be left to your own devices outside the safety of the Academy's gates amongst the Z's. Do you all understand me?"

"Sir, yes Sir!" the room's white walls reverberated as the cadets all answered as one.

He paused, staring hard at the cadets, silently inventorying those that he deemed potential trouble or those that could be leaders as only a combat veteran could assess. Seeing no questions and hearing no comments, the Officer continued.

"I was not stationed at the Apocalypse Academy for you to like me, nor are your drill sergeants." He said motioning with an arm to where all five drill sergeants stood at the position of Parade Rest against the wall.

"I do not give a rat's ass or a wooden nickel if you laugh, cry, beg, plead or piss 'n moan about your stay here as part of Project Orphan. Your alternative is to have your candy asses booted out of the Apocalypse Academy and into the wide, wide world of the walking dead or what I like to call the "Z" zone. This is your second opportunity to leave the Academy voluntarily. I believe Sergeant Hogg gave you a similar option earlier today. There will not be a third opportunity. For those of you that decide to stay, I will make you warriors. For any of you that decide to depart, you will be given a backpack containing seven ready to eat meals, a knife and ten matches. After a handshake at the gate, you will be on your own. Is there anyone amongst you that would like to take this option? Like I said, this is it. Anyone who stays will be here because they *want* to be here. Anyone want to go? If so, raise your hand?

The Colonel slowly scanned the faces of the cadets. No one raised their hands.

"No? Ok, good. Now that that's out of the way, let's get down to business and talk a little bit about Z Command, the Apocalypse Academy, what you're doing here as part of Project Orphan and what our ultimate overall goal is. Have all of you seen an animated "Z" by now?" The Colonel nodded to drill sergeant Stone. The Sergeant immediately dimmed the room's lighting and activated a projector mounted from the ceiling. The first slide depicted a black and white still frame undead creature from the horror movie Night of the Living Dead.

Most of the cadets nodded yes. A few girls tentatively shook their heads no while several other boys just sat silently; their unknowing facial expressions spoke volumes about their lack of experience.

"A "Z" is also known as a Zombie, Zeke, ZOM, Puss bag, undead, walking dead, cursed ones, Romeros, Reapers, Husks, animated corpses, the living dead or my personal favorite, Mr. Zulu. All are the reanimated corpses of a mammal. Yes, I said reanimated. As in, living and then dead, and then undead but walking around again. It can be a human being, a dog, a cat, a bear, a wolf, a rat, a lion or hell even a dolphin. Anything that once had mammalian DNA can be transformed."

The screen changed to depict a color movie scene of an undead biting into a victim's cranium.

"How many of you watched old movies about "Zs"? You know, they can only be humans, they can only walk at night, they only eat brains, they all move like pond water or they slowly lean in to bite the damsel in distress? That, for the record, is all Hollywood bullshit. Much of the world died and became reanimates themselves because they entrusted their fates to knowledge gained on the Saturday night Creature Feature and the false propaganda that they unknowingly spread. I happen to know this personally as the President of the United States of America's favorite German Sheppard tore out his master's heart, throat, liver, and spleen before savagely biting off the Commander in Chief's genitalia and eating it. You will note that I did not mention the brain although his brain was probably not far away because his head was usually up his ass."

The slide projector clicked to show a dismembered corpse with a gaping hole where the crotch area should have been. The words "TOP SECRET" framed the image at the top and bottom.

"Yes, before you ask, yes...that was the President."

Several boys noticeably cringed at the mental image of their testicles being torn off and eaten by an undead K9 as the Colonel's gruesome description of the President's death caused a reflexive throb to twist their own scrotums painfully.

"To keep the technical stuff to a minimum, "Z's" are the intellectual by product of mankind's search for godhood. In short, a bunch of egghead scientists put their collective geniuses together using a Hadron Collider and decided that mankind could achieve cellular regeneration through the genetic manipulation of a bunch of viruses. Their initial success with a virus, which they dubbed H1N1 – GR for Viral Gangrenal Recession, or more casually as the "HUNGER" virus, was that it could be used in nonsurgical wound repair of even badly infected wounds. New tissues, when fed plasma, grew and replaced the damaged body parts. It was miraculous and had such incredible battlefield applications that they began bonding more and more strains together without ensuring that the appropriate, and in truth, mandated testing was performed. The need for long term psychological and physical testing was ignored. Shortcuts were taken, documents were forged, and pharmaceutical companies paid bribes to be the first to market the miracle drug. Their eventual final product was a self-replicating virus that only survived in nanoseconds but was capable of renewing cellular structures. The problem was that the virus replicated so quickly that it quickly overrode all safety mechanisms and safeguards. That was approximately the same time when the breakdown of the subject's physical and mental state occurred. Degeneration of brain tissue was first followed immediately by wound degeneration. Lesions erupted on the subject's skin and ocular blood vessels and tear ducts ruptured causing bloody tears to redden the subject's eyes and stream down their faces. Brain damage and hemorrhaging caused the victim to become feverous, further destroying brain tissue and leaving the victim in a near catatonic state."

"The virus would then seize the autonomic nervous system and pancreas, overriding the body's pain centers, shutting down the lungs and endocrine glands. Insulin production would cease, and the host would die, seized in crippling convulsions. The entire process start to finish ranged from as little as two to seven minutes or as long as a week to ten days. There is no definite time limit until the change occurs."

Multiple slides changed over as the cadets viewed the bloody transformations of numerous victims of the horrific virus known as HUNGER.

The Colonel again looked at the cadets, now seeing several young faces that were remembering the transformations of loved ones.

"By this time, the HUNGER virus seemed to have developed a sort of awareness. A primal need to survive if you will. Soon the virus reactivated certain pieces of its dead host. Unable to sustain itself, the virus was forced to feed on the red blood platelets of living flesh. To further this end, the virus reanimated the corpse's motor portion of the brain and gave the body a single task. Feed. Rend flesh beneath their teeth and bite to the blood and bone marrow beneath. As best we can tell, with the pancreas shutdown, this is how the "Z's" regenerate their flesh and blood supplies since the body no longer creates insulin or processes proteins.

"I feel compelled to tell you that the next few slides are extremely graphic. They are still frames taken from the security cameras of the Center for Disease Control in Atlanta, Georgia. I must also insist that none of you look away from this projection screen. It is absolutely imperative that you understand the breadth and scope of how the virus escaped into the public and what you will all be facing."

The Colonel motioned to drill sergeant Stone and the next series of pictures slid onto the screen. The slides summarily depicted a doctor and his orderlies being disemboweled and eaten down to the raw bone by an infected patient. Arterial blood splatters stippled the walls in great gouts of crimson dots as the berserk patient ripped through flesh and blood with its savage teeth, flinging torn remnants of flesh against the cinder block walls. The doctor's own blood streaked upward to strike the security camera with almost three-dimensional movie perfection. The last sighting of the doctor or of the orderlies was as the doctor slumped to the floor with the patient ripping at his face and eyes. Approximately two minutes later, based on the time stamp of the security camera, the former orderlies rose back to their feet. One orderly's intestines had been ripped out and trailed behind him on the floor as he walked towards the doctor and began to feed. The slide show stopped on an up-close image of the orderly creature as it exited the open door. Thick, ropy blue veins stood out from the creature's forehead and temples. The blood vessels in both eyes had burst, leaving the entire sclera crimson and the orderly weeping bloody tears, giving the creature a cruel, demonic visage. Lastly, bloody drool ran freely down the undead thing's chin, dripping from the ragged flesh of the doctor that it still chewed between its teeth.

The Colonel left the last image on the projection screen for a full thirty seconds before motioning for drill sergeant Stone to turn on the lights with a nod of his head. The last up-close image of the creature's face was left upon the projection screen. Off to the left, several female cadets were crying in a half-huddle holding each other as if to stave off the images they had just viewed, even though every cadet in the room knew that they would see the images forever, as they were burned indelibly into their brains.

"As I am certain that you have surmised, Patient Z1 killed everyone present. The orderlies rose again, the doctor did not as the physical extents of his wounds were let us say, much more in depth. The orderlies and Patient Z1 then escaped into the surrounding countryside turning every creature that they encountered, which included humans, dogs and cats, into infected parallels of themselves. As we discovered over time the infected follow a standard pattern, a replicating cycle of engagement. It goes like this: *Bite, Die, Rise, Bite.* Hundreds of creatures and people were infected within hours. Within days, the wholesale slaughter of the eastern seaboard, Washington D.C. included, had occurred, and paralyzed the nation with fear. Security checkpoints and quarantine zones were set up only to be overrun by the infected dead as they marched onward towards the living."

A hand raised in the front of the classroom. Dancer. The brown eyed girl waited to be recognized before she asked a question.

"Yes?" The Colonel said nodding his head at the girl.

"Sir, why wasn't the National Guard or even the active-duty Army itself brought in to quell this infection before it got out of hand? Sir." The girl's accent sounded foreign to Spartan, perhaps British or Scottish. It was hard for him to tell.

"A good and fair question Ms…?

"Dancer, Sir." The girl replied, casting her eyes down at the plastic bracelet on her left wrist.

"Well, twenty thousand National Guard troops were called out and overrun almost as soon as their boots hit the ground, adding thousands more to the massive living dead wave. One hundred thousand regular Army soldiers and Marines were deployed along with air support from the Air Force, in New York City alone. Do you know what that got us Ms. Dancer? The Colonel asked.

The girl shook her head slowly, not really wanting the answer.

"It got us one hundred twenty thousand dead soldiers, Marines and Guardsmen, most of who got back up trying to eat the remainder of us. You see, that's why the disease works so well. It is transmitted by a single bite or the transmission of blood. Then it replicates exponentially. So, imagine if you will, one hundred thousand infected troops multiplying as they marched through cities, biting, tearing and destroying the population."

The entire east coast, from Boston to Miami was infected within days. The west coast from San Diego, California all the way up to Seattle, Washington, fell days later. Any city that flew internationally across the heartland of America fell third. Within two weeks, there was total population infection or TPI. Emergency plans were put into place. The contingency plans and tactical response protocols that Homeland Security developed were never meant to restrain an aggressive viral attack of this nature, only a virus or bacteria that could be treated with antibiotics or a shot of penicillin. In the end, the small rural communities across the country fell to the walking dead within a month. A core group of military personnel to include myself were evacuated and sequestered here in what is affectionately known as "Z" Command. Your Sergeants were all part of that group, chosen for their particular specialties, mental toughness and training skills."

"So why are you all here, can anyone tell me?" The Colonel asked.

Heads slowly turned as the cadets all looked at each other, searching to see if anyone had an appropriate answer that the Colonel was looking for. No one seemed to know.

"Come, come…surely at least one of you, out of a class of thirty young, bright minds can make an educated guess as to why you have been brought to the Apocalypse Academy. You there…" The Colonel said, pointing to a dark brown skinned boy sitting in the third row. The boys' hair was an unruly mop, and he wore what looked like a large dinosaur tooth hanging from a leather thong around his neck. "…state your name, where you are from and your family's status as in living, dead, or undead."

The teen stood up looking angry at being called out in front of the other cadets to answer a question."

"Ma name issa 'Gator. I ah'm from Tangipahoa parish in Louisiana. That's right outside the big city of "Nawlins, right on de bayou. I can hear de bullfrogs croakin' at night and eat de crawfishes all day back dere. Ma and pa, dey is undead. Saw 'em myself." The boy said and began to sit back down, then promptly stood back up. "Oh yeah, I don' know why we issa here, lessen it's to kill 'dem dead 'tings. Suh!"

The Colonel nodded at the answer. "Thank you, cadet Gator. Would you mind telling me what the story of that tooth is that you wear around your neck? Sergeant Surfer has already told me however, I am certain that the other cadets would find the story entertaining."

The teen stood up again and lifted the large tooth high on its leather thong. The anger that he had displayed before was gone. His voice was now filled with pride.

"Dis here tooth, which sounded to Spartan like "toof", came outta de mouth of a big ol' gator-girl named Annabelle. She done been prowlin' de swamps for near onto one hundred seasons and was near as big as de school bus. See, she saw me and my cousin out in de peiro trollin' for de perch. We had caught a whole mess of dem fishes and was hanging 'em on de stringer over de side, when 'ol Annabelle, she takes a fancy to dem fishes. Her big ol'jaws came right outta de water and ate de whole stringer plus half'n our boat. Me and Billie Ray got thrown clean outta the water up into de air. When we landed back, we was in de water with ol'Annabelle an she done looked powerful angry dat we was in her swamp."

"Me, I start swimmin' like de devil was on mah tail, but Billie Ray, God bless him, he ain't got no swimmin' skills. Ol' Annabelle, she go down under de water and take Billie Ray by de waist an shook him. De water turned all red and Billie Ray's upper body floated to de surface for just a second afore dat mean 'ol devil gator done came back an' snapped it up too like a chicken nugget."

The boy paused to wipe a tear from his eye.

"Billie Ray, he was a good 'ol boy. So now I am powerful mad, after all that devil gator just ate my cousin all up. So's, I splash outta de water fast as I can an' run to Pa's pickup truck to grab de shotgun. Just as I turned back around, dere she was, grinnin' a gator smile at me as she came to eat me up too. Know what I did, I jus' smiled right back at her and emptied both barrels of Pa's shotgun into her big 'ol face. Only ting I hurt was her pride and dis here tooth that de blast knocked out. Then she jus' turned around, happy as can be an walked off into de water of de bayou. One day, me an' dat gator, we gon' dance again. Den we will see if she's still a-grinnin'. Dat's why I wear dis tooth. To remind me dat ol' Annabelle, she's still out dere waitin' for me."

Then he sat back down. The room sat in stunned silence.

"Thank you, cadet." The Colonel then selected another boy, this time a dirty blond-haired teenager of approximately sixteen years of age. As the boy stood up, Spartan could see long, lanky muscles flexing in his forearms. He was not muscular like the body builder Freak, he was more of the type of boy that looked like he had worked on a farm his entire life bailing hay and mucking out stalls.

"Sir, my name is Cowboy. I come from the great state of Texas. My parents are dead. Been dead 'een before "Z" night. Got killed by a drunk driver on I -10 outsid'a Dallas. I am fifteen years old. Sure as shootin' don't know why I am here." The boy said with a strong drawl to his words.

"Now you" the Colonel nodded to an Asian boy that was Techno's antithesis in the third row. Where Techno was a pudgy, overweight boy, this teen was thin and wiry. Like someone that you might see in an old martial arts movie.

"Sir, my name is Dragon, and I am originally from Osaka, Japan. I was living in Little Japan, outside of Los Angeles as an exchange student when "Z" night happened. I do not know the status of my parents, sir; however, I am assuming they are dead. Japan is just too overcrowded for an infection not to kill a majority of the population and my parents were not fighters. I do not know exactly why I am here Sir; however, I am grateful to be alive and safe."

The boy bowed deeply to the senior military officer of the Apocalypse Academy, showing respect for both rank and person. Much to Spartan's surprise the Colonel returned the bow just as reverently.

"Domo Arigato Dragon-san." The Colonel said, and then looked around the room repeatedly selecting random teenagers before finally coming to Spartan last.

"Alright son, you're the last one. Tell us your story. Go ahead."

Spartan gnawed on his lip as he stood up. Looking down at the bracelet on his left wrist, he silently hoped for an answer to pop into his mind. Slowly but clearly, he spoke.

"According to my identification bracelet, my name is Spartan. As to the rest of your question's sir, I am afraid that I cannot answer them. I do not know exactly how old I am, I cannot remember anything beyond a few days ago. My parents may be alive or dead and I have absolutely no idea why I am here."

The Colonel looked confused, glancing sidelong at the drill sergeants. Taking a single step forward and resuming the position of attention, Sergeant Hogg spoke up in a powerful voice.

"Sir! The cadet is a Code Eight Sir!...Stress induced memory loss. Cadets' age is sixteen years of age according to the birth certificate paperwork located within his residence. Parental status is undead but destroyed by this cadet. Place of origin is a small town in central Wisconsin known as Sparta, Sir! The drill sergeant resumed his place in line with his peers.

"Thank you, Sergeant." The Colonel said, turning to look back at the cadet. "If you survive this training cadet, then perhaps you can get with Sergeant Hogg and ask him to fill in some of the blanks in your memory for you."

Spartan nodded and sat back down, wondering at what he had just heard. He couldn't have killed his own parents even if they were "Z's" could he? Why couldn't he remember? The Sergeant had said that his memory loss was from stress. What could have happened that was so stressful that his mind had shut down to block it out? He needed to find out. Hearing the Colonel resume speaking, Spartan refocused his attention back to the Commandant.

"The answers to all of these questions, except for cadet Spartan's memory loss are all clear except one. Why are you here? The answer is really quite simple. You are all orphans. Children left behind when your parents died, were turned or in some cases, even abandoned you. That is reality. Deal with it now so it doesn't haunt you later. Billions of people have died or been turned into the walking dead by contracting the "Z" plague. You are not unique or special by being left behind. What you are is lucky."

"In the 1980's, the face of warfare began to change. The Berlin Wall was dismantled. The Cold War ended, Cuba became a non-threat and warfare was personalized into terrorist events. Airline hijackings, murders, assassinations and religious jihadism led to the first Gulf War. Weapons of Mass Destruction became the central focus of militaries as conflicts spread from Iraq to Afghanistan to Yemen. While the concerns had initially been nuclear in scope, the focus was quickly changed to include biological terrorism as well."

"In 2001, the World Trade Center was attacked and destroyed, killing thousands of innocent civilians. The attack did much more than kill a bunch of people. It demonstrated

America's weaknesses and opened the door to new terroristic vulnerabilities. On May 02, 2011 a United States Seal team killed terrorist leader Osama Bin Laden. The news was televised on every station and every radio broadcast. What was not announced was that when the SEAL team invaded Bin Laden's compound they found dozens of chemical and biological weapons. Among them were Saran gas, Anthrax, Typhoid, H1N1, and H1N1GR also known as HUNGER. The concerns of the World Health Organization and the other various Centers for Disease Control were well heard, and hundreds of scientists began to study the deadly compounds and viruses. Virals and anti-virals were created, judged and eliminated as potential cures for the HUNGER, in the event that some half-baked third world dictator decided to go off the reservation and use the virus on one of its neighbors, for instance Israel in the Middle East or the Ukraine as it stood opposing Russia."

The Colonel paused to offer a deep sigh and a solemn shake of his head.

"But in the end, it was our own loss of safety controls that allowed the HUNGER to be introduced into the civilian population. We had drawn up dozens of contingency plans for invasions and attacks against the U.S. We identified every chemical weapon using terrorist group in the world and targeted them for extinction. We ran drill after drill based upon generic response plans for Anthrax attacks, Ricin, abandoned property filled with explosives and active shooters, but somehow, we forgot about the HUNGER. Maybe we didn't forget at all. Maybe we allowed our nation's leadership to be childlike and decide that by not seeing the virus that it simply did not exist? I don't know. I just know we were fools."

"I was responsible for one such contingency plan. Not a plan to create an anti-virus or conquer a nation. No…my orders were much simpler. I was to create a contingency plan to help the populace survive in the event of a large-scale biological attack. The Apocalypse Academy and your inaugural class are that contingency plan. You see, I am a fan of history. I have studied the greatest warriors of our world and those most able to survive. What I have found is that while the skills and abilities of such highly trained gentlemen such as your drill sergeants exemplify the modern world, the devastation brought on by this plague will take us backwards hundreds of years in the past. It will take us back to a time when Celtic warriors roamed Northern Britain, the Romans conquered Gaul, Mesopotamia was a war zone and the greatest warriors to ever live ruled by might and wisdom. To a time of the Greek Spartans and the Battle for the pass at Thermopylae."

"The Spartans became great for several reasons. First and foremost, they had one single job: they were warriors. Spartan children were taken from their homes at an early age and taught weapon prowess. They were taught how to steal and how to survive in the harshest of environments. Just as importantly, they were taught how to kill without feeling, and how to conquer their foes mercilessly. In essence, this is how you were all found. Alone, starving, stealing to survive, and unthinkingly killing "Zs" to stay alive. You had regressed from the children of the tech era where your every waking moment was spent with a cell phone, tablet or computer in hand to a far more primal state of self-preservation. A state in which you had to kill to survive. A state in which you can exist either on your own; alone or as a larger part of the inaugural class here at the Apocalypse Academy."

"You that have decided to stay and learn from the cadre of experts here at the academy, we will teach you everything you need to survive in this dead new world. We will teach you skills such as weapons training and first aid. We will teach you how to kill and dress out a deer as well as how to eliminate a Z-Bear. You will be taught to become predators. Your prey will be the undead and the living that worship them."

"Do not misunderstand me Cadets. Your training will be the most difficult thing that you have ever had to do in your lives. There is more than a little chance that one or more of you will die during the various phases that you will be expected to complete. It never gets easier, and some of you will die before ever completing the entire training process. This is the realism that you will be trained in. That is how the Spartans of old trained and is therefore how we will train. We deal on realism. When you learn to shoot, you will shoot a "Z". When you train with martial weapons, it will be slashing and bashing against "Zs". If you get bit during the training processes, you will die…from a "Z"."

The Colonel paused to allow his words to sink in, his eyes hawking the room, looking for the weak or infirm to speak, to cry or to panic. No one spoke a word. The looks on the Cadet's faces around the room looked grim. Overall, the emotions ranged from a prevailing sense of excitement or anticipation to anticipation and trepidation, before finally rolling down the range to confusion, horror, and all-out terror.

"You're training officially begins at 0500 tomorrow morning. I would strongly recommend that you all get some rest while you can. God bless you all and good luck." The Colonel turned smartly on his heel and walked toward the exit.

Sergeant Hogg bellowed "On your feet!" in a voice that rattled the buildings windows and the cadets leapt up to the position of attention as one, silently standing beside their seats.

The Colonel paused at the open doorway and silently did an about face. He looked over the assembled cadets standing tall and proud before him and nodded once grimly, and then he turned without another word and strode out of the room, followed by all of the other drill sergeants except for Sergeant Hogg. A wide grin split the Sergeant's face.

"Alright sweethearts. It's time for beddy-by with ol' Uncle Hogg. Have sweet little dreams of sunshine, rainbows and lollipops…BECAUSE TOMORROW YOUR CANDY ASSES BELONG TO ME AND WE GOT "Zs" to kill!!!!!!!"

The Cadence of Sergeant Surfer

Up in the morning in the pouring rain!
Up in the morning in the pouring rain!
D.I. Surfer done gone insane!
D.I. Surfer done gone insane!
Lead us up a hill, down to another!
Lead us up a hill, down to another!
Telling us all he's nobody's mother!
Telling us all he's nobody's mother!

Brought out his M4 and brought out his knife!
Brought out his M4 and brought out his knife!
Tells us all, that he's fit to fight!
Tells us all, that he's fit to fight!
Aims at the undead, shoots it in the liver!
Aims at the undead, shoots it in the liver!
Cuts off its head and throws it in the river!
Cuts off its head and throws it in the river!

Runs to the next one, kicks it in the head!
Runs to the next one, kicks it in the head!
Doesn't give a damn if it's living or dead!
Doesn't give a damn if it's living or dead!
Teaching us all how to run and how to fight!
Teaching us all how to run and how to fight!
Destroying them "Zs" both day and night!
Destroying them "Zs" both day and night!

CHAPTER FOUR
NEEDLES AND BLADES

The morning began in pure agony as the Drill sergeants led physical training or PT as they called it, for the entire platoon of cadets. Drill sergeant Stone was the resident PT guru and seemed to take endless and apparent delight in seeing the sweat dripping down the faces of the cadets as they pushed, pulled, and lifted what felt like the weight of the world in a combination of exercises. The sergeant was especially fond of pushups, mountain climbers and boot beaters. The latter was a squat-based exercise in which the cadets were forced to squat until their buttocks was just above their heels and then touch the outer ankle areas of their boots without bending over at the waist. The first ten were not bad. By fifty, the cadet's legs were burning madly. By several hundred, which was where they were currently, the cadet's legs were like jelly. By the end of the exercise period, which had lasted for two full hours, four cadets had passed out and another dozen had puked up their scrambled eggs, sausage and orange juice that had comprised their breakfast that morning. This had the added noxious effect of permeating the air with the stench of sour vomit for the rest of the cadets. Only Freak seemed to be hanging tough with the exercises. Everyone else felt and looked absolutely destroyed.

Just when Spartan didn't believe that the torture could get any worse, Drill Sergeant Stone turned the entire platoon over to Drill Sergeant Surfer for a morning "fun run".

Sergeant Surfer's idea of fun quickly did not match up with those concepts held by the cadets. As the run began, Sergeant Surfer led the pace, maintaining a steady airborne shuffle. Calling cadence, the drill sergeant led the cadets up and down hills and repeatedly around the campus of the Apocalypse Academy. Turning onto River Drive in front of the former High School, the Sergeant gave instructions for the cadets to begin an "Indian Run". An Indian Run consisted of the drill sergeant yelling "GO!" and the last person in the platoon from both ranks would sprint full speed up to the front of the formation. It was grueling because the sprint disrupted the cadet's breathing and rhythm that had been established during the cadence jog.

Despite Sergeant Surfer's blond pony tailed hair and beach bum good looks, Spartan would have sworn to anyone that asked that the man was not human. While the cadets rotated through the Indian run sprints, the blue-eyed drill sergeant ran the sprint with every cadet, from the back of the formation to the front, jogging casually back to the rear to prepare for the next sprint. Several cadets would later swear that they overheard the drill sergeant saying, "Hang Ten Dude or Dudette!!" as he ran back to pick up any stragglers that had fallen out of the formation. His endurance was phenomenal.

The end of PT and of the not so fun run was achieved five blistering miles later as Drill Sergeant Surfer issued the Quick Time March command slowing the platoon back to a walk, followed almost immediately by "Platoon Halt!" Steam flowed over and from the cadets like souls rushing from their bodies. The moist morning riverfront air cooled the cadets as they stood quietly waiting for their next batch of instructions. A small, non-descript white cinderblock house bearing a large red cross on its side walls and door, stood before the cadets. Sgt. Surfer jogged over to the building and spoke with someone inside. Several moments later, a very pretty, Hispanic woman in her mid-thirties came out of the building and walked down to stand before the sweaty and gasping platoon. Dancer unconsciously brushed her hair from where it hung drenched with sweat upon her cheek and tucked it behind her ear. Several other female cadets did the same. Everyone waited for the woman to speak, but instead were incredibly surprised when a familiar gravelly voice called out from within the building.

"Whatsa matter ladies!" Drill Sergeant Hogg said as he walked out of the little cinderblock buildings' doorway. "Can't handle a fun little jog? Hell, I take my dog for longer runs than that every night!" The man's laughter echoed off the waterfront behind the cadets.

"Don't worry cadets, the PT will get easier for you day by day. This here is Nurse Ortega. She is our resident nurse, doctor, dentist and veterinarian. You get a boo-boo, you see her, lessen' of course you get bit by a "Z". That's a whole 'nother story." He paused to make certain he had every cadet's attention and that all were accounted for. They were.

"This here nice lady is gonna be givin' you your inoculations. For all of you uneducated types that means you're getting' shots in the arm and in the ass and hell yes, it's gonna hurt! So, I want everyone to strip down to their skivvies without breaking ranks and await those same shots.

I better not hear any whining either. I goddamn hate a pansy. Take it like a man or a woman." He said, placing a thick unlit cigar between his teeth and clamping down on it.

"After you are done, get your asses redressed and form back up with Drill Sergeant Surfer at the rear of the building by the baseball fences. Any questions cadets?" The drill sergeant asked, looking over the platoon's collective faces. Immediately, all of the female cadets' hands shot into the air.

Hogg selected a petite little blond girl of about sixteen years of age.

"Name, age and question cadet!" he thundered, spitting chewed cigar tobacco from his lips as he spoke.

"My name is Princess, drill sergeant, and I am sixteen years old." She squeaked in a timid, high pitched voice. "You…you… want us to take off our clothes and strip to our underwear IN FRONT OF THE BOYS?!"

The drill sergeant sucked in air through his clenched teeth and around the gnawed cigar. Reaching up he grabbed the cigar between his thumb and first two fingers and began to point it at the cadet as he spoke to her. Irritation clearly punctuated every word that he spoke.

"Awwww, Whatsa matter *Princess*?" his voice emphasized her name heavily, dripping with sarcasm. "You afraid of the needles or are you afraid that one'a these here boys from yer platoon is gonna see yer little pink girly-goods? While I am certain that some'a these young men may find you cute, I can promise you one thing. There ain't a "Z" out there that gives a rat's ass if your snatch is as bald as a cue ball, has a fur lined landing strip or is bushy like a Wookie. In our world, a world where the dead walk, modesty leaves you alone; unprotected by your partner and vulnerable to attack. Alone you *will* die! So, do me a favor and take your little fairy tale dreams of Prince Charming riding in on his white stallion and being the first to see your little pink precious love box and toss them right out of your enchanted castle's fucking highest window WHILE YOU STRIP OUT OF YOUR GODDAM UNIFORM! AM I PERFECTLY FUCKING CLEAR CADET?! The drill sergeant screamed, turning a bright crimson, sending flecks of spittle to leap from his mouth.

"Yes, drill sergeant." The girl replied meekly, tears falling from her eyes as she methodically began to strip her boots and then her uniform. Finished, she modestly tried to cover herself with her arms and hands.

A snicker came from the rear ranks of the platoon as Cutter and Lotus Jane stood giggling in their underwear at the shy girl's dilemma. Apparently, Jane had no issues with modesty at all.

As the scowling drill sergeant turned around to face the remainder of the platoon, miraculously every other hand that had been raised for a question dropped.

"Good" the sergeant huffed a little calmer than moments before "Maybe now we can get some goddamn work done."

Filing into the white cinderblock house one by one, the injections were administered by both air gun and needle.

Since there were no medical records available any longer since the world's collapse, every cadet received a full spectrum of inoculations ranging from measles to tetanus. The actual shots consisted of one air gun shot in each shoulder, and two injections into the buttocks area with needles: one on each cheek. The result was a very sore platoon that continually rubbed themselves in pain as they left the nurse's station and formed back up under Drill Sergeant Surfer's watchful eye.

There was only one other incident beyond Sergeant Hogg's verbal tirade at Cadet Princess. A cadet by the name of Meatball from Bravo squad went through the compressed air injections without a problem, only to take one look at the liquid filled syringe in the nurse's hand and passed out face first onto the floor. Sergeant Hogg brought the boy around with a series of facial slaps and steel toed kicks to the boy's butt that revived the cadet rather quickly. Of course, the drill sergeant accompanied the physical abuse with a string of profanity and curses about what he intended to do to the cadet's Grandmother if he did not get immediately to his feet. To Meatball's credit he stood up and took the shots without even a sound. Through it all, Nurse Ortega seemed nonplussed by the drill sergeants tirade.

As he dressed, Spartan gently touched the golf ball sized knot that was forming on his left upper butt cheek. The injected medication had conglomerated into a throbbing mass which left it on the painful side of uncomfortable to say the least.

"What the hell did she inject into us?" Spartan asked Freak quietly "Syrup?"

Freak just chuckled.

After the cadets had redressed, Sergeant Hogg reformed the platoon. Marching the cadets out in formation slowly at first, the drill sergeant began to steadily pick up the pace. Keeping a slow but steady rhythm, the sergeant began moving to their next location. Approximately half a mile down the road, the whining started. Several of the younger cadets began to complain about the "distance they were marching after receiving the shots", "having to run so much" and that "they were sore and tired."

Hearing the complaints, Sergeant Hogg called for a quick time march, reducing the cadets to a slow walk and immediately followed it up with "Platoon Halt!" Spartan didn't know what was coming but did know that it couldn't be good. Turning to face the platoon, the drill sergeant spoke loudly.

"It sounds like at least one of you little pukes have decided to complain about our little march and feels the need to rest your dainty little tootsies that have become so weary on this little trek. The time has come for all of you little ass-wipes to understand that this is not summer-fucking-camp! You need to persevere rather than complain. Find ways to succeed rather than reasons to fail. As such, the remainder of the day will now be spent at double time everywhere we go. No breaks will be given. Any of you little bastards that fall out of the formation will result in your immediate expulsion from the Apocalypse Academy and become a castaway in the dead zone beyond the walls. Understand this cadet's! This training is not a fucking joke. There are no goddamn yellow cards to be raised if you get tired. Everything we ask you to do has a purpose, all of which is centered upon keeping your currently useless asses alive."

"Physical training makes you all equal. If you cannot keep up with your squad mates, you will do one of two things. One, you will slow them down so badly that your entire team will become vulnerable to a "Z" attack or two, you will fall behind and they will leave your worthless ass to become "Z" chow, which is what I would do. At the least, use you as a distraction so those worthwhile can get away. Either way, you are a liability to your team. As such, I would rather kick your sorry ass out the gate and sacrifice only you now than to allow you to potentially get your entire team killed, torn apart, eaten or even worse turned into puss bags. So now do one of you little fuckers want to man up and tell me who was whining about the goddamn run in my formation or do I break all of your balls?"

Time passed incredibly slowly. A few seconds seemed endless to the platoon. Finally, a voice spoke up.

"It was me drill sergeant." A small red headed boy said as he stepped forward. There was an amazing resemblance between the boy and the son of Sheriff Andy Taylor on the old Andy Griffith television show. The teenagers' red hair glowed in the afternoon sun.

"No shit." The drill sergeant said simply. "What the fuck is your name cadet and what is your problem?""

"My name is Rooster, drill sergeant. I really hate to run, that's all."

"Holy Jesus carrying a handbag full of pineapples and land mines! A scrawny little shit-fuck like you ought to be able to run all goddamn day! What the fuck is your malfunction dipshit? You just lazy or do you think that you're just too goddamn good to be running around with the rest of us?"

"No drill sergeant." The boy said simply.

"I thought Roosters were supposed to be tough. Are you tough boy or are you just a whiny, snot nosed little bitch?" The drill sergeant goaded.

"I am tough drill sergeant."

"Really? Really… Why don't we just test how tough you are cadet? I reckon that's the only fair way to prove if you are or if you're not."

"Yes, drill sergeant."

Sergeant Surfer called out from the rear of the platoon. "Platoon, open ranks. Form a large circle around cadet Rooster.

As the cadets completed the instructions, Sergeant Hogg stalked around the circle, eyeing each cadet. Finally, he stopped in front of one of the boys that Freak, and Spartan had tussled with in the bathroom on the first day inside the

Apocalypse Academy. The beefy boy sported two black eyes and a crooked nose from that day.

"You…front and center." Drill Sergeant Hogg called. "Looks like you like to fight boy…is that right?"

The pig faced boy just got a grin and shook his head yes.

"What's your name cadet?" The drill sergeant asked.

A quizzical look crossed the boy's face as if he did not understand the question.

"ON YER GODDAMN BRACELET DIPSHIT!" Sergeant Hogg exploded.

The boy seemed to finally comprehend what was being asked of him.

"Oh…uh…my name is Orc, drill sergeant."

"Obviously, a genius. Good name. Fits you both in looks and in brains. Orc you know how to follow orders don't you?"

"Yes, drill sergeant."

"Then I am going to give you a series of orders. Do not act on any of the orders until I give you the command to do so…am I clear cadet?"

"Yes, drill sergeant."

"Ok, good. Here we go. Order number one: I want you to walk over and stand directly in front of cadet Rooster in the center of the circle. Order number two: you are to repeatedly pummel cadet Rooster about the face and body. During this time, cadet Rooster will be proving just how tough he is by standing still and absorbing the blows but will not fight back nor protect himself in any way. You may punch and kick but no biting or groin shots. Am I clear so far cadet?"

"Yes, drill sergeant."

"Order number three: You will not cease striking Cadet Rooster until either I give you a direct order to do so, or Cadet Rooster is either unconscious or dead. Am I clear cadet?"

"Yes, drill sergeant."

"If so, then move to the center of the circle as instructed and prepare to begin."

The drill sergeant turned to look at the small red headed cadet.

"Cadet Rooster. Do you understand the purpose of this exercise??

"Yes, drill sergeant. To prove how tough, I really am."

"Very good cadet. Assume the starting position at the position of attention in front of Cadet Orc."

"Yes, drill sergeant." The boy yelled and sprinted over to stand directly in front of his future assailant. Fear shown in Rooster's eyes, yet he stood unwavering in front of Cadet

Orc. Orc outweighed the diminutive Rooster by at least sixty pounds.

"This is gonna hurt man" Freak whispered to Spartan. "Kid's got balls though."

Spartan gritted his teeth together in frustration. He hated senseless violence, especially the type perpetrated by bullies like Orc. It was especially painful to watch when the physical abuse was handed out to the defenseless to prove a point. But at the same time, he knew that this would be a lesson that the other cadets would not soon forget. On top of that, it was necessary. What the drill sergeant had said was correct. Weakness or a lack of cohesiveness in the unit could and probably would result in death. There was no longer any place for weakness in our world, either emotionally or physically. Only the strongest, smartest, and most agile warriors would survive.

"Begin!" The drill sergeant commanded to Cadet Orc and the pig-faced boy leapt to begin the attack of the defenseless cadet. The larger boy attacked with a zealousness that bordered on reckless abandonment, knowing that he had nothing to fear in the way of return blows or punishment for his actions. Orc's first blow was a front snap kick to Rooster's solar plexus. The toe of Orc's boot sank deeply into the defenseless cadet's belly, driving the air out of him with a *whoosh* and bending him over at the waist gasping for breath. Orc followed this up with a strong downward right cross that struck Rooster behind the ear and floored him. Gasping for air, the boy struggled wobbly back to his feet,

Rooster nodded to the drill sergeant that he was ok to continue. Then he looked over at Orc.

"That all you got big man?" The little Rooster crowed at his fellow cadet. "Your sister hits harder. I should know, I porked her last night! Man was she tight!" the boy goaded.

Orc apparently had a sister because he responded with a snarling flurry of blows, smashing his fist repeatedly into Rooster's head, neck and shoulders, growling with every punch like a wild animal. Steadily, Orc drove the boy down to his knees as punch after punch landed savagely onto the boy's upraised face. As the semi-conscious cadet fell over onto his side without so much as a whimper, Orc switched tactics and began kicking the downed boy in the ribs as hard as he could.

Still Rooster never complained and never asked for the beating to stop.

A hand reached over and softly gripped Spartan's forearm. The brown eyed girl that had silently implored him to intervene for Techno now did the same for Cadet Rooster. Without a word exchanged between them, he knew exactly what she wanted from him. If he didn't intercede, Orc could permanently maim that kid or even kill him. Looking down at the fallen cadet, Spartan saw that Rooster was no longer protecting himself from Orc's blows and just grunted in place as they landed. Still Orc's savage attack continued.

Spartan broke ranks without a word and walked up behind Orc as the Cadet drew his leg back to deliver a savage kick to the bloody and battered Rooster's face.

"He's had enough Orc…Stop." He said quietly.

"What, you his mama or sumthin'?" The boy said to Spartan "Drill sergeant said beat the boy, I'm gonna beat the boy. Plain and simple." Orc replied, rearing back, and delivering a kick directly into the downed cadets' cheekbone.

Spartan felt the red fury that was his battle signature rise through his heart and into his brain as his endorphins kicked into overdrive. Grabbing the back of Orc's jumpsuit with one hand, Spartan shoved Orc over the prone Rooster, face first into the ground and stepped protectively over the unconscious boy, straddling the red-headed Cadet.

Glaring down at Orc, Spartan spoke with deeply implied menace.

"I said stop. I won't ask again." He said, snarling through his teeth as his body smoothly transitioned into a fighter's crouch, and doubling his fists. "I promise…you will find out that I *DO* fight back, and I will hurt you." Looking down at the bloodied and prone cadet, his tone softened. "Besides…he's learned his lesson."

Orc looked around, confused. Following the orders of the drill sergeant was one thing but Spartan and that big black kid had severely hurt him, Cutter and Savage during the fracas in the bathroom. He was in no hurry to get into a fight with the muscular teenager again. On the other hand, pissing off Sergeant Hogg promised to be a very bad thing. He decided to let the drill sergeant have the final say. Looking over at Sergeant Hogg, the burly cadet was surprised to see the big drill sergeant calmly chewing on his cigar, just shrug his shoulders. Having no support, Orc decided that retreat was the better part of valor and began to back away. Trying to save face, the pig-faced boy attempted to trash talk Spartan as he withdrew.

"Gonna get you one day Spartan. You ain't always gonna have everyone around you. Then the Echo's will see what the real deal is! I'm gonna get you! I swear it!"

Spartan just snorted in amusement at the boys' idle threat and knelt next to the unconscious Rooster.

"He's breathing but unconscious." Spartan called over to the drill sergeant.

Hogg just nodded, idly chomping on the cigar between his teeth.

"First aid station is back where you got your shots, over by the weapons field hero. You ignored my orders and broke ranks to save his skinny little ass. He's your baggage and now it's your problem how to get him there."

Spartan half slapped; half prodded the boy back to semi-consciousness. Orc had really done a number on the young man's face. Swelling closed both eyes and his nose was definitely broken. Both lips were split in a single jagged line across his mouth. An echo in his memories held a voice that said there was a time to put up and a time to shut up. The fiery Rooster now knew which was which. Hoisting the boy into a fireman's carry across his shoulders, Spartan requested and received permission to take Rooster to see Nurse Ortega. As Spartan bent to grab Rooster's rucksack, he was surprised to see Techno bend over and dutifully take the bag himself.

"I've got it. I will carry it back to the barracks for him." Techno said.

Spartan nodded his thanks and set off with Rooster over his shoulders, dangling and unconscious.

Back in formation, Freak fell into step behind Techno. Techno's legs wobbled under the additional weight of the second rucksack, but he plodded steadfastly onward. As the Asian boy staggered and swayed under the weight of the two rucksacks, Freak covertly reached out and lifted upward on the two camouflage bags; applying just enough lift, probably about twenty pounds with each arm, for Techno to maintain a steadier gait. At one point, Freak thought he was busted again for helping another cadet. He would've sworn Sergeant Surfer looked dead at him as he silently helped Techno from behind. But then the drill sergeant just turned around and jogged back to the rear of the platoon without a word.

"Wow, I must be getting stronger." Techno called over his shoulder at one point. "These rucks only feel about half full."

Freak flashed Dancer, who marched beside him, a huge grin. "Must be all the P.T. you've been doin' 'Dawg!" Freak replied, boosting the boy's ego and then sharing a conspiratorial wink with Dancer.

Twenty minutes later, the road turned north of the river near a boat ramp and began to slowly go uphill. After being treated by Nurse Ortega for a possible concussion and broken nose, Rooster and Spartan met back up with their platoon at the old red brick fire station that sat beside the green and white striped tennis courts atop the hill. The large, brick building held four metal bays with roll down doors that until "Z" night, had contained fire trucks. Beside the parking bays, was a second smaller building with a flagpole standing out front. Upon the flagpole a single, battered American flag flew. Raised and lowered every night by the drill sergeants, it was a small symbol to all of them that America was not dead. Around the base of the flagpole, dozens of purple and white striped petunias had been planted, adding a strange splash of color to the otherwise dreary, and dead landscape surrounding them.

Marching the entire platoon directly in front of the closed gunmetal gray vehicle bay doors, Sergeant Hogg called for the formation to halt. Stepping off to the side, the two drill sergeants spoke amongst themselves. Although Spartan could not determine every word, he was pretty certain that the drill sergeants were discussing Cadet Rooster's status and ability to continue at the Academy. Without facing the platoon, Sergeant Hogg called out over his shoulder.

"Cadet Rooster! Front'n center yafriggin' little maggot!!"

"Yes, drill sergeant!" Rooster screamed the expected reply.

The slight, red headed cadet shrugged off Spartan's supporting grip, turned and took his rucksack back from Techno. Slinging it over his shoulders, the battered and weary cadet tottered unsteadily toward where the two drill sergeants stood waiting for him. As he walked, Spartan noticed that each step wove crazily, like the cadet had the rubbery legs of a punch-drunk prize fighter. He silently hoped that the tough little cadet would make it all the way to the drill sergeants without falling over unconscious.

Finally, Rooster stood before the drill sergeants. Sergeant Hogg towered over the boy; his eyebrows knit into a frown as he glowered down at the boy. Spartan could see the big drill sergeants jaw muscles working as the yellow teeth continually ground the cigar into pulp between them. Those same muscles flexed and released a dozen times before he finally spoke.

"Cadet Rooster" the drill sergeant began "Today you have demonstrated that you are capable of several things. First you demonstrated that you have a big, smart mouth. That is a brash, useless and stupid trait in a survival unit like the Apocalypse Academy. Lose it or we will kick your ass outta the front gates so fast that the "Zs" will think that you had a rocket inserted up it. Do I make myself clear cadet?!"

"Yes, drill sergeant!" The boy screamed in reply. "It won't happen again drill sergeant!"

"It better not." The drill sergeant paused before continuing, pulling the cigar stub out of his mouth and looking over at Sergeant Surfer. The blond drill sergeant just nodded for his partner to continue.

"Secondly, you demonstrated that you could follow orders, whether you agreed with them or not and whether or not they were unpleasant in their consequences. That is not an easy task in the very best of conditions. In a fucked-up world like ours where you may have to shoot a "Z" child or pacify a brother or sister it is a real boon."

The drill sergeant paused to spit out a small piece of tobacco that had broken away from his cigar.

"Lastly you demonstrated that you are indeed a tough little son of a bitch! Probably more than a few fries short of a Happy Meal, but you're not afraid to walk the line and spit directly into the Devil's eye. Not once did you beg. Not once did you violate orders and try to fight back. Not once did you try to quit. Well done. You've earned my respect…for now.

Spartan thought the cadet's posture improved just a little at the praise.

"Thank you, drill sergeant!"

"Judging by the way that you are swaying standing at the position of attention and by adding in the fact that your eyes keep rolling up into your head, it is our assessment that you are in continued need of medical support for a concussion. Since you already apparently had brain damage before all of this began, we do not feel that allowing you to continue with today's activities would be in your best interests. You are to immediately report back to Nurse Ortega at the First Aid station. There you are to be treated until assessed and released by the nurse. At that time, once you are cleared for duty, you will then report back to the barracks, and find Drill Sergeant Stone. You will receive the assignment and expectations as Charlie squad's new Squad Leader at that time. Do you understand me cadet?"

"Yes, drill sergeant!"

"Then you are dismissed. Go and take your cherry ass on up the road and get fixed up. We are training for war. A war with the living and with the living dead. So, I will need squad leaders with brains, balls or just a case of crazy. Fortunately, you seem to have all three."

"Yes, drill sergeant!" The battered cadet then turned in a weaving, sloppy right face maneuver and set off for the aid station back by the baseball diamonds. His orange hair ironically looking like a flame on top of the boys' head as it blew in the gentle breeze coming off the river front.

Spartan's attention was instantly drawn back to the drill sergeant as the man began to speak.

"The rest of you ladies will not be getting off that easily. Now that we put all this silly-ass nonsense behind us we can get down to business. You all heard what I said to Cadet Rooster. We are in fact, at war. We are at war with the walking dead that want to eat our faces and spleens and we are at war with bands of living humans that survive as raiders and bandits. Thugs that will kill ya as soon as look at ya... 'cepting of course you ladies. You they would probably gang rape first, then pass you around for some individual fun until they was tired of you, then they would kill ya. To prevent that we are gonna teach each of you just how to survive. The first course in survival begins today with Sergeant Havok.

For the next two days you are his to abuse, train and carve chunks out of."

Sergeant Hogg gestured to the tree line and the dark-haired drill sergeant slowly uncurled his body from where it was camouflaged at a tree base. He had apparently been there all along and not one cadet had seen him.

"Today you will select and begin to learn how to fight with a martial weapon. A martial weapon is a hand-to-hand weapon meant to kill within close quarters. In the coming days you will learn to strike, block, parry and counterstrike with the weapon that you select. In the former military, we were limited in our selections. A lack of instructional manpower and a need for continuity led to the vast majority of the military being trained with the M-16 and a bayonet. Only the Special Forces units traditionally had more open selections due to their personal preference in the case of martial weapons and the need for insurgency operations in foreign countries where ammunition was not necessarily available for our American firearms."

"Think of your martial weapon as your personal signature. Many, if not all of you, may remember the "Batman" movies and cartoons on television. He had a signature weapon; the Batarang. This weapon was a bat shaped shuriken; when he did his good deeds or defeated the bad guys. A martial weapon should *feel* right in your hand. It should move like an extension of your own body. In fact, it should almost feel alive when you hold it. Some of you will understand this aspect when you select your weapons. Some of you will not and will select your weapons for a variety of other reasons such as size, multiple use abilities, intimidation or even prettiness and usage in movies. But the true weapon masters select their weapons because they feel a bond with them."

"Back down the river, at the Armory, you will be guided by the drill sergeants to eight stalls of weapons. Each contains dozens of melee weapons. Some are modern in nature and some are more medieval in flavor. Many of the older weapons were taken in a gathering raid on the museums in Chicago just after the war started. All have been reviewed and repaired as necessary to make them fully functional. It is a vast assortment ranging from dual purpose weapons such as mining and farming tools, to swords, axes, knives, spears, maces and various missile and exotic weapons. The choices are almost endless."

"You are to select just one primary weapon and one fighting knife or hand tool each. After you've selected your weapon you are to report to the training field directly behind the stalls. Be cautious and selective in your decision. You cannot change your mind later. This is a one-shot process. The weapon that you choose may ultimately decide whether you live or die. Choose what suits you best, not what is the biggest or baddest looking. Good luck to you all in your selection. Echo squad you're up first. Fallout and make your selections. Cadet Cutter, you are to advise when your team has completed its objective.

"Yes, drill sergeant!" Cutter screamed as he led his team at a sprint up the hill and down the river into the Armory.

The Armory was enormous. The worn, stone – faced exterior seemed too ordinary to hold the vast horde of museum quality hand-to-hand weapons that were contained within. Tools, swords, pole arms and knives lined one set of stalls while spears, blood weapons, axes and exotic missile weapons lined the other. Each cadet searched the individual stalls for the one item that met their interest. Several small squabbles broke out as the cadets often fancied the same weapons. Usually, they were the weapons that were with the most noticeable accoutrements or "bling" to them. There was a definite division between looking pretty and deadly efficiency.

When Alpha team entered the Armory, Spartan reflected on this as he slowly walked past each stall. His eyes moved over each weapon, but his hands touched none of them. Spartan knew that when he came to the right weapon, his mind would tell him what he wanted. Slowly he passed the tools and spears, maces and axes. Polearms and more exotic weapons blurred by without sparking an interest. Finally, he stopped in front of the stall containing a bristling collection of swords.

Spartan mentally assessed the functionality and efficiency of each blade. Great swords such as the claymore or katana required the use of two hands to wield; because of their size and weight, they were cumbersome and would limit his combat options in the event he was forced into battle. The long swords of medieval Europe were formidable weapons; but tended to be unbalanced with the blade being much heavier than the pommel. This would cause his arms to tire if he was forced to hold it for any length of time. He passed machetes and parangs, scimitars and falchions, and then his eyes settled on a gray steel curved short sword gleaming in the corner of the stall, a scabbard standing behind it.

Polished metal glinted as he reached out his hand and grasped the leather wrapped, square hooked pommel. The blade, although solid was not nearly as heavy as he would have thought, and it was perfectly balanced. Raising the sword straight out in front of him, Spartan noted that it took very little strength to maintain his grip and the hook at the end of the pommel aided in supporting the weapon. He knew this was the blade for him. He quickly bent and picked up the vaguely green tinted bronze scabbard. Holding the blade of his sword between his knees he buckled the scabbard onto his belt and slid the steel weapon inside.

"An interesting choice." A voice behind him said. "Tell me, did you choose this blade by its merit or by its history?" Drill Sergeant Havoc asked in a low but conversational tone.

Spartan quickly assessed the drill sergeants demeanor, even as his reflexes snapped his body to the military position of attention. He knew that the Drill sergeant expected an answer, but honestly, he was not sure why he had actually selected this particular sword.

"Drill sergeant, I selected this sword because it was the most operationally efficient weapon that I could find. I do not know this blade or its history, it just..." Spartan paused.

"Go on..." The drill sergeant stated. "Continue your thought."

Spartan hated to sound stupid or childish, but he was committed to the thought. "Well… To be honest, it's sort of like… it called to me. I could feel inside of me that this was the right weapon for me to use in battle."

"Interesting." The sergeant repeated looking down at the sword. "That blade came from the Field Museum in Chicago. The legend associated with it is that it was the actual sword wielded by the ancient Greek King, Leonidas as he and his three hundred Spartan warriors battled the invading Persian armies at Thermopolis. I find it ironic that your given codename and your selection of weapons coincide so well. Perhaps it is providence that the legendary sword of King Leonidas is once again wielded by a Spartan.

Spartan did not understand the drill sergeant's historical reference but knew it was significant and silently vowed to research the long dead kings' history.

"Finish selecting your knife and fall back into formation Spartan."

"Yes, drill sergeant" Spartan replied and moved on to the knife stall not fully understanding what had just occurred or the significance of his weapon. Quickly, he selected a ten inch long, black, cold steel forged Tanto combat knife and fell back into formation as instructed.

Drill Sergeant Havok muttered under his breath. "Perhaps the leader of these 30 warriors will not meet the same fate as the last one who led the 300." And he silently walked out to meet the formation of youth.

Drill Sergeant Havok slowly walked in front of each of the cadets, silently inspecting the choice of weapons and asking why they had made that particular choice. The answers he received were wide and varied, but not truly unexpected. Some had chosen their weapons by size, others by the feel of a weapon in their hands. Cadet Princess from Charlie team had selected hers because it was bejeweled with a large red Ruby in the pommel like a princess should own. Cadet Pig had chosen a spear because he had poked himself on the blade. After evaluating the wound, he adopted the spear as his "pig sticker". Cadet Freak, the large black teenager from Alpha team, had been in heaven selecting twin aluminum baseball bats one blue and one black that he immediately named "Jake" and "Elwood" after the movie the *Blues Brothers* which was one of his personal favorites to almost everyone's delight. Freak loved the movie because it was filmed near his grandma's home where he had grown-up in Chicago. The inspection went on and on, with each rank explaining their choices.

Cutter had selected a vicious looking knife with a curved blade and a spiked hand guard. He also selected a Sykes Fairborn British SAS survival knife as his backup weapon. Orc, the burly enforcer of Echo team, sported an enormous two-handed claymore sword of Scottish origin. Cadet Deacon had chosen an ancient mace that bore the insignia of a cross. Perhaps most interestingly of all, Cadet Deadeye had selected a "Razor bow"; a titanium framed collapsible compound bow whose outer edges were forged blades of glistening steel. This intrigued the drill sergeant.

When asked why he selected the weapon, Cadet Deadeye had asked for and received permission to demonstrate his reasoning. Curious, the drill sergeant had watched as Deadeye silently moved fifty yards away from the main group and brought his cupped hands up to his mouth. After just a moment, Spartan heard low warbling sound coming from the boy… not quite a whistle, more of a quivering sound. A moment later an answering call in the same warbling tone, echoed from thirty yards away from where the boy stood, hidden in the tall dry grasses. Patiently, the boy continued his soft call until at last a covey of doves burst from the grasses, flapping into the air. With skill and precision, Deadeye raised his bow, knocked an arrow and effortlessly drew it back to its full extension. A split second later the cables and pulleys released their pressure causing the arrow to streak into the air. Powered by more than one hundred pounds of torque, the arrow bisected the flight path of the dove that passed over head of the Native American youth. So powerful was the arrow that only the slightest quiver could be seen when the bolt struck the bird's breast and exited through its back continuing into the sky.

As the bird began to fall, Deadeye grasped the frame of his bow by the twin handholds. When the bird's trajectory was within reach, he swung the bow horizontally across his body and used the razor-edged frame to cleave the bird neatly in half. Slowly he stood, slinging the bow diagonally across his chest. He picked up both halves of the bird and his arrow that had fallen back to the ground. Slowly he trotted back to the drill sergeant and presented the bird in both of its halves to him. Deadeye explained that the longbow was an art form of his people; the Apaches; and he had been trained to use it for his entire life. The razor bow was merely a modified longbow and as such was a natural extension of his lifelong training.

The drill sergeant quietly said, "Very good."

After Deadeye's show, only two cadets were still unaccounted for: Techno and Dancer.

"Great" Spartan thought. *"Two of my team members."*

Just then, Techno came awkwardly running toward the formation. In his hand he was carrying what looked like a collapsible silver and black police baton fully extended. The drill sergeant stopped the boy just shy of the formation.

"Why did you choose that weapon?"

A shy smile spread across the boy's plump Asian features. "Efficiency and…" He said extending the weapon with a flick of his wrist "technology!" The boy replied touching a small red stud on the rubberized handle of the weapon. As the button depressed, electricity arced and popped as the current crackled up and down the batons extended foot and a half-length. Techno also displayed his backup weapon which was a palm-sized multi-tool. The multifunctional tool set contained everything from the prerequisite knife to wire cutters, screwdrivers and scissors. It fit in perfectly.

Again, the drill sergeant nodded his consent as the chubby Asian boy fell into the formation quietly next to Spartan a smile upon his face. Now only Dancer was missing. Minutes stretched by and while the cadets began to murmur in concern and discontent, the drill sergeant just stood quietly and silently at the position of parade rest, with his feet spread apart and his hands clasped behind his back. His dark eyes remained focused on the buildings' darkened doorway.

After more than ten minutes, Dancer finally emerged from the Armory. Strapped diagonally across her back was a small Japanese blade. In her hand, she carried a five-foot-long staff that ended in a metal point on one end and a samurai sword type blade on the other. She quietly came and stood directly in front of the drill sergeant before surprising them all by taking a knee in presenting the weapon to him in an articulated gesture of honor reminiscent of feudal Japanese society. The drill sergeant further surprised the cadets by bowing as he took the polearm from the girl's outstretched hands.

Drill Sergeant Havok tested the blade, the weapons balance and spear like point. After several twirling and slashing maneuvers, the drill sergeant, weapon master stopped and placed the polearm back in the into the girl's outstretched hands again with a bow.

"The naginata is a fine weapon. It combines power, grace, efficiency and beauty. It is a wise choice." He said to the cadet. "And I see you've also selected the Japanese short sword as well. They shall serve you well in combat I think."

"Thank you, Sensei Havok." The cadet answered in a voice that only the drill sergeant could hear. Cadet Dancer again bowed, this time touching the bladed pole weapon and her head to the ground before rising silently to her feet and returning to the formation. Catching Spartan's inquiring eye, Dancer shrugged and would acknowledge him no more. It seemed there was more to this young lady than just a pretty face and sexy brown eyes. Spartan was determined to find out exactly what was behind the scenes with his teammate.

The next two days were spent in a grueling and muscle splitting series of understanding the cleaning and care of the cadet's weapons, physical training with the cadets' chosen weapons, physical training without the weapons, and individual study. The drill sergeants imposed very strict rules that were incorporated with all the cadets due to the potential lethality of the martial items they now carried. Sparring was prohibited unless directed and overseen by a drill sergeant and heaven forbid; don't drop a weapon on the ground.

Each cadet was expected to learn every nuance of their selected weapon, how to use it, its strengths and its weaknesses, and how to care for it. Some cadets like Freak and Gator for instance had little trouble mastering their choices and only had to study the fighting styles taught by the drill sergeants. Other cadets like Princess and Techno were a hazard to themselves, each other and everyone else around them as they flailed their weapons around dangerously. The jeweled sword and the electrified baton wreaked so much havoc that the two were finally separated from the group for their own safety… as well as everyone else's.

Before sunrise on the second morning, Spartan felt a small hand on his shoulder gently shaking him awake. The platoon had bivouacked under the stars in the fields of a farmhouse far from the armory while the Drill sergeant said Nurse Ortega slept within. A quiet voice said "shhhh…" And Spartan could see the chubby Asian boy, Techno, squatted beside him with a finger held to his lips. Silently, the boy motioned for Spartan to follow him as he maneuvered his way through the other sleeping cadets. Spartan chuckled as he passed the sleeping Freak, whose snores were echoing in the predawn light like a bear hibernating in a cave. As the two cadets reached the edge of the field, Spartan quietly spoke to the smaller boy.

"What's wrong Techno?" He asked leaning in so that his voice was a mere whisper in the boy's ear.

Nodding his head toward the east, the Asian boy whispered back. "I thought you should see this. It's amazing." tilting his head to the top of the hill. The purple, orange and pink sky of the predawn morning had barely lit the horizon, leaving much of the area still cast in elongated shadows.

"Where…?" Spartan said, but cut himself off.

Atop the hill, dressed in battle dress pants and a blue sports bra, Cadet Dancer slowly gyrated. In her hands was her chosen weapon, the naginata, slowly and methodically spinning through a dozen coordinated and interlocking patterns. Around her hands, behind her back, and above her head the bladed weapon flew. The steel blade glistened, reflecting the skies predawn firelight and dawn tones. Faster and faster the blade sang through the air and Spartan felt he could almost hear the thrumming in the air as the blade slashed by. Then, as the first blonde rays of the sunlight peaked over the horizon, the dancing blade stopped; its hypnotizing song ended. Spartan and Techno watched the girl known as Dancer, as if on some unseen movement in time lower her weapon to the ground. Redressing into her uniform, she quietly picked up her pole arm and began trotting back towards the camp.

Not wanting to risk embarrassing the cadet, Spartan and Techno silently agreed to say nothing and returned to their bedrolls. Not sure of exactly what he'd just seen, Spartan knew that there was far more to the female squad mate than he knew, and he intended to find out what it was.

Dawn to dusk training left all of the cadets sore and tired. After two brutal, bruising and bloodying days of training with their new weapons, the march back to the barracks of the Apocalypse Academy by the cadets seemed to pass in the blink of an eye. The file march was much noisier than it had been during their approach to the weapons armory. Weapons of every conceivable size and shape glinted in the sun and bounced noisily against packs and canteens as the cadets marched ahead with a bit of a newfound swagger. Perhaps it was the weapons emboldening the cadets or a newfound confidence that was growing with the training; but the platoon's footing was sure in their step and seemed to march in time much more than before. Spartan imagined what the platoon must've looked like from a bird's eye perspective. Something akin to a navy-blue armored caterpillar bristling with metal spines.

Drill Sergeant Hogg strode into the middle of the road, directly between the two columns. He was accompanied by the soft-spoken drill sergeant known as Havok. They seem to be engaged in another quiet yet serious debate. Sergeant Hogg was holding what appeared to be a foldout map in his left hand, though he did not seem to be reading it; more like crushing it in his fist as the two drill sergeants spoke. There was an obvious sense of anger or tension between the two men.

Spartan glanced back at the squad members, ensuring everyone was present. Freak grinned down at him, casually flipping his ever-present baseball up into the air and catching it again with his own massive glove size hand. The baseballs' leather hide made a soft "thwack" each time it landed in the massive hand. Techno jangled and stumbled along, definitely the least surefooted of the group. Of the entire squad, he was the only one out of step. His "Techno – club" as he dubbed his electrified, collapsible baton rattled in its holster at his waist. Fatigue showing on the boy's plump face, but he stoically endured the march without complaint. Spartan was not sure if this newfound endurance was so much a desire to succeed on his own or more likely, a fear of ending up like Rooster; pummeled and beaten to a pulp.

Dancer was next, her naginata acting in the surrogate role of a walking stick. Her step was light and unfatigued. Catching Spartan looking at her, she gave him a wide, beaming smile and a wink. Spartan felt the heat rush of a blush creeping up his neck like a horde of crawling insects. He nodded to the girl once and turned away. Damned if he didn't feel like a schoolboy when he looked at her. He would really have to focus to get that under control.

Lastly, he looked at Deadeye. The boy's skill with a razor bow had deeply impressed Spartan. Anyone could swing a sword or stick but it took real talent to do anything with a bow. Spartan vaguely recalled going to a camp one summer with his parents for vacation. He could not remember who else had been with him, but he remembered the thin fiberglass bow that he had found there. It'd been a cheap, children's target bow but as Spartan pulled the memory from his mind, he recalled innumerable hours spent shooting arrows at a hay bale with a paper bull's-eye attached to it. By the end of the summer, he could hit the paper in about one out of three shots, but he never could consistently hit the bull's-eye. To hit a flying bird overhead and then cut the bird in half on its way down, took some serious skills. He would have to remember to talk to the young Native American for advice on the weapon when they were alone.

Deadeye's facial muscles looked tense. Actually, Spartan thought the boy never seemed to relax, always appearing wary and on guard… Always looking for the next battle or obstacle ahead. Of all of the squad, only Deadeye moved silently. There was no rattle or jangle to his movements, only stealth masked with silence. The deadly looking Special Forces tomahawk hung from the boys' belt, was quite eye catching. The young Apache seemed to honor the ways of his elders, even as he accepted more modern versions of his ancient tribal equipment. Spartan nodded once to the teen and was acknowledged by a single return nod. Deadeye was doing okay; no further conversation was necessary.

Spartan's attention returned to the front of the column as a roar echoed out over the fields far in the distance. The sound of numerous engines revving up with the throaty "varoom" was immediately followed by the constant chattering of dozens of exhaust pipes. The sound of possibly one hundred or more motorcycles starting in unison just beyond the rise of a nearby hill echoed throughout the morning air.

"Cover!" The drill sergeants instantly called in unison as they ran to the ditches at the roadside, directing the cadets simultaneously to do the same. Spartan hurried his team into the ditch; however, the hulking Freak might as well have been standing in the middle of the road. His muscular bulk, even lying down was still completely noticeable.

The roar of the motorcycles grew louder as the engines engaged. Down the road, beyond the chain link fencing and just beyond the bend, Spartan could see a rising dust cloud as the motorcycles entered the roadway that they currently hid beside. Looking around quickly, Spartan noted a grove of elm trees about forty meters behind them and across a set of long unused railroad tracks. The drill sergeants and Spartan looked at each other and back at the grove. It was their only chance. Spartan did not know what this band motorcycles was about, but he knew that his drill sergeants had all automatically become deadly serious at the first indication that they were present. That was enough for him.

"Into the trees! Stay low!" Sergeants Hogg and Havok called down to the squad leaders "Pass the word!" With that the drill sergeants took off a full sprint, running for the woods. Spartan noted a drawn pistol in each of the drill sergeants' hands as they ran. As word was communicated down the platoon, the cadets followed suit, running for all they were worth. Halfway to the wood line, Spartan heard a small cry and a crash as one of the cadets fell. Turning he saw Techno sprawled out on the ground. Spartan knew his time was short and that the encompassing fence would provide absolutely no cover. The throaty roar of the motorcycles sounded as if it were only seconds away. Left alone, this boy was going to die. He did not know why he knew this, but the raised hairs on the back of his neck told him that this encounter was deadly serious and that the riders of the motorcycles would be upon them in mere seconds. Ten meters from the woods, Spartan stopped and called out to Freak. As the big man turned, Spartan hurled his rucksack towards him. The muscular black teen snatched it from the air effortlessly and continued into the woods. Time was running out the sound of the engines was much louder now. The throaty chop – chopping of the motorcycles' engines reverberated in Spartan's chest.

Looking around frantically, Spartan finally spotted what he was looking for. Casting a final glance at Techno; still sprawled and unmoving, Spartan whipped out his sword from its scabbard and raced to a nearby boxwood bush. Two quick swings of his razor-sharp blade and the four-foot bush separated from the stump and roots. Grabbing the severed bush in one hand and his sword in the other, he sprinted for all he was worth to his fallen teammate's side. Dropping the bush next to Techno, Spartan used the blade in his hands to excavate a three-inch wide, six-inch-deep hole. Dropping the sword, he grabbed the bush's stump and slammed it into the hole, propping it up right in front of him. He pulled the unconscious boy behind the improvised camouflaged hedge beside him just as the first motorcycle roared into view.

Peering through the makeshift hedge, Spartan watched as the procession of more than one hundred motorcycles roared onto the road at a high rate of speed, filling it completely with frames of steel and motors of oily power. Each motorcycle was ridden by a single or sometimes a male and female pair of black leather clad riders. Black leather spiked gloves worked the clutches and throttles of the steel horses and shining black leather boots led into heavy black leather chaps. Straining to see as the motorcycles roared past, Spartan noted that every person that rode the motorcycles was armed to the teeth, bristling with a vast assortment of knives, guns, axes and in some cases even sledgehammers. In addition, each motorcycle had a bleached human skull affixed to its back plate.

Slowly looking back at the tree line, Spartan could just make out the shadowed form of Drill Sergeant Hogg, hunkered down next to a huge elm tree. The drill sergeant slowly raised his hand in a clenched fist, silently telling him to be still. Sweat dripped down Spartan's face as he fought back both his fear and his impulse to run. He nodded slowly back to the drill sergeant. At least he knew that the Academy instructor had his back if it came down to a confrontation.

As the last of the motorcycles paraded past, Spartan felt himself once again begin to breathe, exhaling slowly. He hadn't realized that he had been holding his breath during the entire encounter. He managed to remain still as more than a hundred-armed motorcycle warriors had ridden past. He was feeling surprisingly good about his chances of survival until the very last motorcycle pulled to a stop at the side of the road, fifty meters directly in front of him. As the leather clad motorcycle warrior turned off his machine, he swung his leg over his bike and a three-foot-long, black machete slapped hard against his leather clad thigh. Walking to the side of the road, the man unzipped his chap's covered jeans and began to urinate through the fencing and into the ditch where just minutes before Spartan's team had been lying.

Demonically spiked shoulders glistened in the sunlight as he concluded his personal business. Turning back, the warrior began to walk to his motorcycle. Spartan noticed the club emblem emblazoned on the back of the vest. A scorpion with its tail stinger raised high, sat poised upon a white human skull. The entire image was wreathed in orange and red flames and above it in large sewed on letters where the white lettering L.O.D. Just as the man began to raise his booted foot to remount his motorcycle, a low moan came from beside Spartan. Of course, Techno would choose now to wake up. The man spun back around, drawing the machete in the blur of an eye.

Spartan slowly snaked his hand across the quasi-conscious boy's chest and clamped it down across Techno's mouth.

"If you move or make another sound, we are fucking dead!" He whispered urgently into the boys' ear. "Blink twice if you understand."

The Asian boy blinked twice as he had been told; fear showing in his eyes as Spartan released the pressure on his mouth.

The leather clad warrior looked around warily from the ditch side, scanning the immediate area for threats. Apparently unwilling to jump the fence and enter the woods alone, the man slowly backed up to his motorcycle. Hearing nothing else, the man re-sheathed his blade, and mounted the bike. With a half jumping motion, the man kick started the machine, engaged the gears and roared off after his fellow bikers.

Spartan fell onto his back feeling his muscles un-tense. Looking over at Techno he asked, "What happened?"

The boy looked back at his squad leader and sheepishly replied. "When we were told to run, I drew my baton. I just knew we were about to be eaten by a horde of "Z's" and I wanted to be ready. I stepped into a woodchuck hole and fell. I guess that I landed on my baton's activation button because there was a stinging jolt and then I woke up with you smothering me."

The remainder of the platoon emerged from the wood line. Both drill sergeants walked up to Spartan as he stood up from the ground. Drill Sergeant Havoc retrieved Spartan sword from where he had dropped it in the tall grasses diving for cover, and handed it back to the boy, pommel first.

"Your actions were brave and insightful Spartan." Drill Sergeant Havoc said as the boy took back his sword.

"And stupid!" Drill Sergeant Hogg added. "Instead of one dead cadet, I almost had two. Next time you want to be a hero, don't…"

"But…" Spartans started to reply looking over at Drill Sergeant Havoc.

"Drill Sergeant Hogg is quite right." The quiet man replied "while your actions showed courage and quick thinking, they also risked the safety of the entire platoon. There is no place for heroes here. Even if you had battled the man and possibly won, his friends would have returned to look for him. Finding him dead would have sparked their need for vengeance. Outmanned and outgunned, the platoon would've been slaughtered."

Spartan spoke "I understand. May I ask a question?"

Drill Sergeant Havok nodded.

"Who were they? Obviously, they were definitely not "Z's" driving motorcycles. Why would we be at risk from other humans?"

Drill Sergeant Hogg spoke up, his gruff tone even more annoyed. "Those useless pieces of monkey shit are a motorcycle gang. They've been screwing up what's left of humanity through criminal activities such as drug dealing, prostitution and various other entertainments like murder for hire since before the fall of the world into what we call the freakin' Apocalypse. Now they have a freakin' cult following among survivors in the abandoned lands. They profess to worship Satan, if you can believe that shit, and see the walking puss bags as undead avatars from their Lord and Master; ol' Scratch himself. They even call themselves the

L.O.D. or Lords of Death. I've heard that they took the idea of the acronym from some old-time wrestlers. I call 'em Lot of Douche bags." He said with an annoyed growl. "Rumor even has it that they are cannibals." He added with an afterthought, spitting a wad of tobacco juice onto the ground. "Bunch a pussies!"

Drill Sergeant Havok interrupted with a quiet "ahem".

"We need to get back to the Academy. If the LOD is moving out of the abandoned lands, we need to warn Colonel Slade."

The Drill sergeants ordered the squads to form up, followed by a double time run the remaining ten miles to the Apocalypse Academy. Upon arrival the cadets were immediately dismissed while the drill sergeants and their commanding officer met to discuss the newest turn of events. As they walked back to the dorms, Alpha squad all went together in a group. As they rounded the corner, Dancer suddenly stopped and turned to face Techno.

"What's wrong?" The Asian boy asked.

Without a word of explanation, the brown-haired girl's hand flew up from her side and open palm slapped Techno in the face raising a four-finger welt instantly upon his cheek. Tears of surprise formed in the boy's eyes. Rage was apparent on the pretty girl's face.

"You stupid bloody git!" She raged, eyes burning with fury. "The bollocks you pulled today could've gotten yourself; or worse, all of us killed. Get your shit together Techno. There's no place in a survival scenario for a wanker!"

Techno looked around at each of his squad mates in turn. All of them glowered back at him. Freak looked like he would pummel him senseless. Deadeye seemed to want to scalp him and Dancer had already paint brushed the taste out of his mouth, leaving a red handprint across his jaw line. The Asian boy looked over at Spartan, hoping for some clemency.

"It was an accident. I…"

Spartan cut him off. "Shut up Techno. Dancer's right. You risked us all today. Next time I leave you for dead."

With that they all turned and resumed walking, Techno walked far behind, his heart heavy and his cheek still stinging. Deep down, he knew they were right, and the thought troubled him deeply.

Dark Interlude

Lost Nation…A fitting name for the localized headquarters of the Lords of Death. Once it was a place of tranquility. It had been a clubhouse where grown men and women went to share in the sport of golf and to tell semi-fictional tales of athletic prowess over cocktails and beer. Now the social area had been converted into a den of debauchery and violence. Oak top tables had been marred by the rape of dozens of women. Knicks and gouges of varying lengths created miniature canyons in the bar top, stained red from where knives and axes had torn through the soft flesh of the biker's victims. It was a true perversion of the recreational intent of the clubhouse and that in and of itself made the Red Baron feel a sense of pleasure.

A bonfire burned brightly, illuminating the night around the first green. Raucous laughter arose from the surrounding shadows as the Lords of Death found their individual pleasures in sex, drugs or alcohol. Those that were committed to deriving pleasure from the pain and suffering of others sat with rapt attention to the bonfire and its spectacle.

A pair of teenagers hung above the fire; spitted as a farmer would impale a pig for cooking. The Lords of Death had captured the youths as they fled across the cornfields west of the town. They had carried no weapons, so the struggle had been brief. The boy had been strong; defiant and protective of his younger sister, and had refused to provide any information, even under the threat of death. The girl however had no such illusions of machismo. She had cried, and begged, and pleaded for mercy. She had offered sexual favors and information if the Baron would only let her and her brother live.

The Baron had always found the correlation between fear and pain to be exquisite. The art of breaking someone's spirit before destroying their body was intoxicating to him in a way that alcohol was to others. So, the first thing he did was to plunge his knife into the boy's stomach. The wound was deep and ultimately fatal. He had no use of the teenager anyway. But the wound was of a sort that would take days, perhaps even as long as a week, for the boy to die. He was certain that he would break the girl's spirit much faster than that. Promises of medical aid would drive her words. She would reveal anything to save her beloved brother.

Fear and panic usually made people talk. The girl was no exception. Two hours after his blade had speared through the boy's intestines, she revealed the purpose of their travel into the dangerous lands of the modern world. They had been told by a random survivalist of a place of safety nearby. A place of sanctity that the undead could not breach and that would provide the youths with the training and weapons needed to survive. She had called it an "*Apocalypse Academy*". To her credit she had resisted telling the Baron of the academy's location…at least until he had plunged his knife a second time into her brother's already lacerated guts. Then she had screeched the location through her tears in an effort to save him.

The Baron knew the place that she spoke of. He remembered the soldiers there from his life before he had welcomed the Demon King Xerxes to guide his blades. He had considered them all fools. Doomed idealists in a world gone mad. Now perhaps he had misjudged them.

Kneeling in the grass before the fire, the Baron used his knife to draw arcane sigils into the dirt. As he completed the last magical mark, the symbols flared red and the flames licked higher, gaining a purplish hue at their tips. Flesh from the two young corpses crackled and popped as the flames began to engulf the bodies. Fat sizzled as it melted away and dripped into the crimson coals.

Standing, the Red Baron drew forth his serrated sword and eviscerated both corpses with single slashes to each body. Freed from the confines of the blackened skin, the organs spilled down into the mystical flames, flaring the fire with arcane power. Space and time seemed to tear as a portal into the netherworld opened and the demonic visage of the Demon King Xerxes glared out of hell and into the unholy soul of the Red Baron.

"You were not summoned. Why do you seek audience with my greatness? Speak and if your words be not useful, I shall cast you down into the pit of despair where you shall languish in torment for all eternity!" The Demon King raged, his voice tearing into the Baron's mind as surely as a knife would rend his flesh.

"Yes, my King!" The Baron spoke, averting his eyes from Xerxes' unholy visage. "I would not disturb your most exaltedness without the greatest of purpose."

"Speak then or know my wrath!"

"We have received intelligence of a human training ground that has been established to train the survivors of your apocalypse. It is intended to be a bastion of humanity whose intent is to resist your exalted designs and to rebuild mankind."

The Baron paused for a moment, considering if he should reveal the nexus between himself and the Apocalypse Academy. Perhaps it would be best if he spun it as continued intelligence rather than personal knowledge. The Demon King did not seem to be the type to forgive any type of failure, including not providing knowledge of an enemy. Besides…Hogg and Slade were idealistic fools. They would not be hard to destroy with his Lords of Death.

"We have performed initial reconnaissance on the location. There appear to be minor defenses such as fencing and a small, occupied force of ex-soldiers. They will not provide a major source of resistance to your plans."

"Then destroy them before they can become entrenched like ticks upon a cur hound. Lead forth a force of the undead into their midst and destroy them utterly. Do not leave a single soul alive. This I command!!"

The Red Baron bowed. "As you wish my Lord… It shall be done as you say."

The last of the fat and flesh melted from the twin corpses, dropping the burnt flesh chunks into the sizzling coals. As the purple hue faded and the connection to the netherworld was severed, the Baron noted the blackened and charred skeletons still bound to the spits. Reaching down into the smoldering coals, he plucked out a sizzling gobbet of flesh and popped the morsel into his mouth. Ignoring the burn, he savored the flavor on his tongue. Human always tasted like bacon to him. Without a word he turned and walked away. He had plans to make and an undead army to raise.

Chapter 5
First Aid & Pacification

Spartan sat on the edge of the olive drab colored canvas cot. Definitely surplus military issue by the look of it, it now served as both a barracks bed and field hospital bed for the current training exercise. Basic first aid was "entertaining" to say the least. They were now eight weeks into the Academy curriculum. By now many of the cadets had suffered the tender ministrations of Nurse Ortega with injuries ranging from a vast variety of scrapes, cuts and sprains to Orc's first day broken nose. The cadets to a man or woman swore that the nurse was the direct emissary of the devil himself. Bones were cheerily set with a wide smile and a wink. Gashes of flesh were stitched with no more of a painkiller than a colored red, green or yellow lollipop "if you were brave" as she plunged her curved needle and coarse black suture thread into the flesh to sew it up before anyone could voice a concern.

Common rumors even had her amputating limbs with axes and chainsaws as well as dental work being performed with pliers and a flathead screwdriver for leverage. These were obviously gross exaggerations but still, the woman was brutally efficient and far from delicate. Spartan listened intently to the nurse as she recited the correct method to splint a broken forearm. To the best of his understanding, the concept was to apply enough pressure to the splint to ensure that the arm was truly broken before applying the securing bandages at three, six-inch intervals for stabilization. This was followed by the application of a sling that elevated the damage to a level above the heart and was just shy of choking its owner.

Spartan returned to the group of other cadets. He had been forced to sit down after Freak had applied a head-bandaging compression dressing simulating the treatment of a skull fracture. Under Nurse Ortega's direction, Freak had wound the bandage so tightly that it had cut off the blood flow to Spartan's brain. Spartan lasted about thirty seconds before his eyes rolled up into his head and he had blacked out, pitching forward onto the dirt floor. Freak had wisely removed the bandages immediately, but it still had caused him one hell of a headache.

To his surprise, Spartan saw the drill sergeants all file into the tent followed by the Academy Commandant, Colonel Slade. Slade's appearance apparently surprised the other cadets as well. They had not seen him since the very first briefing when he had welcomed them all to the Apocalypse Academy for the first time. Drill Sergeant Boomer hollered "Officer on deck!" and all the cadets now used to the military decorum had leapt to their feet, snapping sharply to attention.

"At ease, cadets." The short and lanky colonel replied walking to the center of the room. The Colonel still wore his dress green uniform that he had worn on their first visit with him at the Apocalypse Academy, his shoes gleamed in the light as if he was on his way to a military ball rather than an abandoned high school surrounded by teenagers and "Zs". Stepping up onto a wooden crate to provide height and oversight, the officer addressed his troops.

"Ladies and gentlemen, I am here for two things. The first is to welcome you to the second phase of your training at the Apocalypse Academy. If you recall in the first phase, your training consisted of basic physical fitness training and basic weapons familiarization with your chosen weapons. This training will continue throughout the remainder of your stay here at the Academy."

Groans came from the crowd as they all contemplated the additional physical training; however, the few muttered comments were ignored by the commanding officer as he continued his monologue. Spartan thought it was pure ignorance on the part of the cadets to assume that physical training would end anyway.

"You can never be too physically prepared. The second phase of your training consists of more specialization. It begins here with learning the various aspects of first aid. Since there are very few true doctors left in the world and none here the Academy, I strongly urge each of you to learn each and every technique and then practice it to perfection. Your ability to provide care to a teammate or civilian could mean the difference between life and death. The world has become a hostile and unstable place and we must be ready to deal with every eventuality. We must be able to heal the injured as efficiently as we eliminate the undead."

The Colonel paused and withdrew a thick cigar from his inner jacket pocket. Lighting it from an old worn Zippo lighter, Spartan noted the faded insignia as the Colonel snapped the lighter shut. It appeared to be a pair of crossed swords with a mountain in the background. Exhaling a thick plume of blue smoke, the Colonel again addressed the assembled cadets, holding up the burning cigar as if it were a pointer.

Turning the cigar sideways, he spoke calmly to the cadets.

"Who can tell me what this is?" he asked the cadets.

Cadet Gator raised his hand and spoke as the Colonel selected him by pointing the cigar his way.

"Why that's a Cee-gar Colonel!"

The Colonel shook his head. "That is only partially correct son. Anyone else care to try?" The Colonel looked around the barracks room but saw no other offers of an answer, so he continued.

"This is a *victory* cigar." He said, "So who can tell me what we won?"

It was Dancer who spoke up next. "We bloody well survived the blokes on motorcycles?" She stated in a soft voice.

"Exactly!" The commanding officer replied, "I was starting to think that my command was filled with mentally handicapped children. Very good, young lady."

"And why did we survive? Can anyone tell me that?" The Colonel waited silently for an answer. Receiving none he continued. "We survived due to three things. Number one: instinct. Danger was imminent you reacted accordingly. Number two: training. Your training provided you with the reflexes to adapt to the situation. Number three: luck. Isn't that right, Techno?" The Colonel asked directly to the portly Asian boy. The embarrassment evident on the teenager's face.

"Sir yes sir!" The cadet answered.

Returning his gaze to the assembled cadets, the Colonel paused to take a long, slow drag on the cigar. As he exhaled the Colonel looked over at Drill Sergeant Hogg and nodded once.

"Cadet Spartan! Front and center!" The Drill sergeant hollered.

"Oh crap." Spartan thought as he weaved his way through the cadets toward the Colonel and the Drill sergeants. *"I am dead meat. They're going to kick me out of the Academy."*

Spartan stopped directly in front of the Colonel at the position of attention and saluted. To his confusion, the Colonel ignored him to speak to the other cadets again, leaving him standing, holding a salute.

"For every action, there is a consequence. An equal and opposite reaction is certain to occur for each and every decision that we make."

Spartan felt his heart drop. Where would he go? He couldn't remember even where he was from much less have a destination. He was so screwed.

"The choices that we make in our lives define who we are and what we will become. The decision to leave a partner behind never has positive consequences. There are few enough humans left on this planet and fewer still of high moral character."

Spartan could feel the sweat popping out on his forehead and slowly rolling down his temples and his upper lip. He knew he was hip deep in shit.

"This cadet failed to follow orders. He was instructed to fall back to the tree line, yet he did not do so. His actions were reckless and bordered on direct insubordination."

"Here it comes!" Spartan thought *"A one-way ticket to the abandoned lands."*

The Colonel continued. "In doing so, he risked every cadet in this platoon as well as himself. This event alone is a sufficient reason for expulsion from the Apocalypse Academy."

This brought an appalled murmur from the cadets that rippled, like stone striking water throughout the barracks. Dancer began to the openly protest but was stopped short by the Colonel's gesture.

"However, he also exhibited courage, ingenuity and leadership in saving another cadet's life. In mitigation of this event, I have had to weigh my decision and have reached an agreement with the drill sergeants' here at the Apocalypse Academy. So, it is with a stern heart..."

"I am so dead."

"... I sentence you..."

Spartan steeled his jaw, bracing for the words of expulsion that would effectively be a death sentence.

"... to the heaviest of personal burdens..."

The silence of the impending words hung in the air like an invisible signpost over the tavern of doom. The Colonel paused, taking another drag on the thick cigar before he continued.

"... promotion to the rank of Corporal."

"Okay, I understand sir. I'm outta here... I can survive... I... I... What?" Spartan blurted out loud. His brain was splitting worse than it had been from Freak's head dressing. The Colonel came and stood directly in front of him returning the salute that he had been holding for so long. "Did you just say... I was... promoted?"

"Well done son. You saved that boy's life. It was a very brave thing to do." The Colonel said, offering his hand to shake waiting for Spartan to bring his hand down from his brow. As Spartan shook the Commander's hand, Drill Sergeants Hogg and Havoc came to either side of him and began to attach the two Chevron bars to his collar. Waiting as the drill sergeants pushed the small spikes through the coarse material, Spartan barely felt the pain as both drill sergeants slammed their fists down on the freshly attached rank insignia, affecting the age-old tradition of "blooding" his rank by shoving the twin points of the securing pins a quarter of an inch deep into his skin.

A round of applause began from one or two cadets or possibly even Nurse Ortega who had been quietly standing off to one side of the room. The applause quickly became a thundering roar as the majority of cadets cheered for him. Only Echo team stood without applause. Their team leader's face bent into a sneer of contempt. The thought of Spartan receiving a promotion for saving that fat fool from his own team made him want to puke. After several moments, the Colonel raised his hand and the crowd quieted.

"Pay close attention to what happened here today. You must all learn to protect each other. There is little enough humanity left in this pathetic world. Between "Zs", raiders and infected wildlife, your chances of survival are low enough. Any chance to save a life, no matter how desperate, is worth the risk because when we refuse to act… when we ignore our humanity, we become no better than a "Z" ourselves, staggering through life one step at a time, only worrying about our next meal."

"That is not to say that Spartan's actions were not without risk. He could've easily been killed or captured. The risk he took was calculated to save his teammate's life. I would like to believe that each and every one of you would have done the same if the circumstances had been similar. The training that you do here each and every day is difficult. But it is not without purpose. You saw firsthand how important that training is. Do not forget that lesson. It may save your life one day."

With that, the Colonel turned and clapped Spartan on the shoulder then walked out of the door of the training area. It was Sergeant Hogg who broke the silence.

"If we're all done being mushy and holding hands, perhaps we can get a little training done. I don't think you'll find the next block of instruction quite so cheerful."

PACIFICATION

. . . . .

Three days of being wrapped, poked, prodded and bandaged in a plethora of positions and angles left the cadets ready for the next portion of their training. The cadets were now confident in how to fix sprains, set bones, run IV fluids, and even seal a punctured lung in the event of an emergency. After eating MRE's morning, noon and night, the cadets sat by squads at the chow hall eagerly eating a ground beef and noodle combination that the cook had affectionately termed "ghoulash". It was a bland meal, and the beef was tough, but it was a hot rarity while the cadets had been training. The cadets had, of course, had several other terms of endearment for the repeatedly served meal to include "barf entrée", "beef noodle hell" and "Yuck!" This last term was especially popular among female cadets.

When the meal was concluded, which was when the instructors had finished wolfing down their food; the cadets reformed their ranks and marched back to "the Morgue" as Nurse Ortega's training tent had come to be known as. As they entered the tent, the first thing the cadets noticed was that the chairs had been rearranged into a "U" shape in the center of the room and that the cots had been removed. Upon each chair sat at the paper blue surgical mask, blue latex rubber gloves, and a set of safety glasses.

"What the hell d'you think that's about Dawg?" Freak asked Spartan, inclining his head at the assembled chairs and supplies.

"Don't know bro," Spartan replied, "but it can't be good."

After all of the cadets had entered the training room, Nurse Ortega walked through the tent flap, her black ponytail flipped over to one side. Over her fatigues she wore a pale blue paper smock with white latex gloves on both hands. Safety glasses sat high on her forehead and a paper mask rested just below her chin.

"Cadets." She said acknowledging the students for the first time as her brown eyes carefully scanned the room. Her voice sounded strange, almost strained. They were used to her cheerful demeanor but now she was carefully enunciating each word and seemed to be struggling for control. "Sooner or later, either one of us or one of you will fall victim to the toxic bite of a "Z". As we all know, the "HUNGER" virus is highly contagious to our systems, with death and reanimation always occurring within twelve hours. What you don't know, and what I am here to teach you today, is how to keep that inevitable return from happening. How to make sure that the end of your individual roads in life does not just turn out to be a U-turn onto the highway of undeath."

Snickers and muttered comments could be heard from Echo team although they were low enough to be ignored.

The nurse turned her upper body and motioned to the open tent front. A moment of quiet but tense expectation was broken as the Drill Sergeants Boomer and Havok slowly pushed a four wheeled metal hospital gurney into the tent and placed it at the center of the "U" of chairs. Dutifully, Nurse Ortega pulled the safety glasses and mask into place. Her eyes carried a hardness to them that made the cadets uneasy. The answer to the unspoken curiosity of what to expect during this lecture was quelled, as well as the several others that went unasked when the cadets viewed the cadaverous undead that was securely strapped down to the medical cart. Wide leather straps and thick metal buckles pulled taunt across the corpse's chest, waist, sides and arms. An additional heavy leather and steel muzzle was strapped to the undead's face making it appear as if it were some sort of nightmarish version of Hannibal Lecter. Blood red eyes stared blankly ahead as the creature's strapped down arms flexed mindlessly against their bindings attempting to get to the living flesh surrounding it within the room. The "Z" was dressed in military fatigues but was mostly unrecognizable having decayed severely, eliminating an immediate chance of recognition. White strands of hair pushed outward from the creature's pale gray flesh giving the appearance of a grotesque mad doctor. The creature, thankfully, was completely immobilized.

Nurse Ortega walked over to the surgical tray that had been wheeled into the tent and had been stood over in the corner. Turning around, she slowly wheeled the surgical tray in front of her until she stood beside the undead corpse that lay strapped to the table. She spoke slowly as she adjusted the tools on the tray laying a certain few nearest to the animated cadaver's chest. The way that she was placing them into orderly rows spoke of years of surgical experience.

"You all know, or should have at least guessed by now, that these creatures are not truly alive; at least not in the traditional sense of the word. There is no heartbeat to force blood through arteries and veins to the organs and muscles. There is no formalized autonomic system any longer. Despite what the idiots in Hollywood would have you believe, the undead do not breathe. They will not sniff you out like a dog looking for a treat. These creatures do not feel pain of any sort. Injury based on nerve damage and subsequent impulses do not disable them. Physical pain such as having a limb crushed with a lead pipe or amputated, only serves to disable that specific limb. In addition, physical trauma to the arms, legs, back, chest, hands and feet will not permanently disable one of these creatures. It may knock them down briefly, but make no mistake, they *will* get back up."

To prove this, Sergeant Boomer stepped forward at Nurse Ortega's gesture. He was holding a four-foot-long length of metal pipe in his meaty hands. Nurse Ortega took a step back as the drill sergeant raised the pipe high above his head and brought it slamming down on top of the creature's right shin bone just above the ankle. The tibia shattered with an audible crack instantly splintering bone to jagged pulp and flattening the lower leg to the width of a cheap dime store novel. Collective gasps of horror echoed through the crowded cadets, coupled with the gurgling chuckle coming from the seats on the far right of the surgical table where Echo team sat. The husky boy known as Orc guffawed loudly at the creature's debilitating injury. As a team, the Echoes' elbowed each other excitedly, pointing at the mangled leg, whispering and enjoying the carnage. To Spartan, the Echo team's snorting laughter sounded very similar to a group of pigs rooting for truffles.

Blackened blood had spurted outward from five or six angles in the undead creatures crushed limb where broken bone had penetrated the skin in compound fractures, painting the stainless-steel gurney and the cadet's legs seated in the front row of the "U" with a necrotic version of a bloody Rorschach test. As gruesome as the injury was, the creature exhibited no sign of physical or emotional pain. Looks of disgust and revulsion were clear even beneath the surgical glasses and pale blue masks that the cadets now wore.

At a second nod from Nurse Ortega, Sergeant Boomer drew his combat knife from its sheath. Dropping the lead pipe to the ground with a clatter, Sergeant Boomer rammed the combat knife into the creature's upper chest cavity, skewering its heart and burying the razor-sharp blade all the way to the hilt in the creature's torso. The only reaction from the "Z" was to moan from deep within its throat and glare hungrily at the drill sergeant through crimson eyes; its teeth clacking together viciously beneath the hardened leather and steel caged muzzle as it strained to bite him.

One would've thought the drill sergeant had told a joke as Echo team all began to copy the teeth clacking noise of the "Z" and laugh hysterically as it vainly tried to bite the black Drill sergeant.

Spartan looked around the circle at the collection of cadets that were assembled there from the various teams. The expressions of curiosity, anger and outrage were paralleled on every face; except by the Echo team members who were displaying mirth, joy and humor. Only two cadets sat without emotion. Techno, who studied the creature analytically with a stoic, scientific curiosity and Spartan himself who did not spare the creature a second glance; already knowing what he would see. Silently he looked at the ground.

After allowing the grievousness of the wounds to mentally sink into the cadets, Nurse Ortega spoke once again.

"Since the H1N1GR infection began, which you now know as the HUNGER, scientists have sought any and every manner to cure and then destroy these poor empty souls. First, the humane approach was applied. Antibiotics, anti-virals and exploratory surgery to isolate the pathogens were all attempted. These methods were met with complete and utter failure and dozens of unintentional infections. Neither complex chemical compounds nor any variety of chemical cocktails known to man could neutralize or even arrest the growth rate of the Hunger infection. If someone was bit, they died. No ifs, ands or buts. No exceptions."

"Next, we tried more invasive and aggressive treatment such as radiation, cellular implantation and stem cell treatments. Apart from an increase in hair loss and cataracts, the failure rate remained at one hundred percent for mortality. If you were infected then you would die, plain and simple."

"So, we began to study why the infected were so driven to attack the living. Did their decaying bodies need nourishment? Was it a chemical imbalance in the brain or body? Was there another external force causing the creatures to become violent? Perhaps magnetic or sonic influences on the brain or was it something even more sinister, like a chemical or toxic agent in their bloodstream? The scientists hypothesized and theorized, then agonized over their repeated failures. The infection was similar in most respects to mad cow disease, but prions were such a new field of study that the best that they could do was try to make a comparative analysis between the two. Needless to say, that came up fruitless."

"The answer that was best formulated by scientists was actually first formed by an eight-year-old little boy, as he watched as his infected father and mother devoured his infant sister. *"His parents were hungry."* Basic, primal, instinct carried to the brain on a viral infected neurological pathway that overrode every other instinct including pain, the need for sleep or the need for procreation. The name stuck.

H1N1GR or HUNGER was the name given to the prion-based virus that had infected and overran the earth in a pandemic worse than any ever seen before."

"So now that the malady had a name, the remnants of the CDC and the World Health Organization began to search for a cause. What was the origin of this devilish disease? How could it cross mammalian species when no known viruses or bacteria could do so with equal expectations of infection to every kingdom, phylum or genus? How could the disease equally affect man and women, young and old, healthy or ill without *EVER* running into any type of genetic barrier that could hold it in check, even for a short time? The answer went back to that same brilliant; little traumatized eight-year old's observation. It was the brain. It was the primal portion of that complex organ that existed to control our base functionality. It was our built-in survival instinct that told us when we were hungry."

"The disease initially began its infection by invading the blood stream through a variety of methods. Transmission vectors included bites, sneezes, scratches by infected flesh, and contact with feces, kissing and even sexual intercourse. Yes, sex. You would be amazed at just how many people were infected because they felt the need to kiss an infected loved one goodbye one last time or to make love before death overtook their spouse, partner or friend. Of course, those are purely human emotional attachments; the animals had no such compunction. If they were infected, then they went about their normal routines until they died and reanimated. If another animal was in heat, there was still the primal drive to copulate. According to a study prior to the beginning of the outbreak, there were an estimated two hundred and fifty million rats living in New York City alone. Think about that. Two hundred and fifty million infected rats just in one city. That estimate was made within the first month of the outbreak. If calculated exponentially then the rate of infection caused by a single rat until the entire population within that city was decimated and resurrected as an undead beast, took roughly a month."

"Through thousands of autopsies performed on the long dead, but reanimated corpses, brought in by scientists that were aiding military operations around the globe, as well as the still living humans and animals that had been recently infected, but had not died and reanimated yet, one commonality was found. Again, it was the brain. The center of our ability to think, to reason, to feel, to react and our foundation of pure, primal, survival instinct. Some say the brain is the core of our very soul if you believe in religious rhetoric. The brain in each and every instance was perforated with millions of microscopic holes and had transformed from a soft, pink mass of tissue into something that more closely resembled grayish-black sponge-like matter. The frontal and temporal lobes decayed first as the infection set in and for lack of a better term dried out those areas eliminating aspects of the self, such as personality, ethical behavior, memory, expressive language and all emotion. The parietal lobe failed next destroying the subject's ability to read, write and calculate. Lastly, the occipital lobe falls under attack removing the victim's ability to discriminate people facially and ends when the savage rupturing of the blood vessels within the eyes occurs, indicating that the person has fully transitioned to a reanimated state."

"To the best of those honored men and women's findings before they were either devoured or were turned into the undead themselves, the area of the brain that appeared least affected by the disease was the hypothalamus which coincidentally controls hunger. For those of you that are not familiar with anatomy and physiology, the human brain generally weighs between three and four pounds while the hypothalamus in a human is roughly the size of an almond. That's pretty damn small."

"The brain in each and every case was altered. Mammals of every ilk were affected. If it had a brain, then it was at risk. Male and female, carnivore, herbivore and omnivore, every nationality, every breed, every religion. Only one abnormality was observed in the reanimation process and reported by the educated folks at the CDC. Children reanimated faster than adults. Why? Does anyone have a guess?"

No one raised a hand to answer.

The nurse shrugged her shoulders. "No one really knows. I sure as shit don't. Maybe they had stronger circulatory systems to pump the infection through the body? Maybe they had more muscular vigor? Hell, it could even be a divine selection process for all we know but the reality was that the young of every species animated much, much faster and were just as lethal as their older counterparts. No exceptions were noted before the CDC and the WHO were overrun. Now, it's just people like me and the few medical doctors that take a WAG at it."

Dancer raised her hand. "Beggin' your pardon Ma'am but I do not understand. WAG?"

"It means "wild ass guess". It's a military acronym cadet." Sergeant Boomer answered in his baritone voice.

"Copy that drill sergeant. Thank you." Dancer replied. She seemed slightly embarrassed by not already knowing the answer.

"Finally, the decision was made by the first and only universal meeting of the world's leaders that the infected could not be saved and must be destroyed unequivocally to have any chance at all to save humanity. Primary targets were selected by the governments of the world in an attempt to minimize casualties. Major cities that were considered "lost" were the primary targets. New York, London, Moscow, Beijing, Mexico City, L.A., Paris, and Rome to name just a few became tactical strikes in an attempt to quell the growing infections.

Sergeant Boomer snorted at this and muttered that it took the infected ten days to travel around the globe and contaminate every god damn country." He said shaking his head "that wasn't bad enough, so we nuked ourselves and so did every other country. Fucking idiots!"

Nurse Ortega nodded her head in agreement, the pale blue paper gown crinkling with her movements then she continued. "So, the way that I see it as I mentioned earlier, the problem was our own humanity, our own sensitivity and compassion for friends and family in the face of adversity. Some people blame the various churches of the world. Before you ask; not some cross jockey or towel head started the infection. Not even the Chinese or the crazy ass people in the Middle East have that kind of technology. But the constant rhetoric of caring for the sick and infected rather than putting them down mercifully resulted in families hiding family members and friends that had been bitten from the government patrols rather than resorting to say goodbye and keeping their homes sterile. The result was sweet hugs to the dying that became throat tearing bites of the infected. Final tender moments gazing into brown, blue or green eyes became horrific battles for survival as the victim's optical colors faded first to a milky white and then to a bloody red as the blood vessels in the infected person's scleras burst. Emotion became death."

"As such, it became a dire vulnerability to the survival of the human race. Mothers and fathers bit children and parents. Neighbors slaughtered neighbors and infected teachers ambushed unsuspecting students creating enormous roaming packs of the undead. Even the political leaders, who knew what was happening, refused to let emotion be subjugated by reason. In the end, one thousand years of civilization was destroyed in twenty-one days, as our passion for compassion allowed the dead to claim ownership of our world."

Every sound within the barracks had ceased except for the continual creaking of the undead corpse's leather bindings. Even Echo team was silent for once, listening to the nurse. Looking over her shoulder, the bronze nurse noted the creature's bloody red gaze of hatred glaring up at her. Nurse Ortega picked up a scalpel and deftly plunged it directly into the corpse's occipital socket. With a deft circular flick of her wrist, she severed the optical nerves and ejected the amputated eyeball through the air where it landed at Cadet Princess's booted feet. The cadet lurched over backward landing on her back, shattering the silence with her panicked screams of revulsion, as her metal chair clattered to the floor.

If the brown skin nurse noticed at all, she gave no indication as she set to work removing the creature's other crimson eyeball and ejecting it with a second plop onto the floor. When she finished, blood streaked her blue paper smock and she slowly turned setting the scalpel back onto the surgical tray and returning her gaze back to the cadets. Peeling off the latex gloves, she tossed them down beside the surgical implement. Reflexively she flipped her ponytail back over to the side of one shoulder and brushed her bangs out of her face with her forearm careful to avoid the blood that streaked the material.

"I hate their eyes the most. Soulless, lifeless yet full of bloody malice and hatred. If the eyes are truly the windows to the soul, then it is no wonder these creatures are fogged over with the red of blood because there is nothing left but evil beneath them. Whatever humanity they had is gone and that is all that made them human beings. Now they are nothing but infected meat."

With that, she brought her combat booted foot down on the first optical orb that she had plucked free. The ensuing pop and splat as the eye split beneath the rubber of her boot sole could be heard across the entire room.

"Madre de Dios, I hate them!" She hissed venomously looking down at the ground and the pulped eyeball that oozed from beneath her combat boot.

Sergeant Boomer quietly laid a hand on the nurse's shoulder from behind. Spartan thought he saw a single tear dribbling down the medic's face beneath her safety glasses as she turned and walked out of the room without saying another word. After a brief pause and a deep breath, Sergeant Boomer donned a pair of latex gloves and safety glasses, then picked up the lesson and began to talk to the cadets, continuing where Nurse Ortega left off.

"Why do you need to know all of this information cadet's?" He asked.

As a unit the cadets responded. "To know the enemy's weakness is the key to victory, drill sergeant!" They called.

"True, but that is not the reason for today's lesson." The drill sergeant turned to the surgical tray and picked up a small steel mallet and what looked like an eight-inch-long, razor-sharp, gleaming steel twisted railroad spike. The spike was attached to the mallets handled by a three-foot length of thin metal chain.

"The only way to truly kill a "Z" is to rupture the hypothalamus in the brain. It is the "almond" that Nurse Ortega described for you. As you've seen demonstrated today, massive traumatic injury, amputation or disfiguring events have no effect at all on the undead. To kill a "Z" in the field you may use a bullet or a bat to the skull, fragmentation grenades or even a sharp blade like a sword severing the cerebral cortex and hypothalamus. That type of destruction is good enough for the "average" Z" to be sure. However, when one of our own falls victim to the infection we owe them a final debt for their service in the preservation of mankind. They deserve to be pacified. To be put to rest without fear of being eternally damned to walk the earth as one of these filthy soulless monsters."

The muscular drill sergeant walked to the head of the gurney and placed the sharpened steel tip of the twisted railroad spike against the corpse's forehead. The "Z" began to writhe and fruitlessly rise against its bonds attempting to bite the drill sergeant through the heavy muzzle. Perhaps it was sensing its end was near. A beleaguered moan escaped from beneath the leather muzzle.

"Rest in peace Doc." The drill sergeant said quietly and raised the mallet high above his head. Swinging the mallet downward, there was a metallic chunking sound as it drove the spike through the creature's forehead. The "Zs" diseased body spasmed once and ceased thrashing on the table. Sergeant Boomer slowly withdrew the spike from the corpse's skull. Grayish-black, rotten brain matter pulled at the corkscrewed spike as if not wanting to let it go. Finally, it slid free with a sickening suction sound like a bathmat being pulled from a shower. Sergeant Boomer frowned as he was wiping the spike clean on a sterile cloth and replacing the pacification tool on the surgical table.

"Driving the spike into the brain and disrupting the hypothalamus will pacify the individual instantly and permanently. Do not forget today's lesson." He said pausing as he faced the cadets. Outside the hysteric sobs of a female could be heard. Spartan was certain that it was Nurse Ortega. "It is not difficult to kill a "Z" that you do not know. Most of us have already done so. Failing to pacify one that you do know because of love or friendship could be disastrous to us all. Failing to pacify a fellow warrior that has been infected and that has turned is a grievous insult and will get you cast out of the Apocalypse Academy with no second chances. Steel your emotions. Master them and only let them loose when it is truly safe to do so. Class dismissed."

Spartan and the other cadets rose as one and departed the barracks somberly, single file. Pausing beside the corpse on the gurney, Spartan gently pulled the restraining chest strap downward and read the name so on the right side of the creature's camouflage fatigue jacket. A realization struck him across the face at what he'd just witnessed. Looking at Freak, Techno and Dancer who had also stopped beside him, Spartan showed them the name.

"Ortega" he said quietly putting two and two together in his mind. "Doctor Ortega. Nurse Ortega just mangled and destroyed her own husband's undead corpse to teach us this lesson. Never forget it guys. We owe it to her. That had to be hell for her." He said releasing the strap back over the nameplate. Together they filed silently out of the room. Dancer, Freak and Techno silently stifled the pain of love ones remembered from their own harrowed pasts and felt pity for the nurse who was always so kind to them, the nurse with the nerves of steel yet a broken heart.

Chapter 6
Hand to Hand combat, Land Navigation and Knife Fighting

Physical training had intensified incrementally since the first week at the Apocalypse Academy. Now in week ten, hundreds of miles of asphalt had churned and burned beneath the cadets booted feet as they ran in formation repeatedly behind the Academy's riverside grounds. Now that the cadets were less of a hazard to themselves, everything was done in body armor while carrying their chosen weapons. The drill sergeants called it full battle rattle, a none too imaginative name, yet precise words for full gear up and movement. Every cadet benefited from the exercise, weekly vitamin injections and flexibility training that built endurance and fortitude.

Spartan mentally reviewed his team as his booted feet rhythmically pounded the pavement during this morning's ten-mile run. Freak, who had already been huge, was now a hulking beast. Veins emerged from the mountains of muscle crisscrossing his arms and shoulders like a human roadmap. The feats of strength that Freak had displayed were truly awe inspiring. One swat from either of the Blues Brothers was enough to reduce even the toughest of cadets to a timid mouse even in training and that was when padded. Once while performing hand-to-hand combat drills; Freak had been partnered up with Cowboy from Charlie team. The lesson had been judo style hip throws to address getting rid of a "Z" that was attacking from behind before he could infect you. For the scenario, Freak was identified as the "victim" while Cowboy was to play the part of a "Z". While the other cadets watched, Freak walked casually across the training mats. Cowboy pounced when the big man was dead center in the room. Rearing his head back, "Cowboy Z" prepared to bite Freak's trapezius or upper shoulder area on his right side. Freak's left-hand shot across his body, grabbing "Cowboy Z" by his right forearm. Shifting his hips, Freak pivoted and in one motion yanked Cowboy from his feet. Cowboy's body inverted as his skull and shoulders crashed into the-inch-thick training mat with an audible thump. "Cowboy Z's" eyes rolled up into his head and the air burst out of his lungs and through his mouth in a rush. Freak swiveled and resumed his combat stance preparing for his next maneuver.

Looking down at the fallen cadet's face, Freak immediately began to holler for the Drill sergeants' and Nurse Ortega. Cadet Cowboy had not moved. His eyes were fully rolled up into his head and a trickle of deep, red blood slowly dribbled from the corner of his mouth. After securing him firmly to a stretcher, the drill sergeants had Cadet Gator from Delta team and Meatball from his own team, carried the litter to Nurse Ortega's office. The big cadet felt horrible about injuring his teammate.

As training resumed, Dancer walked softly up to Freak and Spartan where they sat on the sidelines watching the other cadets spar. The big cadet was still obviously upset.

"Just what the bloody hell did you think you were doing out there Freak?!" She hissed through gritted and clenched his teeth. "You could've killed him out there, you tosser!"

"I was just training like we were supposed to Dancer. I never meant to hurt him none. I just got caught up in the moment." Freak held his hands up defensively in front of him.

Spartan took a step back as the brown-haired whirlwind stepped directly into Freak's personal space, jabbing her index finger into his chest repeatedly as she spoke. Each jab was like an angry little exclamation mark.

"The… (poke)… next… (poke)… time… (poke)… You… (poke) hurt… (poke) a cadet… (poke)… I will… (poke)… hurt you! (poke)

Freak held his hands up looking to Spartan to save him. Spartan stood silently off to the side with his hands and feet at the position of parade rest. His eyes were shifted far away from the conflict in front of him. Catching his eye, Dancer glared at him also, but Spartan only shrugged his shoulders in response. Whirling on her heel, Dancer took two steps than spun back to Freak. The big man looked like he had been chastised by his grandmother.

"We are all on the same team Freak. The human team! "Z's" are everywhere. We cannot afford to hurt our own people. Control yourself you oversized plonker." She said in a sage voice.

"Yes ma'am" was all the big man could say "I'm sorry."

"Me too guvnor." She replied and snapped a lightning-fast kick into the hulking cadets' genitals, dropping him to the floor with a moaning grunt of pain and a look of utter shock.

Dancer looked over her shoulder at Spartan. The team leader had not moved. Looking her directly in the eye, Spartan gave a single nod. Dancer turned without a word and stalked away.

"Yep" Spartan thought *"the team is shaping up nicely."* Then he, as well as Techno and Deadeye helped their hulking friend back to his feet.

The remainder of training in hand-to-hand combat resulted in no further injuries. Cadet Cowboy returned by the end of the day no worse for wear beyond a severe headache.

The next morning after PT, the cadets were marched to the edge of the wooded area; where many of the cadets had been proving themselves to be experts at direct, in your face combat. Deadeye demonstrated his skills and ancestral prowess moving swiftly and silently through the various training grounds that had been created for training at the Apocalypse Academy. Urban, rural and wilderness movement appeared to be second nature to the young Apache. The other cadets, especially the larger ones like Freak, Orc and Meatball lumbered through trees and buildings, clanking and crashing like proverbial bulls in a china shop. To Deadeye, every little noise told a story. Every footfall held a location. Every scent identified a target.

In an effort to impress the importance of silent movement upon the cadets, the drill sergeants had created a challenge drill where the cadets attempted to "tag" each other with red paint filled, hollow training knives. The cadets were allotted thirty minutes to find a hiding place or ambush spot. When the whistle blew, it would be every cadet for themselves.

Orc lasted exactly one minute, as he tripped over a chair in the first building that he entered and was promptly "knifed" by Bravo team's Dragon, much to Sergeant Boomer's delight. Freak did not last much longer when he attempted to creep up a staircase only to find Delta team's Knight waiting on the high ground of the landing and Charlie team's curly haired Cadet Popcorn closing off his retreat back down the stairs. In the end, Knight and Freak eliminated each other simultaneously while Popcorn bounced away taking the steps two at a time and returning to his hiding place waiting for another victim, like a trapdoor spider.

Throughout the battle, no one saw Deadeye lying low and watching from the deep shadows between the furniture. He was nothing more than a ghosting shadow following the movements of his teammates and his enemies. As time passed, cadets eliminated each other continuously. Dancer eliminated Princess only to be immediately put out of the contest by Gator as she tried to cartwheel out of the way. Techno fell to Lightning and Vulture put a red X on Deacon's back from behind a tree. Cutter, who was extremely skilled with his knives, eliminated several cadets including Pig, Vulture, Medusa, and his own teammate Skull. Moving swiftly, Cutter paused only long enough to pick up Skull's knife despite his teammate's complaint. Now armed with two training blades; Cutter raced off to find the others. Again, no one saw Deadeye move. With ninja-esque stealth and unerringly balanced footsteps, he flowed from his shadowed concealment to where he now perched, crouching high in the branches of the trees… Silently watching like a hawk studying a rabbit exiting the safety of its burrow.

Spartan also fared well, eliminating several opponents with a quick series of slashes, faints and thrusts. Delta team's afro – wearing Cadet Jive, Echo team's Cadet Savage and the diminutive Popcorn from Charlie team never had a chance. Even Cadet Lightning, who was skilled at stealthy movement, fell to a quick leg sweep and thrust of Spartan's training knife.

Zero company was down to less than ten combatants in a sum total of thirty minutes. Cutter and his Echo teammate, Lotus Jane had formed a temporary truce; agreeing to work together until they were the only two cadets left, then they would battle to determine the winner. Their partnership was very productive. Together they eliminated the fiery redheaded Rooster with a combined ten paint field slashes across to his head, throat and back. Cadet Gator was eliminated next with a single well thrown blade from Cadet Cutter.

Cadet Deadeye silently watched as Cutter squared off with Dragon in the front yard of an abandoned house. As the two cadets slowly circled each other, they jabbed and feinted with their training blades. Red paint simulated bloody damage of previously fallen foes. Cutter's twin blades whirled in a red dance of dripping paint amid hollow plastic knives. Dragon's martial arts allowed him to flip, tumble, twist and turn out of harm's way repeatedly while he sought to penetrate the dual knife defenses of the Echo team leader. Despite several close slashes, Dragon was unable to find a weakness in Cutter's defense. Similarly, Dragon's skill prevented Cutter from striking a killing blow with either of his training knives. Strike met strike…block met block… and both combatants punched, kicked, and dodged until they were exhausted.

Finally, the two separated, Cutter leaning against an abandoned car that stood on the roadside, his breath coming heavily. Dragon backed away literally, leaning against a tree on the opposite side of the yard. Sweat poured down both cadets faces as they both gasped for breath, exhausted from their combat. Cutter was the first to regain his feet, moving slowly back towards the Asian martial artist. As Cadet Dragon stepped back into the yard from where he had leaned against the tree and assumed the fighting stance, he felt the slap of a blunt plastic sting against his Achilles tendons. Looking down he saw Lotus Jane lying on the ground holding her paint knife and grinning up at him.

"Yer out, Bruce Lee!" She quipped twirling her paint knife between her fingers. Dragon could only watch as Cutter and Lotus Jane gave each other a high five and then ran into the wood line. Zero Company was down to four combatants.

Spartan came around the corner of the house as cadet Dragon was walking slowly away towards the neutral zone. Quickly, Spartan assumed a fighting stance preparing for battle with the Asian martial artist. Dragon held up a hand.

"Already out" he said matter-of-factly. "Watch for Cutter and Lotus Jane. They are working together. He attacks from the front and she ambushes."

Spartan nodded. "Typical of them to cheat; seems like their style. Thanks for the warning." He held out his hand to Dragon. The Asian cadet took it and shook it firmly. "Good luck Spartan. Avenge me."

"I will."

With that, the chase ensued. Spartan entered the wood line following Cutter and Lotus Jane's tracks. No one saw the Apache cadet concealed upon the house's roof; hiding in the shadow of the building's brick chimney. Nor did they see the lithe Apache slide down the drainpipes and follow Spartan, Lotus Jane, and Cutter silently into the Apache's native forest killing grounds; a ghost entering the splash of darkness, pausing only to study the footprints in the dirt. His quarry was close. The hunt would end soon.

Ahead, Cutter stood in a clearing surrounded on every side but the entrance by tall pine trees and moss-covered oaks. Shadows littered across the evening grasses. The ground was raised: slightly hump-like, as if the earth were somehow deformed here. Several stacked piles of rocks littered the ground in lines and circular patterns. Hidden from view, Lotus Jane looked up from beneath one of the tall pine trees lowest bows. Waiting for her next chance to strike, a rattlesnake in the pine straw.

Spartan entered the clearing cautiously, knife at the ready, slowly scanning for his opponents' side to side. His eyes settled on the Echo team leader who stood calmly and brazenly upon the mound at the center of the clearing. Cutter, knowing the advantage of the high ground, began to taunt the Alpha team leader.

"C'mon Corporal." He jeered emphasizing Spartan's rank with a sneer. "Not so brave without your walking, muscle bound clod to back your play, are you? Don't worry; I'm not going to hurt you… much."

Spartan chose his words carefully, hoping to enrage the Echo team leader into making a tactical mistake.

"Seems to me that you have been hiding behind the skirt of Lotus Jane, at least that's what I heard from Dragon. Speaking of her, where is your personal little Goth bimbo? I was hoping to show her how a real man fights one-on-one, rather than like you. Or did your inbred personality finally wear on her nerves and she ran off?"

Cutter stiffened visibly, then started laughing and sank into a fighting crouch, both blades laid flat back against his forearms.

"Enough talk. The last thing I need is a girl to fight my battles." He said coldly, his eyes glistening in anticipation.

Spartan tsked at Cutter, taunting him further. Although they were almost equal in height, Cutter was the more agile of the two boys. The two team leaders circled slowly, the single plastic knife of Spartan held upward; his offhand raised to block or defend. Cutter held both his hands upward with the blades running down the insides of his forearms. Spartan could tell this was not Cutter's first knife fight. Watching his opponent, he wondered where the girl was hiding waiting to ambush him.

Smooth confidence showed in Cutter's combat stance and the training blades moved up and around his arms, flashing individually from blade down to blade up, making figure-eight motions smoothly as he maneuvered around the hilltop.

Block… Parry… Return strike… Block…

Cutter's footwork flowed unerringly as he danced up and down on the high ground constantly pushing the dueling pairs positioning, driving Spartan before his slashing blades like a herdsman steering a sheep. Soon he would have his rival where he wanted him. Soon, Lotus Jane would strike from her hiding spot at Spartan's back and the dual would end in his victory. Perhaps not the cleanest win in history but a win was a win, was a win. Then, there would only be Jane's dispatch. She might even forfeit due to her unfettered loyalty to him. If not, oh well, he knew how to take care of her.

Spartan worked his single blade furiously, parrying and blocking each cut from the pair of Cutter's swirling and slashing blades. Sweat poured profusely down the teen's face as he read and countered each attack from the Echo team leader. He needed to end this quickly. He was getting tired fast. If fatigue set in, he was doomed. Cutter seemed to sense his fatigue, and was really pouring on the assault, slash after slash whistled high then low, followed by twin stabs to his midsection. Each attack, although turned, forced him further back towards the tree line to where Spartan knew Jane had to be hidden.

A particularly vicious double slash from Cutter forced Spartan back to the tree line. Left, right, left, Spartan twisted and dodged as Cutter's blades flashed in. The stitch in Spartan side was so severe that he was starting see spots from a lack of oxygen and overexertion. A dual stab from Spartan's left side was followed by an arcing sidekick that Cutter drove deep into Spartans ribs. Although the pain of the kick was minimal, the maneuver pushed Spartan hard to his right and directly into Lotus Jane's position where she had hidden behind the large trunk of a birch tree. Red paint lined Spartan's ribs as he was eliminated from the dual by the girl's thrust to his back and side. Exhausted and angry with himself for not seeing Lotus Jane's ambush, Spartan glared at Cutter.

"Couldn't win on your own, could you Cutter?"

"Doesn't matter, I won, didn't I?"

Cutter raised his arms in victory turning slowly three hundred and sixty degrees like a prize fighter who had just won the world heavyweight title. As his back was turned, Cutter did not see the light brown fist that reached down from the tree branches to wrap itself in Lotus Jane's long black hair. It was only Jane's startled yelp of pain as her head was painfully jerked upward that gave Cutter any indication that anything was wrong at all.

Turning to look back at his injured teammate, Cutter sought Lotus Jane and saw her standing with her arms outstretched in her palms turned upward and a quizzical, panicked look on her face, as if to say, "what happened?" Then, Cutter noticed the thin red stripe of paint across his teammate's throat, streaked from ear to ear and he instantly knew that he was not alone. The fight had not ended with Spartan's defeat as he had thought. Somewhere in the darkness, someone was hidden. Somehow, he had missed someone. Whoever that person was, he or she had talent in both blades and stealth. As the realization that the battle was to continue came over him, a shadow in the branches of the trees behind Lotus Jane moved and began to unfold behind the girl like a demon emerging from the shadows of Hell. Deadeye dropped to the ground, face and arms streaked with camouflaging mud. He looked like a vengeful forest spirit from an age long gone.

"You are not the only one capable of a silent attack. You have skill with your knives but no heart to provide bravery to your actions." The Native American cadet said softly.

The Echo team leader slowly backed away, fear evident on his face. It had been easy to challenge the other members of the Apocalypse Academy when he had known Lotus Jane was always there to strike from behind. Now he faced someone who had as much skill or more with the blade than he did.

"You can't intimidate me Indian!" The Echo team leader spluttered. "I'll beat you just like I beat your team leader."

The teenager's bravado did not match his actions. Cutter slowly circled to his left, edging towards the opening in the clearing. He wanted an avenue to run if it became necessary.

The Apache teen squatted down; his weight carefully balanced on his toes. This training knife held loosely in his hand, red paint dripping like blood from its tip.

"Perhaps instead of Cutter you should be called "*running dog*!?" Or maybe "*pack mate*" as in… "He who cowers and misuses his Pack!"

The insults stung Cutter. He didn't need to hide behind some skirt to win his battles. His movement to his left slowed, as the anger of the insults became evident on his face.

"I don't need anyone else to beat you Indian. I'm better than you. I'm faster than you."

"We shall see." The Native American said softly and began to advance at the blond-haired boy, his knife held at the ready.

The fight with Spartan had taken a lot out of Cutter. If he was going to win this fight, it would have to be quick. Gritting his teeth, his jaw muscles clenching, Cutter tightened his grip on his two blades.

"C'mon Tatonka," Cutter insulted "I can take you, and maybe you'll just bleed a little for real."

Deadeye stood before him, still as a statue. His eyes slowly followed his opponents every movement, noting every change of body posture as Cutter tried to maneuver to the

Native American cadet's flank. Still Deadeye did not attack as Cutter achieved a forty-five-degree angle from the brown skin cadet's back. The Echo team leader let loose a screaming war cry and charged forward. Cutter's blades spun back and forth, upward and downward into wind milling blur of plastic and paint. Still Deadeye did not move. The Apache was silently counting the Echo team leader's footfalls in his head. He had estimated the length of the boy's stride to be twenty-two inches, foot to foot, when running. Just shy of two feet, heel to toe. To cover the ten feet between them, Cutter would need approximately five seconds.

Four seconds… Still the Apache waited, completely immobile, muscles clenched and coiled like a serpent about to strike an unsuspecting bird.

Three seconds… He silently steeled his nerves, despite the Echo team leader's savage war cry, and the advancing blades whirling like fan blades through the air. Still the Apache waited.

Two seconds… Deadeye's muscles bunched like steel cables, coiling in anticipation. Time slowed as if to lend adrenaline to his actions. His lips felt dry and stuck to his teeth. It took all of his self-control to not charge the Echo team leader from the moral high ground. Inherent tribal rage begged for action.

One second… The Native American cadet exploded into action. He dove low and backward, catching his weight on his forearms whipping his legs around in a double leg sweep. The Apache's heels connected with the shins of the Echo team leader, as momentum brought the two boys' bodies' together, Cutter tried to leap over the maneuver, but only succeeded in raising the height from which he fell. As his legs were struck, his arms pin- wheeled attempting to catch his fall.

Deadeye's outstretched legs caught Cutter just above the ankles, driving them backward and the boy's face forward. For the briefest of moments, the Echo team leader appeared capable of flight; his arms outstretched, and his body parallel to the ground. Then gravity returned with a vengeance, smashing the teenager to the ground with a vicious impact. The boy's breath exploded from his lungs, and his knives skittered away into the dirt to either side of him. The impact of his face into the hard packed dirt instantly split Cutter's lip leaving him dazed and confused as to what had happened.

His vision spun crazily as he shook his head side to side, trying to clear his head from the impact. Scrambling blindly Cutter attempted to find his training knives. He knew that without the knives he would be helpless.

The Native American kipped nimbly back to his feet and silently stalked over to the wheezing and gasping Echo team leader. Taking the two training knives from where they lay in front of the breathless boy, Deadeye place a booted foot in between Cutter's shoulder blades, shoving him downward into the earthy leaves and pinning him to the ground. The maneuver forced the boy to struggle even harder for the much-needed air that had been blasted from his lungs by his impact with the hard ground. Despite his struggles, Cutter could not free himself from under the boy's boot.

Looking up at the drill sergeants that Deadeye had seen standing atop a tower overlooking the training; he slowly drew his thumb across his throat in a symbol of execution.

Reaching down, the Apache grasped a firm handhold in the Echo team leaders sweat soaked hair, his fingers wrapping tightly around the blond locks. Pulling the cadets' head back, he continued to press down with his boot making the execution as painful as possible. Cutter grunted in pain as Deadeye drew his training knife across the cadets' forehead horizontally from temple to temple. The knife left a wide, deep Crimson smear as it passed over the Echo team leader's skin. Red paint flowed quickly down the boy's forehead, merging with his sweat into rivulets of simulated blood. Still holding the boy beneath his boot, Deadeye let loose a traditional Native American war cry of his own. Cutter had just been "scalped."

Standing victorious atop the Echo team leader, Deadeye of Alpha team had won the training event.

After allowing several free moments of celebration and congratulations to the Apache cadet; Drill Sergeant Boomer reformed the platoon and marched them back to the Apocalypse Academy. Seated back in the classroom, Sergeant Boomer began to review the drill sergeant's after-action report from the training exercise with the cadets. The After-Action Report or AAR was based upon observations made by all four drill sergeants. The result was not what the cadets had expected. Drill Sergeant Boomers' critique held none of the enthusiasm that had bubbled from the cadets. In fact, it rode the hard edge between congratulations and open contempt. His dark eyes were hard as he looked out over the congregated cadets.

"With the possible exceptions of Cadet Deadeye and the teamwork displayed by Cadet's Cutter and Lotus Jane; that may be the single, most pathetic attempt at a survival class activity that I have ever seen."

The drill sergeant paused to let his words sink in, his eyes defying any comments from the assembled cadets.

"Have any of you even heard of the word *tactics* or the phrase seeking the *tactical advantage*?"

"Drill sergeant" the Bravo team leader, Dragon spoke up as he raised his hand, "We were instructed to silently eliminate our competition. Did we not achieve this?"

"You call that silent boy? Hell, we could hear most of you from the Sergeant's tower. The only one of you that was hard to track was Deadeye. Most of you just crashed through the trees, unmindful of where your feet stepped, uncaring of the snapping of a twig or the rustle of leaves until you were prepared to strike. Shit, Freak sounded like a wild buffalo stampeding around. A skilled hunter would have and did eliminate most of the company in less than an hour. Can any of you tell me why Cadet Deadeye was so hard to track?"

The drill sergeant paused, looking around, everyone seemed reluctant to answer. The drill sergeant slowly shook his head in disgust.

Cadet Freak raised his beefy hand.

"Because he is a bad-ass M–F'er, drill sergeant!"

A mixed group of gasps and chuckles came from the crowd of cadets. Freak just shrugged. The truth was the truth.

The burly, black drill sergeant looked nonplussed by the comment.

"Okay, respect is good, even healthy in this environment. Now, why is he in your words, to quote your phrase, a bad-assed MO-FO?"

No one answered, so the drill sergeant continued.

"Did anyone even see Cadet Deadeye during the exercise except when he was fighting the final battle?"

A murmur broke out from the crowd as everyone compared notes, comments, and thoughts. In the end, there was a consensus that Deadeye seemed to melt into the shadows of the house at the beginning of the exercise and almost magically appear out of the woods when he eliminated Lotus Jane. None of the other cadets could remember seeing him at any other time during the exercise. Then Spartan raised his hand.

"Since I don't believe it was magical in nature drill sergeant, I would like to know how he moves the way he does. Can you teach this to us?"

"I would tell you what I saw Corporal Spartan. You can learn from my words if you want to live. As for teaching you to move silently through the woods like an Apache warrior, I would say you have a far better instructor than me for that if he is willing to teach you."
The drill sergeant looked over at where the Native American cadet sat leaning back in his chair silently. Spartan followed the drill sergeant's line of sight and locked eyes with his teammate. The boy sat with no expression, no acknowledgment or denial, as if to say, *"you can never be an Apache."*

Drill Sergeant Boomer continued.

"You all *died* because you are simpleminded. You think only in one dimension. Your only focus was what was directly in front of you on the ground or behind a tree, not in a three hundred sixty-degree radius. To survive in the wilderness filled with "Zs" you will need to know how to recognize danger from the front and the back; to both sides, from above and below. You all followed the worn dirt paths due for the ease of movement, barely checking your surroundings. Light discipline was nonexistent as flashlights shone like light sabers from a Star Wars movie, throughout buildings, and in the forest making you all easy targets."

"Cadet Deadeye never used any additional light as he moved from shadow to shadow, from the ground to the trees, and ultimately to the rooftops in a concerted effort to break a tracker's rhythm. Finally, Cadet Deadeye only engaged with the target when he had achieved tactical superiority ***and*** the operational need to do so. His skills were not about ego. They were about success. While several other cadets had multiple kills, Cadet Deadeye had only two, Lotus Jane from an ambush position and Cutter face to face. However, his stealth, tactics and kills were enough to gain the victory for Alpha Team when straightforward attacks, trickery and brute force could not. It seems to me that strategy should be the word of the day for all of you to learn. If not, you will not survive long in the world of the undead."

"I want you all to think about this and think about the lessons of the day, as you fallout for chow. No questions? just think about everything that you saw and learned today. Fall out!"

Chapter Seven
Deadeye's Story

At two am, Spartan silently walked fire guard and approached his teammates bunk only to find the Apache missing. Worry filled Spartan's mind, as thoughts of the Native American cadet leaving the Apocalypse Academy were considered. Quickly, Spartan searched every room including the lavatory, with no success. Several long minutes of searching eventually led to Spartan finding Deadeye outside lying in the grass. The tough Apache cadet was wrapped in his olive-green wool blanket for warmth against the cool night air.

"Hey man" Spartan called softly "Are you okay? What are you doing out here? You do realize if you get caught outside of the barracks it's both of our asses."

The young Native American took a deep breath and sighed.

"I miss the moon and the stars. I feel separated from my ancestors. I cannot see them from my bed in the center of the barracks, so I sneak out here every night to speak to them. I've been doing it since we arrived here. Congratulations, you are the first fire guard to notice that I was even missing."

Spartan knelt on one knee in the grass across from the boy, allowing him a moment to collect his thoughts.

"Today's exercise made me realize how much I miss my people. How much I miss my family and my tribe. As a boy I learned all of the skills I used today, tracking animals during hunts with my father in the northern woodlands of the United States. By the age of four I could recognize the tracks of deer, rabbits and fox. By the age of eight, I could identify predators such as the wolf, bear and cougar as well as any bird native to our lands. By the age of twelve, I knew how to live off the land, stalking silently, using the wind, finding fresh water and foraging for edible roots and berries. It all became second nature to me because my father cared enough to teach me our ancestral skills. Unfortunately, I took that time with my father for granted."

The dark-haired boy paused, looking up at his team leader for understanding. Spartan did not say anything because he could not remember his own father, so he only nodded once when Deadeye continued.

"My father and I were hunting on "Z" day. School was out for fall break and he had planned this elaborate hike deep into the forest of northern Washington. We had been walking and camping for two days when we saw the bird of ill omen."

Seeing Spartan's questioning look, Deadeye elaborated.

"What you would call a vulture. Its wingspan was enormous, and it blotted out the sun as it flew past our position in the forest."

Again, Spartan only nodded, not wanting to break his teammate's concentration.

"It's slowly circled overhead us, flying high over a clearing of tall pine and oak trees that stood a quarter-mile in the distance. We should have turned back. In fact, my father told me to turn away and wait in the forest for him while he investigated to make sure no one was hurt or worse. He was a Forest Ranger. It was his job to keep the woodlands safe. But I was young and headstrong as most teenagers are. I thought I knew everything so I ignored my father's instructions and ran ahead, determined to prove that I was a man; that I did not need my father's protection and I would face down the foolish superstitions of terror that belonged to this bird of ill omen."

The Apache youth paused, steeling himself mentally to finish the story. Spartan sensed that the recollection would not end well, but still he said nothing. It was the youth's tale to tell.

"Leaping across a small stream, I burst through the trees and blackberry bushes heedless of the scratches. Had I taken but a moment to look at the surrounding area I would've known that going forward was a bad idea. I could have recognized the tracks, feeding grounds and my surroundings. Instead, I found death, covered in coarse brown fur. Strangely enough, the first thing I noticed was all the blood. Blood had been splattered and splashed for three meters surrounding what I first thought to be a small deer carcass. Intestines hung from the bushes like purple ropes of sausages and chunks of meat were splayed into several different piles of bloody carrion. Standing over the deer corpse was a six-hundred-pound mother grizzly bear, and two-year yearling cubs. Bloodstained their fur, from their caked muzzles to their stubby tail flanks, as if they had completely savaged the deer with such ferocity that the blood had exploded outward from the creature to coat their pelts."

"Seeing me as a threat to both her kill and her cubs, the mother grizzly rose up on her thick hind legs, towering eight feet into the air. Raw meat dangled between her fangs as she roared her challenge to me. The sound deafened me, eliminating all other forest noises for a full ten seconds. In those seconds I noticed several things. It is amazing the sense of clarity that you get when you that know you are about to die."

The Apache youth took a deep breath and then continued.

"The "*deer*" on the ground was actually the headless corpse of a man wearing a brown doe skin jacket. His left arm and left leg were missing, but the remaining boot and clothing showed them to have belonged to a hunter. Pieces of camouflage pants leg and an orange net vest had been torn away and hung from the nearby blackberry bush. To me, that was pretty big indicator that the bear's victim had been familiar with the woods. Also, a 30-06 rifle lay in the dirt next to the corpse's remains. It had been clearly bitten in half and the barrel was bent to the side."

"Secondly I noticed that the bear had been savaged in several areas along its neck and torso. Flesh and fur appeared to be flapping loosely as it displayed its rage; like fur flags blowing in the wind. The skin and fur hung in three-inch wide flaps and thick black coagulated blood oozed from the wounds. I mistook this damage from the feeding frenzy with the cubs. I thought perhaps the yearlings had attacked their mother in a moment of excitement and that one or both of the baby bears had taken a bite out of the mama bear. Although the wounds were extreme it was not out of the question for bears to act in this manner. But then I noticed that the mother grizzly was also missing an eye and its remaining eye was glowing an almost demonic red from the blood vessels that had burst inside its skull. As the creature looked down at me, the hole in the creature's skull where the orb had been removed looked to be a mile deep. Terror paralyzed my legs and I stood gasping in fear."

"Finally, I realized as well that the eyes on both of the cubs were also crimson red, glassy and fogged over. I knew then that the rumors of the dead rising had come to fruition in the forests of my home. These bears were all dead, but they were still hungry for the living and I was about to become an Apache snack."

"As I slowly began backing away, returning the way I had foolishly run in my hurry, a black feathered arrow streaked past my head and buried itself in the nearest bear cub's left's eye socket. The cub flipped over in a death roll, driving the arrow deeper into its skull and snapping it in half as it fell. Some sense of parentage must have remained in the mother bear, because upon seeing her cub murdered, she dropped to all fours and charged. Arrow after arrow streaked from the woods as my father screamed at me to run. I spun and fled into the tree line at a sprint, yet I could feel the ground tremble as the massive grizzly bear pounded along behind me. The whuffs and snorts of its undead body chasing me inspired fear like I have never known. As I ran, I silently prayed to the gods of my ancestors to guide my footing and not let me fall."

"How did you get away?" Spartan asked.

"I didn't entirely."

"I don't understand."

"The grizzly finally got close enough in the chase to swat me with its massive paw. Its undead claws dug into my ribs, snapping several of them on impact and digging four bloody furrows from my side to my spine all the way down to the bone."

The Apache youth lifted his shirt and turned his back to Spartan displaying the four long scars that ran horizontally across the boys back and ribs.

"It is only by the grace of the great Spirit that that grizzly bitch didn't break my back. I remember that I flew through the air and landed in a blackberry briar thirty feet away. The last thing I saw as consciousness fell away was the massive, she bear as she rose back up on her hind legs, claws fully extended, coming towards me for the killing blow. As my eyesight faded, I saw my father leap from the tree branch where he had been firing arrows upon the grizzly's back trying desperately to save his stupid son. The last thing I saw was his Bowie knife flashing in the sunlight as he stabbed the beast repeatedly before I lost consciousness."

"Why didn't the bear eat you?" Spartan asked feeling guilt for his insensitivity but wanting to finish the story before a Drill sergeant found him off post.

"I don't know. A family of four was fleeing into the woods from Seattle, running from the infection that had immersed the massive city to a grip of the living dead. It seems while my father and I hiked and hunted, the entire world had gone insane. They found me by chance while they were foraging for berries. The father of the family, Sven, bound my wounds and cared for me until I could be passed on to a passing military unit for proper treatment. They never found any trace of the one-eyed bear, her remaining cub, or my father. I came to assume that the first corpse the bear had attacked was infected. I assumed it was already dead when the bear attacked it, but I can't be a hundred percent sure.

Perhaps one of the cubs attacked first. That would explain the torn flesh and fur that I had mistaken for bites from her cubs during the feeding frenzy. It probably didn't take long for her to turn; a day, maybe two."

"You said you missed the signs? What did you miss?"

"When you grow up in the woods, you learn where animals eat, sleep and mate. You learn to look for telltale signs like paw prints, scat and tree rubs where the animals scratch their fur. You listen to the sounds of the forest and you follow the omens. I did not do any of this. I ignored all that my father had taught me in my childish effort to show him I was a man and now he is dead or possibly even worse."

Spartan thought silently for a moment, then spoke.

"We cannot bring back your father Deadeye, but you can pass along his teachings to protect your new family… your team. Then, if we ever graduate from here, one day we will all help you on your one-eyed bear hunt together. If it is still out there, we will find it and destroy it. Then, maybe your father's spirit can rest in peace."

The dark-eyed boy regarded his team leader, jaw muscles bunching in the light as he clenched his teeth fighting his emotions. Silently he nodded.

"I would like that very much."

"Can we go and take our asses inside please?" Spartan asked, "It's damn cold out here." He said rubbing his bare arms and shivering.

Deadeye grinned suddenly, flashing white teeth as the tension broke. "First lesson paleface, cold is a state of mind." He said with a laugh.

Spartan rolled his eyes.

"Whatever." Spartan said as they walked back to the barracks.

Chapter Eight
Prelude to Dante

The first day of week ten at the Apocalypse Academy was spent doing menial barrack chores spit and polish due to the continual rain and sleet that had moved into the area the night before. Dripping ice coated the trees and brittle icicles hung from the power lines in a brutal display wind and rain.

As midday approached the icy rain had subsided into a steadier rainfall, and the cadets were called into the recreation room for an impromptu meeting with Drill Sergeant Hogg and Colonel Slade, the latter of whom they had not seen since the day of Spartan's promotion at the Apocalypse Academy.

The call of "Officer on deck!" echoed throughout the rec room as the Colonel entered the area. All of the cadets leapt to their feet instantly, snapping to attention. Their heels clicked together audibly, and the snap of their bodies echoed throughout hall.

"As you were, cadets." The Colonel said, looking over the group. "Please be seated."

The recreation room was traditionally not the area for their meetings. Most often the classroom had been used whenever the drill sergeants or on the rare occasion, Colonel Slade wanted to speak with the cadets. Instead, the rec room represented the Academy's ideas of rest and relaxation. Painted olive drab green, there were gun cleaning kits, knife sharpening whet stones and battle armor repair stations. Everything was tactical or pragmatic except for the single ping-pong table that stood in the center of the floor. The game table had been justified due to its ability to increase hand eye coordination, reflexes, as well as tactical thinking. If legend was to be believed, Drill Sergeants Boomer and Stone had carried the ping-pong table back to the Academy from two miles away, while Sergeant Hogg and Sergeant Surfer killed every "Z" that had crossed their path.

It was directly in front of this table the Colonel Slade stood. Drill Sergeant Hogg silently stood by the wall, at the position of parade rest, his square-cut jaw clenched, and his blue eyes focused straight ahead on nothing.

"Cadets," he began "tomorrow morning at 0600 hours you will engage in the single most difficult and potentially deadly training taught at this Academy. This training is known as the "Dante Course" after the medieval author Dante Alighieri. His visions of Hell will seem tranquil compared to what you will find beyond the fencing. Upon entering this sophisticated obstacle course, you will be expected to solve individual and team problems, employ tactics, demonstrate courage and for those of you in team leader roles, show leadership. This event will be timed; the fastest team's completion earning them first selection from the firearm Armory which will be held on Monday of next week.

A quick murmur surged through the assembled cadets. This was the first time firearms were even mentioned to the cadets. The excitement was palpable. While the martial weapons they currently owned were practical, guns were cool.

Spartan raised his hand to ask a question of the Colonel. After the crowd quieted, the officer acknowledged him with a nod of his head.

"Yes Corporal?"

"Sir, what's the catch? It can't be as simple as just a timed event. This isn't a track meet."

The Colonel looked pleased at this question, a slight smirk twitching at the corners of his mouth.

"Very good, Corporal. I knew that you were promoted for a reason. Deductive logic is always a boon."

Spartan caught a glimpse of Cutter murmuring to his crony Orc. Both cadets were glaring daggers at Spartan. He suppressed a smile because he was absolutely certain they were saying something snide about him and probably plotting ways to take him out. Oh well he thought, let them try.

"There is indeed "*a catch*" if you wish to call it that. The entire course is contained within a fifty-five-hundred-meter chain-link fence. The fence is eight feet high, topped with triple strands of double spooled concertina wire. There is only one point of entrance into the obstacle course with a door that opens inward and cannot be reopened from the inside. There is also only one exit at the completion of the course, four hundred and forty meters from end-to-end. Almost 3 full miles of challenging and deadly obstacles for you and your teams to complete."

"Piece of cake Sir!" Cutter piped up, a smug look upon his face. "My team and I will ace this!"

The Colonel chose not to respond, however the look of immediate, complete and agonizing death that Drill Sergeant Hogg flashed to the arrogant cadet warned that he should not speak again without permission. Cutter immediately looked down at the tabletop, withering under the drill sergeants steely gaze.

"You'll be expected to complete the obstacle course in full battle gear, while carrying your martial weapons. This includes rucksack, gas mask and martial weapons but no firearms."

Spartan thought he heard Techno groan from the crowd. Although he was learning slowly, he was still a hazard to himself and others with his stun baton.

"You will need every skill that you have learned thus far, fitness, discipline and teamwork. Potentially, you may even need your first aid skills. Tactics and leadership will be paramount for the completion of this event."

Spartan again raised his hand. It still didn't sound that hard. Difficult on endurance level maybe, it still didn't seem to meet the threshold of a medieval hell as described in Dante's Inferno.

"Sir, what are you not telling us?"

A hard look crossed the Colonel's face. The lines around his eyes and mouth seem to deepen visibly. After taking a deep breath he spoke.

"The course will be populated with free roaming "Z's". To complete the course you must evade, neutralize or pacify your way to the finish line and out of the gate that you'll find there. If you fail to clear the obstacle, you will die. If you are bitten, you will die. If you panic and freeze up, you will die. There are no safe zones, no areas of protection, and nowhere to just sit and hide. This is your first real test to ensure that you can react as you are expected to react when dealing with a "Z" attack in the field."

The room had become so silent; it seemed as if everyone in the room had stopped breathing. Each cadet's eyes mirrored his thoughts and emotions. Terror, resignation and determination were all written as clearly on their faces as their blackboard lessons had been on how to hotwire a car. Freak sitting next to Spartan, flexed his huge bicep and rolled his neck from side to side as if warming up for battle already. The cracking sound sounded like small arms fire in the silence. Spartan thought about the implications of what the Colonel had said. This was the first time that either he or one of his teammates could be killed since their arrival at the Apocalypse Academy ten weeks ago. Granted a lot had changed in both their abilities and awareness since then, but the situation was still daunting.

The silence was suddenly broken by the sound of a sliding chair on the linoleum, running feet and the retching splatter of daily chow being regurgitated all over the floor. Although Spartan could not see who had just thrown up, he strongly suspected that Techno had just lost his lunch. Colonel Slade looked at the teen with evident empathy in his eyes. Conversely, Sergeant Hogg glowered at the teenager's heaving body with obvious contempt. The man absolutely despised weakness in any form, especially in a public setting.

The Colonel chose to continue rather than embarrass the teenager in front of his peers.

"Are there any further questions?"

No one raised their hand. As a whole, the cadets of the Apocalypse Academy remained silent. Even the normally boisterous cadets of Echo team sat stunned by the knowledge that they would soon be facing their own mortality by battling "Z's" up close and personal. The only sounds to penetrate the room were the occasional sniffles and sobs from several of the female cadets.

"Then, I wish good luck to all of you. It is my fondest hope that you will all survive this challenge unscathed. If there are no further questions, you cadets are dismissed."

As the various cadets slid their chairs back from the various tables, and the Colonel and Sergeant Hogg exited the room, Spartan quickly gathered Freak, Dancer and Deadeye.

"I need all of you to meet me in parking bay number four in fifteen minutes." He said, "Alone. No friends and no one to hear what we discuss. I will meet you all there."

"Do we need our weapons?" Dancer asked.

"No, we just need to talk this through. We need to make sure that we are fully prepared for what we're going to face tomorrow."

Receiving nods of agreement from all of his teammates, Spartan turned to walk back into the room.

"Where are you going?" Dancer asked.

"To talk to Techno." Spartan said solemnly.

Chapter Nine
Techno's Story

Spartan found Techno kneeling; hunched over a concrete bench at the far end of the courtyard. The boy sat with his elbows on the bench in his fingers intertwined through his hair at the front of his head. Techno's body shook with each of the wracking breaths that he took, and Spartan could see the tears dripping from his downturned chin. He quietly sat down next to his beleaguered teammate. The boy was clearly terrified.

"Talk to me Techno."

"I don't wanna die Spartan. I don't want to get bit and have to be pacified. I'm scared to death." He sobbed.

"That is not going to happen Tech." Spartan said. "Alpha team looks out for its own. We've got your back."

"Uh huh, just like the cop had my back on "Z" day?" The Asian boy responded.

"What do you mean Techno? What happened?"

The boy's sobs became harder for a moment as he mentally recalled the personal horrors that he'd experienced on "Z" day. Slowly he composed himself, his sobs easing as he prepared to tell Spartan what he remembered about the world's most infamous day. He subconsciously swiped his forearms across his nose, drawing a mucous trail upon his blue sleeve and smearing a line of tears across his cheek. Techno never noticed. Quietly he spoke to his team leader, his voice quivering as he told his story.

"I was working as an orderly at the Blue Pines Nursing Home just north of Sacramento, California. I had just turned fifteen and it was my first job after school; just a couple of days a week and on weekends. Basically, I was a gopher for the nurses. I would carry towels, get dinners and walk with the patients when they wanted to go smoke or get out of the confines of their rooms and go into the garden. It wasn't much pay, but I really enjoyed working with the old folks. They always had awesome stories and they were so eager for the company, and they liked to talk a lot. Most of their families put them into the home and just forgot about them; basically, considering them already dead."

"I played checkers and cards with them to help them pass their days and it always made me feel good to make them smile. So many of them seemed lost; just left alone to die, ya know? Like their families thought they were a bother. Just like old horses that had been put out to pasture."

"I was especially fond of one old guy. I mean all or at least most of the folks at the nursing home were pretty nice. There were only a rare few that were contentious, nasty and overall spiteful old bastards, but usually it wasn't aimed at me just at their families, their situation or maybe life in general."

"For instance, Ms. Kellogg's was a retired kindergarten teacher. Every day I would go see her and every day she would give me a Tootsie Roll. Free candy. Awesome! What a nice lady. I would've loved being in her class. I remember how she really liked to read those old romance books and would talk about how things were so much better in the days after World War II. I swiped several of my mom's books for her and she treated it like it was the biggest secret in the entire world."

"Another guy, Mister Johnson, lived in B wing over near the elevator. He was an elderly black man, who enjoyed his newspaper every morning and Kool cigarettes as he worked the crossword puzzles. I liked to help him solve them every day. Occasionally he would forget what he was working on and start telling these really funny jokes. He was always happy, ya know? Always clowning around and hitting on the pretty, young nurse's aides. He made me laugh a lot."

"Mister and Mrs. Carter lived in adjoining rooms on C wing. They were a husband and wife that spent their days arguing over who was the better baseball team in Chicago… The Cubs or the White Sox, all the while drinking Pabst Blue Ribbon beer together. They always tried to draw me into the arguments as I went to each of their rooms. So, I always chose the side of whichever room I was going to at the time. I'm actually a San Francisco Giants fan."

"Even the staff at the Blue Pines was pretty cool. Doctor Sedgwick the head physician, Mister Mike the maintenance man, and big Tully John, the driver for the transport vans all treated me really nice. I mean after all; I was like a stupid adopt-a-kid project and they all looked after me. Doc Sedgwick helped me with my homework, especially science and health. Most of the time he didn't even need to look up an answer. He just knew the stuff out of his memory. Mister Mike would pay me to be a lookout while he smoked in the garden. At a quarter a cigarette, this added up pretty quick. Big Tully John would drive me home if the weather was bad or if he wanted to talk about the Raiders or Giants depending on the time of year."

"Even Nurse Abernathy was nice in a no-nonsense, professional, business only manner. She was the one that assigned my daily chores, reviewed my work and acted as my boss. If I did anything wrong, she made me redo it over and over until I got it right. "*Teaching young people to be responsible*" she called it. But when no one was around, she would talk to me about my hopes and dreams and give me advice on how to achieve everything I had set my heart on."

"But my favorite person in Blue Pines was a cantankerous, wheelchair-bound, grouchy old guy in Suite 214. His name was Albert Simmons. He was ninety-six years old and a veteran of both World War II and the Korean War. I don't remember in which branch of service he served but I do remember that he had a whole shoebox full of medals and ribbons that he had earned during his time in the military that he kept under the nightstand by his bed. Al was great. Every day he had a new story for me. Adventure, excitement, intrigue… It was like meeting Indiana Jones or James Bond in person. I mean… This guy did everything; including being vicious at chess and backgammon."

Spartan nodded, allowing the boy to continue uninterrupted.

"When the first news of the infection spread, it was Al who knew how bad it was going to be. He told me that people were stupid because they kept going places in groups rather than isolating themselves from infections that were transmitted by the transfer of bodily fluids. He thought the infection had to be viral because the antibiotics that the governments were using seemed to not have any effect on the infected people, at least according to the media. He thought that the virus must've been some sort of mutated strain of an already known pathogen. He also thought that it was probably man-made; maybe a version of rabies or Ebola or even one of the lesser-known viral infections which he called "vectors", in remote places like China, Africa and South America."

Techno unconsciously wiped away another falling tear from his cheek where it hung waiting for freefall.

"It was Al that also carefully watched the news as the infected people mingled during their daily activities, died and eventually returned to life as walking corpses. After ten days, when New York, Philadelphia and Washington DC all fell to the infection, it was Al that figured out that not all of the undead were the same."

"What you mean Techno? The infected are all the same. I mean, they all want to eat the living."

"That's true." The boy replied. "But the infected are also very different. For instance, not all corpses rise back up. Only the ones with the head and brain intact returned to their semblance of life. And there are differences in how they come back when they do. For instance, freshly risen corpses move faster than the older, more rotten ones. Al said they tend to have large purple or black areas on their body where the blood settled when they died. This was because the newer dead had not developed mortis yet to slow their movements. Also, the fast ones, "Reapers" as Al called them, often vomited when fighting the living. This was due to the natural expulsion of bodily gases from a corpse as it decays, however, also was exceptionally more dangerous as it served as a way to also help spread the plague. One drop of bloody vomit in an open eye or mouth and you were doomed to change into the very creature that was trying to kill you."

"The slower, shambling type of "Z" are undead that are between about five days to six months old since the time of their death. Mortis has set in, tightening the tendons and muscles, which Al said reduces their ability to move beyond a fast walk. The flesh and muscles have also begun to break down, so that's why they have huge festering sores on their body. Interestingly, Al noticed that the slower moving undead seem to develop a pack instinct to offset their lack of speed. Being able to surround the living with an enormous group of the walking dead, offset the greater speed efficiency that their victims often had as an advantage. Al called these types of undead "Romero's" after the movie director that had created an almost prognostic series of movies of what was then entertainment about living dead. They are essentially immune to pain, and the loss of limb only slows them down. As with all of the types of undead, where only decapitation or extreme damage to the brain or cervical vertebrae seem to end their existence."

"The third type of infected, Al called "husks". These were essentially corpses who could not feed on living tissue to replenish blood, nutrients or whatever the fuck they get from eating us and have essentially dried up and appear quasi – mummified. They move super slow and are extremely brittle. When struck in battle, they disintegrate into a sticky, powdered bone dust. The virus is contained within this dust, which then becomes airborne, floating on the wind until it finds a new host to latch onto. Al said that although these undead were the slowest and easiest to evade, they were also the most dangerous because you needed a level V self-contained hazmat suit and a flame thrower to avoid the infection. I didn't know exactly what that was, but it sounded serious, so I nodded a lot and talked about it like I understood. I wish now I had asked more questions."

"Where's Al now Techno? He should be here at the Academy teaching if he knew this much about the undead. Is he still alive?" Spartan asked.

"I don't know." Techno replied. "The day before "Z" day was officially declared, soldiers burst into the nursing home waving guns and giving orders. They drug Al out of his wheelchair forced him from the home to a helicopter. I remember Al had a resigned look upon his face, almost as if he'd been expecting them. As he was leaving, he hugged me and shook my hand. As I held onto his neck and cried like a baby, I heard him whisper in my ear "We did this. Be safe boy. Trust no one."

"After he had been loaded into the chopper, I stood there watching him fly away. When he was fully outta sight and I was sure no one was looking, I opened my hand and looked at the coin Al had pushed into my palm as he shook my hand. It was a metal challenge coin, like the military used to recognize high performers and super soldiers. I had seen a lot of them at the nursing home, each different from the next. Different branches, different units, different designs. As I looked at the coin, I remembered Al's whispered words. He had said "we did this." I searched his room, looking for anything that might explain what he had meant with those cryptic words. The coin bore a likeness of a caduceus on one side and the American flag on the other. Around the edges of the coin, surrounding the image on both sides, were four words: Center for Disease Control. I think that Al was telling me that the CDC had caused the plague. I never saw the old man again. I have often wondered what happened to him. Maybe he survived and is tucked away at some secret government facility, learning about the plague. Or maybe they executed him. I just don't know."

"The next day, the first of the "Zs" arrived on the grounds. I was helping serve lunch in the dining room when three patrol cars arrived in front of the building. My parents had always taught me that when we needed help to find a cop. Holding Al's coin tightly in my clenched fist, I dropped the lunch tray on the counter and ran outside to see what was happening. Surely the police would help me. I ran from officer to officer trying to explain what I knew and what I had surmised from Al's coin and comment. All I got was "No time kid!" or "Get the hell out of the way kid!" I didn't know why but they didn't want to take the time to listen to me. Finally, I found an officer that would listen. He was a Captain directing his people from place to place as if preparing for something. I told him everything I knew and showed him Al's coin. Do you know what this fine public servant did?"

Spartan shook his head.

That dumb bastard told me that I should be ashamed of myself for stealing the coin from an old person and making up lies. Then he told me to put my hands behind my back because he was arresting me for theft."

"What did you do?"

"Before I could do anything, a man's voice came over the patrol car loudspeaker. I looked up and saw a walking wall of undead at the top of the hill. There had to be hundreds of them. The voice over the loudspeaker announced "Here they come. Prepare to fire." As the officers' attention was diverted, I turned and ran. I knew from Al's descriptions that these were "shamblers" or "Romero's" and that I could outrun them, even as fat as I was back then. Al had always insisted that it was best to run if we could. I raced through the building as fast as I could."

Out of breath, I found old Nurse Abernathy. I paused only long enough to tell her about the approaching "Zs" and to tell her to run as the gunfire began to pop outside in long streams of sound while the police fired at the advancing dead. I sprinted out of the back door and up the hill towards where I lived. Reaching the summit of the hill, I looked back and all I could see were "Zs" surrounding the nursing home. That's when I realized that patrol cars with the flashing lights were all gone. The policemen had fled and left the elderly that were trapped in the home to die. The fucking bastards! I could hear the screams from the hilltop. All of those poor, defenseless old people being eaten alive because the police considered them expendable based solely on their age. I will never forget the sound of hearing the elderly friends that I had made, dying beneath the tearing claws and crunching teeth of the undead. The last thing I saw was Nurse Abernathy trying to get Ms. Kellogg into the building while Mister Johnson feebly swung his walker back and forth, valiantly trying to keep the undead at bay. Then they were overrun by the wave of rotten flesh and they were gone."

Techno's tears again flowed freely. Spartan patted the boy on the back. He could not remember his own pain-and-suffering from "Z" night, but he empathized with his teammate's heartache.

"I sprinted all the way home. When I got there, I found the door torn off the hinges and blood stains splattering the walls. The house was in shambles and the only trace of my family that I found was my mother's left ring finger. It still had her wedding ring on it where a "Z" had bitten it clean off of her hand. From where it lay on the floor, it seemed to be pointing at the front door as if telling me to run for my life. So, I grabbed my book bag, stuffed in six cans of tuna, a loaf of bread and some clean underwear. Putting on my jacket, I headed out into the street carefully watching for "Z's" and trying to be quiet. The military found me the next day hiding behind a dumpster. Shell-shocked they said. Then I was brought here by helicopter two days later."

Spartan took a deep breath, looking over at the sad Asian boy. "I'm sorry Tech. But no matter what, I will not let that happen to you or anyone on Alpha team. Not as long as I'm alive."

Techno wiped away the last of the residual tears upon his cheeks.

"Thanks Spartan. I mean it. Thank you for listening and also for what you did on the first day here. It's been a long time since I thought I could talk to anyone."

"Besides," Spartan added. "You're too ugly to be a "Z". No sense giving them additional scare powers from your ugly mug."

A broad smile spread on the boy's faces and Techno stood up from where he had been sitting.

"Screw you Spartan!" He laughed.

Spartan looked seriously at the boy.

"Our team is waiting for us at parking bay number four. We need to talk about how we're going to run this course tomorrow. The sooner it's over, the sooner you'll feel better about the future of Alpha team. Are you okay to do this or do I need to go and talk to Sergeant Hogg about preventing you from running the Dante course?"

"Are you crazy? That mean assed son of a bitch would put me straight out the front gate and I would be an instant "Z" dinner! That man has no compassion for anyone. It's either do as he says, or you get the boot; sometimes quite literally."

"He's training us to survive Tech. It can't be easy to take a bunch of teenagers that don't know a damned thing and turn them into warriors. I mean, would you want to have to try to change Cutter and his crew?"

"I never thought of it that way. They can't be easy. I don't think Orc can even spell his own name much less think tactically."

"All right then, let's go and meet up with our team." Spartan said as he led the boy to the parking bay where the rest of Alpha team stood waiting.

Halfway to the bay Spartan pulled up, almost stopping his movement in mid stride. So abrupt was the change of pace that Techno bumped into him from behind. Spartan turned and looked back at Techno.

"Go on ahead. I have to take care of something really quick. Tell everyone that I will be there ASAP."

"Now?" Techno asked. "Are you serious? Shouldn't our meeting be the priority?... Our team?"

Spartan took a deep breath and blew it out. He really didn't want to waste time explaining his private thoughts to

Techno but if he didn't then the boy would burn up more minutes digging for answers.

"Look Tech, you have imparted some important and potentially lifesaving information to me about the specifics of the Z's as Al told them to you. Knowing what they are capable of could save lives. I am going to get the information to the other team leaders for dissemination to their teams."

"Even Cutter?"

"Yes, even Cutter. He may be a shit stain, but he's still human. In the grand scheme of things that puts us all on the same team. If I failed to pass on the information to everyone and someone dies then that would be on my shoulders. In my book that would make me barely better than an Echo team member and no better than a "Z". I don't want that on my conscious for the rest of my life."

Techno looked deep into Spartan's eyes. There was often a warrior's fire smoldering in the underlying layers of his soul. No there was only a look of compassion. He was truly a leader that cared about people as much as he cared about battle.

"Okay. I understand. I will tell the others that you'll meet with us in a few minutes. Go do what you need to do." He said and turned to walk away. "But if Cutter is an asshole and gets bit anyway, I am not shedding any tears for him…and Spartan?..."

"Ya?"

"Do me a favor and make sure Jane knows too. I don't trust Cutter and I don't want anything to happen to her." He said sheepishly, his face turning red with embarrassment.

"It's a deal." Spartan turned and ran back towards the barracks as fast as he could, hiding his smile from the boy.

Techno watched him leave then headed back to the Bay to meet with his partners on Alpha team.

From around the corner, Jane listened to the two sets of receding footsteps. She had been sent by Cutter to spy on the Alpha's; to listen in on their plans for engaging with the obstacles and undead within the Dante course. Spartan's comments had been as she expected, brimming with loyalty, honor and leadership. But it was Techno's words that had stolen her thoughts and breath. When she knew it was safe, she peeked out from around the corner and watched the Asian boy walk away until she couldn't see him anymore, then she raced back to the barracks.

Sergeant Hogg's Cadence

Up in the mornin' way too soon,
Killin' Zs before its noon.
What are we gonna do when we get back
Take a shower and hit the rack.

NO WAY, GOTTA RUN
PTs LOTSA FUN!

I wanna be a Drill Instructor
I wanna cut off all of my hair
I wanna be a Drill Instructor
I wanna earn that smoky bear.

NO WAY, GOTTA RUN
PTs LOTSA FUN!

I went to the armory on my knees
I said Mr. Z killer won't ya arm me please
He looked at me with a big ol' grin
Said if ya wanna be a Z killer ya never give in.

NO WAY, GOTTA RUN
PTs LOTSA FUN!

Up in the morning at the break of day,
Training so hard that we never play
Running through the Academy all in a line
All I do is double time.

NO WAY, GOTTA RUN
PTs LOTSA FUN!

CHAPTER TEN
THE DANTE COURSE

Alpha team's meeting in parking bay number four was short and to the point. During the Dante Course, no one was to go off on their own, time was not a factor, and everyone agreed to cover each other's asses. The night flew by in a fit of restless sleep for all the cadets. Alpha team was the last team to arrive at the course, half drenched from the rain that set in during the night but arriving at exactly 0615. They had been forced to double time it all the way to the fence line to ensure that they made it on time.

As if the Dante Course needed the devil's assistance at causing fear and doubt, the overcast gray sky opened up and a hard cold rain began to fall, limiting vision with thick silvery droplets. Awaiting their turn to enter the Dante course, Spartan looked up and noticed a carved wooden sign hanging over the entrance way to the obstacle course. Seeing what Spartan was looking at, Dancer read the sign out loud.

"*Abandon all hope, ye who enter here.*" She read. "How bloody sweet is that? It's almost homey when you really get right down to it. I mean chain link fencing, barbed wire, and let's not forget the walking dead? I could almost imagine that I was back in London. Now, if only I had some crumpets and tea."

Spartan didn't know what part of London that Dancer had lived in, but he was pretty sure that it had not had a barbed wire fence around it. Looking over at Techno he could almost hear the boy's windpipe locking up as he mentally fought to control his terror. Water ran down the boy's face, matting his black hair but Spartan could not tell if it was also mixed with tears as it streaked down the boy's cheeks. He was determined not to look too hard because it really didn't matter either way.

"Game time!" Freak added cracking his neck to the side. "Time for the Blues Brothers to take the stage." The big teenager began to rotate his shoulders, loosening the massive joints in their sockets. "Gotta bring the pain!"

Deadeye stood silently saying nothing at all. He just stared ahead into the course, focusing on the task yet to come. If the cold, wet weather bothered him, he kept it to himself. Spartan suspected that the teen had been outside in far worse.

Spartan adjusted his short sword at his hip, securing it tightly, and inspected his teammate's gear. Techno's stun baton was in its scabbard on his belt which was probably safest for all of them. The boy fidgeted side to side, obviously nervous. Freak's bats were out and, in both hands casually spinning in alternating concentric circles back and forth to loosen his wrists. Dancer stood with the haft of her naginata stuck into the mud like a walking stick, her blade pointing to the sky as if defying the storm gods to strike her down. Her pretty face was streaked black as her makeup ran in small charcoal rivers over her cheekbones like war paint. Deadeye had knelt down observing the ground, looking for any early signs of the dangers that they would face inside the deadly course. His razor bow was slung across his back, and a deadly looking tomahawk dangled from his hip. They were ready.

A buzzer sounded, followed by an announcement over the loudspeakers fixed high upon the light poles. "Alpha team, you are on deck. Begin on the next buzzer."

"Okay here we go." Spartan said "Deadeye on point. Check for "Z" tracks and rough terrain. I will go second. Techno… Your third, in between us all, Dancer you go forth due to your reach with your weapon. Freak, you are on our six. Don't let us get surprised from behind.

"You got it brother." The giant replied "Ain't nothing getting' by me!"

"All right, slow and steady people. I know this is a race, but it's more important to come out alive. Techno has told me that there are three different types of "Zs" that we need to watch for… Is that right Tech?"

"Yeah right… Reapers, Romeros, and Husks. Reapers run and vomit. Romero's move at a shambling gait but there is usually a shitload of them, and Husks disintegrate whenever you touch them. The powder from the Husks should be suppressed by the rain, but just the same, avoid contact with them or you could end up infecting us all."

"Thanks, Tech."

A buzzer sounded over the speakers indicating Spartan's team should begin the Dante course immediately.

"Here we go. Let's move out, slow and quiet." Spartan said.

Deadeye moved silently through the one-way revolving gate, his eyes alternating between the rain-soaked ground and the open areas ahead of his team. He quietly unslung his bow and knocked an arrow. Holding the readied weapon with one hand, he moved forward the team in position behind him. They had previously agreed to a three-meter interval for movement. Stops would only be taken for a brief breather or if they needed to make important decisions and the team would always position themselves in an outward facing circle to make sure they were not surprised while they talked.

Moving stealthily forward towards the first obstacle, Deadeye led the team to small copse of fir trees. Calling a halt for the team through the use of an upraised fist hand signal with his left hand, the Native American team member dropped to his belly and snaked forward in a classic low crawl. Reaching the edge of the tree line, the camouflaged boy peered between two low hanging boughs. Ahead he saw the first obstacle of the course. It was a single raised log spanning an approximately 10-foot-wide streambed. From his position, he couldn't see how deep the stream below was located. Wandering aimlessly in front of the entrance to the obstacle were two Romero "Zs". Carried on the soft breeze, Deadeye could hear the low moans of several more undead hidden somewhere around the obstacle, but definitely nearby. Quietly the boy crawled back to his teammates.

"Two creepers… or … Romeros are outside the first obstacle. It looks like a log that we have to jump up on and use to then cross the river. I heard several more "Z's" in the area as well but I couldn't see them. It was hard to tell exactly where they were at, with the rain is messing with my sound perception."

Spartan nodded. "How high is the log off of the ground?" He asked.

“’bout three feet. It will take time for each of us to climb up.” Deadeye said, looking specifically at Techno.

“Okay” Spartan said thinking fast. “Let’s lure them away from the log. Eliminate them quickly, and then cross one by one. The last thing we want is one of them taking a bite outta Freak’s big ass as he tries to climb up.” Spartan said with a smile.

“How do you want to go about it? “Dancer asked seriously.

“Divide and conquer. Two teams, twenty-meter interval. Techno with Freak, Dancer you’re with me. Deadeye; you’re looking for additional “Zs”. If you can get them from a distance, take them. But conserve your arrows. We may need them later. Is everybody ready?”

Everyone nodded.

“Okay, move out.” He said quietly and motioned with a four-fingered gesture straight ahead. Then he stalked out into the clearing with Dancer hot on his heels. Glancing to his right, he saw Freak and Techno moving out to engage as well. Halfway across the field, Spartan and Dancer stopped and began waving their weapons in the air at the undead blocking the path to the obstacle. Twenty meters away, Freak and Techno mimicked the action.

The response was immediate. The undead turned as if they were of one mind, drawn individually to each group and began to shamble forward. Low, unearthly moans drifted through the wind and rain as the two teams prepared to engage. Although they were in two separate positions, they looked like mirror images of each other. Freak stood with his left foot forward, twin baseball bats resting gently over each shoulder with his huge hands gripping the twisted faux suede grips. Spartan could almost swear he could smell the faint scent of pine tar in the air from the bat's handles. The team leader could not help but smile as the gigantic cadet broke into a rendition of Cab Calloway's "Minnie the Moocher". His team's colossus seemed right at home going into battle. Techno on the other hand appeared ready to pee himself.

Techno had now drawn his stun baton. Spartan was more afraid that the terrified boy would shock himself and fall unconscious on the ground, than do actual damage to the walking dead. So far, he was hanging tough but as the team leader, Spartan could only hope that it lasted long enough that the boy did not get himself or one of his teammates killed.

Looking over his right shoulder, Spartan caught Dancer's brown eyes with his own. Despite being the smallest and lightest of the group, the girl wore a hard look on her face that spoke of her willingness to passionately destroy "Zs" much larger than her. The butt of her naginata pressed into the mud, like a pike set for a horseman's charge. Spartan had watched this pretty young girl a month earlier twirl, spin and dance with that pole arm in the early morning light with deadly precision. He had very little fear that she would allow any "Z" to get close to her or anyone else on the team.

As the first creature lurched within range, Spartan pivoted on his left foot, spinning out and away from the slow-moving creature. As his momentum swung him past the undead's outstretched arms and behind the creature's left flank, he swung his blade downward to his lower right. The razor-sharp sword slashed cleanly through rotting flesh, severing the tendons behind both knees. Without the structural support, both of the creature's legs buckled with an audible popping sound, dropping it to the ground and onto its back. Spartan allowed his momentum to continue forward, clear of the "Zs" reaching grasp. As the creature's eyes tracked Spartan's movements, it rolled over onto its belly. Dancer's blade winked in the sunlight as she spun it to a striking position then drove the eighteen inches of hardened steel downward, piercing the creature's neck and severing the spinal cord and flesh just below the skull. Black, rotting blood clung to her blade as the creature shuddered once and lay still; pinned into the ground like an obscene exhibit from a bug collection. `A horrible, rotten smell wafted upward on the morning breeze as she wiggled the imbedded blade back and forth, trying to free it from the ground beneath the corpse. Yanking her blade free, the undead's head rolled over into the muck. As she wiped the viscous bodily fluids on the creature's clothing, she saw that the "Zs" eyes were still following her movement. Spartan and Dancer spared no time for congratulations, leaving the corpse where it lay; they turned and raced for the log bridge.

Spartan looked to his right as he ran. Freak was maniacally bashing the "Z" in front of him and Techno. Both of the creature's arms appeared to be broken and stood out at angles where no joints were located and one of the creature's thighs clearly showed a thick, jagged shard of white as shattered bone had ruptured through the skin apparently after a particularly brutal shot from either Jake or Elwood. Techno had circled behind the creature with his baton upraised to crush its skull, however before he could strike, both bats brought the band together on either side of the "Zs" skull, pulping it into a disfigured mass, and sending diseased brain matter splattering outward and the risen corpse to the ground for a final time.

"Hidie, hidie, hidie ho!" The gigantic black man sang, as Techno grinned.

"Freak! No time!" Spartan called from the log bridge and pointed upriver. Several more "Z's" were emerging from the riverbank, dripping with water and blackened with age. They slowly began to shamble their way towards the team. Together, Spartan and Dancer crossed the log bridge.

"Gotta go Dawg!" Freak said grabbing Techno by the arm and propelling him forward.

Techno, who was much less athletic than the ripped and muscular Freak, slowed the run by a few seconds. Seconds that was precious when avoiding "Z's". Looking up, they saw Dancer and Spartan already on the far bank of the river, waving at them frantically. Dozens of "Zs" were clawing their way up both sides of the riverbank in search of living flesh to devour. An arrow zipped through the air, splitting the space between Techno and Freak, and impaling the closest of the "Zs" through the forehead. It dropped silently off the riverbank and back into the water below. Following the creature's plummet with his eyes, Techno saw to his horror that the river below was filled with the undead. They looked like a crocodile pool from the National Geographic channel, thrashing in the water and snapping their jaws hungrily. Paralyzed with fear, the Asian cadet stopped dead still, his body locked with fright as he looked down at the undead, his mouth opening and closing soundlessly. A full yard behind Freak, the big teen didn't notice his partner had ceased running.

The big black cadet hurtled onto the three-foot-high log, never breaking stride. Crossing quickly, he jumped to the ground beside Dancer and Spartan then looked back for his teammate. Techno had not mounted the log yet, standing with his hands outstretched, barely touching the wood. Deadeye was racing up towards him at a sprint. If Tech didn't move soon, he would bottleneck the entrance to the log bridge and both of the cadets would be surrounded by the shambling corpses and they would die.

Freak started to remount the log bridge and go get Techno but was stopped by Spartan's grasping hand.

"You can't help him Freak. If you go back over there, you'll only get yourself killed too. Deadeye will get him moving on his way over. He will move or he will die!"

"C'mon Dawg! Move your ass!" Freak hollered at Techno. If Techno didn't move soon, both he and Deadeye would be encircled by the undead and would be eaten alive.

Skidding to a stop next to the paralyzed Asian, the Native American cadet drew back his next knocked arrow and fired directly into the face of the closest "Z". The arrow flew through the air so fast that it appeared to vanish from view as it covered the ten feet between where the boy stood with the bow and where it shivered to a stop inside of a walking dead corpse. The impact of the arrow into the creature's eye socket, launched by the powerful bow at such a close range, lifted the impaled creature from its feet and drove it backwards into the closest two undead. Together the walking corpses fell in a tangled heap of rotting flesh. The walking undead and the permanently dead rolled back down the bank, buying the boys a few more precious seconds.

"Move your ass fat boy!" The Apache yelled. "If we stay here, we both die!"

Striking like a coiled snake, Deadeye lashed a hand up and slapped the brain-locked boy in the back of the head hard enough to jiggle Techno's eyeballs and hopefully bring him to his senses.

"They're getting up the fucking bank. Move!" He yelled. "Or I will gut you myself and leave you here as bait!"

Whether it was the sight of the "Zs" or the Apache's gruesome threat or maybe just unbridled terror, the chubby Asian boy climbed onto the log on his hands and knees and rapidly scrabbled forward. Reaching the end of the log, Freak's gigantic hand grabbed him roughly by the collar and yanked him forcefully onto the bank. Sand and dirt clogged into the boy's mouth as he smashed unceremoniously along the ground. Behind him, Deadeye had mounted the log but was now fighting a defensive holding movement against more than a dozen "Z's" as he slowly backed away from the encroaching undead. Steadily he slashed with his razor bow at grasping hands and clashing jaws. Balanced on the log over the center of the River, he knew that one misstep and he would either fall backward onto the log bridge or plummet twenty feet down into the "Z" filled river. Either way would mean certain death for him. Even if he made it all the way across the log, the undead were pursuing him and they would be forced to fight again. They needed a way to eliminate the creatures while keeping the team safe.

Quickly Spartan spun and grabbed Freak's arm.

"Can you lift this?" He asked pointing down at the log bridge.

"Hell yeah! Piece of cake Dawg!" The big man said, tossing both of his bats onto the ground and rubbing his hands together.

"When I tell you to, lift and toss this end of the log down into the river. Collapse the bridge to your left! You got it?!"

"I feel ya Dawg. Don't worry I got this!" Freak said as he squatted and wrapped his arms around the huge log. The log easily weighed five or six hundred pounds. Even Freak's vaunted strength would be hard-pressed to lift and throw such a large object.

Turning back to the Apache, Spartan hollered." Deadeye! Listen to me! Keep backing up slowly. Freak is going to collapse the bridge! On my go I want you to jump for my hand on your right. Do you understand? Jump for my hand on your right! On three; One! Two! Three!

The giant's shoulders and biceps swelled as he gripped the log and drove his legs downward into the earth. Steadily the massive cadet lifted the fallen tree clear of its dirt mooring, displaying nearly unheard-of strength. With a roar, Freak heaved the log's end over the riverbanks edge, smashing several undead free from where they were climbing up the riverbank below them. As the end of the tree swung around it, it clipped Freak's chin knocking him backward into a sprawl.

Feeling the log move, Deadeye's razor bow flashed downward severing another hand that was gripping his pant leg. Then half pivoting to his right, he launched himself off of the falling log and out into the open air. Shoving the deadly razor bow further out through the air towards the empty part of the riverbank so that he didn't land on the deadly blades, the Native American reached desperately for his team leader's outstretched hand.

Grasping Deadeye at his wrist, Deadeye's pendulum-like momentum slammed him into the muddy riverbank, crushing the air from the boy's lungs and yanking Spartan half over the embankment with him. The Apache boy dangled precariously fifteen feet above a river full of "Z's". Below him, the undead were thrashing and reaching upward, trying to grab the dangling teenager and pull him into the water below. Sweat and rain threatened both of their grips as they hung dangerously, swaying silently over the moaning dead. Dancer dove onto Spartan's legs attempting to hold him down, but she just didn't weigh enough to counterbalance the two larger boys' weight. Together they were still slowly sliding towards the river's edge, inch by slick inch.

"Where the fuck is Freak's big ass?" Spartan screamed. "Get him over here!"

Another hand shot forward over the top of Dancer and Spartan, grabbing Deadeye by the collar. The hand was not Freak's chocolate brown color but one of pale white. It was Techno. The boy had shaken off his paralysis and was attempting to pull Deadeye up onto the bank with all of his might. The Asian boy's face purpled and strained with the effort. Together, Spartan and Techno hauled the Native American cadet gasping onto solid ground where he lay on his back silently thanking the spirits of his tribe.

Untangling himself from his teammates, Spartan looked around for Freak.

"Freak you okay?" He asked seeing the boy lay prone on the ground.

"I'm okay Dawg," the big man called, rubbing the side of his jaw and head. "The damn log hit me when I flipped it over the edge. Felt like I got hit in the jaw with a fastball. It really rang my bell. I'm okay though." He said staggering as he stood up. "Just a few cobwebs. I'll shake it off. No worries."

Deadeye rose to his feet, swiftly drawing his Tomahawk into his hand. With a look of malice, he slowly advanced on where Techno still lay on the ground, gasping for breath.

"I should scalp your fat ass!" The cadet hissed. "Once again you endangered everyone on the team!"

Spartan, Dancer and Freak held their breath. Although they wanted to intervene, they knew that this situation had to be resolved before they could go any further into the Dante Course. They all knew that Deadeye had every right to be angry. Techno had almost gotten him and everyone else killed with his cowardice.

Several tense moments passed as the Apache stood over Techno. Rain dripped in rivulets down the tomahawk's black blade. Techno's eyes never left the deadly looking hatchet. With a war cry, the Apache cadet lifted his tomahawk high, and swung the blade downward in a flash, burying the blade into the mud next to Techno's head.

"The next time you endanger all of us, you don't walk away." He said with a snarl. "But today, since you saved me in the end; you live."

Pulling the tomahawk free of the mud, Deadeye extended his hand to help Techno to his feet. As the boy stood up, Deadeye reiterated his feelings. "Freeze again and you're dead meat!" He said releasing the Japanese-American cadet. Techno was speechless and only nodded his comprehension to the terrifying scout.

Seeing the drama between his teammates come to an end, Spartan spoke.

"We need to get moving before the undead find a way over the edge of the riverbank. From now on, Techno you're the last in line. Live or die… It's your choice. I won't sacrifice another team member because you can't keep up or you freeze and block the path of the escape."

His tone brooked no discussion and no argument. Techno could only nod.

"Move out!" Spartan commanded and the teens set off toward the second obstacle of the Dante Course.

Alpha team sprinted a full quarter mile in an effort to make up time and to hopefully outdistance any Romero's that may be following them from the first obstacle. Finally, coming to the second obstacle they slowed, evaluating the area without fully stopping.

Before them stood and eight-foot-high log wall, lined on either side of the path by thick trees. Deadeye accelerated and hit the wall at a full run. Leaping up with one leg acting as a springboard on the wall, he used his arms to vault upward, where he grasped the top log and hurled himself over. Twin splashes mud and water jettisoned from beneath his boot's as he landed, razor bow in hand, and instantly began to scan the perimeter for any approaching "Z's".

"Clear!" He called back to his teammates.

Spartan athletically jumped the wall next, assuming a defensive position opposite of Deadeye. The blade of the sword of the Leonidas dripped a steady river of rainwater from its pommel as he held it at the ready. The remainder of Alpha team scrambled over the wall. The only near incident was when Dancer threw her naginata over the wall to allow herself the mobility to climb and it had stuck into the ground inches from Spartan's foot. Straddling the top of the wall, she sheepishly looked down at her team leader, batted her dark brown eyes and shrugged apologetically.

After two unsuccessful attempts, Techno looked over at Freak.

"I can't make it." He said in a dejected tome. "I'm just not strong enough."

"No sweat Dawg. I'll give you a boost. Just jump up there and grab onto the top." The big teen said matter-of-factly as he sheathed his twin bats.

Techno nodded, knowing if anyone could get him over the wall it would be the powerhouse beside him. Jumping up, he barely had time to grab the top log when he was unceremoniously dumped over by a helping shove in the ass from Freak. The Asian boy landed less than nimbly on his buttocks with a muddy splash. Freak landed easily next to him a moment later. Reaching an oven mitt sized hand down, he helped Techno back to his feet.

"Sorry man. I thought you was ready. My bad." Freak said, although a fleeting thought passed through Techno's mind that the overzealous push and subsequent apology were less than heartfelt.

Spartan moved his team along as quickly as he dared. Deadeye, who ran like a gazelle, was allowed to range one hundred meters out in front of the team, searching for any footprints, animal tracks or other signs of "Z" presence. Tracks he did not mind finding; but indications of the actual undead like shambling Romeros or the running, undead bodies of the Reapers, he hoped to avoid as much as possible. The Apache cadet showed absolutely no signs of fatigue or of slowing down as he moved. Glancing forward and back, Spartan studied his team. Dancer ran smoothly, her wet brown bangs pushed to the side and her ponytail slinging rainwater side to side with every step that she took. She seemed to be extremely focused, looking for danger while Deadeye was so far out front. Freak was softly singing the theme song to the old Western television show *Rawhide* as he strode along. He was using the tune as a cadence, keeping his mind from the physical strain on his lungs and legs. To his credit, Techno was also keeping pace, matching Freak stride for stride. Spartan himself was maintaining the pace. Sweat trickled down his back, mixing with the rainwater that had soaked his T-shirt. At least he did not feel worn out. It looked as if they would all be okay as long as the Dante Course did not turn into a full sprint.

Rounding a bend in the path Spartan spotted Deadeye down on one knee holding up a closed fist that told his team to immediately stop. Spartan relayed the hand signal to his team while simultaneously dropping to a crouch and then added additional hand signals to Dancer, Freak and Techno that he was going to move up to Deadeye to see what was ahead or if they should continue to hold their position. After receiving the *thumbs-up* from all three teammates, Spartan moved towards the Apache's position; low, fast and quiet upon his arrival, the scout whispered in his ear.

"Open field ahead with the path running between two heavy clumps of the trees. At least two "Z's" roaming, but there could be more hidden. I think that they are Reapers. This could get bad really quick, especially with Techno slowing us down."

Rapidly searching his memory, Spartan recalled what Techno had told him about Reapers that he had learned from his friend at the nursing home. He remembered that they were fast, capable of bloody, infectious vomit and ultimately extremely dangerous.

"How do you know that they are Reapers?" The team leader asked.

The Native American cadet did not verbally reply. Reaching into his combat vest, he produced a small three-inch long pair of binoculars and handed them to Spartan. Taking the field glasses, Spartan used them to observe and study the two "Z's". The undead shuffled mindlessly side to side, turning in small elliptical formations as if patrolling in an assigned area. As the rotation turned their bodies to face the hidden team, Spartan could see the bloody crimson gore that painted the lower half of the faces and chests of the undead. It was fresh and still wet.

"Their feeding?"

The Apache nodded.

"On what?"

"Look down at the ground." The scout replied.

Spartan angled the binoculars downward. At first, he saw nothing but sticks and tall grasses. Then all at once it occurred to him what he was looking at. He was not looking at branches at all, he was looking at antlers. Judging by the points of the rack, this had been a mature ten or twelve point deer.

Spartan was shocked; his mouth dropped open. "They ran down a fucking deer! They're that fast?"

The Scout nodded silently, and then pointed twenty degrees to Spartan's left.

"Two more carcasses over there."

"You have got to be fucking kidding me!"

"Exactly." The scout replied completely deadpan. "Now you know why I said it was Reapers."

"Fall back to the team. We need to strategize and the clock's ticking." Spartan said.

The Apache nodded and silently began to back away, his eyes never leaving the Reapers. Spartan followed suit, ensuring that every footfall made absolutely no noise, not wanting to draw the attention of the two vicious undead.

Arriving back at the team, Spartan quickly moved his team into a combat information circle. Quickly he explained what he and Deadeye had seen in the glade and the circumstances that lay ahead of them.

"I say we take 'em out. Can't leave no damn Reapers at our backs." Freak said. "There's only two of them. It can't be that hard. Sure, they are fast, but they still can be put down."

Spartan nodded then looked around the rest of his team waiting for other input.

Dancer spoke up. "I say we move through the woods. Silent and camouflaged we may be able to evade their detection. There is no sense in engaging with those bloody things if we do not have to. Besides in the open field, these creatures are too fast. If they can run down the deer, then they can run us down. Better to use the trees and scrub to slow them down if they do come after us."

"I got a newsflash for you. Those trees are gonna slow us down too Cookie." Freak replied not waiting for Spartan to call upon him. "Trip on a root or broken branch and we're all "Z" chow."

"Tech?" Spartan asked. "What do you think?"

The boy looked indecisive, chewing on his lower lip. He hated making decisions. "The woods would probably be safer, but we're also against the clock. I agree with Freak. I don't want to constantly be looking over my shoulder for these bastards. I know that I can't outrun them. We put them down."

Spartan again nodded and then looked over at Deadeye for his opinion.

"Woods." He said simply "Fat boy over there is a liability in a normal flight; against something as fast as this will be, he will be an easy buffet. Then again, the rest of us would all be safe, but he would be dead."

Spartan saw Techno blanch at the comment but suppressed his smile. The Apache was motivating the kid by using fear as a tool. The team leader carefully weighed his options. The ticking clock; the strengths and weaknesses of his team; and the creatures' known abilities. He could hear Colonel Slade's pre-brief of the course in his mind.

"Pacify..."

"Neutralize..."

"And evade."

He made his decision. "We go into the woods." Looking over at the big man, the disappointment was evident on his face and by the slow shaking of his head. Spartan spoke softly. "I'm sure you could beat them down Freak; but I can't defend against bloody vomit, can you? We take the safest path and the time be damned or the competition. This is about survival as much as it is about crushing "Z's". Just so we all get out of this in one piece, know what I mean?"

"We will use the tree clump on the right. Move in deep, and quickly get out of sight. Okay, standard Ranger file. Eight-meter spread. Move out and for God's sake, keep it quiet."

The team rose as one. Deadeye moved into the woods as silent as a ghost followed by Dancer, Spartan, Freak and then Techno. Forty meters into the woods, Deadeye again signaled for a halt. Silently the boy knocked an arrow and drew it back on his bow. Following the scout's line of sight, Spartan spotted his target.

A white spotted, brown fawn had entered the edge of the wood line on the opposite side of the clearing, two hundred meters parallel to the team's location. Its brown ears twitched side to side as its nose scented the air, nervous from the death of its kin blowing in the wind. The undead had not yet noticed its arrival. The Apache intended to rectify that.

Deadeye lined up his shot, took a deep steadying breath and loosed the arrow. Streaking through the trees as if it were a sentient being, the black shaft streaked across the meadow like a bolt of ebony lightning. The broad razor head of the arrow struck the fawn's left rear haunch, ripping out a bloody gorge of flesh before penetrating all the way through and embedding fully into the deer's right leg as well. The effect was instantaneous. Hamstrung; the deer began to bleat wildly, pain and terror bulging out its eyes as it attempted to pull itself along on it still functioning forelegs. The deer's distressed cries immediately drew the attention of the Reaper "Z's". Sprinting at a maniacal pace; blood and spittle trailing behind them, the twin undead reached the fawn in scant seconds.

Unable to run, the deer could only paw at the air and bleat its fear and pain as the undead leapt upon it and savagely ripped mouthfuls of flesh from its hide and entrails from its body. One of the Reapers paused in its gorging long enough to spew bloody, chunk filled vomit directly into the defenseless young deer's muzzle and eyes. Satisfied with the distraction, Deadeye turned back to the team and saw Dancer's horrified look.

"Don't look at me like that." The Apache said. "We needed a distraction; now we have one. We need to move now while the pus bags are occupied." Then the boy turned and trotted into the woods without looking back. Spartan laid a hand on Dancer's shoulder, empathizing with the girl's revulsion to the loss of anything living to the teeth of the undead. However, he knew that Deadeye was right, and the sacrifice had been necessary to ensure their safety. The deer's life would hopefully provide them an opening to pass through the Reaper's hunting ground undetected.

"C'mon Dancer. We have to go." He said softly.

Wiping away a single involuntary tear that rested upon her high cheek bone, the girl took off after the Apache cadet without a word. Spartan and the rest of the team followed suit. Ten minutes later they were free of the woods, the "Z's", and their ravaged venison meal had been left a quarter of a mile behind them. As she finally left the woods behind, Dancer silently hoped that neither she nor any of her teammates would ever have to know the anticipated fear of certain death that the young deer had felt in its final moments. What a horrible way to die.

Far to the west, outside of the obstacle course fencing, Drill sergeant Hogg stood high in a watchtower and observed his assigned squad through a combination of high-powered binoculars and closed-circuit imagery from the cameras strategically mounted throughout the course. Overall, he was pleased with his team's progress thus far, but the worst was yet to come.

Colonel Slade stood silently behind the Drill sergeant, his hands clenched behind his back. His jaw muscles knotted and flexed as he watched the dramatic events unfolding upon the Dante Course.

"No injuries up to this point through three obstacles and two "Z" encounters. So far, so good." The Commandant said between clenched teeth. "Spartan made a good decision on taking to the woods and using the deer as a distraction was innovative, in fact it was tactically brilliant, if somewhat unforeseen."

Sergeant Hogg could only nod. He was worried for his assigned cadets and it showed in the deep creases upon his brow. He would give anything to be at their sides, smashing dead skulls and kicking undead, rotten ass. Sitting on the sidelines and just watching while his charges risked their lives wasn't worth a shit. But for now, he knew that there was nothing he could do to help them. Their survivability was strictly in their hands.

The next obstacle was a cargo net which presented very little difficulty for the team. The fact that there were no undead in the immediate area seemed to signify that this obstacle was only intended to eat up time. Still, the Alpha team members were cautious, not wanting to get surprised by a pack of Romeros while they were entangled with the huge net. Even Techno managed to scurry over it with minimum trouble.

Fatigue was beginning to set in as the team repeatedly stopped and started, sprinted and jogged through the course. Seeing the sheltered overhang of a dozen tree branches ahead, Spartan called a halt to allow the team to catch their breath. Tucked under the relative security of the trees, Spartan reformed the combat information circle with his team facing outward. Looking around, he evaluated the condition of his teammates. Freak was breathing hard and sweating profusely. Dancer was leaning on the haft of her naginata; rivulets of sweat making small "C" shaped rings of her Brown bangs. Techno sounded like a locomotive. Huffing and hissing as he fought to catch his breath, the Asian boy's head hung low; but Spartan did not know if that was from lack of air or the fear of the upcoming obstacles.

"Head up, eyes out Tech. Watch your zone of responsibility." Spartan said softly. The boy soundlessly complied, still trying to control his breathing.

Spartan looked over at Deadeye. The cadet barely looked winded despite almost doubling the running of the rest of the team by scouting well ahead of the team's formation, then reporting back his findings to Spartan. The boy's endurance as well as his stealth and accuracy with a bow were the reasons that Spartan had selected him as Alpha team's scout.

Spartan himself was somewhat winded but still operationally functional. His breath would recover in a few minutes and his legs were not yet fatigued. Perhaps all of the insane running during the early morning PT sessions had actually paid off, in spite of the inclement weather. Positioning himself at the center of the combat circle so that everyone in the team could hear him, Spartan spoke softly over the incessant drip–drip–drip of the falling rain from the tree branches.

"We are about one third of the way through the course. Is everyone okay?" He asked.

Seeing nods from everyone he continued.

"Deadeye; slow the pace a bit. We have a long way to go and not all of us are as untiring out here as a deer." Immediately he regretted his choice of metaphor remembering Dancer's reaction to the sacrificed fawn. "Keep your scouting range down to about fifty or so meters. Freak, I want you to lead the rest of the team on the run. You're the largest so you set the pace. We'll match you."

"Dancer, you and I will bring up the middle. Keep your pole arm at high guard. I don't want anyone getting accidentally stuck on that blade. I know you're getting tired, so if you get to fatigued let me know and I will move you to the front of the file to keep us all safe." The girl nodded as Spartan stood up.

"What about me?" Techno asked.

"Tech, I want you in my hip pocket. Fall behind, fall out or become a liability and I will leave you. Like I told you before, I won't sacrifice the team for you."

The Asian boy looked as if he was going to throw up but said nothing in response and nodded.

"On your feet. Set up a Ranger file in ten seconds. Deadeye… Get us a heads up for the next obstacle when you can. Moving out in three… Two… One. Go."

Deadeye took off like a rabbit being chased by the hounds of Hell, anxious to scout the dangers ahead. The rest of the team rose as one. Together they moved single file into the second phase of the Dante obstacle course.

Freak's pace, while not quite as rabid and merciless as Deadeye's, was brutal, nonetheless. What he lacked in pure speed, was more than made up for by his long, powerful legs. Moving swiftly down the dirt trail, the team rounded a blind spot of trees and almost ran into Deadeye who stood contemplating the scene before him. Literally hundreds of immobile undead stood like desiccated statues in the field in front of them, spanning the area from riverfront to the tree line they had just left. From just behind Freak, Techno identified the mummified creatures.

"Husks…" Techno said quietly.

Spartan recalled that the undead were nearly completely paralyzed and desiccated due to dehydration and the lack of consumption of human flesh, but they were every bit as deadly as the fast, virus vomiting Reapers or the pack-based mentality of the Romero's. Due to their brittle body structure, Husks had to be avoided at all costs. Where a team member may survive a direct contact with the other forms of undead as long as they didn't suffer from an attack that could infect them, any impact, regardless of how minor, could result of the breaking off a limb or rupturing of the skin on a Husk which would subsequently release a powder-based form of the HUNGER virus into the air. If that happened, the effects could be devastating, potentially infecting everyone and everything in its path depending on which way the wind blew.

In his mind, Spartan wondered if this was how the virus had infected the entire planet so quickly since both Reapers and Romero's required direct physical contact to spread their plague. Not that it really mattered now since the world had gone to shit; but hopefully someone had analyzed this and figured out a way to destroy the Husks without further spreading the HUNGER virus.

Looking ahead through the silvery droplets of light rain, Spartan nodded at Deadeye and the teenager began cautiously maneuvering past the outstretched arms and legs of the living corpses. A creaking sound, reminiscent of old leather being bent, could be heard as the closest undead slowly turned to face the much more mobile cadet. Interestingly enough, most of the Husks either had no eyes at all or they were shriveled reddish black orbs that could not possibly have been capable of sight. Spartan silently wondered how they were aware of Deadeye's passage.

Looking to both sides, Spartan noted standing rainwater slowly flowing down a slight slope towards the river flowing briskly to his left. Remembering the floating corpses from the first obstacle, he knew the river was not an option. Moving to his right would only cross back into the area with the dead deer and the two Reapers. There was no way in hell he was going back there. Straight ahead was the only option. He quickly made a command decision.

"Everyone, weapons secured. Repeat… All weapons are to be holstered. We cannot risk physical contact with these creatures. Dancer, if you have to carry yours, make sure that its blade is pointed down. Anything that gets grabbed; drop it. No struggle. No physical contact. Does everyone understand? One punctured corpse and we're all dead."

His team complied wordlessly, sheathing weapons where they could, with Dancer pointing the blade of her naginata towards the ground. As soon as the weapons were secured, the team moved out. Slowly… Cautiously… As they wound their way through the slow reaching Husks, it quickly became apparent that Freak's huge size was going to work against him. Forty yards into the walking minefield of Husk bodies one of the creatures' outstretched claws snagged into the canvas of the huge cadet's rucksack. Pulling itself forward towards the cadet, the desiccated "Z" brought its taut jaws and jagged teeth onto the rucksack canvas strap, tearing at the material, trying to get to the flesh beneath.

Fear loomed in the teenager's eyes. Against any normal human or even a Reaper or Romero, Freak could bring his superior strength to bear, snapping the person or creature in half. But here, against a Husk, he risked not only infecting himself but his entire team if he used to brute force. Nor could he drop the heavy pack as the creature's teeth were locked tightly onto it.

"Help..." He hissed quietly not wanting to attract further attention from the undead. "It's got my rucksack."

Surprisingly, it was Techno that came to the rescue. As the creature slowly reared its head back again to take a bite out of either the canvas strap of the rucksack or possibly out of the cadet himself, the Japanese-American boy carefully thrust the end of his stun baton into the undead's open mouth and activated the electrical arc. The "Z" spasmed as electricity coursed through its dried body, then fell over into the mud with a splash. Everyone held their breath as they look to see if any dust emerged from a rupture in the corpse's fallen body. Seeing none emerge, the team moved quickly on, all of them holding their breaths. After thirty yards, Freak finally took a breath. Carefully twisting, turning and dodging the deadly dust filled and cadaverous Husks, the team passed the remainder of the obstacles without any further incident. Upon clearing away from the last of the Husks, Spartan turned and looked at Techno.

"How did you know what the effect of the electricity would be on the Husk?" Spartan asked.

"Simple biological reasoning really." the boy said in reply. "Electricity short-circuits the motor neurons of the brain. Without those motor neurons, a body cannot function. I simply shorted out what little physical ability it had left. Without it, the "Z" fell to the ground inert."

"But how did you know that the "Z" would not rupture when it fell?"

"I guessed that the rain that had been falling for two days would have added enough moisture to the undead to keep them from splitting apart. I suppose that was lucky in retrospect. I probably should've tested my theory first."

Spartan could only stare at the boy in disbelief. He had just risked the entire team on an untested theory. Fortunately, it had worked out for the best. After this set of trials was over, he and Techno were going to have a very serious talk.

Beyond the rows of the nearly immobile undead, the team approached the sixth challenge of the Dante Course. The obstacle consisted of the sixty-meter-high log tower. Each log was supported on a dual post frame, three feet above the next log with the overall structure creating an "A" frame. The objective of the obstacle was to overcome any personal fear of heights by first scaling logs up, then safely descending on the opposite side. Beginning at the obstacle's base, the teens looked upward. The obstacle appeared to climb all the way up to Heaven just like the Led Zeppelin song; only it wasn't made of a simple stairway.

"Freak, you're up first. Post up at the top of the obstacle. You will serve as our anchorman, provide the team focus and act as a lookout for any wayward "Z's" that may be approaching us from either side. Especially keep an eye out for those Reapers that we left behind. We don't need them sneaking up on us."

The gigantic cadet nodded once and turned to the wall of logs. Placing his massive hands on the logs, he began to climb upward effortlessly, using his superior strength to pull himself along.

Spartan looked over at Dancer. "Climbs well for a big man, huh? Think you can keep up?"

Dancer rolled her brown eyes high into her head and let out a sigh of disgust.

"Puh-lease mate." She replied and began quickly climbing the structure. "He may climb like a bloody gorilla but I am a blinkin' cat." She called back down over her shoulder.

Techno came next, followed by Deadeye and finally Spartan. The only stall to their movement was Techno's fear of crossing over the top of the barrier. Freak's firm grip on the boy's combat harness eased the teen's mind enough to allow him to cycle his legs over the top one at a time as the Asian boy bear-hugged the top log, and then he was able to gather speed and confidence as he got closer to the ground. As Spartan crossed the top of the obstacle, he looked out the tree line and saw the Drill Instructor Hogg giving him a thumbs-up signal from the observation tower. He didn't waste time responding and climbed as quickly down as he could.

The team reassembled quickly at the opposite side of the obstacle. *"So far, so good."* Spartan thought. *"No injuries, no major impediments."* Resuming their Ranger file; the team followed the trail and ran quickly ahead. Three minutes later they came to the edge of the river and the next obstacle. It was there that the lack of problems changed.

"What the hell do you mean you can't swim?" Spartan asked Freak in a loud tone; concern notable in his voice. "It's not as though we can go back to the beginning of this obstacle course and say "I'm sorry, my idiot teammate forgot to mention that he can't swim so can we just leave now? You didn't think you should mention this earlier? Jesus H. Christ Freak!"

"Ain't no swimmin' pools in the ghettos of Chi-town brother. On the south side, you're worried about eatin' each day and dodgin' rounds at night Dawg, not relaxin' in some pretty blue pool. Swimmin' like that is meant for the fish at the Shedd aquarium." The big man replied. "I look like I got gills to you?"

Spartan ran his hand over his forehead, down his face and horizontally across his chin. He was in deep thought when Techno came up with the perfect idea.

"We can use a five-man tether Spartan. Twenty feet of rope between each man, hooked to our combat vests." He looked at Dancer apologetically. "Or woman. Two men cross the river first, Freak goes in the middle; and two men anchor at the shore on this side. We can pull his pack across last. Just like mountain climbing."

Freak looked at the boy skeptically. "Do a lot of that do you?" He asked in a sarcastic tone. "Climbin' mountains?"

"Well no… technically I've never been, but I've *read* all about it. As long as the knots hold, it should be fine."

"As long as the knots hold?... Well, ain't that just comforting." The big man looked concerned but nodded.

"It's either that or get left behind Freak." Spartan said seriously. "So, what's it going to be big man; the water or the "Z's"?"

"Shit Dawg… Let's do it." Was all Freak said.

Spartan and Techno began tying the knots from the parachute cord that they had brought with them. They'd all learned basic knot tying during the first few weeks at the Academy. When they were finished, Deadeye was secured to Dancer. Freak was in the middle with Techno and Spartan acting as the anchor. As soon as all of the cadets were tied together, the Apache scout waded into the river. The current swiftly flowed about his legs and after about ten feet into the river, the ground dropped to waist deep, or about four feet. Walking swiftly, the scout knifed through the water, wading without a word until he reached the natural edge of the river's drop off into deeper water. As the water crossed his chest, he began swimming, moving just as silently in the water as he did on land. The scout was followed smoothly by Dancer. The girl hesitated only a moment as the chilly water crossed her thighs and her teeth chattered involuntarily. As Dancer reached the middle of the river, swimming easily, Deadeye staggered shivering onto the far shore. River temperatures in northern Illinois during the fall were well below being "*just chilly*".

Freak held a death grip on both attaching ropes around his waist. Swallowing a lump, the size of a bowling ball in his throat, he waded slowly into the water. Steeling himself and gritting his teeth against his own fear, the big man's eyes showed the panic that he was fighting to keep down. He hadn't wanted to tell his teammates that he had never actually learned to swim because he was terrified of the water.

"Holy mutha-fuckin' God!" He exclaimed as his genitals entered the water. "It's so cold."

Standing up and securely bracing his feet against the rocks, Deadeye slowly wrapped the rope around his waist and reeled in the slack as the black cadet waded deeper and deeper into the river. The current was strong, pulling at Freaks jumpsuit and weighing him down. It was like trying to a pull a bull steer out of the water for branding. Suddenly, as Freak reached the drop off in the river there was a brief splash and a sharp tug on both ends of the rope. That was the only indication to his other teammates as the muscular teen's feet slid out from under him and he sank beneath the rain-pocked water.

Still exiting the water, Dancer waded toward the shore as fast as she could, trying to pull in the slack of the rope and assist Deadeye by pulling Freak to land. Instead, the big man's bulk was being driven by the current and pulled Dancer back towards the shoreline and into the water. Dragging her feet and hands through the silt and dead leaf filled river's bottom, the lightweight girl grabbed desperately for anything that she could use to slow her teammate's momentum. The sheer power of the river was unbelievable, and the current unyielding. Doing a half flip onto her back in the churning water allowed Dancer to halt her forward progress as she dug her heels hard into the leaves, silt and rock. Quickly, she pulled the rope around her wrists and elbows to tighten up the slack, alternating them one after the other. Glancing up, Dancer saw that Techno and Spartan fighting a similar losing battle on the opposite shore. Freak felt like he weighed half of a ton and his mass coupled with the river's natural force was threatening to pull them all in with him.

At best it was a stalemate. Both shorelines looked like a pathetic game of tug o' war, with Freak acting like the flag in the middle, albeit under water. Suddenly by chance or design, Freak's head emerged from the water, gasping as the frigid water fought his attempts to gain his breath or his footing. The cadet was hanging onto the thin parachute cord with a grip of steel but try as he might; even the powerful young man was not strong enough to pull himself across the river. Both sides of the river could hear the teen gasping for air as the water rushed around his head and shoulders.

"Can you swim?" Spartan asked as he frantically looked at Techno as he shrugged out of his ruck sack, dropping it onto the ground.

"Yeah. I went to the YMCA every year for lessons. Why?"

"I have to get Freak or he's going to drown! I'm going to cut loose of the tether. I will get upstream and let the current carry me to him. You will then become the end man. Keep the tension on the line tight and don't let him sink. You have to hold the line alone! Do you understand? You have to hold the line! When I get to him and I give you the thumbs up, then I want you to cut us loose in front of you. The current should pull us to shore like a pendulum with Deadeye and Dancer holding on the other end. Then you'll have to swim across alone. Can you do that? "

Techno nodded once, wrapped the thin green cord around his waist and braced himself against the added weight for when Spartan cut the tether.

"Do it!"

Spartan did not hesitate. Drawing the sword of Leonidas, he swept the razor-sharp blade across the cord. The line parted with an audible popping noise that was immediately followed by Techno's strained grunt, as Freak's full weight pulled against the paracord wrapped around his waist. Spartan shoved his sword back into its scabbard and raced upstream as fast as he could run. Reaching a stone embankment that overhung the water, he dove headfirst into the cold river. Surfacing quickly, he gauged the speed of the current and the twin bank placements of his team.

Using the current as momentum, Spartan swam hand over hand until he was lined up on a direct collision course with Freak in the center of the river. The water was moving swiftly and already his arms and legs were going numb from the cold. He was only going to get one shot to try and save his teammate. If he failed, then they would probably both drown.

"Freak!" He yelled, riding the current. "Get ready to grab on to me! Freak, do you hear me! Get ready goddamit!"

The big cadet barely lifted his head, and Spartan could not tell if he had understood or not.

Ten feet…

Five feet…

Spartan lunged out and grabbed the cadet's nylon combat harness with half numb fingers, pulling himself close to Freak. Reaching over the cadet's head, he wrapped an arm in the parachute cord on the opposite side of the river. Struggling against ice cold water and strong river current, he reached up his opposite hand and gave Techno the thumbs-up sign.

"Freak, Techno's cutting our tether. We're going to let the current swing us like a pendulum to shore. I need you to kick big man. Hard! Can you do that?"

Freaks mumbled reply was lost in the cold, rushing water. Spartan placed his free hand on the cadet's combat harness above his waistline, just as Techno cut the line with his multi-tool's blade. He hoped Freak had heard him. The effect was almost instantaneous. The rope, held in place by Dancer and anchored by Deadeye immediately began to swing towards the opposite bank, pushed just as Spartan had hoped like a giant human pendulum. As soon as the two boys had reached water shallow enough for them to stand in, Dancer and Deadeye leapt down into the water to help them onto the shore, each grabbing a teammate under the arm.

Spartan looked back to the opposite bank but could see no sign of Techno. Visions of undead ambushing his fat teammate on the waterfront as he stood there alone or of Reapers pulling him under the cold water flashed through his head. He truly hoped that the boy was safe. Scanning the river, he finally found the boy. Using a side swimming technique, the cadet labored to drag something behind him following the current using the same technique that Spartan had. Techno determinedly swam towards the opposite shore. Emerging from the water, he struggled to pull his burden up onto land behind him. Spartan recognized the teeth worn strap on the item. Techno had saved Spartan's and Freak's packs. Realizing that Spartan was staring at him, Techno spoke up.

"I took a lifesaver course once. That was called the "side swim and tow." Besides I remembered what Sergeant Hogg had said to Freak when he had grabbed my rucksack during our run. *"Leave a man without his rucksack and you might as well leave him to die!"* And I knew that you and the big ox would need dry clothes. Mine sure as heck wouldn't fit you guys."

Spartan clapped the boy on the shoulder. "That was smart thinking Techno. You probably saved us from hypothermia. Good job!" Spartan turned to the rest of the team. "Okay everyone. Get dry clothes from your packs and get changed. I'll stand watch and change last. We move out in five. Sorry Dancer, no place for privacy here."

The girl just shrugged and pulled off her wet T-shirt exposing her navy-blue fitness bra. Techno gawked and immediately turned a deep shade of crimson from head to toe before turning his back to afford the girl some privacy. Chuckling at the boy's embarrassment, Spartan followed suit. He figured the boy had never seen a girl semi-dressed, up close before.

Spartan knew that although they were chilled, they had to continue quickly. Right now, they were vulnerable. Sooner or later the "Z's" would find them. Reaching into his rucksack, Spartan handed Freak a crushable hand warming pack and a thick chocolate and peanut butter flavored protein bar. The big black teen shivered but gratefully took the packet crushing it in his massive hand. His teeth chattered so hard that he could not speak.

"Put it under your crotch big man." Spartan said. "The heat will help raise your core temperature and warm your body faster if you put it there."

Freak nodded tearing open the protein bar with his teeth and placing the packet and one of his hands inside the front of his pants. All that he could think of was how much he had always hated water and how now he hated both the cold *and* the water. Teeth chattering, the boy quickly devoured the protein bar in several large bites. After a few minutes, he began to slowly feel warmer.

Seeing that everyone was dressed in dry clothing, Spartan changed and rallied his team. "Look, we are all cold and tired. Stay alert. We started this as a team and we will finish this thing as a team, then there will be hot showers and hot chocolate at the end. Hang tough. Be strong. We will get through this. Everybody ready… Move out."

Despite battling the teeth chattering cold and continued rain, Alpha team set off with determination in their eyes. Spartan used physical movement to reform his team. He set the pace at a brisk jog which rapidly changed the environment from shivering torment to a sweat inducing pleasure. Even Freak, who had bordered on hypothermia from crossing the river, was warmed fully by the time they had reached the next obstacle in their path.

After calling a short halt for water, Spartan sent Deadeye ahead to observe the next challenge for his team. Deadeye, who amazingly still showed no sign of fatigue, sprinted off silently. In his absence, Spartan moved among his teammates checking their status. A mass consensus of tired, cold and fucking miserable (this from Freak) was obtained. All in all, they seemed in pretty good shape; physically and mentally.

Spartan noticed a different look in Techno's eyes. At the beginning of the course the boy had been terrified into immobility, now his jaw was clenched and he looked determined to finish.

Several minutes later, the Apache cadet reappeared and ran to Spartan's side. Kneeling next to his team leader, he spoke softly.

"It looks fairly simple. There's a rope swing over a muddy pool of water about twenty foot in width. It's about ten feet across, give or take a few inches, from bank to bank."

"What's the catch?" Spartan asked, knowing the obstacle could not be that simple.

"There are a couple of "Z's" in the water. It looks like they are chained in place. I could only see the head and shoulders of each of the creatures. Both had been secured with thick chains and metal collars clenched tightly around their necks. From their level of decay, they look like they are probably Romero's so there will be no chance of them jumping up and biting one of us as we swing over. So, all in all it seems simple. Swing over and no problems. Fall off and into the water, you will end up "Z" chow."

Nodding, Spartan moved to brief his team. Their only response came from Freak when the big man grunted in disgust.

"Great, just what I need. More fucking water Dawg!"

Deadeye quickly looked over at Spartan and asked a question as the team prepared to move.

"There are only two "Z's" that I saw. Do you want me to take them out? I can hit them both quickly from a distance, so they will never see it coming and won't be able to start their calling moan to summon other nearby creatures."

Spartan thought about the offer. After considering the tactical ramifications of the limited arrow usage, he then refused Deadeye's offer.

"No, save your arrows. We don't know what is yet to come. We may need all of your arrows before this damned course is over."

Deadeye nodded, and then seeing that the team was ready, took off, setting the pace at a run. Racing across the hundred yards before the obstacle, the Apache let out a war whoop and leapt out into the open air grasping the dangling rope at about its mid-length. Pulling his legs beneath himself to give himself plenty of clearance over the chained undead, he sailed across the water trap containing the animated corpses and released the rope at its apex. His momentum carried him up and over the rotting flesh and gnashing teeth of the "Z's" before depositing him on the far side of the obstacle safely.

Seeing how the Native American crossed the obstacle, Dancer, Spartan and Techno followed suit. Freak, who was both larger and taller than the rest of his team, also sailed through the air but his legs traveled dangerously close to the surface and by association; the "Z's". Pulling his legs up would still leave him vulnerable so the big man went on the offensive instead. Sailing lower and closer to the nearest "Z", Freak rammed his steel toed combat boot into the creature's jaw and teeth. Metal crushed bone with the sound not unlike a ceramic vase breaking and the undead's head snapped backwards against the restraining collar. The entire lower jaw as well as the front teeth on the top shattered, tearing free of the corpse's decaying skull to land glistening on the muddy embankment. Freak landed heavily next to them, a huge grin on his face.

"You see that shit Tonto?" He asked the Apache cadet with a ghetto-fied swing of his head. "That's how we handle business in the Windy City! You play… You're gonna get a boot in the mouth bitch!" Looking down at the jawless corpse still standing within the obstacle he promptly gave him the finger.

The scout merely shook his head, and then answered with icy sarcasm.

"It is a wonder that you ever learned to advance beyond your ancestors' Cro-Magnon beginnings. You have no style, no panache. Just beating and bludgeoning things into submission. I believe primitive man mastered *that* particular skill about ten thousand years ago. It is a true shame that you were unable to continue to learn to use "sophisticated tools" like the longbow. Still, I am sure that you will be useful to the team if we need a sacrificial decoy or if somebody finds a particularly difficult pickle jar to open."

Then without another word, the scout spun on his heel and trotted ahead towards the next obstacle. Freak looked over at Techno.

"Did he just call me a caveman or a sacrificial lamb?" He asked.

"Ummm yes…" replied the boy with a tentative smirk, ensuring that the giant wasn't angry. Seeing the confused look on Freak's face, he quickly shifted into sympathetic laughter. "He did... both."

Freak looked momentarily stunned, and then Techno continued.

"It was probably because you called him a sidekick to an old black and white television show that has been off the air for fifty years." He added.

"Really? He's gonna pay for that shit. I'm better at crushing "Z's" than any of you." Then the big man took off after the lithe Apache. The rest of the team quickly followed suit back into a Ranger file.

"Yes," Spartan thought, listening without comment. *"The team is definitely coming together."*

The initial shock factor and overall awareness of "Z's" had become a norm for the cadets since the beginning of the obstacles. They were an acknowledged, if unpalatable, evil that maligned the earth bringing with them waves of rot, decay and putrid essence. Even so, the cadets of Alpha team were not psychologically prepared for the outlandish world that awaited their team at the next obstacle. It was like something out of a demented butcher's nightmare.

"What the fu...?" Freak said out loud, looking from the obstacle to the Native American cadet that he had just caught up to. The big man had run hard to catch the scout, so his breathing was heavy and labored. "Are you kidding me man? This is wrong on so many levels. Who the fuck even thinks this shit up for training?"

The Apache did not respond, instead he just gaped, truly in shock at the site for the first time since they had entered the post-apocalyptic obstacle course. It took a lot to startle the scout, but he decided the horrors associated with the next obstacle were inhuman and that the images that were currently invading his mind filled his mouth with bile. The rest of the team arrived. The most notable comment came from Dancer whose voice was muffled by the fact that she was biting into the edge of her fist in an effort to not scream in horror.

"Bollocks!" She cried aloud in terror filled with revulsion.

Ahead of them, dozens of undead Romero torsos hung in uneven lines, suspended from nylon harnesses beneath a wooden support beam above them. Row after row of rotting corpses, hung armless and legless from the rafters. The Romeros were diverse, ranging in all sizes, shapes, genders, ethnicities and ages. It seemed as if a thousand pairs of eyes attached to an army of undead amputees stared into their very souls. The image was horrifying and revolting to behold.

Before the line of Alpha team's cadets, the front row of dangling undead began their mournful wailing. The low moan seemed to simultaneously express the need to feed and a desire to have their eternally damned existence ended. In several areas throughout the obstacle, crows rested upon the heads or shoulders of the decaying corpses casually pecking at the maggots that grew within the rotting flesh; piercing eyes turned red with burst blood vessels with a slight popping sound or stripping diseased skin away to quickly gobble down. It was a horrid combination of pecking and flesh tearing sounds that burrowed straight into Alpha team's soul, scarring them forever.

Spartan read the placard of instructions posted to the right of the entrance of the obstacle. As he read them aloud. he became more and more disturbed.

"It says we have to push, pull or move our way through this obstacle without getting bit. The "Z's" harnesses are secured to the overhead posts, but they will swing back to front, front to back, side to side and fully rotate three hundred and sixty degrees in a circle on a swivel."

A small gasp escaped Dancer's lips. When Spartan looked up, she would not meet his eyes but her lip quivered.

"Are we all good?" Spartan asked his team in general, not letting his eyes leave Dancer's face. The question lingered until Dancer finally looked up. Wiping her moist eyes on her forearm, she silently gave Spartan a thumbs-up signal. Spartan paused, looking slowly at the rest of his team, then back at the brown eyed girl standing next to him. "Are you sure?"

Surprisingly, it was Techno that spoke up.

"Hey Dancer…" he said in a lighthearted tone, "just think of it like an old-fashioned fun house attraction. You know where you push the big hanging bags back and forth as you try to get through the room? It used to be one of my favorites when I was a kid. That one and the room with the mirrors that made me look skinnier. That was always cool too."

Then, almost as an afterthought he added, "Of course, I always got knocked down by the swinging bags. But that was usually because the other kids were swinging them at me trying to hit me with them. I was an easier target than the skinny kids my age, so I usually got bombarded by those guys. Sometimes I never even saw the next one coming and once they really got to swingin' they seemed like they hit me from every angle, over and over." His voice trailed off into memory as he replayed the bullying in his mind. "The bastards always found a way to try to hurt me; even when it was something fun. At least these things are only trying to bite me."

Spartan thought about what Techno was saying. It makes sense that the bigger the person, the more "bags" he would displace and start swinging as he moved into or through an area. Size once again definitely mattered here because the swinging "bags" had plague infected teeth. Plus, each neck still had a couple of inches of mobility in either direction. Swinging, spinning, gnashing infected "Z" torsos… This was definitely not Techno's carnival Fun House. Making another fast decision, Spartan advised the team of his plan of action.

"Okay, we are going to move with the smallest to largest through here. Dancer, Deadeye, Techno, me then you Freak."

Seeing the dismayed look on the big cadet's face, Spartan clapped him on the shoulder. "Sorry big guy but you are more likely to set things swinging than the rest of the group put together. Slow and easy, okay? Take your time. We will be ok."

Freak nodded, tipping his neck side to side until it cracked loose in each direction. As he had repeatedly done this before entering obstacles, Spartan had begun to believe it was more of a nervous tic than a needed release of tension or pain. Spartan knew that the big cadet was far better suited to rampaging through an open area, bats flying and cracking skulls. This obstacle would test the muscular teen's patience and sense of calm to no end.

Spartan gave the cadet one more squeeze on his shoulder for encouragement. Pitiful moans, like diseased cattle, lowed from the limbless apparitions, gaining in timbre as the team moved past. At various heights, rotten flesh moved diseased jaws in lunging snaps, as the undead tried to bite the first four cadets. A jerking momentum was quickly established as the hanging corpses began to swing their pendulum like bodies back and forth, to and fro in an almost obscene parody of Edgar Allen Poe's death scene from the classic tale of the Pit and the Pendulum. The creature's thrust their necks forward, clacking their teeth on empty air as they strained to reach the living flesh that was passing just beyond their reach.

Dancer had moved into the miasma of swaying "Z" torsos fluidly, her trepidation now lost in the concentration of the moment. Spinning, pivoting and gyrating in a manner that, had they not been inside swaying literal swinging minefield of undead torsos; the boys would've found to be sensual at the least and probably bordering on the erotic. As it was, she became a dancer of innumerable movements, swiveling twisting, and turning as the various undead strove to take individual bites out of the girl's separate body parts as she passed them by.

"I don't think I can move like that boss." Freak said very seriously looking at Spartan, but with a huge smile. "I'm not built that way. Hell, she just moved like she was made out of freakin' syrup. Just flowing over and around a big 'ol stack of pancakes."

"I'm with you there Freak. There's no way that I can move like that either. Just keep it together. We'll get to the other side." Spartan replied.

Deadeye and Techno went next, navigating their way through the torsos of gnashing undead. One positive aspect of the obstacle was the team was able to use Techno's stun baton. When he held the baton to the base of an undead skull and activated the coursing electricity, the jolt scrambled the corpse's brain to the point that the undead became fully immobile, head sagging downward and diseased drool hanging in ropey strands from the now still mouths. Whether or not this was a permanent effect, no one knew nor wanted to wait around to find out, but the line of immobile corpses hanging from the overhead beams in the obstacle was the first positive sign the cadets had seen since entering the Dante Course. Of course, there was always a downside. The scent of cooking flesh from the electricity flowing through their rotten bodies and the audible bursting of the creature's eyes from their sockets nauseated the cadets and left reddish black streaks of viscous eye fluid running down the corpses faces. Additionally, the smell of the burning skin seemed to incite many of the larger crows. Many flapped huge wings and began circling above the team, surveying them from above. Others cawed loudly from atop their chosen feasts as if to complain that they preferred their meals uncooked and raw.

The continual moan of hunger assaulted their ears as the cadets moved into each new area, punctuated by the occasional crackling sound of electricity as Techno neutralized a gnashing "Z" that got too close. The reverberating sound of the moaning was unnerving coming from every direction around them as they moved into the obstacle and the sickeningly sweet smell of sun rotten flesh gagged them all. The entire experience was more than the little overwhelming and Spartan suddenly realized that this was how it would feel if they were mobbed by a pack of Romeros. Undead on every side, the inundating noise, the perpetual movement, the dead eyes staring into his own, almost mesmerizing as they closed in to tear out your throat or your organs. Bowels clenching, he wanted to get the hell out of there as fast as he could and it took all his willpower to prevent himself from running headlong through the torsos, flinging them aside with reckless abandonment. Though he longed to do just that, doing so would set the pendulum of animated torsos and gnashing teeth swinging, effectively dooming his teammates behind him.

As the teenagers moved forward, the corpses began to sway further and further, to and fro. Limbless spinal columns bent and straightened back and forth, as necks stretched forward, jaws clacking with horrifying power as they sought the flesh of their prey. Displaced ropes of intestines dangled from several of the undead, whipping around like grayish blue snakes as the undead's instinct to feed drove their limbless bodies into a frenzy. This caused the undead to spin or swing from the ropes in a crazed parity of Techno's fun house attraction. The constant jaw clacking of decayed teeth when coupled with the audible grating moan of the undead was disorienting, making it difficult to determine if the team was moving straight ahead or veering off to one side where they would be trapped. As the torsos swung and twisted, the cadets dodged left and right, back and forth trying intensely to avoid contact with any portion of the swaying bodies.

At one point, Techno's combat harness was snagged by the gnashing set of undead teeth near his left shoulder. The undead's glazed eyes stared directly into the Asian boy's face as he tried to steadily chew through the nylon and into the teenager's oh so close chest cavity. The boy's scream for help and wail of "It's biting me!" echoed across the field. Unable to clearly see Techno through the chaotic revolutions and chain jerking torsos, every member of Alpha team cringed with the boy's cry, knowing that if the boy was truly bit, he would turn into one of these monsters himself and they would be forced to put their friend down with the pacification spikes and hammers that they all carried as part of their standard gear.

Deadeye sidled back to the boy's side, deftly avoiding numerous jaws that lunged forward towards him. Amidst Techno's wail of terror, the scout quickly pried the creature's jaws apart the tip of his razor bow, slicing the rotten cheek skin into a grotesque smile. The corpse's brittle teeth shattered into jagged shards of bone, releasing the canvas strap from between them. A quick assessment showed the cadet's screams to have been unfounded and the only evidence of the attack were a few teeth marks and a smear of bloody drool in the cadet's combat harness.

Seeing the look of terror in Techno's eyes, Deadeye held the undead torso at bay with his razor bow's blade still inserted into its mouth. With his free hand he grabbed the shrieking boy by the shoulder and shook him hard. When that had no effect, he reached up and grasped the tip of the boy's nose between his thumb and first two fingers. He squeezed hard until the cadet's panic subsided into the recognition of pain then he let loose a bit. Tears welled in the boy's eyes.

"You got it together now?" He asked looking at the Asian's fear filled eyes. His anger was evident. "If I get bit before we get out of here because you are being stupid, I will cut your head off before I die. Do you understand me? Fuckin' pussy! Man up!"

With that the Apache tweaked Techno's nose hard enough to elicit a squeak of pain from his teammate and his eyes to tear even more.

"I said do you get me?!"

Techno sobbed a weak "Yes" which sounded a lot like "Yeb" with the pressure on his nose. As Deadeye let loose of his pressure, Techno silently offered a small thanks to his teammate. Despite the look of pure derision on the Native Americans face, he lightly slapped the boy on the back.

"Don't mention it. This thing has got me spooked too. Let's get the hell out of here." The Apache said, and they quickly traversed the remainder of the obstacle without further incident, maneuvering through the Romero's and exiting out into the open field beyond the last hanging corpse.

Standing at the entrance, Spartan looked at Freak.

"I guess it's just you and me now big guy!"

Just as they turned as one to enter the obstacle, the sound of machinery starting and gears turning met both boy's ears. The posts supporting the chain linked corpses begin to rotate, causing the undead to raise and lower like the pistons of an engine. The obstacle had just become a hundred times harder and the undead's, seemed to instinctively realize this, snapped their teeth in anticipation of fresh meat.

"Awww shit!" The big man said looking at the moving torsos in gnashing teeth. "Dawg, you've got to be fucking kidding me! What kind of bullshit is this?" Spartan continued to watch the macabre spectacle looking for a way through.

"Remember, slow and steady Freak. Gauge where you move and when you move with the upturn of the piston. The corpses are moving in a rhythm; alternating row after row, back and forth, up and down."

"Dude, if I had rhythm, I would've been the next Michael Jackson. Take a good look at me; do I look like the king of mutha-fuckin' King of Pop to you? I can't even moonwalk! "

Spartan laughed out loud, his eyes glistening with mirth.

"What?!" The big man demanded.

Spartan pointed at one of the "Z's" corpses as it was swinging up and down in the obstacle. The undead torso was wearing a red and black eighties style Michael Jackson jacket with the sleeves torn away. The diseased head still maintained the long curled black hair it had worn in life. This had been a person who had refused to leave a favorite fashion time of their life. Laughter was rolling out from between Spartan's lips at the sight. Finally, he managed to choke down the chuckles, sucking in huge gasps of air. The team leader spoke to his partner.

"Brother, it's just like Thriller!" He said and started laughing again as he pointed at the swinging corpses.

"Aww man that is so messed up. Screw you Spartan!" The titanic youth said with a grin.

Composing themselves, together the two warrior cadets entered the obstacle, weapons at the ready. As the piston bearing machinery holding the Romero's spun the corpses wildly, the two members of Alpha team twisted and turned, avoiding the teeth and defending each other's backs against the swaying undead bodies and gnashing jaws. Freak's twin bats swung brutally, tapping out a bass drum beat on any unfortunate undead they encountered. Spartan's sword flicked and darted, cutting and slashing mercilessly… reducing the swinging "Z's" to severed, crushed and segmented headless torsos lying in a macabre jumble of body parts that they left lying behind them in their wake. Rotting blood and splattered brain fluids splashed across both of the cadet's uniforms. The two cadets emerged from the obstacle victorious, leaving the wanton destruction of the hanging Romeros behind.

Once the two youths were safely out of reach of any of the swaying Romero torsos, Dancer moved over to Spartan. Quickly she tore twin strips of black cloth from her undershirt. Wetting the cloths from her canteen, she carefully wiped the decayed blood from around his eyes, nose and mouth. Taking one of the pieces of cloth from Dancer, Techno did the same for Freak, careful not to let any of the contagion drip into the openings while Deadeye provided overwatch for them. Even after Techno, who started after Dancer, completed cleaning off Freak's face, the girl continued to carefully dab at her team leaders'; ensuring every drop of blood was wiped away.

Glancing to the side, Spartan saw the rest of his team looking on and became somewhat embarrassed by the apparent extended attention. "Thanks" Spartan said gently pushing the girl's hand down. "I appreciate it." Dancer did not reply offering only a smirk and a quick wink to acknowledge her team leader's gratitude. The moment was interrupted a second later when Deadeye quickly approached Spartan.

"Boss, we gotta move. "Z's" incoming. Romero's. It looks like ten, maybe a full dozen in a wandering pack. They're coming at us from behind in the area of that last water obstacle with the rope swing. They may have been following us since the first log crossing."

Spartan nodded, considering what he had been told. If the Romero's were following them then it stood to reason that the two Reapers may be also. Quickly he issued orders to his team.

"Deadeye... Point man, Dancer, Freak, me, and then Techno. Move out. Double time. Let's move people!"

Techno began the formulation of a complaint to be the last man, but one look from the Native American cadet immediately silenced him. The boy truly looked like he would cut his head off. Maybe being last wasn't so bad. At least he would be well away from that razor bow and any "accidents" that could occur with it.

The team raced across the open field. No "Z's" were in sight but the mournful wail of more than a hundred undead was being carried on the wind behind them. Perhaps the sound was from the obstacle that they had just left, but more likely it was a combination of the undead both with and without legs behind them.

The next obstacle was a standard balance beam. There were no "Z's", no water, just a time delay. One by one the cadets rapidly tiptoed across the 4 x 4 beam. Feeling confident that they had outdistanced the Romeros behind them, they maintained a straight Ranger file through the "S" curve on the trail. A quarter mile further they arrived at obstacle number nine; and there they stopped dead in their tracks.

A twenty-foot-high enclosure stood before them, chain-link fencing covered on all four sides and the entire one hundred yards overhead. The entire structure looked like an obscene and deadly parody of a huge professional wrestler's steel cage. As disconcerting as the battleground appeared to be with its links dripping with rain slowly between each silver-gray wire, it was the contents inside that truly took the team's breath away. Torn body parts littered the ground in various stages of decay. Romero's, at least a dozen, tore through sinew and muscle with their teeth, ripping through the severed limbs and eviscerated organs with reckless abandon. The bodies were so ravaged it was impossible to tell if the remains were human or animal. Perhaps most disconcerting to the team was that several of the body parts appeared fresh, still glistening with red blood no signs of sun blackening or rot. Silently, the members of Alpha team prayed that these were not the remains of the teams that came before them. If it was, then it was quite likely that whole teams of cadets had been wiped out during this phase of the obstacle course.

Standing idle, interspersed throughout the field within the cage were a dozen more "Husks". There was no rhyme or reason to their placement other than to make movement through the cage and away from the other "Z's" much more difficult. Not only did they have to avoid the deadly, plague dust carrying undead, but they would have to ensure that the Romeros did not damage one either. That could well be impossible. As they all knew, anything or anyone running into a "Husk" and causing their paper-thin skin to split, would spill the deadly viral spores into the air; potentially dooming them all.

Dancer's gasp alerted the team to the last area of concern. On the far side of the cage, she had spotted a sleek black stallion running past a man suspended high above the ground in a steel cage. The horse whinnied in fear and charged along the perimeter of the fencing while a dozen or so Romero's stood beneath the man, clawing at the air and moaning their piteous moan in an effort to reach his living flesh. Brown and greenish yellow grass flew out from behind the horse as it fled a group of three Reapers that wildly pursued it, knocking Romero's out to the way as they chased their quarry. While rabid in their pursuit of the horse, the Reapers passed dangerously close to several of the Husks.

The horse was lathered, with white foam spewing from its nostrils and mouth. Obviously, the horse had been fleeing the undead and breaking away from their grasping claws for quite some time. It's sprints from the undead were brief, gaining just enough distance to catch a foam filled, snorting breath before having to flee again, as the Reapers relentlessly pursued it. The Reapers on the other hand showed no sign of fatigue as their undead bodies did not register the pain of muscular breakdown like living beings did. Nitrogen, not oxygen filled their cells, and the chemical was being mass-produced as the undead's flesh decayed and broke down into its base elements.

Spartan used every bit of technical battle prowess that he had learned in the classrooms of the Apocalypse Academy to survey the field inside of the cage. Tactical models used for combating the living provided limited insight when dealing with the undead. There was nothing orthodox about how they moved and attacked. He was fairly certain that Sun Tzu did not have animated corpses in mind when he wrote the *Art of War.*

While the living would fight to survive, the walking dead had no such compunction. Because they could not recognize pain, the undead would wade into the lead hailstorm of an M-60 machine gun if they sensed there was even a chance to take a bite of fresh meat. A hard decision had to be made. Why any human would willingly submit to being caged above "Zs" Spartan didn't know, but he strongly suspected that the man was something other than a volunteer, but he kept his opinion to himself. Warmth was creeping into his cheeks and anger was filing his mind. He had experienced enough of this fucked up training course and he intended to slaughter every undead. Romero, Husk and Reaper. It did not matter to him. He had led his team away from every obstacle. If this cage had truly slaughtered some of the other teams as it appeared, then he intended to make certain that it could not do so again. This was war and in war, there were casualties. In war, there were sacrifices. In this war, those casualties and sacrifices would be the corpses of the people who had fallen before him. A battle rage was building into a red wall inside of him. Slight tremors shook his hands as he began to eagerly anticipate the battle that was to come.

Calling his team into a quick combat circle, Spartan laid out his plan of attack for the most vicious and potentially deadly obstacle yet.

"There's only one entrance into and one exit out of this structure. That means we have a fight on our hands. I don't see any way around it. Once we get inside, if we go methodically, we run the risk of getting mobbed by the Romeros and the Reapers. If we try to dodge around, the

Reapers will run us down before we can get across the field. We must do this as a team. Watch each other's back and we will be okay. If you let yourself get isolated and singled out, then you will probably get slaughtered like that young deer had been back by the pair of Reapers that we saw earlier."

"At some point we need to be able to get to that man, but for now he is safe suspended well above the ground. So, for now, he becomes a secondary priority. After we deal with all the danger that the "Z's" present to us inside the structure, then we will get around to getting him out of that cage and seeing just what exactly he is about. But when we do get to him be alert. I don't think he's there voluntarily."

Dancer spoke up. "If he's not there voluntarily, is he a prisoner?"

"I don't know, but good or bad, he's still one of the living. We are obligated to try and save him, not to judge him."

Looking at the titanic black youth, Spartan spoke directly to him. "Freak; you and I are on point this time. Deadeye is faster than both of us but this time we are putting the hammer down rather than performing a run and gun operation. We hit them to kill with a single shot. I want you to put all of your strength into every swing of those bats. Hit them as hard as you can and remember, kills only come from headshots. If your kill shot is unavailable, take out a leg and put them on the ground."

"Tech," Spartan said looking at the Asian boy. "If he puts one of those fucking undead on the ground, then you use the stun baton on its brain to put it out of action."

The boy nodded, wild eyed. Spartan could see the tangible horror of the thoughts permeating through Techno's educated and imaginative brain.

"Focus Tech! If you fuck this up and get one of us or yourself infected, I will personally shove you into that goddamned pack of Romeros and cheer as they eat your liver! Don't let me fucking down!"

"I won't. I'm on it." The boy said turning to look at Freak. Seeing the look of concern on the big teenager's face, he added. "Don't worry; I've got your back."

Spartan nodded. "Deadeye; the Husks are yours. As much as I wish that we could just avoid them, the risk is too high that either we or one of the Reapers or Romeros will run into them. Burst them from a distance with your arrows, preferably as far from the team as possible. Hopefully, the falling rain will push the viral spores to the ground before we move through the area. After the Husks are out of commission, you have free range for targets of opportunity. But we have to put the Husks down first to prevent them from potentially infecting the whole team while the others are chasing us."

The Native American cadet nodded once and looked into the cage, identifying his targets of opportunity and gauging the distance for each shot. In his mind he could almost see the hash marks indicating the space between him and them in meters. He knew what he had to do. Almost lovingly, he pulled a long black arrow from its sheath and knocked it firmly onto his bow string.

"Dancer; you're the rearguard. Nothing comes up behind us. Your polearm gives you reach. Use it to your best advantage. When we get ready to enter the cage, I want you to use the blade of your naginata to hamstring the horse and create a distraction on its next pass, just like Deadeye did with the deer. Pain and momentum should take the horse to the far side of the field before the Reapers can overtake it. With luck, we'll deal with them last if they stay on target with the stallion, or first if they break away to engage us when we enter the cage. They are definitely the immediate threat above all others."

Seeing the miserable pain in the girl's eyes, Spartan offered a brief, quick explanation. "They're fast movement provides them an opportunity to strike us before we can be fully prepared. I'm sorry Dance, but we need the distraction even more than we did before. It worked the first time with the Reapers and the deer so we have no reason to believe that it won't work again. I know that you don't like it, but it has to be this way."

"I know." She said softly, her voice tremulous and barely above a whisper.

Once again addressing the entire team, Spartan spoke confidently.

"Again people, stay together and stay frosty. We'll get through this as long as we each do our jobs and watch each other's asses. Keep the fence line at our backs. This will limit the avenues of approach from the Reapers and Romero's only to our front or sides. Are there any questions?"

No one spoke. A look of grim determination was etched into each of the cadet's facial features. Freak rotated his shoulders and neck in preparation for the impending battle. Dancer's jaw muscles twitched and flexed rapidly as she built up the nerve to take the action that she did not want to have to do, her sweat slicked hands clenching on the haft of the deadly medieval weapon that she held.

"One last point and then we move. That blood out there is red. The meat and organs scattered across the ground are fresh. One or more of our friends from the Academy is potentially lying dead out there from these fuckers. It doesn't matter if it was a member of our team, Bravo, Charlie, Delta or even those screwed up Echoes. It was a human being. A living, breathing, brother or sister-in-arms that these dead dicks slaughtered. We will not leave this field of battle until every walking "Z" has been put down permanently. We owe it to that cadet, whoever he or she was, to obtain vengeance. Vengeance for the living against the undead and that is a debt I intend to see paid in full!" Spartan said through clenched teeth.

Freak's neck cracked like a half dozen gunshots as he rolled it side to side in what Spartan had come to recognize as a pre-battle ritual. As one they waited for the ill-fated equine sacrifice to make its last lap past the doorway to the cage. The horse's undead pursuers raged wild eyed two yards behind it, howling unintelligible screams of pain and hunger. Strands of crimson drool and wind dried spittle hung from the Reaper's torn lips like bloody banners waving in the wind.

Seeing the horse rounding the distant bend ahead of her, Dancer stepped through the gate. Tightening her grip on the naginata against the horse's momentum, Dancer steadfastly stood in the doorway as the stallion raced past. Leaning out she brought her deadly naginata to bear. In the milliseconds before the blade dug deep, the wild rolling horse's eyes met her human stare as if to say "Please... Don't." Then the

British cadet's polearm flashed forward; its silvered blade first stabbing; then slashing through the flank, tearing meat and sinew in a bloody rainbow of arterial mist. As the horse stumbled, Spartan quickly yanked the cage door back closed. The horse cried out in pain and cartwheeled forward, end over end. The beast rose back up to its upright position just as the trio of Reapers leapt onto its back. Rotten teeth tore into the horse's flesh while its lifeblood poured out of its hindquarters. Rearing and bucking maniacally; the horse shook its attackers violently. One Reaper was thrown free up into the air only to have its arm crushed under a savagely flailing hoof when it impacted with the ground like an insane rodeo rider. If the mangling injury hurt the undead creature at all, it showed no outward signs of pain.

With a last wild-eyed look of pain and betrayal towards Dancer, the horse staggered away carrying its deadly burden of Reapers upon its savagely torn back and across the enclosure before finally collapsing from blood loss fifty yards away. The Reapers immediately went into a feeding frenzy upon the dying animal, tearing through its hide. Spartan threw the cage door open and led his team into battle, immediately slashing his legendary silver sword across the approaching neck of the nearest Romero. The diseased head severed effortlessly from the decaying body as the corpse tumbled to the side, its skull landing with a thick splash of mud at Spartan's feet. Quickly the team moved through the fatal funnel of the cage's door structure and closed it behind them.

The thwip and twang of the razor bow's draw and release was followed by a hollow thud as Deadeye's first arrow found its mark into an undead Husks eye socket seventy-five yards away. The creature popped open like a child's birthday balloon only to have the viral spores and dust float on the air currents down to the ground, settling beneath water and grass.

Freak had drawn the Blues Brothers and was bellowing out the chorus from "*Everybody needs somebody to love*" while his Jake and Elwood bats kept time on the corpses of the living dead whenever they came within range. Elwood drove down deep into the skull of an approaching Romero, shattering the bone inward in a splatter of black blood and gray brain matter, while Jake whistled by on a backhand swing to crush the knee of another undead, driving it to the ground. The creature's leg bent into an "L" shape as the leg broke. It was a brutal, efficient battering with excellent rhythm, contrary to Freak's earlier comment about being unable to keep time with his music.

Techno immediately stepped up and smashed his electrically charged baton into the creature's skull just as the fallen monstrosity reached for Freak's exposed calf. Electricity surged and the "Z's" body arced in muscular spasm. The undead's eyes rolled back deep into its skull turning the sockets completely red, its body frozen into neuron-overriding paralysis, jerking from side to side. A second and third smashing blow from Techno's baton put the creature out of the fight permanently, crushing it cranial bone down through the hypothalamus.

As the team moved forward, another arrow leapt forth from Deadeye's razor bow and another husk burst far off in the distance, popping like a leather balloon. Deadeye's eyes continually scanned for new, immobile targets. The boy seemed completely unfazed by the walking dead that milled around him and the team.

Behind them, Dancer spun and whirled. Her deadly naginata turned over and around her body like the propeller on an aircraft. Numerous Romero body parts lay severed in the mud at her feet as three "Z's" approached the team from their right flank. Repeated insults in her native British language rolled out of her mouth with each slash of her twirling blade; like a prize fighter taunting her opponents. Seeing the numbers quickly building behind the brave girl, Deadeye spun on his heel and fired a shot directly into the ear hole of one of the three Romero's that were beginning to surround the British warrior woman. The arrow speared the creature's head, looking comically like a standup comedian wearing a false arrow prop on his head while telling jokes. The "Z" dropped without a sound. The Apache then spun back around and fired an arrow into the chest of the third husk almost 100 yards away. The result was the same as the others. Pop and fall.

Spartan kept alternating his line of sight between the distant Reapers and the pack of Romeros as the team move forward. He and Freak continually slashed and battered approaching Romero's, slaughtering them like wheat before the scythe. Decaying black and bloody body parts lay scattered in a straight line defining the team's path as they forged ahead.

Dancer's blade split one "Z" at a forty-five-degree angle from its left shoulder down to its right hip before reversing her momentum and removing the top half of its head on the back swing with a bloodcurdling scream. The last remaining "Z" fell seconds later as she used in upward stroke with her naginata to sever the creature from its groin to its skull dividing it neatly in half. Pure, unadulterated rage boiled from her lips in a primal scream, having been birthed from the insults and curses she had been previously been using in the battle.

As Freak drove another Romero into the mud with a shattering overhand swing from one of the Blues Brothers, Spartan eliminated it from the combat with a backhanded swing from the sword of Leonidas. Spartan continually slashed with his blade at any and every undead he could see. Bloodlust had filled his veins and his vision was tinted red with rage. Arcs of blackened blood and a plethora of severed virus infected limbs splattered into the air before falling into a red, bloody puddle that had formed at his feet.

A Romero's severed skull stared sightless and silly at him from where it lay half buried in the mud, the sword of Leonidas wedged deep into its skull after a particularly powerful two-handed overhead stroke had cleft the bone in two halves. Daring to glance around, Spartan surveyed the battlefield. At least for the moment, the prisoner in the cage was safe as all the remaining Romero's were converging upon his team.

The sounds of the bloody battle were devastatingly loud. Battle cries and thudding bats, slashing blades and severed limbs, moans of death and the crackle of electricity all met his ears blending into a cacophony of chaos set in time to Freak's singing. As the last Romero approached the team, Spartan jerked his embedded blade free of the "Z's" skull in the mud and bloody muck at his feet. Setting his stance, Spartan wiped the rain from his eyes with his sleeve, careful to avoid any diseased blood and brought his bloody blade low to his side, preparing to rip the sword forward with a killing blow. A hand on his shoulder stopped him as the walking corpse closed within ten feet. It was Techno.

"I got this one." He said and walked between Spartan and Freak towards the undead. The cadet's blood caked stun baton arced with electricity and a steady, sharp, snap – snap – snapping sound. As the "Z" sensed its living prey separated from the larger defensive body of warriors, it reached out mud caked claws, as if beckoning the boy into a savage dance of death. Techno waited. The creature approached closer and closer. Its distance was down to five feet… Four feet… Three.

Spartan screamed for the boy to kill it!

Two…

One…

At the last second, Techno dropped to the ground in a perfect split; a feat that he could not have dreamed of accomplishing when he first arrived at the Apocalypse Academy two months earlier. Legs spread wide to the sides; he avoided the undead's reaching grasp as it passed harmlessly over his head. The stun baton lunged forward, propelled by the Asian boy's thrusting arm and a fierce war cry in his native language.

"Bonsai!"

The heavy electrical prod made contact with the corpse's groin and the tattered jeans that it wore. Water-soaked clothing conducted the one million volts of current charged through the creature's body. The effect was instantaneous as the undead's body seized into total paralysis, trembling as its virus riddled body conducted the electricity from head to toe. Pulling one leg back beneath himself, Techno rose and brought the metal baton down onto the immobile creature's skull just at the crown of its head. The resounding crack drove the corpse to the ground. Two more quick swings of the baton and the undead's skull split like an overripe melon. At five swings, the Romeros skull had been reduced to broken chunks filled with grayish, disease riddled, brain matter. Its movement abruptly ended. Spartan and Freak looked at each other in astonishment but then quickly remembered the Reapers at the far end of the cage.

"When the hell did he become Jackie fuckin' Chan? Shit Dawg, I can't do the splits, can you?" Freak asked.

Spartan just shrugged. "It's amazing what you can do when you're afraid that you're going to die."

Cautiously aware that the Reapers were still occupied with their horseflesh meal far off in the rain; Spartan took a moment to evaluate his team. At that moment the rain began to come down in a deluge, partially obscuring Spartan's vision. Freak was busying himself with administering the coup de grace to any of the undead that were down from lost limbs but still gnashing at the team. Each stroke of his bat punctuated his serenade of the undead with the Blues Brothers song "*Rubber Biscuit*." All the Husks had been destroyed by Deadeye's bow and the Romero's had been efficiently cut and bashed into pieces. That left only the Reapers that were still avidly ripping into the entrails of the betrayed horse.

"Everybody sound off! Anybody hurt?" Spartan called, trying to stem the flow of rain from his eyes with a single hand above his eyebrows. "Tech?"

"Techno; I'm good."

"Deadeye?"

"Deadeye; good!"

"Freak?"

"Freak and the Blues Brothers are all good, Dawg!"

"Dancer?"

The silence from the lack of a response was immediate, but oddly it echoed in their minds as loudly as a gunshot. Looking back and forth, no one saw the British girl. She seemed to have vanished into the pouring rain. Deadeye said aloud that he had seen her just moments before, eliminating a Romero. But now she was gone. Scanning the gray walled horizon, Deadeye's sharp eyes registered movement through the gray downpour.

"Spartan... Seventy-five meters out in front of us. She's going for the Reapers!"

"Oh shit!" Spartan cried and took off at a sprint, running to catch up with the girl before the Reapers saw her. The boy poured on every ounce of speed that he could muster but he felt like he was moving knee-deep in mud. Freak, Deadeye and Techno followed behind, just five yards slower.

"Dancer, stop!" Spartan screamed, but the girl marched on. If she heard him over the deluge, she gave no indication.

Twenty yards from the corpse of the tooth and claw ravaged horse; the Reapers took notice of the approaching girl. The first of the undead raised its rain and blood matted head from where it feasted on the horse's thick belly meat.

Dangling strips of half chewed horseflesh still hung from the undead's rotten teeth. Equine blood washed down the monster's face and neck in a gruesome replica of a man's goatee. The creature roared a primal cry of such savagery that its two companions ceased their bloody feast and leapt to their feet, preparing to sprint to the attack. One of the undead still bore a severed section of the horse's bluish–gray entrails dangling from its jaws and claws.

Planting the haft of her naginata into the ground like a steel battle flag, the living girl faced off with the undead trio in a chilling expectation of bloody confrontation. Emotional tears, streaked Dancers blood speckled face and she slowly widened her foot stance ensuring her center of balance was properly placed and repositioned the haft of the naginata lightly over her right shoulder. Her left hand came up into an open palm defense of martial arts stance, with two fingers up two fingers down and her thumb cocked stiffly to the side.

Spartan poured on every ounce of speed that he could muster, not wanting his teammate to face the triumvirate of living dead alone. He knew he would never make it in time, but still he had to try. He ran for all he was worth; unable or unwilling to lose another member of his friends or family.

The first "Z" leapt over the slaughtered horse, clearing it cleanly and landing in a crouch. It sprinted faster than any living man could, running towards Dancer who stood completely immobile in the field, watching its approach. No emotion showed on the lithe cadet's face, her jaw set, her eyes impassive, almost tranquil. It was as if the rage that had powered her mad dash up to the creature's had suddenly evaporated with the nearness of combat and all that she knew was the weight of her weapon and the approach of her foes. Every other sensation had just faded into background noise, compressed by adrenaline and a desire for vengeance upon these evil creatures.

The naginata extended from her arm like a deadly cybernetic scythe. Despite the weight of the weapon, it never wavered an inch as the girl waited for the "Zs" sprinting attack. As the creature closed within five feet, it emitted a guttural cross between a soul rending moan at the beginning that melded into a primal scream at the end of its charge. Decay infected saliva bearing the HUNGER virus spewed from its lips as it gnashed its rotten teeth at the dark-haired girl, clearly anticipating biting into the soft flesh of the teenager's throat. The creature's scream was met in both volume and savagery by the former flag bearing cadet. Teeth bared; she roared her fury back at the undead being. Snapping her arm outward, the polearm flashed forward in her grip, extending in the blink of an eye out to its full eight-foot length.

Grasping the haft of the medieval weapon near its end, she swung the wicked metal blade across her body with all her petite might. Calisthenics and strength training added force to her strike as the blade clove through the Reaper's body from right to left. Twin halves of the infected undead separated; casting the upper torso three yards to the left and driving the lower torso and legs to the right. Spinning to add momentum to her follow-up swing, Dancer brought the steel blade down with lightning quickness across the bisected undead's neck. Tempered steel sliced through rotten flesh and drove into the soft dirt beneath causing the Reapers head to roll away from his body like an old-fashioned bowling ball down a lane.

Looking up at the remaining two Reapers, Dancer again roared her primal challenge. Her scream cracked and strained as her pain was released into the air of battle. A black war mask of rain-streaked mascara added a visceral savagery to her appearance. The Reapers snarled as one, leaving the mauled corpse of the horse behind and raced toward the isolated cadet. When they were in full sprint, the creatures were hard to follow visually at the best of times. The pouring rain further camouflaged their dead gray flesh, making watching their movements even more difficult. Then, the Reapers did the unexpected and separated; splitting apart to charge the girl from two separate angles. The move created a pincer effect and Dancer knew that she would have to leave one flank open if they attacked her simultaneously.

Long, wicked nails dripped water and gore as they opened and closed reflexively, anticipating their deadly attack on the dark-haired girl who stood defiantly alone before them. Shortening the grip on her naginata by sliding her right hand upward on the rain slicked shaft, Dancer prepared to whip the weapon back across her body horizontally. Swinging the thousand folded steel blade; the teenager was shocked as the closest Reaper twisted its body out of harm's way, avoiding the blade's swing straight at its torso, displaying an understanding of the damage that the weapon could cause. The girl's swing was not without gratification, as the creature having avoided the killing blow, could not withdraw its outstretched claw fast enough. So sharp was the blade of the ancient Japanese weapon that it passed smoothly through the creature's wrist, lopping its clawed hand from its outstretched arm without arresting its forward momentum in the slightest. Unfortunately for Dancer, the loss of a hand did not cause the undead beast even the slightest bit of discomfort and it propelled itself ahead, leaping into the air to pounce upon the British girl.

Waterlogged, decaying flesh crashed into the young cadet with bone crushing force, knocking the girl's weapon free from her grasp. The ancient samurai weapon tumbled through the air to land ten feet behind the grappling combatants, half buried in the mud. Twisting her body as they fell together, Dancer rolled her body onto the top of the undead and into a mount position as the animated corpse attempted to lurch forward with its teeth and latch onto her exposed face. Dancer jammed her hand under the creature's jaw forcing it closed. Her other hand gripped the "Zs" one good wrist, preventing it from digging in its blood-streaked claws and ripping a fistful of flesh from her body.

The undead writhed and whipped its body back and forth, beneath the cadet's mounted position, trying to free itself from beneath the teenager and striking her repeatedly on the unprotected side of her head and rib cage with its gore spewing stump. Focusing beyond the pain of the strikes, Dancer silently prayed that the pummeling attack would not rupture her skin and expose her to infection as she forced her hips into the high mount position; straddling the "Zs" sunken and decayed chest as she had been taught in Sergeant Hogg's ground fighting classes. The problem was now that she had achieved the tactical advantage, she was at an impasse. She could not release the squirming "Z" to grab a weapon without being clawed or bitten. Conversely, she could not continue to be bludgeoned by the "Z's" bloody stump. She was already getting fuzzy brained from the continued strikes to the side of her head. If the creature managed to open a cut on her head and she got infected blood into it, she would be damned.

Glancing up, Dancer spied the second "Z". It had apparently tripped over the corpse of the first Reaper that she had decapitated and had fallen to the ground during its initial run at her, or she would probably have been dead by now.

What the bloody hell had she been thinking, charging off halfcocked like a schoolgirl getting snogged for the first time? It had been foolish of her to charge into battle so recklessly and emotionally. Her father would be so disappointed in her. He had taught her better.

Now the second creature was back on its feet and hunched like a mongoose preparing to attack a cobra, bloody saliva waggling from its open mouth, defying the cleansing rain. The "Zs" mouth widened and released its mournful moan. As the moan built-in volume, it became a full shriek of hell born rage. At its crescendo, the "Z" launched itself through the air; claws and jaws opened to tear the helpless girl from its undead twin. Hopelessness filled the brown-haired cadet as the distance steadily between her and the pouncing undead closed; while she was rendered helpless to react as long as she grappled with its undead kin.

Seeing the attack coming, Dancer knew she was helpless. She closed her brown eyes hoping that her end would be clean and that her team would ensure that she would not come back. Mentally she braced herself for the impact of the attack. Dancer recalled the saying that in the face of death, your life flashes before your eyes in an instant. Visions of her childhood in Britain flew through her brain at a thousand frames per second. Then another second. Then another. Still struggling to hold the undead beneath her, Dancer saw the second horrifying undead six inches away from her, lying in the dirt face down. From the back of its skull jutted the black shaft of one of Deadeye's arrows. Three more arrows had pierced the creature; two in the torso and one in the thigh. The creature had not tripped at all; her teammate had knocked it down with well-placed arrows. The creature had been shot out of the air as it dove for her and it had died in the millisecond before it reached her; instantly turned off like a light switch when the arrow had pierced its forehead. It was a one in a million shot.

The rapid approach of booted feet announced the arrival of the rest of her team.

"Dancer! Clear!" Spartan's voice rang in her ear.

Trusting her training, the Cadet dove from her mounted position astride the undead's chest and rolled hard to her right side. The "Z's" snapping jaws lunged upward attempting to lock its teeth onto the fleeing girl's soft flesh. Snapping teeth were met by industrial rubber and forged metal plating as Spartan's boot smashed the "Z's" head back downward into the mud with a curb stomp that crushed the undead's skull into black and red rotted paste.

Quickly scanning for any more threats and seeing none; Spartan walked over to the pretty brown eyed cadet. Quickly, he issued orders to free the prisoner from the cage. Deadeye and Freak complied, running off while Techno ensured that none of the neutralized "Zs" would get back up again with the touch of his electrical baton and a couple of well-placed swings. Kneeling softly next to the girl, Spartan could not help but feel his heart strings tug as the girl sobbed openly.

"Why?" He asked while he carefully inspected the side of her head for any sign of an open wound beneath the gore.

Tears rimmed the girl's eyes and spilled quickly down her cheeks. The arduous trek across mascara, mud and blood slowed the flow of the tears to a zigzagging trickle. As the pathway became clearer those tears became a torrent of sobbing emotion that paralleled the rain pouring down around them.

"I had a… a horse back home… in England. I don't know. I just…Fuck...I … I don't know. It was like he was mine again. I had to protect him from those savages. I guess I lost it. I'm sorry."

No more needed to be said. He was certain that they would all have to face the demonic images of happiness that came with memories of the past sooner or later. Right now, he found himself thankful for the amnesia. Spartan cradled the girl's head while she fought mentally with her own past and the things that she had lost in a world gone insane. They all saw images beneath the undead flesh. The ghosts of happier times. Everyone but him.

Ten minutes later, after releasing the man from his cage and turning him over to Sergeants Boomer and Havoc, who met them at the exit gate of the obstacle, the team was back on its feet and forging ahead toward the next obstacle. Wild eyed exhaustion was evident on everyone's face. Few words were passed apart from brief encouragement as each team member passed by Dancer. Freak returned the girl's naginata and offered a shrug and a friendly wink. Techno patted the girl on the shoulder and told her that everything would be okay. Deadeye simply gave her a nod and a thumbs-up signal.

Yes, it was certain that they all had their specters of the past. Some more than the others. There was no room for any of them to be judgmental. Dancer's moment of weakness had come and gone and there had been no casualties. For that they were all thankful and, that was the best that any of them could ask for given the world that they were living in. It certainly was not the first time nor the last time that someone had ever done something completely irrational in a combat situation.

Jogging ahead at little more than an airborne shuffle, they came to the ninth obstacle. The challenge was a series of concrete sewer pipes that had been laid out end to end which created a mazelike series of man-made tunnels. They all knew that the maze would be confining and dark. They all suspected what else it could also possibly contain based on the previous obstacles: deadly encounters. Along with the concerns about the cloying darkness and the free roaming undead, the pipe was oval rather than round, with its width wider than its height, so they would have to move hunched over or at a crawl. Crawling would mean small weapons only.

Spartan barked orders "Smallest to largest! Deadeye, you are back on point, but we need light. Does anybody have a chem light or any other suggestions?"

It was Freak that had the answer, producing a well-worn silver Zippo lighter and handing it to his team leader. Seeing Spartan's quizzical look, the huge cadet tried his best to look innocent.

"What?" He asked "A brother with the Zippo is such a shock? It's not like I'm carrying a torch lighter for my crack pipe. Dude, I grew up in the south side of Chicago. I've been carrying this with me since I was six."

Upon seeing the look on his leader's face, he quietly added "Okay man. It was my brothers'. Look at the inscription on the back."

Spartan turned the lighter over and read the engraved writing.

"*To Sergeant Lamarr Jackson, for your service in valor. Hooah!*" And was signed "*Fourth Special Forces group, Fort Bragg, South Carolina.*"

"I'll take good care of it Freak." Spartan said somberly.

Freak nodded adding "He was killed in Afghanistan 'bout a year before "Z" night. It's all that I have left of him."

Deadeye had already sensed Spartan's intent and had torn off his t-shirt and ripped it into separate strips of cloth and wound on two stout branches that he had quickly tomahawked down from a nearby tree. Using the Zippo,

Spartan lit the torches. Handing the lighter back to his teammate, he spoke quickly.

"One torch out in front, one held behind us in back. We will have to move quickly. We don't want these to burnout while we are stuck inside these tunnels. Hand-to-hand weapons only. Knives and hand axes only." Tech make sure you don't zap one of us with that stun baton. I don't feel like dragging anyone out here. Let's go. Watch your heads."

Entering the man-made labyrinth, Deadeye took the lead with one torch held in his left hand and his tomahawk in the other. Techno, Dancer, Spartan and Freak followed. Moving as swiftly as they could, they rapidly came to a T junction where the team needed to make a quick decision.

"Right." Freak said from the rear.

"Always go left," Tech disagreed. "It's a proven rule of puzzle solving. Trust me. I used to do this at the nursing home all the time helping them solve mazes on paper."

Rather than listen to Techno, the team led by Deadeye, turned right. After about forty yards, they ran into a dead end.

"I told you to go left. Next time maybe you'll listen to me." Techno whispered.

Reversing their direction, but unable to realign their order, Freak now led the way back to the T junction, blocking everyone else's ability to see anything up ahead. Reaching the open space, the team resumed their regular marching order with Deadeye out front. Maneuvering left after left, the team quickly moved through the maze. By Spartan's estimation they had to be about two thirds through the obstacle. The pace was maddeningly slow and his thighs were burning fiercely at having to squat down for so long. Rounding another ninety-degree turn, Deadeye called a halt to the team. In a low voice he called back to alert them to what he saw.

"Do you want the good news or the bad news?" He asked the assembled group.

"The good news." Dancer replied from the second to last position.

"I can see the end of the tunnel."

"Okay. So, what's the bad news?"

"There is a Romero chained like a watchdog at the exit, and he does not seem like the mailman or a game show host waiting to give us the grand prize."

"Dancer, can you squeeze by Tech and Deadeye to use your long weapon?" Spartan asked trying to think of a way to use the medieval weapons' length to his advantage.

"Negative" she replied patting the chubby Asian boy on the shoulder "Techno-san has had far too many eggrolls and dumplings for me to get by."

Before Techno could reply, Deadeye called back to the team. "I have a plan." Quickly sitting down in the concrete tunnel, the nimble Apache cadet stripped off his shoes and socks, then handed them back, along with his Tomahawk to Spartan.

"Dude, what the hell you gonna do? Cheese 'em to death with your toe funk?" Freak quipped from the back of the party.

Deadeye didn't bother to respond. Instead, he pulled his bow over his shoulder and placed the body of the weapon against the bottom of his feet. Fully five feet in length, the bow stretched from wall-to-wall, making a scratching noise as the teenager fought with himself to achieve the proper positioning. Using one hand to balance the bow against his feet, he used his free hand to reach back, drawing and knocking an arrow. Sighting the weapon sideways, he pulled the string back to its full draw. The boy's bare toes gripped the weapon at its midsection.

"This is gonna sting." The Apache murmured under his breath and released the tension on the drawn bowstring. An audible *twang* rang out as the Bow's eighty-pound tension pull was released. The arrow leapt forward with the swishing sound that was immediately followed by the bowstring slapping flesh with a sound like a whip-crack. Deadeye threw his head back in subdued agony as the heavy tension line lashed into his toe tops; lining them with a dark and bloody welt that rose steadily across his bare feet. Slowly the Native American scout released his breath from in between his clenched teeth with a stifled hiss of pain.

The arrow struck the "Z" at the bridge of the nose; effortlessly driving first through the facial bone, into the disease riddled gray matter of the brain and through the bone again as it exited the back of the undead's skull. The impact of the yard-long black arrow drove the Romero out of the tunnel's entrance and all the way back to the full extent of its chain. Spartan could not help but think of an old Foghorn Leghorn cartoon as the Romero was jerked up short, just like the cartoon dog always seemed to be.

Exiting the maze, the team stretched to relieve the kinks in their backs while Deadeye put his boots back on. While Freak and Techno kept watch, Spartan checked on the status of the Apache scout. Spartan could see the bloody welt that the bowstring had left across the top of both of the scout's feet. It must've hurt like hell.

"You okay man?" The team leader asked.

"I'm good." Was all that the boy said as he slipped his socks and boots back on.

At that moment Techno walked up and advised Spartan that there were no more "Z's" in the immediate area. His demeanor was animated, and he was apparently very excited by the trick shot that Deadeye had performed.

"Dude, that was freaking awesome! Very ninja-esque. Bruce Lee couldn't have done that shit!"

Deadeye rose to his feet with a grin, slinging the bow back over his shoulder. "Ninjas are pussies compared to Apaches!" The boy exclaimed, accepting the compliment.

Recomposed, the team moved out, back into Ranger file eight meters apart. They knew that the end of the course had to be near because they felt as though they crossed an entire continent. Fatigue had drained them both mentally and physically, but the successful completion of the course drove them forward. Another quarter-mile sprint led them to the final challenge. Standing before them was a twenty-five-foot-high log wall. Hanging from the center of the wall was a single hemp rope approximately 4 inches thick. Beyond the wall the team could see the exit gate built into the chain-link fence.

"Okay team. This is the last obstacle. Up and over and then were home free." Spartan said encouraging his team.

Spartan was not greeted by the applause and cheers he'd expected. In fact, the entire team apart from Deadeye looked downright dejected.

"I can't do it." Techno said. Dancer immediately parroted him saying "Me neither. I've got nothing left."

Freak, who was used to having to sum up the last reserves of strength late in the game, tried to encourage his teammates. "Gotta try Tech. Only other option is to die out here. You too girl. It's just one little wall. You can do it. I'll help you."

Inspired by Freak's pep talk, Techno nodded and walked toward the wall. A quick jump up by the chubby Asian boy was met by a faster slide back down the water-soaked rope. Dancer was next. Running as fast as she could, the nimble teenage girl jumped up, catching the rope at the apex of her leap about nine feet off the ground. She struggled to maintain her grip, climbing an additional few feet, and then suddenly could not pull herself any further. Her booted feet scrabbled for purchase on the wet logs for several seconds before her hands involuntarily released, spilling her hard down onto the cold wet ground. Silently, she rubbed her buttocks in pain and embarrassment. Looking down at his fallen teammates, Spartan turned to the big cadet.

"Freak, you still good?" Spartan asked.

"Ninth-inning baby, I got this!" With that the giant ran towards the wall and leaped upward. With half a dozen Herculean pulls of his massive biceps he reached the top of the wall and swung his right leg over. The big man looked back down at his teammates, grinning.

"Freak, stop right there." Spartan hollered then ran up to the base of the rope. Quickly, he climbed upward, joining the black cadet at the top of the wall.

"What's up boss?" Freak asked.

"We're going to make an elevator." Spartan replied, nodding his head toward the rope." You and I are going to help these guys get over the wall. Freak immediately caught on.

"Deadeye! I need you to attach a branch or a board to the ropes and make sure it's stout and tied tight. We're going to lift Tech and Dancer up and over in a team lift." Spartan said. "When you're done tying off the branch, keep a lookout until we get Dancer and Techno over the wall. We don't want any "Z's" surprising us while were exhausted."

It took no time at all for the scout to return with the thick branch and to tie it off securely. Through the combined efforts of Spartan and Freak, the two physically exhausted cadets were hauled up and over the wall. While they made it up to the top smoothly, the sliding release down the wall on the backside left them both unceremoniously dumped in the dirt, lying exhausted in the thick mud and cold rain. Together they lay there side-by-side completely exhausted.

Looking up from the top of the wall Spartan saw a sight that instantly terrified him. Running hard towards his team were two Reapers. They were dressed like the Reapers from the area where his team had used the deer as a distraction. Apparently, they had finished their free meal and moved on.

"Deadeye trust me and don't look behind you! Just climb this goddamned wall as fast as you can! You've got company." He screamed down at the boy. Then turning to the rest of the team, he continued issuing orders. "Freak jump down there and get Dancer and Techno over by the cage door. As soon as Deadeye gets over, we will join you and we can all get the fuck out of here!"

Freak slid down as fast as he could, barely touching the wall. Splashing into the mud and water, he ran over and grabbed Techno and Dancer by the arms, instantly hauling them to their feet. "We gotta go!" Was all he said, as he unceremoniously dragged the exhausted cadets along beside him towards the gate.

Back at the wall Spartan reached down and held his hand out for Deadeye to grab. Racing forward, Deadeye did not even bother to use the rope, finding natural hand holds between the logs and scaling the obstacle like he had been doing it for his entire life. In seconds, the scout cleared the top of the wall. Swinging his legs over the top in a single motion he quickly let his body hang down from the wall before letting go and dropping to the ground. Spartan followed suit a moment later. Slipping and sliding as they ran through the slick mud, they struggled to meet up with the rest of their team at the exit to the Dante Course. Slinging open the cage style door they exited the ten levels of Hell and left the Dante Course behind them. Just as the Reapers had rounded the wall and leapt for the gate, Freak kicked the one-way gate closed; slamming it forcefully into the first Reaper just as it reached the opposite side.

All the cadets fell into a jumbled heap in the mud, uncaring of the cold wetness that was seeping through their already rain-soaked clothing, so mentally and physically tired that they could barely move. After several moments of gasping for breath, they staggered back to their feet, and were suddenly greeted by a single person's applause. Sergeant Hogg stood twenty feet away congratulating them on their completion of the Dante course.

"Well done!" The burly Drill sergeant said to his team. "You done went and made me proud. Nobody got bitten and nobody suffered any permanent injuries. Of course, you didn't have the fastest time, but you all survived; in the long run that's all that really makes a shit anyway. Now if you would be so kind as to get into some kind of a fuckin' formation that is not a complete cluster fuck, we should be getting back to the barracks. It's getting late and chow is in thirty minutes. I would really hate to be late."

Chapter Eleven
Not Everyone is a Winner

The collective relief felt by his entire team was nothing compared to the personal elation that Spartan felt. Not only had they all survived, but beyond various bumps and bruises, no one on his team had been seriously injured. Moreover, they had acted tactically as a team. Even Techno had fallen into line under the deadly pressure. Spartan had personally seen the boy's transformation from coward into warrior. With the exceptions of the initial fear driven paralysis of Techno at the log bridge and Dancer's meltdown over the sacrificial horse, the group had done remarkably well for their first trip into a combat zone. Granted, the combat zone was a quasi – simulated one even if it did still incorporate deadly parameters, but still they had emerged alive. That was still something to be proud of.

No one had spoken since the end of the Dante course. Mental fatigue, shock and physical exhaustion had removed all social urges from the Alpha team. Silently, the team filed back into the barracks escorted by a grim looking Sergeant Hogg. Even the man's trademark cigar was missing, and he walked with a determined step that was both measured and expedited.

Upon arrival at the barracks, the team was released with a single, simple "Dismissed!" barked by the drill sergeant. Spartan had expected a "good job speech" or even an atta-boy for his team's performance and his decision-making. He was surprised that the drill sergeant would not even meet him eye to eye, almost seeming to ignore him. Leaving the formation area from which his team had been dismissed;

Spartan jogged to catch up with his team. His legs felt like lead as he caught up with them all in the stairwell on the third floor. Alpha team was housed on the fifth floor. As they began to exit the stairway on their floor, Spartan hurriedly called them back to the landing. Casting a quick look around to ensure no one was listening he asked them a quick, quiet question.

"Did anyone else notice?" He asked quietly.

Everyone else was so fatigued that they could barely lift their own heads to look around; however, Deadeye noticed what Spartan had observed and replied.

"We're the only team here, but we were the last to run the Dante course." The Apache said quietly, a frown creasing his brow. "Something's really wrong."

As Deadeye's revelations permeated into their brains, fear broke across both Techno and Dancer's faces. "Perhaps the perimeter fences have been breached by the "Z's." Techno said. Spartan slowly shook his head from side to side in disagreement.

"I don't think so. There would've been alarms, formations, or worst-case scenario… evacuations. We certainly would not have been marched back to the barracks by one of the academy's deadliest warriors. He would've been on the front lines. Whatever it is, it's bad and we need to be ready."

Spartan paused for a moment, his mind lost in a dozen possible answers that could explain the absence of the other teams and their own drill sergeants's withdrawn behavior.

“Whatever’s wrong, we need to stay together.” Dancer said quietly.

“Yeah” Techno added “I don’t want to be alone.” Panic seemed to be lurking just beneath the boy’s skin, like a worm inside of a dog. He fidgeted nervously from side to side. Seeing Freak and Deadeye’s silent nods of agreement, Spartan made a quick decision.

“We need to get cleaned up, changed and get back to an on-duty status as fast as possible. Everybody report to your rooms and shower but keep all of the doors open; stay in audio range of each other at all times. We’ll meet in the recreation room in twenty minutes. Bring your weapons and cleaning kits. We will use the weapon care and cleaning after the Dante course as an excuse for a team activity if anyone asks. If not, then they will be ready for us to use if they are needed.”

Everyone agreed and walked directly to their rooms. Spartan caught up to Dancer. Placing a hand lightly on her shoulder, he spoke to her softly.

“Sorry about the open doors during showers but I didn’t think anyone should be alone and out of contact. Especially you…” He added gently. “I know you were really upset out there over the horse. I just wanted you to know that if you need to talk… I’m always here.”

Dancer stopped suddenly and turned to face him. Large tears slowly rolled down her cheeks from her big brown eyes. Spartan felt his chest clench at the sight of her pain. He silently wiped a hand across her cheek, brushing the teardrop away.

"I can stand guard outside your door if you want me to, so that nobody..."

His words were cut off as she leaned forward and firmly kissed his lips. Then she turned and strode into her room, never once looking back nor saying a word.

Spartan stood as if mesmerized; his mind awhirl with about thirty different emotions. Despite all of the confusion, rage and anger he had felt throughout the day as he had run the Dante course, none of it compared to the elation that he felt at the touch of Dancer's lips against his own. He was entirely awash in the heat of the moment, struggling to accept the new emotions such as hope and trust and maybe even something deeper... Shaking his head he chided himself aloud.

"Stop acting like a schoolboy. Get your mind off of your teammate and move your ass. You've got a team to lead."

One last time he subconsciously touched his lips as he started to walk towards his own room. He was filthy, battered and exhausted and he suddenly realized that he also felt like a million bucks.

"What the hell?" He muttered as he shook his head and entered his quarters. He was still wondering at how such a horrible day had ended so perfectly when he stepped into the scalding hot shower.

Twenty minutes passed in the blink of an eye. Individually, the team all took scalding hot showers in an effort to cleanse the blood and rot from the battles with the living dead. They had all scrubbed their bodies at least twice and still felt dirty even though they were cleaner than they had been all day.

Dressing quickly, the only sound was a "Clear!" call from each room at the five-minute mark and every five minutes subsequent to that. Alpha team was very dedicated to the idea of ensuring that they stayed safe. Meeting back up in the recreation room, carrying their weapons cleaning kits and weapons, Spartan noticed that very little physical damage showed on the cadet's bodies from the day's trials and tribulations in the obstacle course. Nothing more major than a few bruises, especially the large purple one on Freak's chin where the massive log had clipped him, were showing at all. Emotionally, they all seemed to suddenly look older. More seasoned. The veneer of youth had been stripped away in a single day and their eyes seemed to be sharper, more critical of life.

"So… does anybody have any clues as to what happened to everyone else?" Spartan asked.

Freak spoke up without looking up, his hands slowly rubbing an oiled rag over his black metal bat. Spartan could just make out the word "Jake" in white lettering on the barrel before the cloth covered it in a smooth sliding motion.

"I had a coach look at me the way Sergeant Hogg did one time when I was back in Chicago. I'd been in a batting slump for about six games. My average had gone from .486 to a sickly .220. During the first half of the season, I had forty-two home runs. During my slump, I had none. I was really losing my confidence."

"What did you do to fix it?" Techno asked. Secretly Techno enjoyed the computer world of fantasy sports before the dead had risen and started eating his favorite players. His interest was genuine.

Freak chuckled. "The coach called me over to the dugout, just before my first at bat of the next game. He told me that I had two choices that I could make it in this world. Hit the God damn ball or go sling crack back in the hood. I would never be good at anything else. Mean ass bastard!" The big man muttered.

"So, what did you do?" Dancer asked.

"What do you think I did? I was so pissed off; I crushed the first pitch into the fifth row of the centerfield seats. When I crossed home plate and went back to the dugout, the old man was waiting for me."

"Remember that lesson boy." He said "Be sure of yourself. Doubt takes you out of the game. It makes you a loser."

"So, you think what? That Sergeant Hogg doubts us? That he doesn't think we have the confidence to survive?" Deadeye asked.

Freak just shrugged and said "Maybe."

Spartan didn't think so. "That doesn't seem to fit; doubting us *after* we survived. Maybe beforehand, but not after. Anyone else have any ideas?"

Deadeye spoke quietly from the corner, where he sat carefully cleaning and sharpening the blades of his razor bow.

"Something must've happened during the Dante." He said quietly. "Something bad. I don't think that the issue is us at all. Look around here. No one else is even in the building. Maybe there's been an incident or possibly even a death. There were a lot of body parts flying around at some of those obstacles. Maybe a cadet was killed. Maybe more than one. Remember all of those body parts that we saw in the cage?"

Spartan nodded grimly. It was definitely a possibility. "Anyone else? Tech? Dancer? Any theories?" His voice trailed off. For some reason he felt like he was staring at the girl. Then he realized with embarrassment that he was. He purposefully turned away to face straight at Techno.

Techno spoke up.

"It could be just the opposite of what Deadeye said. Maybe they were *trying* to kill a bunch of us off, you know, culling the herd. Survival of the fittest and all that."

The notion was chilling and something that they hadn't considered before that moment. What did they really know about the Apocalypse Academy? Perhaps they viewed weakness as a liability towards overall team survival. Training thus far had been mostly team oriented but that didn't mean that times didn't change. Someone that was a liability in the field usually meant a higher chance of dying for that person and the higher likelihood of death for the person trying to rescue the liability. Hero complexes in war got people killed. Plain and simple. Spartan felt that it was unlikely that they were actually trying to kill some of the cadets off but still they had nothing more to go on. They decided as a team that they should be watchful, nonetheless.

"Dance?" Spartan looked over at the girl; studying her as she paced back and forth in the room. She in turn kept her eyes on the polished wooden floor of the recreation room, never once looking up at him until she was ready to speak several moments later.

"Maybe it isn't Sergeant Hogg at all." She said in a voice just above a whisper. "Maybe his superiors are upset about something. Anything. The race times were too slow or too fast on the Dante course. Too many or not enough cadets died or maybe the Colonel was just busting the drill sergeant's balls because we made it out of their sick, satanic shitehole of a death trap."

They knew next to nothing about the history of the Apocalypse Academy or the Command staff beyond Colonel Stone. It had to be assumed that there were other people involved in the Academy's creation but none of those people seem to have survived "Z" night. In fact, beyond the initial briefing and one other meeting, they had not seen anyone besides the Drill Instructors and Nurse Ortega or the other non-training support staff unless you counted the chow hall staff.

Kevlar gloved hands carefully held cleaning cloths and wet stones as the cadets of Alpha Team silently worked on their weapons. Time was lost as they all lapsed for several long, silent moments deep in personal thought. The almost silent swish of a polish cloth over the metal bats seemed to clash in antithesis to the grinding slash of the sharpening stones on the blades of the various swords, knives and Dancer's polearm. The sounds were alternately amplified and muted based on the occupation of each cadet's thoughts. After an hour of rigorous cleaning, Alpha team looked as good as new at least on the outside.

Suddenly, the announcement speaker buzzed to life from the ceiling where it rested. A deep voice that was unfamiliar to the cadets spoke into the microphone. As it spoke the voice carried a strong and demanding undertone.

"Cadets of Alpha team; you will fall out for chow immediately and then report to the parade deck at 2030 hrs. You will be briefed at that time on a sensitive matter. Upon completing the briefing, teams Bravo through Echo will meet you at a pre-designated destination. You will receive this information at the formation area. Do not be late or you may be too late. Bring your weapons."

The speaker clicked off.

"2030 hrs…." Spartan thought aloud "that's one -hour people. Let's make sure that we eat and that we are ready."

Where their twenty minutes of shower time had passed within the blink of an eye, the pre-formation dinner and wait crawled by with maddening slowness. Spartan could not help but compare the two times of apprehension to be a parable to the story of the tortoise and the hare. A beeping noise sounded, breaking him out of his reverie. Looking down at his black tactical watch, Spartan acknowledged its Day-Glo green light and blinking bell-shaped alarm symbol on the watch face. He had felt it to be in the team's best interest to set the alarm due to their exhaustion. He needn't have bothered. Upon hearing the repetitive beeping, his team was up and moving for the stairwell; adrenaline and nervous anticipation powering their steps.

Pushing open the steel stairwell door the team found Sergeant Hogg standing on the quarterdeck waiting for them.

From his creased forehead and the way, the drill sergeant's eyebrows seemed to meet at an angry point in the center of the man's nose; the team knew to form up quickly and quietly. Sergeant Hogg was not a man to be trifled with on the best of days. Right now, he looked like a captured wild animal that was ominously pacing back and forth within his cage, waiting for the door to open. Closer examination showed the drill sergeant to have bloodshot eyes and a faintly puffy look to his face. As if someone or something had upset this man to a high level of emotional explosion; Spartan felt true sorrow for that person.

Calling the team to attention, the drill sergeant marched in a formal, crisp step to stand directly in front of the team. In a voice that clearly conveyed that no questions were to be asked, the drill sergeant spoke.

"Today has been a day of trials and triumph. It has also been a day of tragedy. You are about to embrace the unpleasant reality of what we are training you to do and the devastating consequences of failure and poor decision-making. After we depart this quarterdeck and we are at our destination, you will not speak, you will not volunteer, you will not cry. Just watch and learn. You survived today due to your skills and a healthy portion of luck. Others were not so fortunate. Conduct yourselves as soldiers. Show no emotion in public, no acknowledgment of loss. Make the sacrifices that these cadets made mean something. Do this correctly and I will escort you back to your barracks when it is all over with and release you to a two-day furlough from duty. Do this incorrectly and I will throw your fuckin' asses out the front gate myself. Are we clear?"

As one the cadets of Alpha responded with a low but clear "Yes drill sergeant! …Permission to ask a question drill sergeant" Spartan added.

"Go ahead."

"Drill sergeant, who was the man in the cage during the horse obstacle? Why was he there?" Spartan asked, knowing that this was in actuality two questions. He had a feeling that this impromptu meeting and the deaths of other cadets may have been related to that individual.

The burly sergeant huffed, snorting in derision. "That scrote-bag is a member of them piece of shit bikers. That particular crazy fucker believes that the Baron is the next coming of Jesus Christ."

"And for that alone he deserves a death sentence?"

"Well, that and the fact that he broke into the Academy by cutting the fencing, assaulted Nurse Ortega and attempted to steal twenty vials of morphine from the infirmary so that his biker buddies could get high. Yeah, he does. His actions jeopardized us all."

"I understand. Will he be pacified?"

"No, he won't." The drill sergeant said with a hard look in his eyes after a moment's pause. "How do you think we restock the "Z's" in the obstacles?"

A cold chill ran down Spartan spine. The man was to be damned to an eternity of hell because of his poor decision making and a lack of self-control. It was a cold harsh reality into the world beyond "Z" night. Friends helped friends. Enemies would be executed or infected.

The march to the assembly hall where the cadets had first in processed was silent and methodical. No cadence was called; no verbal commands issued yet the cadets footfalls fell in perfect rhythm with both their hard-faced drill sergeant and with each other on the asphalt despite their fatigue. Rain continued but had slowed to a drizzle from its previous downpour.

Entering through the twin metal doors at the front of the main conference building, Alpha team filed one by one into the main meeting room following by Sergeant Hogg. Where there had previously been chairs and tables around the room for the initial briefing with the Colonel, the room had now been emptied. Bravo, Charlie, Delta and Echo teams were already standing in formation, eyes forward. No one spoke. There were no hidden smirks cast at each other when the Sergeants were not looking or hints of smiles at other people's suffering, even from the Echoes. Everyone was deadly serious. The anxiety was so high that to Spartan it seemed almost palpable. Almost as if a living, breathing specter of Death lingered over the formation like a ghost that had reached out with ethereal tendrils of suffering to envelop the entire collection of cadets within its icy embrace.

Drill Sergeant Hogg moved his group to the area that had been pre-designated for Alpha team and then silently left the room. As the teams were organized alphabetically, this put Spartan and his team at the very front of the room. Several silent, uncomfortable minutes passed. Only an occasional dripping sound broke the silence as rainwater fell from the formed-up cadets clothing, to puddle slowly on the floor.

The silence was broken as the front entrance to the room was opened and Colonel Slade walked into the meeting hall. The senior officer looked much as he had during the cadet's initial briefing and option to depart the Academy. Impeccable gray flat top and a perfect dress uniform with a chest full of ribbons, medals and badges. His polished shoes reflected the halogen lights above like small mirrors. But Spartan could see that there was a difference in the man. Puzzling within his own mind, Spartan sought to identify the variance; then it came to him. When the cadets had first come to the Academy, the Colonel's eyes spoke of hardness. Strong, tough, no-nonsense. The man commanded respect with just a look. Now, although the toughness was still there, it appeared to have been subverted by other emotions, sadness, pain and grief. This was a man who had lost someone within his command and was not used to it.

Walking silently to the center of the room the Colonel looked over the cadets; searching the faces for any trace of conduct that did not belong. A noise at the rear the room signaled that someone else had come in, but Spartan dared not look. Then the Colonel spoke, his voice was low but projected force before it.

"Today you are to be congratulated. You have survived your first live encounters with the walking dead in a controlled environment. Some of you displayed innovation and tactics, others utilized stealth and cunning and still others, brutality and savagery. All are traits that you will need to survive in this new world of death during the days, weeks and months to come. Team leaders, the leadership skills displayed by each of you were superior and you all demonstrated advanced problem-solving, creativity and teamwork. You are all to be commended and I applaud you."

The Colonel and the assembled drill sergeants gave the cadets a full round of applause.

"However as with every battlefield there are casualties. Although it is to be expected, it's never easy to acknowledge the death of a valued team member. Tonight, you'll have to see the unfortunate side of our new lives. Pain, suffering and death are very real consequences for the decisions that each of us will choose to make in the coming days. I ask that you all remain professional, stay focused and pay close attention to the next bit of time. I will not lie to you. The remainder of tonight will be terrible. What you see and what some of you will be required to endure will stay in your mind for the remainder of your lives. But it is necessary for you to all truly understand what your futures hold. Be strong."

As if to accentuate the Colonel's statement, lightning flashed in a blindingly close burst of light followed microseconds later by the crack and bass rumble of thunder. The sound was immediately followed by a roaring sound as the rain outside began to fall in a deluge.

Looking over to his left, the Colonel gave a single, small nod to an unknown cadet that stood silently by the side hallway door. Spartan's interest was piqued with curiosity; both from the unknown behind the gun metal gray door and by the mystery cadet. The cadet held the door wide as Drill Sergeants Stone and Havoc pushed forward two sheet covered medical gurneys. Atop the gurneys sat an array of three boxes. The largest, a wooden crate about three feet in length by two-foot high sat alone upon one gurney. The remaining two wooden boxes were evenly spaced on the second medical cart. Of the latter two, one was about two-foot long by one foot high and the second only about eight inches in length and three inches in height.

Placing the carts evenly spaced directly in front of Colonel Slade, the two drill sergeants exited out of the metal doors only to return seconds later. Sergeant Stone pushed a third gurney into the room. The wooden crate upon the gurney was a full six-foot in length by two foot in height. This cart was wheeled behind the Colonel and placed up against the dry erase whiteboard at the front of the classroom. Drill Sergeant Havoc then entered the room accompanied by Drill Sergeant Hogg to his immediate left and Drill Sergeant Boomer behind them by about a yard.

Between the triumvirate of drill sergeants shuffled a hooded individual. The person's wrists and ankles were sturdily chained together, and an additional chain connected the two sets of manacles effectively holding the person's hands no higher than waist height and preventing any movement faster than a slow shuffle. The three drill sergeants moved their prisoner next to the six-foot box at the front of the room. It was not lost on any cadet in the room, that the prisoner wore the blue Lycra jumpsuit and AA insignia of the Apocalypse Academy. Obviously, this person was a cadet and not the prisoner from the cage. Nor was it lost on anyone that Sergeant Surfer was not present for the proceedings. A murmur immediately erupted across the assembled students. Only Alpha team stood stone still, remembering Sergeant Hogg's words and threats on the parade ground. No one on Alpha moved.

Techno cast a glance over briefly to Spartan as if to say something, but a scathing look and a subtle shake of his team leader's head told the technologically capable cadet to shut his mouth and be silent. Now was not the time to talk.

Drill Sergeant Surfer's voice cut through the din of the dismayed cadets ordering them all back to the position of attention. The crisp harshness in the drill sergeant's normally laid-back tone immediately affected the assembled cadets. The triangle of drill sergeants at the front of the room never flinched. The cadets may not have known that the drill sergeant was standing in the back of the room behind the formation, but the Instructors certainly did. The Colonel's stance never shifted and any emotion that he may have possessed at the cadet's apprehension before him was internalized, never to be seen by his subordinates. As the crowd of trainees snapped into attention, the Colonel again addressed the cadets.

"I know that you are all worn out and with good reason to be. Physically and mentally, you have exhausted yourselves in an outstanding display of fortitude by completing the Dante course. It is to be expected after what you have all endured and persevered against today. But what we do now and what you should always do after a battle when it is safe to do so, is to honor our fallen dead. Regardless of our personal needs, we owe a few moments of our lives to recognize the sacrifices that our teammates have made to continue making the world a better place. In addition, fate has chosen to let us see the darker side of our own existence." The Senior Officer said nodding his head slightly at the cadet standing placidly against the front wall escorted by the trio of drill sergeants.

"What could he have done to deserve such harsh treatment? Could he have intentionally killed another cadet in the Dante course?" Spartan wondered to himself looking at the cadet. *"And who is it?"*

The Colonel's voice drew him back into the assembly room and out of his thoughts.

"Three of your brothers and sisters-in-arms have fallen today. Before you grieve, I remind you all, that each of you was afforded an opportunity to leave the Apocalypse Academy on the very first night when I addressed the entire assembly. All of you chose to remain despite the warning that some of you may die. For these three individuals…" The Colonel said waving his outstretched hand toward the boxes on either gurney. "Their fears are over. Death has claimed them and although it may seem cruel, at least they will not be sentenced to an eternal damnation of walking the world forever as an animated monstrosity."

Pausing for just the briefest of seconds, the Colonel looked over at the unknown cadet posted by the double doors and issued a brief nod in his direction. The cadet then walked towards the gurneys in front of the formation. As he got close, the cadet reached a hand into the cargo pocket on each side of his jumpsuit. From which he removed a handful of folded white paper strips from one side and three small, horizontal "L" shape strips of wood from the other. They looked like the kind used to hold a name plate on a school desk. Arriving at the boxes, the Cadet first placed the strips of wood atop each crate. Then he paused as if awaiting further orders, white paper strips held carefully at his left hand.

The Colonel continued "Some of these cadets you may have known and been acquaintances with. Some may have even been on your team, or they may have been your friends…"

"Not my teammates." Spartan silently thought. *"Thank God."*

"Some may have been complete strangers to you. However, whether or not you knew them is not important. What matters is that they lived and died as human beings, fighting to restore humanity in a deranged and sickly world. What lies within these boxes are the mortal remains of those cadets; at least what there was of them left to salvage. I will address each coffin in turn to tell you how they died so that their final act as a human being will allow you to learn from their mistakes and hopefully, if the time ever comes and you find yourself in a similar situation, you will recall this last act of kindness and fare better than they did. If so, then the sacrifice that they made today will not have been in vain and you will live because they died."

The Colonel looked over at the cadet standing at parade rest next to the smallest box and gave a slight nod. The cadet snapped to attention, performed an about face flawlessly and then placed one of the white paper strips upon the wooden block. The cadet saluted and returned to his original position. The Colonel's voice read the name off the paper at the same time Spartan's eyes focused on it from a distance.

"Cadet Meatball! Team: Bravo. Born date unknown, found in Phoenix Arizona. Died on this day during training in the Dante obstacle course – in the tri-infected area. Final cause of death: disembowelment and dismemberment by Reapers. Situation: Cadet Meatball was knocked unconscious to the ground by the fleeing horse as his team attempted to run through the area, there is uncertainty as to whether or not the initial cause of death was due to equine impact or from "Z" action. Lesson learned: live animals are unpredictable. Warriors should not cross an area containing a frightened or injured animal; especially one of greater size than man."

Again, a nod from the Colonel and the cadet strode over to the midsize coffin/crate and placed a name tag upon its holder before returning to his initial post by the gurney.

"Cadet Knight! Team: Delta. Born date: unknown. Found by the Apocalypse Academy staff in Seattle, Washington. He died this day holding back the undead from advancing atop the log bridge over the river obstacle. Situation: Due to the slow movement of his team crossing the obstacle, Cadet Knight, the rearguard, was forced to turn and fight a holding action upon the log bridge. Though he fought valiantly, allowing his team to cross in safety, Cadet Knight was overwhelmed physically and fell from the bridge into the corpse infected water below. Cause of death was due to dismemberment from underwater "Zs". Lessons learned are twofold: "Zs" do not breathe. They can and will kill you from places like waterways, ponds, lakes and oceans. Secondly, when a decision is made to cross an obstacle or a limited access pathway, movements must be quick and efficient. Hesitation or indecision can lead to death."

Spartan recalled that Deadeye had almost suffered a similar fate due to Techno's terror and that his team had narrowly averted that same tragedy mostly through Freak's massive strength. Luck it seemed had truly been on their side. A small sob came from the rank two rows behind out the team. Spartan judged the sound to come from Cadet Princess, who had been rumored to be romantically involved with Cadet Knight. There would be no fairytale ending to their story for sure.

A final nod from the Colonel and the cadet walked over to the three-foot long box.

"Corpsman Band-Aid." The Colonel announced. "Field medical volunteer team. He was probably unknown to most of you. Born in nineteen hundred and ninety-seven, found at the CDC Institute in Atlanta, Georgia. Died this day on the Dante obstacle course when trying to assist a cadet that had fallen from the sixty-foot high log climb. Situation: while treating the cadet for a broken arm, Corpsman Band-Aid was attacked from behind by a pack of Romero "Zs". Knowing that the cadet with a broken arm could not fight, Corpsman Band-Aid engaged eight "Zs" in hand-to-hand combat. This allowed the injured cadet time to flee and catch up with the rest of her team who had opted to leave her behind due to the overall team liability of an injury. Cause of death: evisceration and dismemberment of both legs. Lesson learned: know your environment before you treat an injury. Had the cadet's team been standing guard, then the broken arm could have been set, splinted and the cadet returned to mobility quickly and safely. Instead, when the cadet's team opted to leave her behind, the Corpsman still felt obligated to attempt to render medical aid. While this act was brave to be sure, in the end it was foolish and a waste of a valuable resource. In this world there are many people; survivors, that could become cadets. There are very few that have had training in a pre-apocalypse setting to become a medical doctor."

Spartan thought he heard the slightest of snickers coming from the rear ranks where Echo team was in the formation. It would not be too difficult to determine who the injured cadet had been. The Colonel had repeatedly said "her" during his eulogy and Spartan knew of only one team that would leave a member behind willingly. Echo team. That meant Lotus Jane would have the broken arm by virtue of being the only female on the team. Silently, Spartan thought about placing a fist in Cutter's mouth in remembrance of

Corpsman Band-Aid. He had not known the boy, but anyone that would sacrifice himself to save a member of Cutter's slimy brigade, deserved to be recognized because Echo team would surely not do it. Perhaps a split lip or two, a busted nose or a blackened eye would serve as a memento that would cause them to reflect on their callousness. Perhaps not. Either way, Spartan would enjoy dishing out the pain. Perhaps he would invite Freak along as well. It would be fun issuing the ass whipping together like they had the first day in the bathroom.

At a nod from the Colonel, the unknown cadet wheeled first one box laden gurney then the other back out of the double doors. No one spoke as the remains of their comrades departed from the room. The only noise was the soft squeak of one of the gurney's rubber wheels on the polished marble floor that sounded much louder than it was. As the metal doors closed behind the unknown cadet, all eyes shifted to the hooded individual escorted by a six-foot box and three drill sergeants. The only noise in the room was the soft hum of the overhead lights. Everyone seemed to have stopped breathing.

"Bring the cadet forward." The Colonel instructed.

Escorted by the drill sergeants, the cadet obediently shuffled ahead before being stopped beside the Colonel by Drill Sergeant Boomer and the other two drill sergeants.

Today we have an uncommon opportunity. In the plague infested world that we live in, or in any real war, rarely do we control our own destinies. Even rarer is the opportunity to ensure our own peaceful rest in the afterlife if we suffer from infection. Unlike the three previous cadets that you may have known as we reviewed their cause of death and the intrinsic lessons that we learned therein, this cadet was bitten, infected and is slowly dying. Yes, I said dying. A fact of which he is well aware. As you know when the heart stops beating the HUNGER virus takes full effect and the turning will begin. Nothing can prevent this. Within moments, this cadet will change into a Reaper. Over time it will evolve into a Romero, then slowly devolve into a Husk attempting to spread its disease at every stage until finally its rotten body will decay to the point of collapse and it will fall to the ground inanimate but never truly dead."

The Colonel looked out over the assembled cadets, his hard, gray eyes reading the outspoken body language of each cadet standing in front of him. Emotions were strong. Sadness, anger and disbelief were the prevalent emotions that he saw. He empathized with the cadets. He had lost teammates before himself. He knew what they were feeling.

"This is the reality of what we are training you to do. We are all destined to die. Today, tomorrow, next week, next year or fifty years from now. Sooner or later, the Ferryman comes for us all. So, it is not the fact that we are going to die that we should be focused upon. That is inevitable and while we may have the ability to make certain tactical considerations which may delay it, ultimately death's icy hand will reach out for us all."

Several sniffles and sobs came from within the formation, but no one spoke.

"What we can control," the hard-eyed officer continued "is when we *know* that Death's skeletal hand is closing around us and that our doom is unalterable; those of us that are truly fortunate can decide *how* we will die. By doing this we can ensure that, although our bodies will perish, our souls will not be damned to walk the earth for eternity. We can be certain that no infection will ever be spread due to our involuntary actions, potentially damning our friends or loved ones. Today this cadet is fortunate enough to have that very option due to a very unique situation."

The Colonel paused to take a deep breath and a sip of water from a bottle beneath his podium. The water was not so much to quench his thirst but to wash down the emotions that were rising like gorge into his throat. Even after all his years in the military, he still found it very difficult to see one of his assigned troops perish.

"This morning, this cadet's team completed the Dante course with no injuries and no fatalities. As the team formed up outside of the last obstacle and prepared to march back to its dormitory, the restraining bolt on the end gate of the obstacle course failed. The Romero's that prowled the ground of the final obstacle burst through the chain-link restraining gate, lurching for the back of a drill sergeant that did not know they were coming. Hearing the metal gate break and seeing the "Zs" moving towards the unaware drill sergeant, this cadet broke ranks and intercepted the undead by tackling and killing several of them with his hand to hand weapon. The cadet fought bravely but was ultimately thrown to the ground by the overwhelming numbers of walking corpses. His actions prevented the inevitable infection and death of a drill sergeant. Together with the drill sergeant, they managed to protect the other cadets and kill the remaining "Zs". This cadet even managed to snap one creature's neck while on the ground, ending its threat. In doing so, this Cadet was subsequently bitten three separate times on the forearm and bicep areas."

Spartan now understood the chains around the young man. They were not there for punishment at all. They were there to prevent the cadet from changing suddenly in the middle of the Colonel's speech and potentially attacking and infecting the other cadets.

Freak spoke softly next to Spartan, were only his team leader could hear. "Shit Dawg; that is just fucked up." Spartan silently agreed.

"So, the choice as I stated earlier is not whether or not we will die. I will. He will. As will we all eventually. No, this heroic cadet instead must choose who he wants to honor him with the task of ensuring that he does not come back to infect the others among you. Who he wants to help him let his soul rest in peace. To do this, he has requested to stand in front of you all, evaluate you personally and after selecting his executioner, to die before you. I have decided to honor this valiant young man's final request. The selected person will then use their pacification spike or their hand-to-hand weapon to release this hero's soul to eternity."

The crowd immediately erupted into a raucous clamor. Words were exchanged. Tears were falling accompanied by the sobs of horror. Explicit comments flew from rank to rank as disbelief at the situation surged across the assembled cadets. Turning to Freak, Spartan spoke directly into his ear while the crowd continued to rage.

"Remember what Hogg said!" He half yelled into the big man's year over the din in the room. "Shut 'em up. Be professional! Hurry!"

Freak turned and grab Techno's arm in a vice like grip to get his attention. Squeezing firmly, he spoke to the Japanese

American teenager. "Man, Sergeant Hogg's watching! Square it away and shut the fuck up. Pass it down the line to Dancer as well."

Techno's words to Dancer were quick but effective as Spartan saw her square her jaw and fight back the tears yet again. Looking further down the line, Spartan saw that Deadeye was as silent and brooding as ever; never uttering a single word.

Looking back over at the hooded cadet, Spartan could not imagine what he must be feeling. Bound in chains, effectively blind from the hood, dying slowly, moment by moment from the infection and yet the cadet stood there absolutely immobile, the rock of stability in a storm of circumstance. A quick glance back at his team showed them back at attention. Spartan allowed his eyes to move back to the cadet at the front of the room and then to the drill sergeants as he followed suit and assumed the professional stance. His eyes met with Sergeant Hogg's and for the briefest of instances, Spartan read real pain behind the harsh looks and lantern jaw. The drill sergeant gave the slightest of nods acknowledging Spartan's leadership, and then returned his focus to the remainder of the cadets in formation scowling fiercely.

Drill Sergeant Surfer had left the rear of the assembly hall and was alternately slapping, cursing and shoving cadets back into formation. The normally smooth tempered drill sergeant was clearly incensed and determined to restore order. After several moments and numerous slaps to skulls later, the formation was resumed. And once again silence filled the air.

Were they really asking one of the cadets to kill one of their own ranks? Was it murder if the cadet had already been infected and was slowly turning into a "Z" anyway? Was it better to have a clean, quick warrior's death than to slowly and inexorably change into one of the walking dead? To feel your internal organs slowly shutting down as the body begins to fail beneath the HUNGER *virus before finally taking your last breath and settling into peaceful death, only to be jerked back into unlife as an animated corpse. No, that truly had to be hell. It may have been different if the "Zs" had proven to be capable of at least quasi– sentient thought processes. But some, especially the* Reapers *had shown at least primal thought processes as they identified slower and weaker targets to attack, hunted in pairs and even occasionally set up ambushes, using their often-superior numbers to force their victims into alleyways, cul-de-sacs and rooms with either no or limited egress avenues.*

"No," Spartan thought. The Colonel was right. *"It would be far better to know that when your end came there would be no return."*

As order was finally restored to the cadet's ranks, the Colonel cleared his throat and prepared to speak.

"Sir!" A loud voice called from the rear of the formation. "Permission to speak, sir!"

Spartan knew that voice. It was Cutter. What could that useless piece of shit possibly have to say at a moment like this? He better hope and pray that it was not something that he would regret or Spartan would make him pay in spades.

"Granted. Make it brief cadet."

"Sir," the sound of two quick footsteps as Cutter stepped forward out of ranks to reply. "Sir, this cadet would like to volunteer his services to end the suffering of the cadet standing before the assembly. I will make it quick and painless, Sir!"

Murmurs again raced through the formation, but they were quickly quelled by another series of stinging head slaps and shoves from Drill Sergeant Surfer who was now prowling in between the ranks. The last words to be heard aloud before order was restored were of a female cadet clearly saying "That fucking gits' codename should be *Butcher*, not Cutter! Stupid arsehole!" in a very loud and very clear English accent. Spartan realized it was his own teammate Dancer who had made the statement, since he did not know of any other British cadets and while he could not show it when standing at attention; he made a point's in his mind to congratulate her on the acerbic perception later. Without a doubt, Echo team's leader was probably fuming at the comment. The thought produced the briefest of twitches of a smile at the corners of his mouth. Fortunately, his full smile was cut short by the Colonel's point-blank reply before anyone saw it.

"Cadet Cutter; while death is something that we will deal with every day and the necessity of our lot in life dictates that we must be efficient and precise in our methodology towards accomplishing our long-term goal of rebuilding a foothold for humanity, we should never reach a point where we *enjoy* the killing or even performing the pacification of another human being. For if we reach that point, then we as a species, are no better than the walking corpses of the damned that currently possess our world. Perhaps those people who have fallen to such a murderous level to accomplish their own happy place of sanctity have in fact, lost their hold on humanity and sanity. It is a thought to consider as you review your own conduct."

A pin could've dropped in the room and made more noise than the collective breathing of more than twenty-five cadets and instructors. Even though his stance didn't change the cadet seemed to have stopped breathing and his face had turned a vaguely purplish hue. Everyone waited; anticipating Cutter's inappropriate reply that they were sure would come.

"Sir!" Came the awaited response. "This cadet understands and will reflect on the Colonel's wisdom, sir!"

Two more quick steps and Cutter fell back into formation without another word.

"I have done enough speaking." The Colonel followed up as though Cutter's remark had not mattered at all to him. "It is now time for this honored cadet to be identified and allow him to select the individual who will grant him final pacification. Please make no mistake; this is not an optional duty. If you are selected, you *will* perform this duty. Failure to do so will result in disciplinary action up to and including expulsion from the Apocalypse Academy. The Colonel turned and faced the trio of drill sergeants around the hooded cadet.

"Remove the hood. The chains are to remain in place." He said in a quiet, but clear voice.

Drill Sergeant Boomer reached up and pulled the drawstring from around the cadet's neck. In one smooth movement, he pulled the hood free. Spartan could not initially see who the cadet was as the Drill sergeant stood between the formation and the other cadets while removing the hood. Then, as the drill sergeant stepped away, Spartan saw the unruly red shock of hair standing straight up upon the boy's head and the freckled face. The doomed cadet was the tough little teenager Rooster.

Chapter Twelve
The Decision

Rooster: the tough as nails, midsized, smart mouth teen that had taken a severe beating from another cadet at the drill sergeant's instruction just to prove that he was tough enough to make it at the Apocalypse Academy. Spartan could not believe that the boy had gone through so much only to perish so ignominiously.

Despite the obvious discomfort of the infected bites that he had suffered on his hand, forearm and bicep, the boy still stood tall and proud. Thankfully, the other cadets could not see the bites due to the gauze and surgical tape that covered the wounds, but it was not hard to imagine the savage, rotten teeth of a "Z", especially a Romero, tearing into the soft flesh beneath the bandages. The bite to the hand was even more visual as the two bloody stumps had been bandaged where the boy's pinky and ring finger had once been on his left hand. If there had never been any doubt as to the cadet's toughness before, no one could say it now. His pain had to be overwhelming, yet here he stood.

Slowly and with great effort, Cadet Rooster raised his head to meet the eyes of his fellow cadets. Slowly he scanned the teams, looking… looking… As if reading the souls behind each of the eyes that stared back at him. After several long moments, he spoke out loud.

"Y'all know me. Ya know I ain't a sissy nor am I afraid to die. I'm a Rooster with a strut like Ric Flair and a temper like a tornado (which sounded distinctly like a cross between a tornado and tomato to Spartan's ears). What you ain't been told is how I got here. I want to share that before I go, an' the Colonel said I could, just so's someone will remember.

When the infection came, I was watchin' my little sister while my mom and dad was at work. My dad worked as a field boss for a local beer distributor and my mom was a waitress down at Jackie's diner in town. We were just plain ol' middle-class country folk, happy at making a livin'. My sis and I were playing hide and seek out by the creek that ran across the back of our property. She was really good at it because she was so small and could bend up like a pretzel to get into the tightest little spaces. Since we ain't supposed to have known names at the Academy I will call her Lily. That was her favorite flower.

Lily had hid so good that I looked for her for over an hour trying to find her. I searched in the hollow log back in the woods, and up in trees and behind bushes and fences. I even checked under the porch and over at old Mrs. Hackmore's backyard next door too because sometimes we would sneak over and snitch apples or mulberries if no one was looking. She wasn't there either. Finally, I gave up and called out to Lily that she had won and that she could come out; I give up I says. I remember hearing her laughter in the air because she had beat me at the game."

"Come on Lily" I said. "I'd done give'd up. Where you at?"

"Again, laughter in the air, this time from the other side of the yard. The little sneak was cheatin'! Hidin' then movin' to where I had already searched. Ooh, I was gonna get her good for that. I ran across the yard but when I got there she was already gone. Laughter came by the creek, so I changed directions and tore off towards the creek full speed, determined to get her good. Maybe I would toss her right in the four inches of water that always bubbled through the creek bed, just to teach her a lesson about being sneaky. Then we would laugh because we knew mom would be furious over the muddy clothes. Maybe we would get a fudgesicle to eat as we sat out in the sun to dry off."

"Halfway to the creek, I heard Lily scream. It was not the scream of a little girl who had seen a cockroach or a spider or a snake. It was a scream of pure terror. I ran as hard as I could, I had to protect her. She was my baby sister. Crashing through the tree branches and splashing through the cool water, I looked and looked for Lily. A red strip of T-shirt lay on the ground with the cat head symbol of "Hello Kitty" stamped on to it. I picked up the piece of cloth and felt the moisture. This couldn't be Lily's because her shirt was white. She must have picked this out of the creek because of the Hello Kitty symbol. That was when I realized that it was not water on the strip of shirt. It was blood. I screamed Lily's name over and over, running everywhere that I had already searched. I ran into the house and checked the living room, the bedrooms, under the beds and even the bathroom. She was nowhere to be found. I ran next door to Mrs. Hackmore's house, but found the door was locked. Before long, dark began to settle in. I never stopped looking. By midnight, I was wet and cold. I had to tell my parents that Lily was missing and what I had found by the creek."

"Running back to the house, I expected to find my parents worried maybe even angry at us. My father would be pacing, maybe smoking a cigarette or drinking a beer. Maybe both. My mom would be on the telephone trying to find us at the neighbor's houses or at other family member's houses; hoping that we had gone for a visit."

"Instead, I returned to a dark house. No lights, no cars, and no parents. Days and days passed. I never saw Lily or my parents again. I later found out that this was "Z" night. The Academy cadre found me in town, raiding old apple pies from an abandoned McDonald's. My family is still out there somewhere, Lily and my parents, alive or undead. I know they're there."

The fire haired cadet stood as a silent tear rolled down the side of his face, weaving its way between his freckles to finally drip from his chin like a single raindrop. After a moment of profound silence, the Colonel walked to Rooster's side and quietly asked the cadet if he had made the pacification determination.

"Sir, yes Sir ah have." Rooster replied puffing out his chest ever so slightly, as if preparing himself to make the announcement of which cadet would be given the honor... and the horror... of ending his time on earth.

No noise came from the ranks of cadets. Even the sobs and sniffles that had resulted from Rooster's tragic tale had been silenced as every cadet, apart from those within the ranks of Echo team, genuinely hoped to be passed up for this *"honor"*. The general expectation was that Rooster would probably pick a member of his own team to do the deed. Mentally reviewing them, Spartan assessed Charlie team's roster to see who he expected to be selected. Cowboy, the tough Texan, would be the obvious choice. As the team leader, he had demonstrated class and guts. His weapon was a Bowie knife though. While it would do the job, it would not be quick or painless. There was no way Princess was going to be up to it, especially since the loss of Cadet Knight during the Dante course. Popcorn was a walking stick figure; a hyperactive bundle of energy that never sat still. Spartan did not know what his weapon of choice was, but it couldn't be too large. That left only Vulture. Vulture was capable with his longsword but seemed so glum and even a little slow mentally, the Spartan doubted his selection. He had gotten the name Vulture due to his resemblance to the Looney Tunes character "Beaky Buzzard" when he was standing around. His posture was slouched, his long neck pushed his head forward making his large nosed resemble a beak. The resemblance was amazing if you were a cartoon fan before the normal world ended.

Perhaps Rooster would select someone with a demonstrated propensity for violence. Certainly, there were several cadets that had shown that they could bring a blade to bear without too much of their conscience being compromised. Bravo team's martial arts expert Dragon was capable of using several different weapons. Stiletto and Gator from Delta team were both handy with knives and Gator carried an exceptionally wicked machete that would end the issue quickly. Even his own Dancer had to be a consideration because of the deadly efficiency of the naginata, although Spartan thought the damage to her psyche if she were forced into putting Rooster down would surely be devastating to his brown eyed teammate. Of course, any of the maniacs associated with Echo team would volunteer. They seemed to relish the idea of bloodshed at any time.

The Colonel's voice brought Spartan's mental focus back to the front of the assembly Hall.

"Which cadet has been selected to perform the pacification for you?" The senior officer for the Apocalypse Academy asked quietly but firmly again.

"Sir, I've selected Alpha team's leader, Corporal Spartan."

Spartan felt his jaw physically drop to the maximum extent of the ligaments holding it to the skull. His mouth felt as though every ounce of moisture had been sucked out of it by an invisible vacuum.

"Corporal Spartan, step forward!" The Colonel ordered.

Training in professional bearing kicked in as Spartan snapped to attention, took two strides forward and executed a left face maneuver and marched to stand in front of the Apocalypse Academy's Commandant. Snapping a crisp salute that the Colonel returned, Spartan stood at attention.

"Corporal Spartan. You've been selected by your Academy teammate to perform the honor of his final pacification. Do you accept this honor and responsibility?"

Spartan looked into Rooster's freckled face trying to read the redheaded cadet's thoughts through his green eyes. The boy's eyes were hard and seem to mirror the pain that Spartan felt at being requested to perform this duty.

"Sir, yes Sir. I do." Spartan replied though the pain of this duty, knowing that doing so would surely haunt him for life. He knew that it was necessary and that he was a soldier and as such, he had to be willing to take horrific actions and follow orders. But there was nothing saying that he had to like it. That was exactly the case with this assignment. He felt dread down to the very core of his being.

"Very well, Corporal Spartan you are to remain with Cadet Rooster until the end of his living time on this planet. At that time, you will be expected to deliver the pacification ritual to your teammate. The option of the pacification spike or your sword will be decided between you and the condemned."

Turning to the remaining cadets, the Colonel's voice notched up several decibels.

"The remainder of you are all dismissed back to your barracks. Due to the rigors of the Dante course and the loss of several teammates, you will be released two days non-duty furlough. You're not allowed to leave the barracks area during this period, and you will be expected to be available in the event of an emergency. I would strongly recommend that you spend at least a portion of that free time cleaning your weapons and reflecting on how you will respond if and when your own time for pacification comes. It is my sincerest hope that we will all face it as bravely and honorably as Cadet Rooster. Drill sergeants; dismiss your teams."

As one the drill sergeants converged on their respective teams. Spartan saw Sergeant Hogg briefly discussing what he assumed to be command orders in Spartan's absence with Freak. Then, his team was marching off. A quick look from Dancer caught Spartan's eye. The sorrow and sympathy that she felt for both her team leader and the fiery Rooster was evident in her eyes. Then they were gone through the metal doors.

"Corporal Spartan, Cadet Rooster. I will leave you two alone to discuss what needs to be discussed. I caution you Spartan not to stand too close. Cadet Rooster was bitten multiple times. His turning is at an advanced stage. You can see the reddish tint already beginning to alter his eyes as the blood vessels are starting to rupture and although he would not be caught complaining, I have seen enough people turned to know that his muscular pain must be extensive.

When he turns it will be initially as a Reaper. Your actions must be quick and decisive. Do you understand what I am saying Corporal?"

"Sir, yes Sir!" Spartan replied.

"Very well. There will be guards posted on the outside of each door and the room is being monitored through closed-circuit video if you get into trouble. Cadet Rooster: you are a fine, brave young lad. I cannot say that any soldier ever under my command has demonstrated a greater amount of bravery then you have. I promise you that I will place a memorial on the grounds of the Dante, in tribute to your unselfish bravery and devotion to your teammates. May you pass on in peace and never know the anguish of undeath. Farewell."

The Colonel offered the chained Cadet his hand to shake. Reaching to the full length of the belly chain, Rooster shook it firmly.

"Thank you, sir."

The Colonel nodded once, turned and walked out of the double metal doors without ever looking back. They all understood that there was no need for further conversation about the matter. Emotions would just make the situation worse, especially from the Commander of the Apocalypse Academy. When the doors closed with an audible click, Spartan looked back at Rooster and was stunned to see him grinning from ear to ear.

"What the hell is so funny Rooster?"

The boy began to chuckle out loud and for a moment Spartan was afraid the doomed Cadet was mentally breaking down.

"Well, by placing a memorial to me in the Dante course, they are effectively making me immortal. Do you mean to tell me that you did not see the humor in a death trapped, "Z" filled obstacle course having a plaque dedicated to an immortal chicken? It's hilarious."

Spartan immediately visualized the cross between the legendary god Zeus and the famous Looney Tunes cartoon chicken; Foghorn Leghorn presiding over the deadly obstacle course. Rooster was right. It was a hilarious mental image. After several shared moments of laughter, Spartan asked Rooster how he had gotten bitten.

"It was kind of ironic actually. See, the Colonel only told you the part of the story about Corpsman Band-Aid. The part about saving Lotus Jane, well that was true. Cutter, Orc and the rest of them assholes left her to die when she fell. Band-Aid ran out on the field and fought like a maniac. What the Colonel failed to mention was that Band-Aid was not alone. When the Corpsman ran out into the Dante unarmed, Drill Sergeant Hogg ran after him, about ten steps behind. We had finished the Dante and were watching from outside the fences. I reasoned that Sergeant Hogg was most worried about the potential loss of the medical specialist which as you know is somewhat rare nowadays. I didn't figure he did it for honorable or personal reasons. I was wrong."

Band-Aid and Sergeant Hogg were fighting "Zs" at every turn while trying to protect themselves and Lotus Jane. She just sat there on the ground, all crunched up into a ball.

Band-Aid told Jane to run, and then dove into a swarm of "Zs" to cover her retreat, Hogg went berserk. The Colonel lied about the number of undead that were present. There were at least twenty with more Romero's staggering in that gate every second. Sergeant Hogg did not see the pack of Romeros that Lotus Jane evaded on her way out of the obstacle course. Eight Romero's were coming up behind him. He was going to be slaughtered. I tried to scream a warning to him but the moans of the undead and Hogg's own war cries drowned me out. Man, that big ol' bastard can fight! So, I did what any red-blooded American boy would do. I jumped up and ran over to the fence and slammed it shut keeping any of the Romero's from escaping the fencing. Then I dodged and ran forward towards Sergeant Hogg and Lotus Jane. I clipped one of the Romero's in the back of the skull with my sword as I sprinted by. Bone, scalp and brain flew forward splattering Hogg's back with enough impact to get him to look behind him. Even though he saw the "Z's" coming up behind him, he turned back to help Band-Aid. He left his ass completely unprotected and if I didn't do something, he would've died for sure."

"I couldn't let that happen. I got my ass kicked to prove to him that I was tough. If I saved his life, he would have to tell everyone about it and then I would be a real life, movie star type badass! So, I ran all the way to him, put one Romero in a rear choke hold and turned it back to meet the wave of "Z's" head-on. I did okay, kicking them away and slashing with my sword while I hung from that critter's neck until one fat bastard that I killed fell into my legs. Off-balance, I stumbled. My choke hold slipped, and that damned "Z" sunk its teeth in seconds later. Quick as a whip I dropped my sword and broke the thing's neck but by then the damage was done." He said, holding up his bandaged arm.

"The last thing I saw was that I was being dog piled by "Z's". I don't know how long after that but probably seconds, and "Z's" were flying every which way offa me. Daylight reemerged as the dead flesh was carved like a sick Thanksgivings turkey. When I got back to my feet, the "Z's" were all slaughtered by Hogg, and Band-Aid was gone. I guess the Colonel missed a few details huh?"

The normally stalwart Rooster looked visibly shaken. Spartan gave him a moment of silence to compose himself before continuing the story.

"I found out later that Sergeant Hogg had found Band-Aid first, about three weeks before "Z" night and the formal declared outbreak of the HUNGER virus. Band-Aid was a teenager. Fifteen, maybe sixteen years old. Sergeant Hogg had dumped all his equipment out of his rucksack, tucked the extra ammunition into his belt and pockets, and then he put the boy into a fireman's carry. Hogg had carried him like that, on foot, across half the entire state of Georgia until he finally met up with the core group of survivors that eventually became the Academy staff here. He considered Band-Aid his surrogate son and has raised him ever since that day. It's no wonder hard ass Hogg went nuts when he saw Band-Aid in trouble."

"Oh shit." Spartan said softly. "I'm sorry Rooster."

"Nah, ain't no sense being sorry Spartan. At least I finally got to prove to 'ol hard ass Hogg that I really was a bad ass. It sure beats standing still while an ape like Orc beats on me. Besides, I have a secret."

"What?"

"I'll tell you right before, you know… the end, on one condition."

"Sure Rooster. Name it. Whatever I can do."

"That when I take my last breath and my eyes roll over all red, you'll never let me stand up as a "Z". One shot. Keep it clean. As hard as you can."

"Do you want me to use the Pacification spike or my sword Rooster?" Spartan said almost choking on the words.

"Are you kiddin'? It's the sword all the way man. You miss with that pacification spike, maybe not go deep enough and I just end up as a lobotomized" Z". Drooling, unable to move and retarded as a jar of Aunt Annie's applesauce, thanks but no thanks." The redheaded cadet pulled a thumb horizontally across his throat. "Don't forget… One shot and don't turn pussy on me Spartan. You swing as hard as you can!"

"Okay" Spartan said swallowing the lump in his throat. "I promise".

The teenage boys sat on the floor, conversing openly. Two more hours passed as the boys talked about pre—Z life. Spartan mostly listened because much of his past was shrouded in the brain haze of his amnesia. It turned out that Rooster loved apples, especially the sour green ones, that he had a Rottweiler named Rocco and that he truly hated Colonel Slade.

"The man reminds me too much of my fourth-grade teacher. He was a stuffy prick too. Maybe I shoulda put a bite on him, you know, on principal when he shook my hand." He said with a laugh.

"Don't even joke about that." Spartan said. Silently he remembered the closed-circuit TV that was recording every moment above them.

"Yeah, he probably would've tasted like shit anyway." Rooster replied, the grin still on his face.

A small seizure clenched the boy's body, causing the belly chain and cuffs to rattle. A gasp escaped Rooster's throat and he clenched his teeth against the pain.

"Spartan… I think… it's almost… time. Oh shit… This… Really hurts!"

"My secret… its Philip…"

"What?" Spartan asked confused.

"Philip… Garretson… My… Name. That's my… secret."

Another seizure slammed into the boy, making him shrink into a ball of pain. Spartan could see the muscles rippling under the boy's flesh as the HUNGER virus began to transform him into one of the walking dead. It was brutal to watch and Spartan silently hated Colonel Slade for making him perform this duty.

"Okay… Philip. I'm here. "

"Spartan… Other part… My secret…"

"Tell me."

"I'm from… Farm… Dubuque, Iowa… Lilly's story is… real. Real name is… Lilly… Garretson. I know… she's alive… Lords… Of… Death took… Find… Her for… M…save…"

The sentence was never ended. Rooster's final breath rattled through his chest before wheezing out of his plague infected lungs. Spartan stood up solemnly, drawing forth his razor-sharp sword as he did so. The slinging grate of metal dragging across metal was the only sound in the room as the sword came free of its scabbard. In one motion he raised the shining silver blade above his head, preparing to and the boys suffering.

"Goodbye… Rooster. Be at peace and don't worry, if Lilly's out there I will find her. You have my word on it."

Gritting his teeth and blinking back the unexpected tears of sympathy for a boy that he hardly knew, he wiped the back of his sleeve across his eyes, clearing the moisture that threatened to blur his vision. Spartan tensed to strike, the muscles of his forearms tightening as he slowly raised the sword of Leonidas above his head. His two-handed grip was sweaty but sure upon the wrapped leather pommel of his ancient sword. A final thought came to his mind as he held the blade upraised unwaveringly above him. It only seemed right to say goodbye to the boy by his real name which he had entrusted to him in his final moments of life.

"Goodbye Philip." He whispered under his breath so that the audio or visual sensors within the room would not register the sound.

Screaming a battle cry, the leader of Alpha team brought the heavy blade down across the dead cadet's skull, aiming for the area that he had been taught the hypothalamus was located. With one sure, powerful stroke Spartan prevented him from ever becoming one of the undead. The only sound that followed was the hollow thunk as the upper two-thirds of Rooster's head fell to the floor and spun like a flaming red top three feet away.

Walking away slowly, his heart heavy at the needed action that he had been forced to take; Spartan approached the double grade metal doors with his sword still in hand. Using its pommel, he beat on the metal until the Academy guard opened the locked door. Looking once at the blood and gore splattered sword in Spartan's hand and over his shoulder at the headless corpse still sitting chained hand and foot on the floor, the guard stepped aside without even a word of apology or sorrow.

Spartan walked alone back to his dorm room, pausing only long enough to clean his weapon off at a water spigot outside. Silently he climbed the stairs and moved past his teammates toward his bunk. He couldn't talk to them right now. He needed time to think. He lay in the dark for a very long time committing his conversation with Rooster into his memory. At some point, sleep finally brought him into oblivion and he slept the restless sleep of someone who would forever endure a horrible cascade of nightmares.

Chapter Thirteen
The Funeral

Alpha team assembled two days later, for the laying of Cadets Knight, Meatball, and Rooster as well as Corpsman Band-Aid into their final resting places. Blue jumpsuits had been replaced by dress blue military uniforms; spit shined shoes and white gloves. Each cadet also wore a black beret that bore the double A patch of the Apocalypse Academy on its crest.

Dancer's hair was pulled up into a tight bun and stood out just below the beret's lip on the back of her head. Deadeye was similarly clad as the other cadets except for two additional tribal blue and yellow stripes of "mourning paint" crossing horizontally across his cheek bones and the bridge of his nose and vertically from his lower lip to the point of his chin. Additionally, within his hair the Apache teen had braided a single brown and white eagle's feather, similarly wrapped in blue and black thread as a tribute to the fallen teenagers' courage. Spartan knew that the Command staff would be pissed but he didn't give a shit. Let each of them mourn in their own way. If there was a problem with it, then he would take the heat as the team's leader.

Freak and Techno stood quietly by. If the whole thing bothered the muscular cadet, he never showed it. Techno had clearly been crying as the eyes behind the round glasses that he wore were swollen and red. For now, though, he was quiet and composed. Calling his team together, Spartan spoke quietly to the group.

"This is a miserable day for all of us. Each of us is hurting in our own way. We need to keep our shit together. No emotion, no feelings in public. Pay our respects and let's get the fuck out of here. When we get back, we can let loose if we need too. Until then keep it together for the cadets we lost and for Sergeant Hogg. Remember, he lost more than any of us did."

Spartan had privately told his team about Rooster's revelation regarding the drill sergeant and his secret promise to hunt for the boy's sister; Lily, the next morning after the pacification had been completed. Reassurances came from all of the cadets of Alpha team and as a group they solemnly filed out into formation. Spartan immediately noted that the formation was smaller than usual. Apart from the loss of the three cadets during the exercise of the Dante, several more were missing. Seeing no drill sergeants in the immediate area, Spartan took a moment to do a quick visual headcount. All of Bravo team was missing. Cadet Pig, known to be a friend of Meatball from pre-apocalyptic life, was also missing. Spartan surmised that the cadet was on funeral detail. As there was very little left of the Italian cadet after the "Z" attack, the detail would not need more than one member.

Cadets Gator and Jive were gone from Delta team, presumably on the same detail for Cadet Knight. That was when Spartan noticed that all of Charlie team was absent from the formation, offering him a direct view of Cutter and his band of rabid dogs from Echo team in the rear rank. Echo team seem positively jovial, laughing, making jokes about "Z's" eating, *'spaghetti intestines and Meatball'* for dinner and how Cadet Knight was definitely not a *'one Knight stand'* for Princess.

Spartan felt his blood begin to boil. Red tinting beginning to haze around the corners of his vision, as seething rage and the need to hurt someone began to overwhelm his thoughts.

Seeing Spartan glaring at him, Cutter made a noise like a rooster crowing that drew his thumb across his throat in a slashing motion, side to side. Spartan watched as his vision became tunneled, focusing solely on the face of the disrespectful punk ass bitch that was the Echo team leader. Just as he took a step forward towards Cutter with his fists closed and fury in his heart, he felt the gigantic meaty paw of Cadet Freak as he gripped his shoulder firmly, stopping him in his tracks.

"Not here brother. Not now. But rest assured, every fuckin' word will be paid for. Remember your words inside. Remember why we are here. No emotion. No feelings. Muthafuckers will get theirs. I promise. That's the Chicago way." The big cadet whispered directly into Spartan's face.

Spartan's brain whirled. His every instinct told him to fight, to draw blood, to hurt those arrogant, self-righteous pricks and their skanky team whore for the things that they were saying and doing at such a reverent time. But Freak's hand and the big cadet's words did what they were meant to do and Spartan's blood rage slowly subsided.

Looking at his leadership counterpart from Echo team dead in the eye, Spartan said a single word. "Soon."

Cadet Cutter produced a small thin throwing knife from inside of his sleeve and ran his tongue over the blade while he stared back at Spartan.

"I can't wait." He said his tongue leaving a wet trail along the metal blade.

Before the cadets could say more, the barracks door crashed open and out walked Drill Sergeant Hogg. He was wearing his dress green top with a bottle of whiskey in one hand and completely missing his trousers. Unsteadily, the sergeant marched forward to stand in front of the formation. He was obviously quite drunk. Freak and Spartan immediately broke ranks, running up to assist the inebriated drill sergeant before he could fall while the entire Echo team guffawed at the drunken soldier. White foam oozed from the corner of the man's mouth. Each grabbing an arm, Spartan and Freak held the burly drill sergeant up.

"Shee?…Sheewhatchugitt for being a… hero?!" The drill sergeant snarled with a slur to his voice."

Nobody else moved, even the normally sarcastic Cutter knew better than to challenge the deadly drill sergeant although he was snickering and pointing openly from a distance. Even drunk the Special Forces soldier could probably kill them all and wouldn't even remember it in the morning.

"Ya git dead! Thaswhatchu git! So stupid…Sho… fuckin' shtupid!" The man sobbed.

Freak and Spartan slowly guided and turned the drill sergeant back towards the barracks. Over his shoulder, Spartan called a single word out to Deadeye. "Ortega!" The fleet footed Apache cadet never said a word but broke ranks and took off at a sprint across the roads and lawn of the academy campus.

Spartan and Freak maneuvered the thick bodied drill sergeant through the barracks doors, the trio careening from wall to wall as they supported Hogg's bulk. It was quite a feat as Spartan, who was not small and Freak, who was like a walking, talking wall himself filled up every inch of available area. That fact alone, coupled with Sergeant Hogg's considerable mass made it a very crowded and painful knuckle scraping venture. When they arrived at Sergeant Hogg's room, the door was blessedly still standing wide open. Spartan kicked aside at least two dozen beer cans and a black wine bottle lay in their path to the sergeant's bunk. Obviously, the sergeant had been drinking ever since the loss of Band-Aid in an effort to drown his sorrows. As booze was a rare item in the post-apocalyptic world and judging by the massive amount of empty beer cans, the wine bottle, and the whiskey bottle in the warrior's clenched fist, not to mention the various spilled puddles of beer and liquor on the floor, the sergeant had probably spent every penny and favor that he had and then some to obtain such a vast collection.

Crowded to a point of immobility, Spartan held the man's whiskey bottle and allowed Freak to muscle the sergeant's bulk onto his bunk. Stepping off to the side, Spartan looked around the room and he noted a large variety of weapon types strategically placed for easy accessibility in an emergency. Even in a drunken stupor, the drill sergeant had had enough sense to stay to his routine and not remove the weapons from where they could be accessible.

Nurse Ortega rounded the corner at a run followed by Drill Sergeants Surfer and Boomer. Deadeye was nowhere to be seen and Spartan assumed that he had returned to the formation after completing his assignment. Reaching into her black medical bag, the Hispanic nurse produced a small flashlight and quickly began to check the unconscious drill sergeant's pupils. Shaking her head to the heavens and muttering a curse aloud in Spanish, she placed the flashlight between her teeth and reaching back into her black medical bag producing an enormous syringe. She motioned to the drill sergeants to hold Sergeant Hogg's arms. Then she hiked up her white skirt above her knees, kicked off her shoes and stood up on the bunk straddling the drunken warrior. Dropping down and placing her knees on either side of the Sergeant's abdomen on the bed, she placed the syringe vertically above the man's chest and quickly pulled open the man's dress green uniform top with her free hand.

Spartan and Freak decided this was the time to leave and turned as one for the door. Glancing over his shoulder Spartan saw the nurse with the syringe in her right hand high above her head. As if sensing the cadet's retreat, she allowed the flashlight to fall from her mouth, striking the quasi-unconscious Sergeant in the middle of the forehead with an audible thunk and called out to them over her shoulder.

"Boys!" The nurse called "I need you to hold his legs. When I give him this adrenaline shot, he is going to thrash violently for approximately sixty seconds. We have to hold him down to prevent him from hurting himself."

Spartan and Freak both looked at each other, unsure of what to do.

"Que chingados!!! He has alcohol poisoning! Either I give him the fucking shot and we hold him down or he dies! Now hold his goddamn legs like I said pendejos!" She shouted.

So stunned were the cadets to hear the normally passive nurse yelling and cursing at them in her native tongue that they ran back to the bunk, each grabbing a leg on the drill sergeant and holding it down to the bed with all their might. Without another word, the nurse plunged the six-inch-long needle into the Drill Instructor's chest and injected the contents of this syringe directly into the sergeant's heart. At first nothing happened. To Spartan, the drill sergeant seemed to be barely breathing which was no real surprise since he was dead drunk, and the pretty Hispanic nurse had just harpooned his heart. Then the first tremors came, subtle but strong across Sergeant Hogg's muscles. The man's fingers open and closed and his green sock covered feet rocked side to side and the Sergeant's eyes flew open before rolling up into his head. Fifteen seconds later, the adrenaline-charged sergeant bucked from side to side, veins straining to burst from his skin.

Sergeant Boomer lost a grip on one arm and was subsequently smashed in the ear and jaw by Hogg's flailing arm. The unintentional blow knocked him backward and onto the floor with a crunch of aluminum cans and rattling the big black man's eyes in their sockets. Seeing the drill sergeant go down in a heap; Freak wrapped both of his massive arms around the sergeant's legs just below the knees.

"I got this bro! Help up Top. Sergeant Boomer's down!"

Hogg's thick thrashing arm wove dangerously close to Nurse Ortega's head, trying to grab a hold of anything that it could. Spartan dove for it and was greeted with a forearm smash to his lip that immediately had him seeing stars. Shaking off the blow, Spartan re-secured the arm to the bed with all his might. He knew his lip was split because he tasted the coppery blood, but he held on doggedly. Approximately sixty seconds later, the seizure came to an end and the drill sergeant stopped swinging about. Everyone slowly and cautiously let go and the nurse climbed down off the bunk. Silently, she slipped her shoes back on and finger combed her now wild brown hair back into some semblance of order.

Spartan looked around the room. Sergeant Surfer was helping Sergeant Boomer back to his feet. Catching Freak's eye, Spartan jerked his head towards the door discreetly. Freak nodded, the bald dome of his head catching the room's light and reflection. No one said a word as the boys exited. Everyone knew grief. That demon was an old acquaintance that had visited them all at one time or another and probably would again. Unfortunately, he tended to stay longer during some visits than others, making the impact of his torturous stay that much more agonizing. Grief and Sergeant Hogg had been having a few cold brews and emotional pretzels together all night long and this day looked like it could be a long one.

Spartan quietly shut the metal door to the drill sergeant's barracks behind them and walked in silence across the polished marble floors. Spartan's lip throbbed and a gentle touch of his tongue indicated that one of his front teeth was a little loose. First Freak, then Spartan exited the barracks building falling silently back into formation. All the other cadets were silent, eyes front, standing at the position of attention. Walking behind his Alpha team, Spartan saw why. Drill Sergeant Havoc stood engaged in conversation with Cutter from Echo team. The boys' sneer had resumed and the occasional glance towards Alpha team left little to guess what the two were discussing.

Several minutes passed before Drill Sergeant Havoc walked to the front of the platoon. Standing directly in front of Corporal Spartan, he reached up a hand and examined the split lip.

"Looks like you could use a few stitches Corporal. Do you need medical attention at this time cadet?"

The word *cadet* was annunciated very clearly and was intended as a demeaning term coming from Sergeant Havoc rather than identifying him by his rank of Corporal. In his eyes, Alpha team was not nearly in his league. The contempt that he had for Hogg and his team as well as most cadets at the Apocalypse Academy was palpable. They were children, not soldiers. Spartan steeled his reserve and decided to not give the ass–munch the pleasure of seeing his discomfort.

"Drill Sergeant, permission to speak, Drill Sergeant!" he hollered.

"Granted." Sergeant Havoc said. He was going to enjoy hearing the boy request first aid for such a minor injury.

"Drill sergeant, I've had worse pain sitting and waiting for a dry MRE turd to pop out of my ass! Sergeant Hogg taught me to adapt to pain just fine drill sergeant! I can take it! Thank you for your concern though drill sergeant!"

The response infuriated the drill sergeant. He did not come out and say it in words, so much as let the banner of his eyes display his thoughts like an accountant's tickertape. They seem to bore cold fury into Spartan's forehead. Spartan knew he would pay for his remark. Insulting or disrespectful conduct in front of a drill sergeant always had consequences. Somehow, someway Spartan would pay for being a smartass and he was certain that it would not be pleasant.

"March the platoon over to the graveyard corporal. Just before the Dante course on the right side of the road. Follow the worn path." Sergeant Havoc said. "We can and will talk about the *virtues* of Sergeant Hogg at another time."

"Yes, drill sergeant. Platoon; right face! Single column; forward march."

The march down the river's edge and up onto the hill was quiet and uneventful, but Spartan could not help but feel that his survival was now a whole lot more complicated. Sergeant Hogg was down and maybe out. Sergeant Boomer had been incapacitated by his own man and Sergeant Havoc clearly, if silently, hated him. It was less than a banner day for the cadre of the Apocalypse Academy.

"Great" he thought to himself as his boots methodically marched in time with the other cadets. *"Just fuckin' great. Just couldn't keep your mouth shut could you genius?"*

As they arrived at the graveyard, the rain began to fall again in thick gray lines splattering the muddy puddles with fresh water nonstop. An open field surrounded by a high chain-link fence stood empty except for a freshly erected flagpole and four even fresher piles of black grave dirt that piled high next to the newly dug graves. Hanging from the flagpole was the blue on black flag of the Apocalypse Academy. As the wind whipped a deluge of falling water side to side, the flag would snap open revealing two flags: the red, white and blue of the classic American flag and the white AA symbol on a blue background for the Apocalypse Academy beneath it. Each gust of wind cast a fresh wave of cold-water droplets over the assembled cadets.

Beneath the flagpole sat four full-size caskets. Each contained the remains of a cadet, regardless of how much or more correctly; how little was recovered from each person. The caskets represented the end of that person sorrow for the world that had been lost in the plague of the HUNGER virus. Spartan silently wondered when his time would come for a similar ceremony.

Colonel Slade stood before the assembled cadets as he had done thrice before. The falling rain ran from his uniform, tumbling over and around ribbons in rivulets before puddling on the ground around his highly shined shoes. If the rain bothered him in the least, he never acknowledged it. The platoon was reformed as both Bravo and Delta team joined Alpha, Charlie and Echo teams that were already in formation. Mud splatters across their dress blue uniforms, as well as on their hands and faces indicated that they had just completed preparing the fallen cadet's final places of rest. If any tears had fallen, they were hidden beneath the cold misery of autumn's sorrow and by the incessant downpour.

Off to one side stood the assembled drill sergeant, including a very ragged but conscious Sergeant Hogg with Nurse Ortega standing directly beside him. A huge shiner shone upon Sergeant Boomer's left eye, swelling it almost completely shut beneath the brim of his round brown hat. Sergeant's Stone, Surfer and Havoc all stood at attention; eyes staring straight ahead at nothing but seeing every movement around them. As the Colonel began to speak; he had to almost shout over the din of falling rain to be heard.

"Today God's tears fall from the sky to parallel our own tears that fall from our eyes and hearts. We have had the privileged of knowing these fine people and now we have the unfortunate duty of laying them to rest as the first heroes here at the Apocalypse Academy."

As if on cue, lightning flashed in the distance and a deep rumbling thunder rolled across the field, its vibration shaking the internals of every cadet. It was almost as if God was saying *"Pay attention boys and girls. This is important."*

The Colonel continued.

"As I have said before, in every war there are casualties. There are men and women; no scratch that, *brave* men and women that were willing to lay down their lives for the protection of their brethren in arms, their loved ones and their countries. In this war, we fight not only to prevent death from occurring to ourselves, our teammates or our loved ones, but also to prevent the eternal undeath that accompanies that ending through the infectious contagion of a "Z"."

"So it is that the heroes laid out before you had chosen to die. Though young, they displayed courage far beyond their years by the selfless actions that they each took, and in the end, they faced their deaths proudly and fearlessly. Though each person died in a different manner, they all displayed the spirit and honor that being trained as a cadet and member of the Apocalypse Academy has come to symbolize. I can only hope and pray that when each of our individual times come and we face the specter of death headlong, in whichever form he or she may take; that we each have the courage to look at that specter deep into its black, soulless eyes and spit directly into its face in these cadet's memory. Then may we all pass into eternity, bearing the Lord's grace and a smile upon our lips."

"In final prayer, Lord please grant the souls of Cadet Meatball, Cadet Knight, Cadet Rooster and Corpsman Band-Aid the peace and grace of your eternal blessing as we inter them forever into this hallowed ground. Amen."

As if to punctuate the senior officer's words, lightning again splashed across the sky dividing into a twenty-split fork; illuminating the gray sky to a brilliant white and making the falling rain seem prismatic for the briefest of seconds. Thunder rumbled less than a second later as the sound raced along the ground to catch up with the light. Through it all, the Colonel never blinked, never twitched and never said a word. As the last echo of thunder faded into the distance, Spartan thought he heard another amen come from the Colonel, but he would never be sure.

"Platoon!" Came the hollered command of Drill Sergeant Stone. "Present arms!"

As one the cadets all threw up their best salutes, holding their fingers rigidly together with the tips meeting the outer edge of their beret just above their brows. From an unseen speaker system, the soulful sound of Taps reverberated. The bugler was slow and strong and clear with each note reminding the cadets that they were ultimately only human and that in a world full of "Zs", making mistakes equivocated to being dead. Spartan noted that a soft sob came from Dancer who stood directly next to him. This tough girl clearly still had a tender heart.

Off to the right side of the formation, the five Drill Instructors shouldered M-16 A2 rifles. Colonel Slade executed a left face maneuver then strode purposefully over to the drill sergeants' position and took an additional M-16 that Nurse Ortega had been holding down at her side. Together they brought their weapons up to their shoulders, and the Colonel barked orders as the last sounds of Taps faded into the hissing plops of the falling rain.

"Ready!"

All weapons came to present arms in front of the sergeants, the nurse and the Colonel.

"Aim!"

The M-16s were hoisted to shoulder level, barrels pointed to the sky at a forty-five-degree angle.

"Fire!"

The seven rifles fired as one, echoing through the rain and sending the souls of the departed cadets onwards to heaven. Twice more the sequence was repeated as the honor guard fired off the customary twenty-one-gun salute to their fallen comrades-in-arms. When it was finished, the Colonel handed the smoking rifle back to the nurse and resumed his place in front of the formation.

"Though this day has been indelibly etched onto our souls, today is not the end of all that we will face. Through these trials and tribulations, no matter how painful, you are stronger and more mentally capable of enduring what the post-apocalyptic world has to offer. As we have seen, it's not pretty but it is reality. With exception of the funeral detail, you are all dismissed back to the barracks for the remainder of the day. May God bless you all."

"Alpha team stand fast!" Spartan called down the line. None of his team moved.

"Sir!" Spartan called to the Colonel as he slowly walked towards the congregation of drill sergeants. The officer had to turn, looking at the corporal over one rain-soaked shoulder.

"Sir, Alpha team is requesting to assist in the burial detail, Sir!"

Interest piqued, the Colonel looked Spartan directly in the eye, searching for any sign of motivation. "Why would you do that Corporal? These men were not from your squad. There is no need for you to put your people through this."

"Sir, I very respectfully disagree Sir! We are all humans. There's not that many of us left as far as we know. In addition, though our team designator may vary, we are all part of the inaugural cadets for the Apocalypse Academy! Lastly Sir, it is our way of showing respect to the fallen and even more so to their surviving teammates. Call them what you will Sir. They were cadets, survivors, code names, tag names, insults, misfits but most of all; they were humans. In the end, we called them friends and as a friend this is the right thing to do, Sir!"

The Colonel nodded ever so slightly, a smile tugging at the corner of his lips for the first time since the world spanning orphans had come to the Apocalypse Academy. The falling rain quickly hid the emotion before anyone could verify it was there. "At least one team has a leader." the Colonel said aloud.

"Permission granted Corporal!" And the Colonel turned to walk away. Three steps later however he was greeted by calls from Bravo, Charlie and Delta teams, all requesting to help the burial detail. It seemed Spartan's leadership was infectious.

Lotus Jane looked over at Cutter, her Echo team leader. Her thoughts went to the brave Corpsman that had saved her life when her own team had abandoned her. The icy rain was making her broken arm ache. As she remembered the tragedy, her cast which was wrapped in translucent plastic wrap to prevent the rain from getting in and softening the plaster, itched maddeningly.

"Cutter?" She said softly.

Cutter continued to walk away, never bothering to look back or to even acknowledge Jane's call. Orc and Skull walked right beside him, with Savage walking one step behind. None of them seemed interested in what she had to say nor what the other cadets were doing back at the graveside. Lotus Jane ran up and grabbed Cutter's arm to get his attention.

"Ain't ya gonna help 'em?" She asked to his back. "Seems like everybody else is pitching in. Shouldn't we, ya know, show respect too?"

Cutter wheeled around, slapping Jane's hand away from his arm so hard that it left a stinging handprint across her forearm and stared at her hard in the face through the downpour of rain.

"Let's get this straight. Two of them cadets are dead because your stupid fucking ass fell crossing over a simple obstacle. They tried to be heroes and rescue the damsel in distress and got what they deserved. You heard the Colonel. The only hero out here is a dead hero. You only feel guilty because they died for your worthless ass? Well, that's your problem bitch. We're going back to the barracks to get dry."

The blond team leader turned and began angrily stomping through the rain-soaked mud, heading back to the academy.

After about twenty paces Cutter stopped and turned back around to face the girl. Raising his voice above the wind and the rain, he shouted at her.

"If they would have done what I did and left your sorry, broken ass behind then the medic and that stupid chicken kid would still be alive, and we would only need to be dropping dirt down onto what was left of you! At least the medic had value. What are you good for? So, unless you're in a real big hurry to join them under the dirt, I suggest that you fall in line! Besides, they weren't on my team anyway. Why should I care about them? If you're not an Echo; and you're not part of Cutter's Cutthroats, then you might as well be dead anyway."

Tears fell from Jane's eyes, but she knew Cutter well enough to know that he would kill her as soon as look at her if she openly rebelled against him. Instead, just as she had in the pre "Z" world with her father, she just let whatever happened happen and wished for a pill or a needle to make all her fears and pain go away afterward.

"That's what I thought. Dumb bitch…" Cutter said as Jane obediently stepped back into line and Echo team turned as one, leaving the muddy burial ground behind. Waiting until the rest of the cadets had walked by them; Cutter grabbed Jane by her broken arm squeezing painfully and maliciously whispered into her ear.

"If you ever challenge my authority again in front of anyone or grab me when I haven't given you permission to do so, then I will cut your head from your body and scrimshaw my name onto your bleached-out skull!" He hissed.

Jane shuddered against the pain and the threat. She was certain that Cutter would do it, so she just nodded and silently bore the pain.

"Let's go! We're out of here!" Cutter called to the rest of Echo team and turned around, leaving the burial detail behind him. Glancing back over her shoulder Jane noticed the Asian boy from Alpha team, holding a shovel and watching her through the rain with his mouth slightly agape. As she slowly walked away, he raised his hand in greeting, as if to say, *"I am here."* She turned her head quickly away hoping that Cutter had not noticed the kind act. She could only imagine his anger if someone else started paying attention to her.

As she walked with Echo team, she wondered how much the boy had seen to make him act so kindly to her. She had never even met the boy, other than seeing him in formation yet he seemed to be willing to accept her as she was. It was all so confusing. She had never been treated with kindness in her entire life. She continued to think about it all the way back to the barracks, hoping the whole time that Cutter did not see the tears that fell from her eyes.

Chapter Fourteen
Replacements

One of the simplest rules in war, especially in the post-apocalyptic world was that there were always orphans to be found. Since the Apocalypse Academy had been founded, one of its principal missions besides establishing a Command Post or CP, had been to collect orphans in the various towns and cities that the patrols passed through. The patrols would then deliver the orphans safely to the hallowed halls of the Apocalypse Academy for training and development of their survival skills. While this did not exactly replace the nurturing breast milk bond of a mother and the ball catching skills taught by a father, it did at least give the orphans a chance to survive in the abyss that had become the modern world with both purpose and stability.

Bravo teams' replacement came in the form of a black haired, black eyed girl who reminded Spartan of Deadeye, at least superficially. She had the same wiry build and the same razor-edged look to her eyes. She seemed constantly ready to bolt off somewhere. As the first morning of physical training together with the new recruits demonstrated, she could run like the wind and did not seem to get tired. In a five-mile run, she easily smoked eighty percent of the platoon, outrunning even skilled runners like Charlie team's Cadet Popcorn and Delta team's Cadet Jive; both of whom could outrun almost everyone else except the truly talented runners like Deadeye, Dragon and Lightning. Her codename seemed to fit her, because as she raced along, her long black hair fanned out loosely behind her, flapping like a raven's wing in the breeze. As such, she was promptly called "Raven."

Cadet Knight of Delta team was replaced by a child that was something of an enigma. Codenamed "Skunk", the caramel skinned boy was of mixed parentage. His kinky black hair was cut short, but he also had a stripe of white that ran right down the middle of his scalp. Nurse Ortega called this a "fear lock", saying that if someone was scared bad enough, their hair could turn white. Spartan did not know if it was fear or genetics that had altered the boy's hair but found that he could easily believe in either justification as being plausible.

It was not until the first run together; the same run-in which Raven so excelled; that Spartan and the rest of the platoon came to understand Skunk's codename in its fullest capacity. The boy seemed to be built of bodily gas. From the first stride through the end of the run, Skunk was floating air biscuits that abused everyone else's sense of smell. Finally, Sergeant Stone had moved Skunk to the rear of the formation when a stream of the peculiarly potent gas had hit Cadet Deacon and left him retching on the side of the road.

Lastly, Rooster's billet on Charlie team was filled by a short, tanned boy codenamed "Taco". The codename was not hard to figure out as the boy's south Texas drawl was so bad that he sounded like a commercial from a pre "Z" fast food chain. He and his team leader; Cowboy, immediately hit it off. The two were immediately almost inseparable, always talking and smiling. Probably remembering Texas and pre "Z" life. While Spartan was glad for Cowboy to have the camaraderie, it was exceptionally dangerous because familiarity could cause dependence on each other. The Drill sergeants had said so from day one. If one of them was bitten or died, it would not surprise anyone if the other did also; trying to save the other. That was why regular names had been discarded and codenames developed in the first place. To help eliminate identity in a world that almost guaranteed a brutal or gruesome death.

No one knew if Corpsman Band-Aid had been replaced. Medical personnel were rare, but it was feasible that someone else could be trained by Nurse Ortega or, since the pacification of her husband, perhaps another doctor could be found if one happened to have survived "Z" night, managed to evade the undead, find the Academy and volunteered to take care of God knows how many teenagers out of the goodness of his heart.

"Yeah right..." Spartan said out loud to no one in particular. "As if that's gonna happen."

As evening set in, the cadets were given some free time. The post Dante weapon selection was to occur the next day, so teams were encouraged to strategize over what type of weaponry they wanted. Each cadet would be allowed to select a rifle and a handgun of choice. Despite Echo team's injury to Lotus Jane, they had been the fastest team to complete the Dante obstacle course without a "Z" induced casualty. They would select first, followed by Alpha team, Charlie team then Bravo and finally Delta team.

Spartan thought this was somewhat unfair since, the pathetic actions of Echo team had resulted in not one but two deaths when they had abandoned Lotus Jane. But he was reminded conveniently by Drill Sergeant Havoc that those deaths were voluntary actions from outside of the course participants and that Echo team could not be faulted for unsolicited deaths or other people's poor choices. Though it pissed Spartan off from a moral point of view, he could not argue the logic. You could not control someone else's unpredictable actions, but that still seemed to be wrong to benefit from it.

Hearing footsteps behind him on the quarter deck, Spartan turned around. Standing before him was Drill Sergeant Hogg. The sergeant's round campaign hat was pulled low down towards his eyebrows and he spoke quietly.

"Corporal Spartan; walk with me."

It was not a request. Spartan immediately fell into step behind the sergeant as they marched across the academy lawn.

The drill sergeant walked at a pace that was just shy of double time. He did not speak, nor did he look at Spartan. He just walked and walked and walked. Mile after mile passed with the only sounds being the rhythmic pounding of the drill sergeant and his own boots striking the pavement. The academy buildings fell away and the cleared off kill zone that surrounded the Apocalypse Academy's core buildings began to be replaced by trees and shrubberies. In the pre-night grayness, the woods appeared to be blacker than the green that Spartan knew them to be.

Stopping before a locked cattle gate at a nearby side road, Sergeant Hogg produced a key from his dog tag chain around his neck and opened both the lock and the gate. Reaching down into his cargo pocket, the drill sergeant produced a small but powerful flashlight.

"Got yours?" He rumbled at Spartan, the first spoken words in at least ten miles.

"Yes, drill sergeant." Came Spartan's quick reply.

Some things were standard issue and were always expected to be carried, a military grade halogen flashlight, a full canteen of water, water purification tablets and the cadet's personal knife selection. This provided the opportunity to survive in most emergencies, even if food was unavailable for several days. This was especially pragmatic since the HUNGER plague had caused many situational evacuations and sudden flight from the undead had become the norm. A man could live without food for several days. Without water, you were doomed to die a very thirsty death in a very short amount of time. You'd become weak, then delirious. In the new world, this often led to suicidal walks out among the living dead, or worse you would collapse as your organ's shutdown, one by one, and you would just dry out, not much different in the end from a Husk "Z".

Sergeant Hogg led the way down the dirt pathway in the dark. Overhanging trees blotted out the remainder of twilight as they walked forward. A wooden sign came into view ahead on the left. Spartan read it silently. "*Survival Run*" and suddenly he knew exactly where he was. The last time he had been here had been on the training day when every cadet had been forced to try to "kill" each other by stalking each other through the woods with paint filled training knives. On that day, Spartan had been "killed" in the final rounds through treachery and teamwork between Echo team's tandem of Cutter and Lotus Jane. Cutter had been the aggressor, distracting his opponents, while Jane had struck from concealment, "killing" several cadets.

On that same day, Spartan had learned just how deadly efficient his own teammate Deadeye was when he had slashed Lotus Jane's throat from behind and then scalped the

Echo team's leader. The cold look on the Native American's face as he shrieked out his war cry still gave Spartan chills, even in memory.

So why had Hogg brought him out here? Did he intend to try to kill Spartan, perhaps due to the embarrassment of the day's events prior to the funeral? Spartan hoped like hell that was not the case as the sword of Leonidas stood propped in its sheath back at the barracks and all he was carrying to defend himself was his survival knife. He really doubted that even the eight-inch-long blade would be sufficient if he was forced to fight the deadly drill sergeant.

"Inside." Was all Hogg said to Spartan with a slight nod of his head towards the dark house.

A quick million thoughts flew through Spartan's head. The house was dark and isolated. If the burly drill sergeant had gone insane and was going to try to kill him, then this would surely be the perfect place for such a heinous act to occur. The Academy leadership would just think his blood was from a paint knife if they didn't find a body. Spartan's paranoia surged as he stepped cautiously into the entry area of the old home. His left hand held the powerful flashlight, while his right hand rested lightly on the handle of his combat knife; his thumb ever-so-gently easing open the Velcro retention strap. Slowly scanning the living room ahead with the flashlight, he simultaneously listened for the footsteps coming up behind him that would let him know that his sergeant was coming to kill him. A bead of sweat slowly wound down his forehead, across his temple and further down the line between his jaw and ear, before slithering to hide under the neckline of his academy jumpsuits' collar.

When he heard the door close behind him with a muffled thud and click, he felt the muscles of his body tense in a conditioned response to the combat adrenaline that his heart was now pumping throughout his system. Everything was hypersensitive. His eyesight, his hearing and even his sense of smell all seemed to be in overdrive. His palms were wet and sweaty in anticipation of the fight for his life that he was certain was coming at any second. As expected, the heavy footfalls of the drill sergeant began to approach from behind him. Closer… Closer… Spartan strained to hear if the sergeant was taking out a weapon. He listened for the rustle of clothing or the muffled scrape of a gun coming out of the leather holster. Immediately, he made up his mind to dart right, through the living room and into the adjacent open doorway when the time came. He didn't know what was through that doorway, but he needed to create distance between the two of them in order to assess the threat. Hogg was an insanely powerful, highly trained drill sergeant and could be armed with anything from a knife to a gun or even a grenade against him.

So, when Sergeant Hogg walked right past him and plopped down in a nearby overstuffed chair, Spartan could only watch in confusion. Maybe his weapon of choice was staged over there under a cushion or on the floor? Spartan tensed even more as the burly man reached over towards a coffee table; certain that he was going for the weapon that his mind was insuring him was there. Instead, the drill sergeant reached over the nearby coffee table to the bookcase and picked up a box of stick matches, striking one on the rough side of the box. Soft yellow light flared from the tiny flame as if battling for space with the two halogen flashlights. Then the match was applied three times to the separate wicks of jarred candles that sat upon the table. As the candlelight rose in the room, the drill sergeant clicked off his flashlight. Confused, Spartan did the same.

Flickering light and shadows crossed the room. Standing where he was, he could see that the room contained twin recliners, each blue green and white striped. Old lace doilies hung across the arms of the sofa, a touch that Spartan did not attribute to the hard-assed drill sergeant. A single picture hung upon the wall above the flickering candles. It was a picture of Sergeant Hogg and a pretty, if shy smiling, blond haired woman standing arm in arm inside of a church. She wore an elaborate wedding gown and he, a tuxedo. Ornate stained glass and a large crucifix could be seen behind them. Spartan's head swam as the realization struck him that he was standing in the drill Instructor's home pre-Z night.

"My wife, Catherine." The drill sergeant said following Spartan's gaze. Gently he shifted himself in his large chair, placing a cushion behind his back for comfort. The dilapidated chair creaked under his bulk. Reaching over the edge of the chair, the drill sergeant slowly opened the red plastic cooler that had been hidden up to now. Pulling out a blue and silver can, the big sergeant popped the top with a hiss and tipped the can up; not stopping until he had drunk every ounce of the can's contents. Reaching back into the cooler, he removed two more cans and shut the lid. He indicated to Spartan that he should sit on the sofa.

"Might want to re-secure your knife first. It seems like the velcro came loose. I would hate for you to lose it in the cushions. I used to lose my television remote control like that all the time." The sergeant said opening another beer. Spartan suddenly felt very foolish. Why had he thought that the drill sergeant would mean him any harm? Re-securing the velcro on the knife's handle, he sheepishly sat down with a nod.

"Hell boy, if'n I was gonna kill you, I wouldn't do it in my own house. Catherine would've been furious if I got all that blood on her furniture. Here!" The drill sergeant said, and Spartan barely had time to register the blue and silver can flying through the air before his reflexes reached up and snatched it on the downward arc. It was ice cold. By the candlelight he read the label. "Busch." It was a pre-Z night beer which was hard to come by in these current hard times. Spartan was suddenly very confused. Then the drill sergeant began to speak, slowly, almost dreamily, talking of the past.

"I've been in the military longer than you've been alive. I've seen the marvels of the pre-apocalyptic world, people going out into space, computers that can do anything, vaccines for almost every disease and then again, I've seen the horrors of the apocalypse. I soldiered for the good old US of A for twenty plus years, across four continents and in seven wars, conflicts, peacekeeping missions and performed covert operations in foreign countries that I couldn't even pronounce the names of."

"Through it all, I always came home to my girl, Catherine. I'd be gone for months on end but when I came back, she would greet me like a new lover, running up and jumpin' into my arms. She was the best thing that ever happened in my life. Sad thing was we never got around to havin' kids. Always talked about it, just never happened, mostly 'cause I was servin' good 'ol Uncle Sam in some crummy third world country. I should have been here more with her. It was on "Z" night, when whichever dumb fucker loosed the HUNGER plague on the world, I was pulled from active duty and ordered to assume a new post for the Illinois

National Guard as their commanding First Sergeant. I was in charge of all of the noncommissioned soldiers in the state, somewhere around four hundred thousand troops in all. Madison, Wisconsin and Chicago, Illinois both fell within hours because they didn't know what they were fightin'. I lost over fifty thousand troops in the first week. Quadruple that in a month. We were ordered to withdraw from both major cities and to assist the Wisconsin National Guard in Milwaukee, where the outbreak was just beginning to show. They firebombed Chicago to hell two days later, burning it to the ground worse than the fires of the early 1900s. Madison was the same four days later, reduced to a pile of smoldering ash by thermobaric bombing."

The drill sergeant paused to take a large slug of his beer then continued.

"The eggheads thought that they could contain the infection by burning it out. They were wrong. The dead just got up, charred and toasty, looking like burnt campfire marshmallows, and walked to the nearest town where they started eating people all over again. It didn't take long for Milwaukee to fall either. We were slaughtered at every turn. We evac'd the fuck out and regrouped at Fort McCoy, a small camp in central Wisconsin. When the first signs of "Zs" started cropping up across the cornfields I was issued direct orders to assist a small unit that was going north to the neighboring city of Sparta. We were to provide a six-man team for fire support, ordered to help evacuate any uninfected personnel and get back out. Supposedly only a couple of dozen "Z's" had been seen in the area up to that point. It should have been an easy Op."

Sergeant Hogg again paused to drain the remainder of the can, placing it beside its brother on the coffee table and opened the top of yet another.

"That beers' gonna get warm. It's not as good if it does." He said to Spartan. Spartan took the hint and opened the can's tab and took a small sip. The burn of the carbonation took him by surprise, but overall, it wasn't bad. Sergeant Hogg continued.

"We set out at daybreak. For some reason the dead fucks do not move as well in the chilly air. One Humvee and a deuce and a half truck to evacuate an entire town. When we got to Sparta, the roads were empty. No civilians, no police, no "Zs". We began a house to house sweep of the dead town, but each house brought the same results. Empty, undisturbed. In some cases, dinner was still sitting on the tables. We methodically swept everything. Houses… stores… schools. No one was to be found anywhere. The only sound in the air was an occasional gust of wind or the rarer bird fluttering off when we startled it from its perch."

"Finally, we came to the northern end of the town, the last building for us to check. It was St. Vincent the Savior's church. Methodist place, I think. The church had been barricaded, complete with barbed wire and boarded windows. Light shone from behind the stained-glass and silhouettes could be seen within. One of my scouts approached and listened at the doors. It only took him a few seconds to report back that the inhabitants of the church all appeared to be undead. I asked for another recon for confirmation. This one was to enter through the bell tower and visually confirm the first scout's opinion from a high and hopefully safe position. Sergeant Delacruz, a half Mexican, half Texan, climbed up the side of the tower and made the confirmation in simple terms after a brief foray down into the church."

"The fuckers are all dead First Sergeant."

Rather than leave three to four hundred undead behind us, the decision was made to burn the church to the ground with white phosphorus. I can still smell the burning flesh to this day when the wind catches me just right. Probably just in my memories but to me it's as real as you are."

"As the fire roared, that's when I heard someone screaming off in the distance. Pulling off my gas mask and hood, I listened hard trying to determine which direction I had heard the scream from. In the wind I heard it again. It was the anguished scream of an angry and terrified child. I guess I have always been sensitive about kids. Catherine and I had always talked about having a large family one day. We used to laugh about how fun it would be to have half a dozen kids running every which way. Our plan had been to have our first child during my tenth year in the military and one every other year after that until we had six in total. Unfortunately, my year ten in the Army took me overseas. Year twenty crept up even faster and exploded into the HUNGER virus infection. It was also the year that Catherine died in an infected outbreak at a shopping mall, looking for new shoes. How fuckin' unfair is that?"

Sergeant Hogg stopped speaking long enough to kill his third beer entirely. Before he resumed speaking, he popped the tops on two more beers from the cooler and set them on the coffee table next to the three dead can soldiers that were already resting there.

"Hearing that child screaming I guess broke something inside of me. I ran away from the tactical response team with no backup towards the sound of terror that I had heard. The farther from the church barbecue that I got, the louder the screaming became. Down the road I ran, almost a mile before I finally found where the child was crying out from. It was a farmhouse straight out of a painting, complete with a white picket fence in the morning light. There were "Zs" everywhere and screams of anger being raged continually from within the home."

"I don't know how many undead I killed getting in the front door. A dozen or so would be a fair enough guess. But my kill number was nothing compared to the boy who stood on the second-floor landing of the house. He had fought like he was possessed. The downed corpses of eight undead lay at his feet. Another dozen were scattered around the interior of the house. Unfortunately, there were about thirty or so more of the pus bags still trying to reach the boy as he stood on the landing with a bat in one hand and the cord of his mother's iron in the other, screeching out his pain, his horror and his suffering into the face of every undead that approached. An empty shotgun lay on the floor at his feet. Blood splattered the walls in an archaic pattern of stippled scarlet rain. Little rivulets of decayed blood could be seen dripping down the stairs like an obscene parody of a "*Slinky*" toy."

"Fortunately for me, my fire team was loyal and opted to follow my insane run into the country roads of Wisconsin or I probably would've been dead. As I fought my way up the stairs, and the boy fought on from above, I knew that we were in trouble. "Zs" poured in through the house. I killed, reloaded and killed some more. I was determined to keep this child alive. I don't know if that was due to mine and

Catherine's dreams of family or if it was the fact that the kid had a serious warrior spirit that appealed to me, but I knew I couldn't let this bloody; gore encrusted child die that day."

"I could hear the fire team chopping through the walking corpses outside with automatic weapons. Unlike me, they had no intent of charging headlong into a farmhouse of death. When they finally burst through the front door in a standard wall flood tactic, I was screaming just like the boy. Bodies lay all around me. I had run out of ammunition and had eliminated the last ten "Z's" up close and personal with my knife."

"As the team swept through the downstairs, I heard a door slam up above. Looking up, I saw the brave kid grappling with an adult female "Z" in a nightgown and a fluffy pink bathrobe."

"Hang on kid, I'm coming!" I yelled; my voice hoarse as hell from screamin' at the dead. Instead, the boy fell to the ground beneath the gnashing Reaper. Frantically I climbed over the bodies of the dead that I had killed and up the stairs that were slick with gore, desperately trying to get to the boy in time. Getting to the top of the stairs, I was just in time to see the boy beneath the biting pink terrycloth blob shove his butcher knife straight into the creature's open mouth and scramble its virus rotten brain from the inside."

"I grabbed the pink robed "Z" from behind and heaved its body over the balcony railing to the floor below. The boy's screaming had stopped, and he lay on the floor, eyes wide open, knife still in his hand, covered in blood. Looking deep into his eyes, I wondered if maybe the last fight had taken him over the edge of sanity. I talked and talked, letting the boy know that I was a soldier and that I was here to help.

Taking the knife away gently, I did a cursory check for bites or scratches. To be honest, I really couldn't tell if he had been bitten at all. There was so much gore all over the kid; I thought that even if he hadn't been bitten, the chances of infection due to exposure to all that diseased blood were pretty high."

"It didn't matter. I wrapped my arms around the brave boy and held his trembling body, trying to stabilize him through strength of will more than anything else. When my team arrived on the balcony, we knew we had to evac the boy asap, even though he was soaked in blood and we couldn't confirm if the child had been infected or not. I made the decision then, that if the boy turned into a "Z" then it would be me and *only* me that put him down. The boy's warrior spirit deserved pacification from a senior noncommissioned officer if it had to happen at all."

"Reassembling my gas mask, I put it back on. I remember Corporal Zimmerman, my second-in-command, talking to me as we transported the boy onto the waiting military vehicle and prepared to leave the now dead town of Sparta, Wisconsin."

"I heard he put up a hell of a fight."

"That description doesn't even justify what this kid did. Twenty-six confirmed "Zs" on his own as well as the pacification of his own father, mother and three siblings. This kid is hard as nails. He will probably make a good team leader one day if he survives this."

Spartan thought he understood finally. Taking a drink of the quasi-warm beer that he had been holding, he asked a question for the first time in the conversation.

"That boy that you saved was Band-Aid, wasn't it?"

The drill sergeant gave him a look that was somewhere in between "you're dumber than a dirt sandwich" and "it's obvious you're mentally retarded". Spartan decided to shut up before he said something else that was obviously stupid. Irritation flared behind the pain in the Sergeant's eyes at hearing the dead child's name. Spartan instantly regretted having brought the dead cadet up.

"Are ya just dense?" The Sergeant said in a matter-of-fact tone that was more of a statement than a question. "Band-Aid was from Atlanta Georgia at the CDC compound. Didn't ya hear the Colonel say that at his wake? Shit! I was talking about the day I found you boy. *You*!" Then grumbled "moron" in a disgusted voice under his breath as if an afterthought and punctuated it with a deep bass beer belch.

Spartan could hardly believe the bombshell that had just been dropped on him. Hard as Sergeant Hogg was, he was the one who had saved him?

"I almost lost you on the way back to the base. Shock shut your brain down, dropping your vital signs to a cunt hair above being dead yourself. Instead, you went into a coma while your brain tried to process and deal with everything it had seen and done. We took bets back and forth that you would or wouldn't survive. In fact, thirty days into your little nap, I actually had 20 to 1 odds that you wouldn't pull through. But I always knew you would. When you actually woke up a couple of days later, I made a shitload of money. It was a good thing too because I was down to just a couple of bottles of booze and a dozen cans of brew left in my personal stash. At least I did have the stuff that's made in a little battlefield hooch to back up my supplies if I desperately needed it."

Reaching over with one massive hand, the Sergeant grabbed the fourth beer and allowed it to flow smoothly down his throat. This apparently opened an invitation to drink the fifth one as well because before the man spoke again, he'd killed off half of it.

"Since I found you, I got to pick your codename when we got back to the Apocalypse Academy. It was actually really easy for me to choose. A tough ass warrior child from a city in Wisconsin actually called Sparta? Are you kidding me? You were born a Spartan through and through. You never quit fighting until the fight was won. Losing was never an option for you and as your actions have shown thus far through the Academy's inaugural class; you are a natural born leader. It was really kind of ironic that the martial weapon you chose was the sword utilized by another Spartan against overwhelming odds and almost certain death. At least they didn't have to worry about a single bite turning them into a walking corpse; just fighting against the entire Persian army. Lucky fuckers! I'll take them odds any day instead of dealing with this virus shit that I can't just reach out and kill with my bare hands!"

The fifth can soldier died in his hand as the Drill sergeant toasted the ancient warriors of Thermopylae and tipped up the silver blue can, draining its contents. Tossing the can over his shoulder, where it landed in the dark with a tin clatter, the Drill sergeant reached into the cooler and pulled out two more cans.

"'Nother?" He asked with the faintest slur dragging the end of his words.

Understanding the drinking obligation that was implied in return for all this information; Spartan said "sure" and drained his own first can. The replacement was flying through the air before the empty made it down from his lips. Spartan smoothly snatched the can and popped the top before taking a long sip. Cold beer tasted better than warm, so he wouldn't let this one gets hot like he had the last one. The first tingle of alcohol induced loose tongue came out as he quietly asked how Sergeant Hogg had found Band-Aid. The drill sergeant's face was clearly sad as he remembered his adopted son. He spoke slowly, as if translating the memories from his alcohol infused mind more than actually remembering the time.

"When the HUNGER virus blew up and the people of the world began seeing their friends and relatives first being eaten like Sunday brunch, then rising from the dead themselves to share in the human buffet, a lot of people turned to the various specialty organizations for safety and assistance. Many people foolishly believed in a cure and thousands turned to the CDC for a miracle if they had been already infected. Cries for help and pleas for assistance fell upon deaf ears or so the civilians thought. In reality, there was literally nothing to be done for them. No miracle cure, no redemption, no saving them. Anyone bitten was doomed to die. The HUNGER virus had a one hundred percent mortality rate."

"When the Pope, seated inside the Vatican, proclaimed the undead plague had been caused by the joint efforts and research of the World Health Organization from Europe and the Centers for Disease Control in the United States, literally all hell broke loose. Instantly the man created animosity between the religious sectors of the world and the state-run governments. To make matters worse, the Pope proclaimed that the centers that oversaw trying to find a cure for humanity's survival were in reality run by agents of the devil himself and that the search for cures were all faked. That they were nothing more than false propaganda from governments that wanted nothing more than to create a new form of population control."

Overnight, the cries for help became screams of hatred and anger. Despite denials by the governments of all seven continents, frustration and fury rained down on every office in both agencies as well as every hospital, doctor's office, emergency clinic and medical personnel like ambulance drivers and firemen. The civilian population murdered doctors, scientists, technicians and secretaries. Anyone associated with the health organizations, even the fuckin' janitors and daycare workers were targeted by the mobs. It was the insanity of mass hysteria in its purest form."

"My unit was mobilized after a high profiled scientist was forced to barricade himself inside of his office at the CDC compound in Atlanta to prevent his own execution. Can you guess what these crazy fuckin' ignorant ass bastards were using for their preferential method of execution?"

Spartan shook his head.

"Fuckin' "Z" bites! Here we are, afraid of the undead plague so let's go out and fuckin' make more of them while we get revenge! Stupid rat bastards!"

Beer number six disappeared at the end of the Sergeant's tirade. Spartan was certain that the reason he drank the beer so fast because the Drill sergeant was risking dehydration from all the spit that flew from his mouth while he screamed out his outrage and needed to keep his fluid levels up. With a new beer in hand (Spartan had not noticed him reach into the cooler to retrieve one) the Drill sergeant continued a little more calmly.

"By the time we were boots on the ground twelve hours later, the infection had flooded through the crowds and the scientist that we were risking our asses for was found hanging from his own necktie in the corporate toilet; a suicide note at his feet. The poor bastard was so scared of being turned into one of the undead that even though he knew we were coming to get him, he offed himself. His note was short and simple. It read, *"I swear, it's not my fault!"*

"So, with mission failure hanging over our heads, we began maneuvering to the roof for chopper extraction. Running and shooting we made it to the roof, a bloody trail of permanently dead "Z's" behind us. The time of extraction came and went. No bird came. We tried communications. There was no answer. After a quick huddle we knew that we were on our own and that we needed to un-ass the CDC building quickly most Riki-tic or we were dead meat."

"So, back down the stairs we ran, coming out onto the second floor of the main building. Passing the receptionist and break room areas, we rounded the corner, and my Corporal ran headfirst into the teeth of the two daycare workers. As they ripped off chunks of his face and neck, we scooped up his M4 and shot both the teachers through the head. The Corporal stood back up completely nonchalant, unfastened his web gear and handed it to the Private standing next to him. Then he pulled out his .45, stuck it into his mouth and ate a bullet. Just like that. No goodbyes, no bitchin'. Just acceptance. When my time comes, I hope to hell that I have the balls to be that brave."

"We lost two more team members to the undead brats that the HUNGER virus had infected after their teachers had chowed down on them. I don't really know why but the three of us took the time to pacify every one of the little bastards. When we were done, the only sound in the room came from a television set that was playing a looped Sesame Street video of an annoying, furry little red monster going "La LaLaLaLa" and singing a song. I shot that little bastard too."

"Searching around quickly, we gathered all of the fallen troops' ammunition and put all of them down for good, then prepared to move out. That's when I heard the crying coming from the cabinet below the television that I had shot. Jerking open the door; I found this teenage boy bent over into a space that no adult could ever achieve. His knees had been covered with four Power Ranger Band-aids as well as the bridge of his nose. Various scrapes were also visible at different spots on his body where he had contorted himself into the cabinet. I coaxed him out, wiped away his snot ropes and asked the kid why he had so many goddamned band-aids. The boy replied that he had fallen down the stairs going out to help Ms. Jenny (I suppose that was one of the teachers we shot in the face) with the children on the playground. When he'd come back upstairs to bandage the cuts, the mob had assaulted the front of the building and he had hidden himself in the cabinet. Having seen the news and hearing the sounds and screams of terror in the classroom, he had stayed hidden in there for almost two days with no food or water."

"I don't know why but I dumped all of my excess shit outta my rucksack and stuffed any items that I would need later into my side cargo pockets. The boy could not stand up on his own because his legs were so cramped up from his long stay inside the cabinet. So, I picked him up and threw him over my shoulders in a fireman's carry. Again, I don't know why I did that. Maybe it was because Catherine and I had always talked about kids and their innate purity and innocence. But take him I did. We evac'd on foot, hauling ass out of Atlanta. We avoided firefights with the undead where we could, conserving ammo and preferring retreat as a defense was our standard tactic. By nightfall we decided to hole up in an old yellow abandoned school bus, with still ten miles to go until we reached the edge of town. Taking individual watches, I fed the kid a Milky Way bar to take the edge off of his hunger and then I tried to rest. Morning came and both of my teammates had chosen to try to make a food run into a Quick Mart that we had seen back down the road. I couldn't blame 'em. We had not been prepared for an extended land operation, and we needed food. I stayed behind to feed the kid another candy bar and make sure that he got some water to fight dehydration. Twenty minutes later I heard an insane amount of screaming and gunfire. My guys had drawn an enormous pack of Reapers to them by searching for food and were now boxed in on all sides with no less than fifty of the freshly walking dead surrounding them."

"Shoving the teenager down into a seat, I raided the soldiers ruck sacks from where they left them on the bus. I took two boxes of 5.56 ammunition, two full canteens of water and one unopened MRE. The ammunition I put into my weapon, topping off all my magazines and the remaining rounds I dumped into my cargo pocket. The MRE and canteen I stuffed into one of the other backpacks that I had emptied and shoved it to the kid with instructions for him to put it on. Strapping the pack securely over his shoulders, I quickly re-shouldered the other pack and moved silently out of the bus and into an alleyway across the street, motioning for the boy to do the same. From the darkness of the alley, I looked back down the road at my men. Although they had been untouched so far, they were surrounded and had to be close to running out of ammunition. I did the only humane thing I could do. Lining up the red dot sight on the soldier standing to the right, I shot him through the ear, exploding his brains across the sidewalk. He never felt a thing. The second soldier heard the shot over the moans of the dead and quickly pinpointed my location. We locked eyes for the briefest of seconds, then he gave me a thumbs-up gesture just before the "Z's" grabbed him. I shot him through the eye. At least they would never come back. I figured that I owed them that much."

"Then I turned and ran, dragging Band-Aid with me until I was out of the Atlanta suburbs. For two weeks that kid and I traveled the country, dodging "Zs" and living off the land. We drank at rivers and streams and caught fish or birds to eat. We crossed Georgia, Alabama and Tennessee like that. Finally, we met up with the Colonel and a small squad as they drove out Interstate 55 through Missouri and into Illinois. We've been here ever since."

The old house was silent for a time as Sergeant Hogg made a point of not speaking until beers number seven and eight had followed along the path of their fallen teammates. With an almost magical ease that would have made Harry Houdini proud, the burly sergeant produced two more cans of cold beer from the cooler. This was immediately followed by a disappointed sigh of resentment.

"Last two. Guess I should at least offer to share. Given the way you've drank the first two, I stand a fair chance of you refusing anyway." Holding up the silver and blue can,

Sergeant Hogg offered one half of his remaining beer stock to Spartan. Spartan politely waved the drink away which brought a rare smile to the drill sergeant's face. As he popped the first can open, Sergeant Hogg resumed speaking.

"The kid wasn't like you Spartan. He was a seriously clumsy teenager. Awkward like he hadn't had a chance to grow and balance himself on his oversized feet. He had no weapon skills, no athleticism. He was much more likely to injure himself than a "Z" if he ever drew a blade. What the kid did have was brains. He was so smart that he probably would have been an honest to God doctor in the pre—Z world. Instead, he became an impromptu Corpsman, learning everything that he could from Ortega and treating basic non -"Z" related injuries like sprains, lacerations and the occasional bullet wound. He also really believed in what we are trying to do here at the Apocalypse Academy. Band-Aid donated many hours to individual cadets to help them pass first aid training and make sure that they honestly learned the skills needed to treat a battlefield injury whether it was a knife wound, shock or even something as simple as a toothache."

"Lotus Jane was one of those subpar cadets that he had tutored. I think maybe that by having physical contact with the girl during the making of splints, and practicing sealing sucking chest wounds, somewhere in there Band-Aid became enamored with the girl. I tried to tell him that the cadets of Echo team were a bad lot and that association with them was likely to end badly. Like a fox hangin' out with a pack of huntin' dogs. For a while he seemed to believe me and pulled back from Jane and the rest. Then came the night that he had gone to tutor her in the setting of dislocated limbs and digits. The training is normally an hour to an hour and a half depending on the length of time needed to master the practical applications. This *training* was *nine* hours long from 1900 hrs. until 0400 the next morning. When he finally drug his bedraggled body through the door I was sitting there waiting. I thought that I deserved an explanation. I took one look at the disheveled hair, the flushed face and the silly shit-eatin' grin and I didn't need to ask anything else. It was all written right there on his face."

Spartan spoke the obvious conclusion to the story. "She slept with him?"

"Yeah, two days before she ran the Dante course. I don't know the reason, maybe a relationship truly developed or maybe she was using her body as leverage for her team's sake. Get the corpsman on your side and they will help take care of you. It's an old adage. The three most important people in the military units are the cook, the corpsman and the quartermaster. Anyway, he was smitten with her. When I packed up his belongings after he was killed, I found poems that he had written to her invoking her beauty, her soul and his love. He never had the chance to give them to her because two days later, he died saving her. What a fucking waste. I lost a surrogate son to a trashy little gutter whore. The team lost its best Corpsman to love or to pussy, whichever way you choose to see it."

Cans eight and nine topped the stacked rows on the coffee table forming a small pyramid of silver and blue aluminum.

"So, by now you're wondering why I brought you way the hell out here to my pre-rising home, told you about your own past, and tossed back a few cold ones with ya. It's really pretty simple. You saved my life. I owed you a debt for your actions and I knew that you had not reassembled your own memories since the shock of the night when I found you standing over a pile of "Z's" including your own family. I wanted you to know the truth of your internal strength and the willingness and determination to persevere against overwhelming odds. Those are the traits of a great leader."

"To date here at the Academy, you've shown strength of character, moral turpitude, physical prowess and tactical thinking. You have yet to learn to prepare for the potential death, the need for pacification of one of your own teammates and the brutality that it will bring to your own soul. You got a small sample of this with Rooster, and I must admit that seeing that brave little bastard change will be something I will never forget as well. Tough as nails that kid was. But ask yourself if you could have swung that sword down on Freak or Dancer's neck. Because in this screwed up world, where death is almost a certainty, then you may have to do just that to one or all of the members of your team."

As Spartan sat pondering Hogg's words, the big sergeant stood up and walked unsteadily into the next room. Spartan could hear him rummaging through cabinets, plates and glasses clanking and a soft swearing coming from the immediate proximity. A moment later Sergeant Hogg returned carrying a bottle of clear liquid in one hand and two shot glasses in the palm of his other. A smile split his face giving the sergeant a seriously malicious look of pleasure.

"I knew it was here somewhere." He said holding up a clear bottle and shaking its liquid content slightly. "If you're gonna be a Greek warrior of legend, then you should drink what they drank."

Setting the shot glasses between them on the coffee table, he poured both glasses full to the rim. Taking one glass, Sergeant Hogg indicated that Spartan should do the same.

Holding up the glass in front of the candles flame, the Drill Instructor offered up a toast.

"To the brave warriors of the past. May their lessons never be forgotten, and their heroic deeds live on forever… in you."

The burly drill sergeant threw the shot of liquor into his mouth and sucked a short breath in through his teeth as the liquid burned down his throat. Spartan knew he was expected to return the toasting, and carefully smelled the liquor in his glass. It smelled like black licorice. Following the sergeant's example, he threw the liquid into his throat. Instantly the initial flavor of licorice was overwhelmed by the blaze of molten fire that burned all the way to his stomach. His eyes became blurry as they watered in a reflexive response and he gasped for breath.

Seeing the teen's reaction, Sergeant Hogg began to guffaw aloud in a deep baritone; his laughter echoing through the emptiness of the house. Immediately he poured them both another shot.

"It's called Ouzo. It tastes like licorice, burns like hell in a bottle. It's a pre-rising liquor. It's your turn to toast." He said happily.

Spartan thought about the burned flesh in his throat and looked at the glass uncertainly. Feeling bound he took up the tiny glass anyways, holding it up in front the candlelight.

"To the fallen warriors of the Apocalypse Academy: Cadets Rooster, Knight, Meatball and Corpsman Band-Aid. May their memories never be forgotten and may their bravery inspire those men and women yet to come."

Sergeant Hogg hollered a "Hooah!" In an old army tradition and whipped back to shot, then slammed the empty glass upside down on the table. Spartan followed suit. The liquor didn't burn quite as bad the second time and there was a strange but not unpleasant warmth that had begun to flow through his veins. And so, it went, sergeant and cadet toasting back and forth until the bottle and glasses sat empty and the walls of the room had begun to bend, spin and twist in Spartan's vision.

"I know what you need!" The drill sergeant roared, slapping his hands on his own thighs before standing up and immediately lurching sideways into a wall; his shoulder punching a hole the size of a basketball into the sheet rock. Spartan heard the big man muttering under his breath.

"Awwww fuck a duck! Cathrine's gonna kill me." Then he staggered off into another room. When he returned, he had a leather-bound hardback book in his hand. He tossed it to Spartan in the air. Spartan could barely coordinate his hands to catch the book and his hands closed on empty space while the flying book slammed into his chest. Picking it up he looked at the blue leather cover with silver embossed lettering. At first, he thought it was written in a foreign language, but as his mind swam through the numbing liquor that was fogging it, the words began to take shape.

"The Odyssey." He read carefully. "Thank you."

"Yesshur, stories 'bout heroes. Ancient Greeks, traveling around fighting monsters and finding their way home again. Maybe one day there will be a book like that about you. Spartan; the "Z" warrior's journey into hell!" The drill sergeant fell into a fit of laughter, as did Spartan. As the laughter died off, Sergeant Hogg somberly spoke.

"Thanks for saving me kid."

Spartan nodded then replied with a curt smile. "Thanks for saving me first." Then almost as an afterthought Spartan added "I wish we could've saved the rest."

"Me too kid, me too. But you know what they say: Wish in one hand and shit in the other and see which one fills up first! You just make sure that we don't have to sit here and drink to the memories of any of your teammates on Alpha team. The rest will have to take care themselves."

Chapter Fifteen
Weapons and Armor

Spartan did not recall getting back to the barracks; he awoke on his dorm floor to the early morning sunlight burning through his eyes and a mysterious, masochistic dwarf hammering on a forge within his skull. PT that morning was brutal. Every exercise movement brought a new and unique pain to his frontal lobe. The standard five mile run which was normally not even a challenge suddenly became torture in the purest sense of the word. Looking over at Sergeant Hogg, Spartan could see no indication or sign of discomfort on the big man's face. Finishing the obligatory physical training, Spartan returned to his room, showered and walked silently with Freak down to the Chow Hall. Eating toast seemed to help the roller coaster in his belly and before long he began to feel at least marginally better. To his team's credit, no one said a word nor asked him any questions about his impromptu meeting with the drill sergeant.

Returning from chow, the teams formed up on the quarter deck and waited for the 0800 arrival of whichever drill sergeant was working with them that day. The rain that had consistently fallen over the past week had subsided, leaving puddles across the ground and diamond brilliant sunshine in its wake. The latter seem to be a new form of punishment to Spartan as the reflected rays seared into his optical nerves, but he stoically endured it.

Sergeant Boomer walked out of the barracks doors a few moments later and addressed the formation.

"Good morning sweethearts; I trust you all got your beauty sleep?"

Spartan couldn't be sure, but he was relatively certain that the question, while it had been asked to all, had been intended for him.

"Yes, drill sergeant!" Came the platoon response.

"Good! Today we will be marching back to where you received your martial weapons. However, we will not be needing those particular tools this morning. We will be going to the armory to select firearms for your teams. As you were advised before you entered the Dante obstacle course, your teams will be allowed to select their weapons by order of time completion from that course. That means Echo team will select first, followed by Alpha, Charlie, Bravo and finally Delta team. You are encouraged to select wisely based on the dynamics of your particular team. You'll need to select one side arm and one long gun.

In addition, once you've all selected your weapons, your teams will be fitted for the first -generation zombie attack protection armor. It is better known by the acronym "ZAP". You go into the field; this armor will hopefully help to save your life as you face the various forms of undead and even some of the more wicked surviving members of humanity. While it is not impregnable, it is superior to clothing or leather such as jackets, or even police and military grade body armors.

Lastly, you will be expected to announce a team name for your squad. For instance, "the Delta team Titans" or the "Bravo team warriors." This team name will be a part of your identifying signature which will be immortalized on the plaque in the lobby of the barracks following your graduation in two weeks. The name is your choice. There is no right or wrong but remember once chosen it is permanent."

"Team Freak–a–zoid!" Freak murmured with a smirk next to Spartan. A short snort came out of Spartan's nose as he held back his laughter.

"Any questions cadets?" No one seemed to have any. Sergeant Boomer then ordered the platoon forward in single file by order of their times on the Dante. Cutter preened like a peacock as he led his Echo team at the front of the platoon. As if Spartan needed something else besides Sergeant Hogg's liquor to give him a headache, having to watch that bastard really made his head throb. Down the road beside the river they marched, single file. One by one. No cadence, no formality. Just a route step enabling the cadets to walk at their own pace as long as they maintained the appropriate interval between each of them. Off to one side, a fluffy red squirrel chattered at them from a nearby tree, its body inverted upside down defying gravity as it held on to the trunk with its claws, head pointing towards the ground.

Spartan knew they had arrived when they crossed the fields where he and Techno had watched Dancer practice with her naginata by dawn's light and they saw the round topped building that had housed the sword of Leonidas until he had claimed it for his own. Up on the hill, he also saw Nurse Ortega's home and office beyond the weapons corral. Sergeant Boomer marched them straight past the martial weapons corral and further up the Hill before finally standing before a dome shaped concrete building. The formation stopped directly in front of the structure. A faded sign read U.S.A.N.G. off to one side of the paved road.

"Form up!" Came the order from the drill sergeant, and the individual teams reformed into a platoon structure standing at the position of attention.

"You will fall out by squad when called. Upon selecting your weapons, you will reassemble at the rear parking lot. When all of Delta team has formed back up, we will continue marching onto the firing range for target practice. Echo team; fall out."

Inside the armory, Drill Sergeant Stone waited for the incoming cadets. Cutter stepped forward and reported in, announcing his team's presence.

"Echo team reporting for weapons issue, Drill sergeant!"

"Very good cadet. Handguns are off in the left wing, long guns to the right. You are to select *one* of each. All items are carefully inventoried so taking more than the allotted amount could have dire consequences including expulsion from the academy. Fallout and make your selections. Once you've completed that task, you are to meet me in the rear the auditorium for armor fitting and reformation."

Hearing the drill sergeant conclude his speech, Cutter eagerly led his team into the side arms area. Cutter, who preferred blades, selected a Walther PPK pistol. The weapon was small enough to conceal, but deadly in the hands of a professional. In addition, it could be adapted with a silencer which was invaluable in the modern dead world. Orc was at the other end of the spectrum. He had selected a fifty caliber Desert Eagle. Strapping on the thigh holster, the gun had literally reached from his waist to his knee. Lotus Jane selected a small twenty-two caliber automatic pistol. Though her ego wanted a larger weapon, her broken arm wouldn't allow it to hold anything larger in a shooting stance, so she stayed small. Skull and Savage each selected nine-millimeter pistols of differing brand names. Skull based his selection solely on a skull that was emblazoned on the gun's handgrip. Having selected their handguns, they moved together over into the right wing to select the long arms.

Seeing Echo team moved to the rifles and shotguns, Drill Sergeant Boomer released Alpha team to the side arm section. Spartan moved several paces into the center of the room and motioned for his team to assemble around him. Quietly he spoke.

"If we are to function as a team, then I propose that we be interchangeable. We should decide on a make and model for a firearm so that our ammunition becomes interchangeable. I think with the long guns, we can be somewhat individual. What do you all think?"

Surprisingly, it was Techno that spoke first.

"What he says makes sense. If one of us runs out of ammunition, we can handoff spare magazines to each other for support. Whatever we select should be durable and not prone to firing problems. Also, I would say that ease of maintenance is important as well. We don't want something too complex to disassemble that we forget the order of how it goes back together or that are so fragile that Gargantua over there breaks off parts." The boy concluded with a sideways thumb pointed at Freak.

The enormous cadet replied after a moment of thought. "Revolvers are okay but they severely limit your ammunition before reloading, even with speed loaders. Mosta' the 'bangers back home either carry for style like an Uzi or Tech Nine or they carry for practicality. Most of the people I know prefer either the Glock or the Sig Sauer pistols. Glock was probably at the top of the list. It was functional and durable. Made outta plastic and shit."

Spartan looked at the big man quizzically. Reading his team leader's thoughts, Freak replied to the unspoken question.

"No, I never ran with a crew. My big brother was into thug life before he went into the Army and always hung out with the local gang. Everybody carried a piece. If you are around it long enough, you learn things, even if you never mean to."

Spartan nodded. He knew that Freak had said he was from the south side of Chicago and it really didn't matter anyway. The past was the past and most of what had happened back then was dead or undead now. He was just glad to have the cadet on his side.

"Deadeye? Dancer? Any thoughts on this?"

The Native American cadet spoke up. "I do not have much experience with firearms. My people preferred the traditional ways of hunting with bow and arrow or spear. Still, what Techno says makes sense. I am not fool enough to believe that I will never need a gun out in the world away from the Academy. I trust those of you with more experience to make a solid selection."

"Dance?"

"Personally, I prefer the Colt single action nineteen eleven semiautomatic pistol. For years it was the standard side arm of the United States military. It is a forty-five caliber, so it has strong stopping power, it is durable having withstood use in seven blinkin' separate wars and it's easy to field strip. The obvious upside, as Freak pointed out, is that replacement parts should be readily available due to the popularity of the pistol." Then as an afterthought Dancer added: "But, the need to carry locked and cocked can be dangerous."

If Dancer had stripped naked and begun singing show tunes from the Man of La Mancha, her team could not have been put into a more stunned position of awe and amazement. They all gawked at her, mouths hanging open, amazed at her knowledge of firearms.

"What?" She asked looking at her teammates confused.

Spartan managed to point and get out a "how?" question, indicating the racks of firearms and empty magazines.

Understanding struck the girl. "Oy, I'm a military brat remember. Mum and Dad are both bloody Military Intelligence, so I grew up on firing ranges. Dad taught me to shoot a pistol by the time I was eight. By the time I was twelve; I was entering shooting tournaments while the other girls were walking stages and swishing their bums in frilly little dress gowns like silly little prats. I would win marksman trophies; they would win pretty, little useless tiaras. Which do you suppose turned out to be more practical after Z night?"

"At sixteen, my friends got cars or jewels like rings or necklaces. I got a beautiful, brand-new, out-of-the-box Smith and Wesson, pink, pearl handled thirty-eight caliber revolver with my name engraved on the barrel. It was bloody beautiful. Besides my trusty ol' teddy bear that I had had since I was born, it was my favorite thing in the entire world. It's probably still sitting in the gun safe in my father's den next to his dozen or so other weapons and my Mum's three fifty-seven, which coincidentally was also a Smith & Wesson. My parents believed in buying American."

Spartan looked her dead in the eye. "We *really* need to talk more." He said with a wink.

"Okay, so we all concur. Glock or Sig Sauer based on what we discussed?"

Together they reviewed both selections. Although the Sig Sauer was dependable as a weapon, the Glock offered a larger variety of size variance to fit each of their hands. As a team they agreed on the forty-five caliber for stopping power. The male cadets all selected the model twenty-one pistols while Dancer took the smaller gripped model nineteen. Then they moved into the long arm area to select the team's rifles.

As they walked, Spartan decided that although it was against the rules, he and his team really needed to know more about each other's past to establish what they would be able to count on each other for in a time of crisis. Then almost as an afterthought, his mind flickered to Dancer; his brown eyed, sensitive little flag twirler, who was deadly with a naginata, an acrobat and apparently a gun fanatic.

Yes, they had much to talk about, even more now that Sergeant Hogg had filled him in on a few of his own memory gaps. He still didn't know who he really was but at least he knew where he was from and that his family was not wandering around idly gnawing on any living humans that happened to pass their way. According to his drill sergeant, he had seen to that in a very up close and personal way.

Choices of hunting rifles, shotguns, automatic weapons and sniper rifles lined a hundred racks around the room in every make, model, style, color and caliber. The weapons stood carefully placed in their own cataloged rack, cleaned, oiled and well cared for. As they walked up and down the aisles, the team quietly discussed the value of each weapon out in a field environment. Normal hunting rifles were generally heavier and longer than they wanted to carry, as were most hunting shotguns. The M-16 A2 was a possibility, as was the AK-47 assault rifle. Both had proven durability around the world and could be fitted with numerous accessories with minimal time and effort.

As a group, the team settled into a decision of three M4 assault rifles; a modernized combat rifle similar to the M-16 but significantly shorter in overall length. Each M4 was additionally fitted with an M203 grenade launcher and a red dot tactical sight above its rail. These rifles were handed to Deadeye and Techno with Spartan keeping one for himself as well. Dancer selected a Dragonov Russian sniper rifle. From an accuracy standpoint, it was effective out to a six of seven hundred yards. Many considered it to be a decent rifle type for long-range shooting, but not in the same class as say the American made Barrett.

That left only Freak. It was no surprise when the team unanimously selected him to be their resident heavy weapons expert. Initially, the muscular cadet had wanted a mini gun or an M-60 machine gun. At over three hundred rounds a minute, the ammunition needed would have to be carried by at least two extra team members; the same applied to the M-

60. Although Freak was strong, the extra belts of ammunition required a second man for hauling them around and feeding them into the gun. That was manpower that the small team could not afford applying. Instead, Freak settled for the Mossberg 590 Combat Shotgun. It was large enough to provide serious suppressing fire, yet portable enough that Freak would be able to easily carry the weapon and three extra belts of shells. They would decide who his assistant breach support man would be later. Whoever it was would get to carry two extra belts of specialized ammunition as well; to include frangible door breaching rounds and less than lethal rubber slugs and pellets. As they prepared to leave, Spartan walked back over and grabbed sixteen empty magazines for the M-4's. After all, the drill sergeants had not prohibited taking any extra magazines, only taking extra weapons. He gave four of the magazines each to Deadeye and Techno before securing his own four magazines into the cargo pockets of his jumpsuit. Having completed their selections, they walked towards the exit from the Armory as a team and towards the auditorium at the rear the building where they were expected to form back up.

Entering the auditorium, the team could see the fittings for the ZAP armor program taking place with Echo team. Cutter looked like he was an arrogant Princeling being fitted for battle by his squires while Orc seemed to be having significant difficulty in telling which was his left foot and which was his right. Moving to the opposite side of the auditorium, Alpha team began to be fitted as well with a series of individual technicians quickly assembling the armor around them. Spartan wondered where these men and women were housed. He had never seen any of them around the Apocalypse Academy. The male cadets were herded left, while Dancer was led off to the right by two female technicians.

The body plate and muscular enhancement and protection fittings for the ZAP armor began with a set of midnight blue, Kevlar woven plates of flexible plastic overlayed onto a titanium mesh chain mail that was worn as an under suit. The plastic Kevlar shell created an airtight seal to the armor while the chainmail created additional structural density against potential injury. Interwoven links connected plates of clear resin, Kevlar, and titanium over the top of the chain mail. Within the armor weave were dozens of micro-fine wires and remote sensors. Each wire led to a specific body area or bodily function and was attached to a micro sensor. The thicker Kevlar plates covered the chest, groin, buttocks, neck, back and leg areas while the chainmail providing hinged protection for the shoulder, elbow and knees. Additional elbow and knee pads allowed mobility as well as maximum protection. Military grade, mid-calf combat boots containing Kevlar shin guards, and steel toes and soles completed the lower half of the protective outfit. Sensor laden, Kevlar chain gloves with blue titanium knuckle guards protected the hands and a full faced helmet with a plastic-coated chain mail neck protector completed the ensemble. Wearing all of the protective gear, Spartan felt like the Tin Man from the Wizard of Oz.

Lumbering and off balanced; Spartan, Freak, Techno and Deadeye stood in a silent line waiting for Dancer to complete her fitting session with the two unknown female techs. She arrived ten minutes later, similarly, attired except where the chest pieces converged. The chest plates were cut at sharp angles to match their pectoral structure and her suit flexed smoothly, adapting to her natural curvature. Spartan thought that she even looked kind of sexy in a deadly, machinated sort of way.

As Echo team exited the building equipped in their blue-black ZAP armor, additional technicians stepped up to all five members of Alpha team, evaluating every fitting, joint, angle and wire. Apart from a few voiced concerns over Freak's massive biceps and the arm segment's pliability, the announcement came that they were "good to go."

"How the bloody hell am I supposed to fight "Z's" in this get up?" Dancer asked out loud. "I can barely walk like a drunken sot, much less fight or shoot."

As if in an unvoiced response, the technicians clipped their battery packs to the combat harnesses on the rear of the armor's Kevlar plating. Neon green LED lettering immediately began to scroll across the helmet's interior faceplate registering temperature, heartbeat, hydration, stress, battery power and targeting computer functions. Additional light bars energized the interior of the suit's display on the HUD to provide the minimal ambient light source necessary to support night vision within the armor.

"Try moving now." One of the technicians said to the group. "The micro servers implanted throughout the armor's plating in the chain mail should respond to the muscular stress that is placed upon them, effectively reacting to boost your strength, speed and stamina far above normal human levels."

Techno, his inherent geek curiosity piqued, was the first to move. His normal gait was slow. Movement within the unpowered armor had been physical hell for the boy. His own weight had been tough enough before he added thirty pounds of armor. Even though the teenager had lost a considerable amount of weight during his tenure at the Academy, he was still no physical marvel like Freak or

Spartan. As his muscles flexed to walk, the micro servers and sensors responded, amplifying his natural ability to move into something akin to an Olympic athlete's level. What started as a strained walk quickly evolved into a jog then into a full-fledged sprint across the auditorium. The Asian boy crossed the one hundred feet of the auditorium in scant seconds.

"Who-hoo!" He screamed as he started running laps maniacally around the gym, his team and the technicians, celebrating his newfound physical abilities.

"Holy Lord Almighty?!" Freak said out loud in absolute amazement. "If that Power Ranger wannabe suit gives Chunky the power to move like that, imagine what I can do?"

Walking over to a nearby technician, Freak grabbed the man from behind with a single hand by the rear of his belt. Exerting next to no effort, Freak lifted the man above his head with a grin inside of his helmet. His LED read "physical exertion .02%." Point oh two percent! This cat was easily two hundred pounds and yet Freak easily lifted him above his head without so much as breaking a sweat. Gently setting the man back on his feet, he patted the startled technician on the back and strutted back over to Spartan.

"Dawg, did you see that shit? I'm like Superman in this shit! Ain't nobody hitting a "Z" skull farther than me if I'm wearing this thing. This is some seriously bad ass tech! I wish my brother could'a seen it! He would've loved it!"

After all they had been through during the last three months; it was nice to hear a little good old-fashioned happiness in his team's voices. Freak sounded like a kid at Christmas that had just got his dream toy from Santa.

"Dancer, what about you? What can you do now that the armor's powered up?" He asked. Spartan could not see her face through the smoky ebony face shield, but he imagined the pretty brown eyes squinting in concentration, her lips slightly pursed. Then she exploded into action.

Martial arts stances flowed from one into the next as the British trained gymnast exhibited some of her father's combat training. The smoothness of the dynamic motions were accentuated by the blue–black glitter of the ZAP combat armor and the whooshing sound that the armor made as it snapped from position to position at the girl's command. Striking with the quickness of a coiled serpent, she snapped off a series of punches, elbows, front kicks and finally a spinning back kick that looked beautifully deadly before settling into a combat ready stance. Finishing her kata, Dancer back flipped into a landing beside Spartan. Turning to face her team leader she bowed formally and waited while Spartan returned the bow.

"I can feel everything." She said aloud. "It feels like I am almost wearing spandex. I hardly even know that it's there when it is powered on. There is no restriction of my movement, no binding in the joints. It's fantastic."

"Deadeye?"

The cadet didn't bother to answer, instead running for the three-foot-tall stage at the front of the auditorium. Halfway there he initiated the special feature that his armor possessed; a secret that the technician had shared only with him. Issuing a low verbal command, he leapt into the air.

"Stealth mode." He said in a near whisper that even the other suits communications systems could barely hear.

Immediately, the glitter and shine of the blue–black armor dulled to a flat, shine less color. Light no longer reflected off its surface, in fact the suit's carefully crafted angles seemed to draw shadow into it. In milliseconds, Deadeye was an unseen part of the stage's shadows and curtains.

Within the armor, Deadeye activated the infrared capabilities of the helmet. Heat signatures blossomed to life around the room as he registered everything from light bulbs to computer generated heat to human being body temperatures. He even noticed a rat hiding over in one corner of the auditorium behind a curtain. He could find anything lurking in the dark with this technology and kill it without them ever knowing that he was there.

Spartan felt a small chill run up his spine. Deadeye was almost supernaturally deadly in the dark *without* the armor's enhancements. With the armor's abilities, he definitely never wanted the boy coming after him for vengeance or with malicious intent. Looking to the stage he called Deadeye back to the formation through the communications link.

"I am already here." Came the response from five feet behind the team. Chatter immediately rumbled across the communications systems. No one had seen him leave the stage yet there he now stood behind them. It was almost eerie. The Native American deactivated his suits stealth mode and it instantly blinked back into existence, returning to the blue and black shine that matched the rest of his team's armors.

"What about you Spartan? What's your suit let you do?" Techno asked.

Spartan thought about it a moment then reached over and took a pencil from the technician's table. Placing it between his fingers, he grunted out loud as if straining and then broke the pencil in half. Everyone laughed knowing that the boy was clowning around and having some fun at their expense. Then, spinning on his heel Spartan took off at a sprint, easily doubling Techno's enhanced speed. Approaching the auditorium wall, he leapt ten feet into the air, ran three steps vertically, kicked off the wall and arced backward through the air before flipping to land exactly back where he started.

"It doesn't seem to do much." He said in answer to Techno's previous question and again the technicians and Alpha team all laughed.

Sensing that the physical demonstrations were done, Techno turned in his armored body to the technician who was inspecting the suits, comparing them to a hand-held computer readout.

"How long do the batteries last? What are they made of? How did you correlate the synaptic nerve response through the muscles and convey it to the enhanced neural stimulation core that must be housed in each suit's helmet? It is in the helmet right…?"

Seeing that the technician, who was surely a science geek of some magnitude, appeared alarmed in the face of a confrontation with the wizard of geekdom, Spartan interjected at the man's defense.

"Whoa! Slowdown Techno. You can give the guy an aneurysm with that many geekism's at one time. How about we settle a simple question like what is the length of time that the armor's batteries can last before they run down first? I promise, at the first chance you can sit down and talk geek–o–neze at length to these guys okay?"

Even with the ZAP armor on, Spartan could read the disappointment in the slump of his teammate's shoulders. It must be tough to want to know everything scientific at a moment's notice; to live in a science-fiction dream world hoping for the day when advances in science would all become reality and then when the day does finally come, you are told to wait just a little longer. His attention was drawn back by the technician's response.

"The batteries last approximately 12 hours." He replied, obviously glad to have avoided, at least temporarily, the mega–nerd trivia contest with Techno. "They last a little less based on extreme usage or adverse conditions such as long-distance running, climbing and possibly swimming. Thermal controls maintain the suit at seventy-four degrees despite current exterior temperatures. This is effective to two hundred degrees Fahrenheit above or below zero and it does not draw any more power. Heightened physical exertion, such as prolonged physical combat, will use the batteries up far more quickly; at least they did in the simulations that we've run so far. Each suit comes with a spare power supply, which are interchangeable so that you could share power supplies from suit to suit if needed in an emergency. The suits are also equipped with solar rechargeable capabilities which are slow to recharge, but good for emergency power." Then excusing himself quickly, the technician turned and walked away before Techno's verbal bombardment could begin again.

Seeing that his team was satisfied with the limited information and data obtained so far with the ZAP armor, Spartan spoke aloud.

"Alright guys, we have one more issue that we need to settle. The Drill sergeants instructed us to come up with a name for our team. Does anybody have any ideas?" Spartan asked. He would swear he could almost make out Freak's grin through his black faceplate. Spartan beat him to the punch. "One suggestion was team Freak–a–zoid. Does anybody have any others?"

No one spoke for a long time, and then Dancer broke the silence with the suggestion of her own.

"How about the Alpha Team Phalanx? It would fit with our team leader's codename and it is explicit in its ability to protect each other from harm. It was also the preeminent formation of the Spartan army."

Spartan could feel the blush rise inside of his helmet as he became embarrassed. He began to reply; to formulate an appreciative refusal but was cut short by the other team members.

"Spartan's phalanx! Sounds pretty bad ass to me Dawg!" Freak said.

"The Spartans of Greece were very much like my own tribe of Apaches. They were trained from childhood to be warriors and in their time, they were the most feared soldiers anywhere in the world for their prowess at arms, their superior armor and their fearlessness in the face of death. It's a fitting title for our team." Deadeye said and then added "unless of course you wish to call us the Apache Braves."

"Are you sure? I mean, this is permanent. It's gonna be engraved on the plaque at the Academy long after we're gone from here. I don't want any second thoughts or complaints later."

Techno was the last speak up. "Just try not to pit us up against three million Persians like the last guy to carry that sword did, will ya? Alive or undead ones; that's a lot of bad guys!"

"I will do my best." Spartan replied, a dry tone in his voice. Then together they all laughed, picked up their weapons and walked out to the formation where Echo team already stood. The issue was settled. Their team was named the Alpha Team Phalanx. Spartan hoped he could only live up to the honor of being chosen as the team leader for such a fine group of people.

Standing in formation with a group of armed maniacs like Echo team at his back for three hours was not Spartan's idea of high-quality entertainment. He found himself constantly glancing over his shoulder to make certain that the miscreants were not up to no good. Despite the fact that they all were wearing fully protective suits of body armor and the additional fact that Cutter's group currently had no ammunition, Spartan was having difficulty keeping his back to anyone who could be jovial when viewing other people's misfortune or that took pride in causing unnecessary pain.

Hell, the bastard had cheerfully abandoned Lotus Jane, their own teammate, due to a broken arm on the Dante course. They had all written her off like old garbage and went on to win the time trials yet they showed no remorse for the loss of life that they had caused. The fact that Rooster and Band-Aid had died saving their teammate was callously viewed as stupidity by them. Additionally, the fact that Drill sergeant Hogg had lost a surrogate son and was miserably grieving from the inside of a bottle or beer can every night was immaterial to their way of thinking. It was strictly survive or die in their book. Kill or be killed. Everything that the Echoes' did was cold and calculated. Spartan did not like them at all.

While Alpha team stood like professional soldiers in formation, Echo team engaged in jokes and laughter which Sergeant Havoc seem to conveniently ignore. Cat calls came from Savage and Orc about how Dancer's and Medusa's body armors fit their curves in all the right places. Cutter and Skull talked about life after the Academy and how it was a shame that some cadets "would never make it out of the training, and that the best thing to happen to the weak or sickly was for the walking dead to tear them open and feast on their intestines. At least then they served a purpose, even if it was only as a distraction while the rest of the team members got away."

Spartan could feel his own internal temperature rising within the body armor despite the computerized temperature control that the suit offered. How could anyone be so uncaring about human life knowing that the world was being overrun by the living dead? Just the thought of Echo team's mirth as they stood there was really pissing him off and he fought for control of his temper.

A fresh round of laughter came roaring from the ranks of Echo team. Listening; Spartan could tell that they had once again turned on one of their own for sport.

"Awwww, what's the matter Janie? You gotta itty-bitty bwoken widdle heart?" Cutter asked the girl in a baby's voice, the mocking tone emphasizing over and over each word.

"Maybe we should get your widdle heart a *Band-Aid.*" He said and began to roar with laughter accompanied by the other Echoes' accept Jane who was now audibly sobbing across the helmet's internal microphone.

"Yeah boss, but she'd have to get it out of the "Z's" stomach first!" Orc added.

"Maybe she could just replace her heart with Band-Aids. He won't need it anymore!" Skull said with his nasally voice.

"Maybe her next boyfriend should be codenamed like duct tape or superglue or maybe even stitches so that when the undead rip him apart, she can put him back together again! Obviously, a Band-Aid won't do it!" Savage called out and the Echoes' roared even louder at their disrespectful jokes showing that they were truly the type of low life's that enjoyed other people's pain and suffering.

Freak's hands flexed and un-flexed in anger, causing the plastic-coated chainmail to creak audibly. "Fuckers need to shut the hell up talking all that trash about the dead folks." Freak growled. "It ain't cool Dawg and it's really pissin' me off!"

Spartan had no doubt that Freak, without his ZAP armor, could probably have dismantled the four boys. With the armor that amplified his strength exponentially, at least tenfold, he might kill them all outright even if he didn't mean to.

"Stand down Freak." Spartan said softly into his helmet's built-in microphone. "It's not our fight. They will get theirs when the time is right. I promise you, but like you said back at the funerals; here and now is not the right time."

"When all of this shit is over Dawg, I'm gonna play the entire concert with the Blues Brothers all over 'em."

"I will make sure that all of Alpha team gets front row tickets to the show and a bucket of popcorn to boot." Spartan replied.

Hearing a fresh round of cat calls, Spartan glanced down the line at his team and saw that Dancer was out of formation. Quickly looking back, he saw that the girl was standing in front of a slump shouldered Lotus Jane. The girl's weapon and helmet now lay at her feet while deep, shuddering sobs wracked her body beneath the dark armor. Twin black rivers of mascara forked off from the corners of her eyes to run vertically down her cheeks until finally dripping away to the concrete below, dotting the ground with black blotches like a new wave Rorschach test.

Through his helmet's enhanced hearing, Spartan could hear Dancer trying to offer compassion to a girl that she did not know at all beyond her enrollment in the Apocalypse Academy and that she fully distrusted as a member of Echo team. Spartan could not help but be impressed.

It was then that Orc made a very, very poor life choice.

"Hey Missy," he called "I think I got a broken heart too. Do you think maybe you could fix it for me? Of course, we'd have to get you out of that armor first, and then you could kiss me all over and make it all better. I keep my heart right here!" He said, grabbing hold of his crotch with one hand and turning his head to laugh with the rest of Cutter's Cutthroats.

The words would've been enough by themselves, but Orc chose to punctuate the request by stepping forward and slapping Dancer on her armored buttocks and then laughing about it furiously with his team while he cupped her armored hip. In retrospect, later back at the barracks, Spartan would have sworn that Dancer's ZAP armor was capable of controlling the weather because the air around all of the cadets plunged forty degrees instantly; its ambient temperature matching the coldness racing through Dancer's martial arts trained brain and heart.

Reaching out with the speed of a viper, the girl locked her hand over Orc's, pinning it against her hip. Pivoting away while she maintained the hand clamp as she had learned in Aikido, Dancer opened a gap between herself and the Echo team letch. With a quick twist of her wrist, she inverted the boy's thick arm and torqued his elbow into a straight arm lock position. Twisting the boy's thumb, wrist and forearm upward, she maneuvered the teen to a point where he was standing on his tip toes to keep his arm from involuntarily shattering in multiple places. The only saving grace was that his armor prevented the over rotation and subsequent dislocations that would've been certain to occur as the girl savagely manipulated the joints.

When Dancer spoke, there was pure icy malice in her voice; her British accent was harsh and clear in its unquestionable hatred for the Echo team cadet.

"Do…!"

"Not…!"

"Ever…!"

"Touch…!"

"Me…!"

She screamed aloud and as she did, her armored boot shot forward in an upward kick directly to the boy's unguarded groin as if it were a physical punctuation to each deadly word. Already on his tip toes from her arm lock and unable to do anything more than absorb the blows, Orc squealed in pain as Dancer's armored boot drove him upward, crushing his sensitive areas against Kevlar chain mail and armor plating. With the fifth successive kick, she released the arm bar and allowed the boy to crash down onto the ground face first. Immediately, he curled almost double into a fetal position, his hands grabbing for his mangled man parts. Spinning around, Dancer faced off with the remainder of Echo team.

"Any of you other bloody prats wanna touch me too? Anyone else got something smart to say? C'mon you wankers! Give it your best shot! Here I am!"

Cutter held up both hands in a position of submission. "Not me babe. You're one crazy British bitch!" He said, "Nice moves though. You ever want a slot on Echo team, you just let me know. Maybe we will trade you for the ball-less wonder you just left lying there." He said indicating Orc with a nod of his head and a smile.

"I would rather die first you pigs!" She said, and then turned back to Lotus Jane. "You don't have to take their shit just because you're a girl!" Then she turned and walked back to her spot in the Alpha team line just as Drill sergeant Havoc rounded the corner and looked down at the now retching Echo team member on the ground. Apparently, sympathy was not an Echo team trait because the Drill sergeant looked down at the injured teenager and then back up at Cutter. The team leader just shrugged noncommittally, and Havoc kept walking figuring that whatever the problem was, the cadets seemed to have resolved it amongst themselves.

Spartan, Freak, Techno and Deadeye were all thankful for the full opaque face shields built into their helmets. At least Dancer would not be able to see the look of horror on her teammate's faces. Fighting "Z's" was bad enough but having your 'nads crushed by karate kicks from powered body armor was horrifying beyond words. No one spoke in either rank of cadets. Echo team's joviality was gone; eliminated with the savagery that they had just observed. The only sound came from Orc as he continued to lay on the ground emitting a high-pitched whining moan and the sound of him vomiting into his own helmet.

"See?" Spartan said aloud to Freak in an amused, conspiratorial tone. "I told you that they would get theirs when the time was right."

Charlie, Bravo and Delta teams all completed their weapon selection and armor fittings. Apparently, although Sergeant

Stone had been standing near the front of the formation, he had also conveniently failed to notice the beat down that Dancer had delivered to Cadet Orc or he also chose to ignore it. Sometimes a little *in ranks discipline* was much more effective than the verbal rantings and occasional head slaps that the drill sergeants could deliver. Nurse Ortega had been summoned and with the help of Drill Sergeant Havoc had lifted the prostrate boy onto her golf cart amidst a wail of agony and departed the area for treatment. How could you treat that particular injury, Spartan had no clue or any inclination to find out, but he didn't pity the boy. He had it coming. Once the teams were fully reassembled, with the exception of Cadet Orc, Drill sergeant Boomer addressed the cadets.

"You all now have weapons and armor. Together with your knowledge, training and hopefully a healthy dose of common sense you have the tools to survive in this world. You all need to understand something. Although the staff here at the Apocalypse Academy is teaching you the proper applications of all the various facets of survival, they are just like any other tool that you could own. If you do not use them, then they will become rusty and eventually worthless. From now on, where you go, your weapons go. All of them. Your armor will become your second skin. You will wear it everywhere except dress formations or when otherwise required to wear specific clothing such as PT gear. For the remainder of this week, we will be at the firing range. You will learn to shoot, clean your weapons, move in a dynamic fashion and develop deadly team battle tactics against the undead and the living. Are there any questions?"

Spartan heard movement behind him.

"Yes, Cadet Cowboy."

"Drill sergeant, I get why we need tactics fer the dead, but why do we need them 'gainst the living? Ain't we all supposed to be fightin' and survivin' and all, to help the other living folks survive too? Seems jus' plain dumb to be learnin' to kill each other when the "Zs" seem to be doing that just fine all on their own."

"The time will come cadet; you will see that there are different types of evil in this world. "Zs" are only one of the many types that you will come to know. It is better for you to know the enemies that you may face in advance and how to deal with them than for you to be caught unaware later."

"Yeah," Spartan thought. *"Just take a good long look at Echo team and you knew that there were malicious, twisted people worse than the rest of the survivors out there. There had to be. People like them who got their rocks off by hurting others, by being sexually aggressive or by stealing things that they had no business ever owning. If there were people out there worse than the Echo team malcontents, then Spartan was glad to soak up all of the knowledge of their strengths and weaknesses and to master the training to deal with the unknown."*

Range week went by without incident. The cadets were taught the importance of weapons cleaning and maintenance, until they could break their individual weapons into their various components and reassembled them accurately in less than sixty seconds. Even the Echo team members seemed to focus on the skill, perhaps innately understanding the need for their weapons functionality when they were eventually released into the field alone.

The M-4's were popular choices for many of the cadets. Collective groups were assembled at various foxhole firing points along the range. Targets were set up from twenty-five meters for weapon sighting or zeroing as it was known and out to three hundred meters for long distance accuracy. In addition, those individuals with M203 grenade launchers attached to the weapons were given a brief class and five practice rounds with the "Bloop guns."

At some point during the training, Techno, who had been struggling all morning long just to zero his weapon, had engaged in conversation with Drill Sergeant Boomer. If Spartan had to guess, it was probably in reference to aerodynamics of the ammunition or the airspeed velocity as compared with resistance when sighting a target judging by the hand movements that the boy was making. That was Techno's style. Geek a topic out before you could recognize and fully appreciate the cool aspects that it had like the fiery explosions or the ability to blow "Zs" into dog food sized chunks.

Whatever the conversation was, late in the afternoon Spartan saw Techno exiting the range with Sergeant Boomer, leaving his M-4 lying on a biped beside the foxhole. Stranger still was the fact that neither the cadet nor the drill sergeant had advised Spartan where they were going. As a team leader, he was expected to provide accountability for his team's whereabouts. At least he knew that Tech had left with the Drill sergeant. For now, that would have to be enough if someone asked.

Further down the range, Spartan could make out a group of cadets standing around Drill Sergeant Havoc, obviously involved in deep conversation. This group consisted of the sniper hopefuls and consisted of one team member from each team selected by each team leader. Spartan's selection had been simple. Dancer could outshoot all of them without even really trying, so she was the obvious choice for Alpha team. Bravo team had sent Cadet Lightning, their fleet footed runner as their representative. Charlie team selected Rooster's replacement: Cadet Taco, although Spartan could not help but wonder if this was so much due to his natural talent as it was because the team did not know or trust the boy enough yet to place him onto their entry team. Delta team's contribution to the group had been Cadet Gator. Since the boy had been hunting alone in the swamps of Louisiana before the dead had risen, the teen had become a solid choice for a sniper. In truth, he and Dancer were very similar in style, and accomplished ability although her skill came from a military endorsed childhood and Gator's had come from the need to put meat on the table for his brothers and sisters while his Papa was serving out an enlistment in the Louisiana National Guard. Lastly, Echo team sent Skull. The thin boy seemed to be relishing the idea of killing anything and anyone from a distance. In fact, he had creeped out Cadet Princess by telling her at lunch time that he had been watching her all morning through his monocular including when she had gone to the port-a-potty when he was supposed to be spotting for the other cadets on his team as a rangefinder.

Looking far out across the field, Spartan could not make out the sniper's targets, but he knew that they were out there somewhere beyond the five-hundred-meter mark. Turning back to Freak and Deadeye, he spoke in a voice loud enough to be heard over the constant pop, pop, pop of weapons firing.

"Do either of you guys know why or where Techno went with Sergeant Boomer?"

Neither of them did.

"Okay, we're up next for Entry team practice at the shoot house. I guess we'll have to go without him. Remember; smooth is fast. Be sure of your targets. Freak: you are our breach man. Hit the door hard with the ram and then fall back to cover our six as we flow by. If the door is secured, blast it. Deadeye, you move off me. I go right, you go left and vice a versa. One room at a time okay, guys? I can't say it enough; smooth and fast. Be sure of your targets. Ready?"

"Hell yeah!" Freak said. "It'll be just like going to a concert at the old Rosemont Horizon in Chicago. There you gotta kick in the bathroom door and move the bodies aside to even take a leak."

Deadeye, who was not known for his sense of humor, fired a stinging quip. "I guess that makes you Freaky Leaky!"

Spartan snorted in laughter.

"Fuck you Tatonka!" Freak replied laughing as well.

Spartan turned, still chuckling and marched his team over to the log and sand filled shoot house were Sergeant Hogg stood impatiently waiting for them at the doorway.

"Are you all done giggling, girls?" The drill sergeant asked. "Because if you are then I suppose that I gotta tell you about this little picnic that yer goin' on." He said indicating the shoot house behind him. "Ya see, this picnic comes with its own special little type of diseased raincloud. Somewhere inside of there is a "Z" or three that just might be waitin' to take a bite outta your cherry asses! I will only tell you that there is *not* a Husk inside but Reapers or Romeros are possibilities, so close-range shots are acceptable without the risk of infection. However, if you get your ass bit or clawed up then you may get to be a future target for upcoming classes! You get me cadets?"

"Yes, drill sergeant!" All three cadets yelled in reply.

From inside the shoot house, there came a roar of delight followed by semi-automatic gunfire. "Yippee-Ki-Yay muthafuckers!" Yelled Cowboy in his deep Texas accent.

Spartan could not help but chuckle again. Although he did not know the boy well, he could not help but like the laid-back, tough guy persona that he always exuded. It was like the boy had stepped out of a John Wayne movie and into the Apocalypse Academy. Looking up and seeing Sergeant Hogg glaring icy death at him from under his round brown hat, Spartan quickly re-secured his smile. Obviously, the man expected… no demanded… perfection from his team. Spartan obliged by putting on his game face and focusing on the task at hand.

Hogg addressed the team one last time before they entered the shoot house. "Line up ladies and remember; *try not to get dead*! Don't fuck this up!"

Alpha team complied. Spartan thought briefly about Techno again. They could've used the extra eyes and gun in the shoot house. Where the hell was he? He considered asking Sergeant Hogg but then dismissed the idea as he focused back on his slot against the shoot house wall. Obviously, the Drill sergeant knew they were a man short of the normal four-person stack but hadn't mentioned it. Spartan wouldn't either, not wanting to appear as if he was making excuses ahead of time. There would be no time to get him set up and into formation anyway. Freak stood in front of him holding a twenty-pound portable steel battering ram and Deadeye stood behind. Each cadet's left hand lightly rested on the combat harness of the cadet in front of them, to allow for physical reaction to the other's movements. This kept their eyes free for target shooting. Weapons ready, the team sunk into a half-crouched stance, affectionately known as a "Groucho" after the legendary movement style of comedian Groucho Marx and waited silently for the drill sergeant to issue the command to go.

"Standby." Came the command. Ten seconds passed.

"Standby." Twenty seconds passed.

"Go!" Came the call from Drill sergeant Hogg.

Freak brought the solid steel ram forward, shattering the door's locking mechanism and driving the door inward. The massive cadet then pivoted to the opposite side of the door frame allowing Spartan and Deadeye to flow into the first room before him. Casting the heavy ram down to the ground with a ringing thump, Freak brought up his Mossberg into a modified firing position and backed through the door behind his team, watching his team's rear for any signs of an ambush.

Upon clearing the doorway, Spartan moved left and entered the first room, his helmet's tactical sight displaying a green crosshair visual display that paralleled the sights of his M- 4. Where the barrel pointed, the crosshair followed. This made quick decision shooting much simpler than the old fashion iron sights had allowed. Pinpoint accuracy could be consistently obtained as long as the weapon could be held steady. Spartan moved smoothly down the wall, methodically moving past various pieces of furniture that had been placed strategically around the room. The only sounds came from his breathing and the soft plastic chink of his chain mail as the Kevlar flexed with his body movements. If his teammate, Deadeye, made any noise at all, it was so minimal that Spartan could not hear it from twenty feet away, even with the enhanced audio sensors of the ZAP armor. Avoiding a small coffee table with a nimble sidestep, Spartan used his tactical light to scan behind and under the sofa. Seeing no "Zs" lurking in either place, he continued forward towards the next doorway. Deadeye was already there with his weapon pointed down the open hallway. A quick flash of hand signals told Spartan that there were three doors ahead. One door on each wall and third door straight ahead at the end of the hall. All the doors were closed.

Spartan lined up silently behind Deadeye. They would repeat the same process as they moved from room to room. It amazed Spartan that they, as a team, had learned so much, so fast and could now implement tactical shooting, movement and communications, in less than a week's time. While they would need continual practice, the motions felt so smooth and natural to them all that they felt like they had been working together for years rather than mere days. Spartan was willing to bet that the perceived smoothness of their actions was due to the lack of internal friction within his team and couldn't help but wonder if Bravo, Charlie or Delta teams with their inherited newbies or Echo team with its inherent dysfunctional attitude were nearly as comfortable going through the shoot house exercise as they were. Freak's massive hand closed over Spartan's shoulder armor indicating that the big cadet had rejoined the tactical stack at the doorway. A small double hand tap on the shoulder plate from the man behind them indicated to the team that they were ready to move onward.

Feeling the tap up reach the front of the stack, Deadeye moved like a ghost into the hallway. A single door stood closed ten feet away on the right side of the hall with the second door five feet further down on the left. The final doorway stood directly ahead approximately 10 yards away. Deadeye reached out and gently turned the doorknob just the slightest. Seeing that it was unlocked, he pushed the door open to its fullest and darted through the doorway to the left. Drill sergeant Surfer had told them that part of surviving on a tactical team was learning to trust the man behind you to cover the area opposite of where you were moving; to know that your back was covered without having to look back and risk running blindly into trouble.

Spartan peeled right, moving out of the fatal funnel inside of the door frame. Due to the close nature of most wooden door frames; the doorway always created a significantly easy silhouetted kill box for anyone that was attacking his team; "Z" or otherwise. If a man went down in the funnel, team members ahead of that person would be isolated and support team members behind would be potentially cut off. Both Sergeants' Surfer and Hogg had been explicit during their training instructions to get the fuck out of the doorway as fast as they could no matter what. If a teammate goes down, go over them, deal with the threat and then render aid if it was safe to do so. If not, leave them behind until the threat was neutralized.

His tactical light flashed across the bedside table then over a queen-sized bed that was covered in a hideous floral print comforter. Spartan smoothly dropped to a low knee position and scanned his light beneath the bed. Seeing no threats, he quickly rose back up and continued his flow along the wall of the bedroom.

“Contact!” Came the quiet call across his helmet’s communication link. “I’ve got sounds of movement in the bathroom ahead of you. It’s the small room off the rear of the bedroom at your two o’clock. It sounded like shuffling feet.”

“10–4, ten seconds to engage.” Spartan replied moving up the wall towards the door. “Freak, you’ve got the hall.”

“Covering.” Came the big man’s reply. Spartan knew the hall was secure. Nothing would get past Freak; living or undead.

Judging by the size of the bedroom, the bathroom should’ve been small. It was probably only a sink and a toilet with no shower or tub area. The space was definitely too tight to effectively fight in. Spartan keyed his microphone twice. Seeing Deadeye’s head swivel towards him at the silent attention call, Spartan flashed hand signals indicating that he would breach the door and the Deadeye would take the shot. The thumbs up reply indicated that Deadeye understood the plan and was ready to engage with anything living or undead that exited the room. No other communication was needed between the two boys.

Moving away from the wall and up to the door, Spartan winced as the scabbard for the sword of Leonidas that was clipped onto his body armor making a loud tick noise as it tapped against his leg in time with his movement. He would have to silence that issue when the training was over. He quickly flashed a hand count to Deadeye. They had prearranged to act on three for any encounters behind closed doors.

“One.”

"Two."

"Three!" And Spartan turned the doorknob, shoving the hollow core inward with a bang as it slammed into the wall behind it. With the door breached, he quickly backpedaled out of Deadeye's line of targeting.

Immediately the bathroom doorway was filled by a rotund woman wearing a fluffy pink robe and wild antenna looking hair rolled up into curlers. Something about the woman's appearance startled Spartan as he gazed at the walking dead matron. The former woman's torn lips and blood reddened eyes widened upon looking up and seeing Spartan and it tottered forward at a shuffle, black feet engorged with gravity laden dead blood and enclosed in matching open toed pink bunny slippers that were obviously part of the set with her robe. Arms outstretched, it moved toward Spartan, its undead moan rising from rot decayed lungs, gurgling out of her ripped open throat with time blackened blood. A long line of unknown bloody bodily fluids drooled from the corner of its mouth.

"Urrgghhh!" It moaned as it advanced, eager to take a bite out of the Alpha team leader. Still Spartan did not act. Waiting in the shadows at the side of the doorway, Deadeye sat immobile with his armor deployed in stealth mode. The armor blended him perfectly into the shadows and dispersed his heat signature, preventing him from being detected by the undead. "Zs" were known to hunt by sound and heat sensory action; perhaps the only beneficial byproduct of the HUNGER virus infection that caused their eyes to rupture and bleed during the diseases initial destructive rampage throughout the body. As the visual acuity transformed from light-based to heat-based performance, sometimes the body could not adapt and the eyeballs would just burst from the change of structure, leaving a blind corpse with empty eye sockets that seemed to be looking inward to hell.

This Romero's eyes were intact; their scarlet orbs focused squarely on Spartan. Blackened and bloody tears had dried down the creature's chubby cheeks. As the creature exited the bathroom, Deadeye shot her through the temple just as she cleared the doorway, causing several of the hair curlers and U – shaped bobby pins to spin off through the air like miniature grenades arming; pins pulled and spoons flying outward. The "Z" fell in a fluffy pink blob onto the floor, a thick grayish-black ooze running out of the three-inch-wide exit wound in the side of her head and onto the soft fabric of the robe. Keeping his eyes and weapon on the open doorway and never looking down, Spartan stepped over the woman's corpse and assessed the bathroom for further threats. Seeing none, he keyed his helmet mic.

"Clear." He called. Quickly the team moved backed into the hallway where Freak still stood guard. Coming up behind him, Spartan again keyed his microphone.

"Deadeye just pacified Grandma. Her hair will never be the same." Feeling Deadeye stack up behind him, he tapped the rear shoulder plate of the big cadet's armor indicating that they were again ready to move forward. Moving quickly but quietly, the team approached the next door on the left. Freak moved just pass the doorway, aiming his rifle ahead of the team in providing overwatch on the hallway. He especially focused on the last door at the far end of the hall. Seeing Freak in place, Spartan and Deadeye repeated the process of entry that they had used in the first room. This time they entered and exited the room, a children's room by the looks of the décor, with negative results or contacts.

Resuming their tactical stack, Deadeye and Spartan both passed Freak's position, allowing the giant to turn and resume his duties as rear guard. Moving to the last room's closed door at the end of the hall, Deadeye pulled the flash bang grenade from his vest pocket. The Apache Scout yanked the pin on the grenade, arming it, but keeping the spoon in place with strong pressure from his armored gauntlet. A flash bang was essentially a stun grenade that emitted a loud noise and a flash of brilliant white light when detonated. The effect was dramatic on the living, causing temporary blindness and deafness. The effect, if any on the walking dead was unknown, but Spartan suspected it would be similar as the animated corpses hunted by sight and sound.

Reaching up with the hand that did not hold the grenade, Deadeye felt the doorknob gently. It was locked. Flashing a quick hand signal to Spartan, Deadeye slid over against the wall, allowing Spartan access to the door. While not in Freak's league for strength, he was still more than powerful enough to kick in the door. Especially when armored. Taking a stride and a half, Spartan used his suit's servos and his own momentum to power his kick forward. Striking the door four inches to the right of the lock with the Kevlar soled combat boot, the door flew open with the crash. In almost perfect harmony, Deadeye rolled the grenade into the room and both cadets quickly averted their eyes.

The low moan of an undead's perpetual hunger began to come from the room as the door slammed open but it was immediately overpowered by the detonation of the stun grenade. Light, sound and gray smoke covered their movement as the two cadets entered the room. Using the targeting system in their helmet's visors, they quickly located the immediate threat. A young female "Z" stood in the center the room; filth covered nails clawed bloody strips of meat from around her eyes as it unconsciously tried to remove the effects of the stun grenade. Effectively deafened and blinded, it did not see or hear Spartan and Deadeye approach at parallel forty-five-degree angles along the room's walls.

Judging by the quickness of the creature's hand movements and the rapid way that it was cocking its head side to side in an effort to clear its hearing, the cadets knew that this "Z" was a Reaper and opted to put it down quickly and efficiently, each with simultaneous double taps to the deadly creature's head. Spartan and Deadeye all sent rounds zipping into the creature's skull vaporizing the bone as the 5.56 rounds chewed through the rotten bone and brain, instantly dropping the undead to the floor. Without a second look, the cadets finished sweeping the room then moved to re-stack at the door clearly marked "exit" in neon red paint at the far end of the room.

From above them, walking on wooden gangways came the call via a megaphone. "End EX!" This indicated that the exercise had indeed ended, and the area was secure.

"Drop magazines and secure your weapons."

All three teammates dropped their magazines and ejected the round from its seating inside of the weapon's barrel, locking the slides back. With a deft flick of their fingers, they then placed the safeties into the on position. Removing their helmets, they gazed up at the voices behind the megaphone and were surprised to see Colonel Slade standing beside Drill Sergeant Hogg.

"Time: two minutes, thirty-second six seconds. Best in the class so far. Outstanding cadets!"

The three boys exchanged high fives, and for just a flickering moment they appeared to be the high-spirited teenagers that the world had known before the night that the dead had risen. Then, the Colonel spoke.

"Whose idea was it to flash bang the last room?"

Spartan replied. "Sir, Cadet Deadeye was on point Sir. He deserves the credit."

The Colonel nodded. "That was a wise choice son. Reapers are nothing to play with. Your actions saved your team from a potentially deadly encounter and turned it into an almost simple elimination. Well done!"

"Thank you, Sir." Deadeye replied quietly.

"Clean your weapons and return to the barracks and then fallout for chow. We will have a nighttime assembly at 1900 hrs. Academy jumpsuits only, no weapons or body armor will be required. Fallout."

As they prepared to walk away, Spartan called back out to Sergeant Hogg. "Drill sergeant! I am missing two members of my team. I know that Cadet Dancer is participating in training with the sniper corps downrange, but Cadet Techno was removed from the range by Drill Sergeant Boomer. Could you advise his status please?"

The Drill sergeant grinned, looking vaguely like the Cheshire cat from Lewis Carroll's *Alice in Wonderland*. "Dancer should be enroute back to the barracks by now. She will meet you there. Techno couldn't hit the broad side of a barn much less the damn targets to save his life, so they went to investigate getting him a weapon that did not require aiming as much. Also, it seems that the boy has extensive chemistry and physics experience, so he will be training with Sergeant Surfer to learn the fine art of blowin' shit up with tactical explosives. If he doesn't blow his chubby little ass into pieces, he will bring your team back a valuable skill. Cadets rarely have that kind of knowledge at his age. Usually, they are just worried about jerking off and thinking about Mary Jane Rotten-crotch."

"Thank you, drill sergeant!" Spartan called, then turned and walked over to clean his weapon with Freak and Deadeye at the wooden station that it been set up for that purpose at the center line of the range.

"So, Techno is learning skills with explosives?" Spartan smiled as he thought to himself. *"His team just kept getting stronger."* Running through each of his teammate's skill sets in his mind, he thought that he had a heavy weapons expert, a sniper, a scout and a demolitions man. Yes indeed. His team was shaping up nicely. The Phalanx was not a team to be taken lightly. Applying a liberal amount of gun oil to his weapon, he began to methodically break it down to its primary components and clean it as he had been taught. *"Yes, Spartan's Phalanx, was definitely coming together."*

Chapter Sixteen
Confrontation

Meatloaf, mashed potatoes, green beans and lime Jell-O decorated their plastic food trays as the team re-gathered for the dinner meal. The air in the chow hall seemed almost happy as the various teams of cadets interacted and talked about their experiences on the firing range or in the shoot house. As far as Spartan could tell from listening to a dozen different conversations at once, there been no casualties and no injuries during the training, unlike the end results from the Dante obstacle course.

Talking casually with his fellow team leader; Cowboy, Spartan learned about Dancer's skill with the sniper rifles.

"She put seven shots into a grouping from six hundred meters that would've fit onto a prairie dog's fuzzy lil' ass!" The Texan proclaimed. "She outshot us all. Good thing we're not back home, Pa would've been pissed. He spent darn near his whole life learnin' us to shoot. Ain't no girl that should be able to outshoot his sons."

Spartan laughed, and looked around for his team. Dancer and Princess sat off to one side of the room talking quietly but seriously. Spartan could not hear the words but assumed it was about the fallen Cadet Knight who had died defending the log bridge on the very first obstacle of the Dante course that so his teammates could cross safely. Emotion was evident on Princess's face and Dancer seemed to be comforting her. Freak was regaling a couple of cadets; Spartan thought they were Jive from Delta team and the new kid, Taco from Charlie team with tales of his pre "Z" feats of athletic prowess. The two cadets looked like they had found their hero, gazing up at the massive teenager with adoration and seemed like they would ask for his autograph at any moment.

Deadeye sat with Bravo teams' leader Dragon, Cadet Lightning also of Bravo team, Gator; Delta team's Cajun Hunter and Bravo team's replacement for Cadet Meatball; the dark eyed, dark-haired girl named Raven. More than likely, they were exchanging hunting stories where tales of woodland valor that seemed to be the common interest between the teenagers. It was good to see the normally silent boy talking with his fellow cadets.

That left only Techno. Looking around, Spartan saw the Asian boy seated with Cadet Popcorn, Cadet Medusa from Bravo team and Cadet Deacon from Delta team. From the way all four cadets talked and animated their hands in various pouring and then exploding simulacrums, Spartan could only guess that they had all been selected as Explosives Specialists for their individual teams.

Yes, all seem to be going well with buoyant spirits bordering on joviality; at least it was until the Echoes entered the room. The open conversations slowed and died out until one by one everyone in the chow hall was looking at Cutter and his crew as they sauntered up the center aisle to get their food.

"Well now," Cutter called out to the general audience. "Don't go stoppin' all the fun and festivities just 'cause we're here. I know that we are a bit late, but everybody knows that the Echoes are the life of the party!"

Cutter stopped walking in front of Techno and looked around at the cadets sitting in the rows and seats around of him.

"Awwww look here boys and girls. Team Geek is all sittin' together. It makes me feel all warm and fuzzy to know that someone still has the know-how to fix a toaster or work complex math problems in a world that's been taken over by the walking dead. At least it looks like each team will have at least one person to use for cannon fodder now that the heroes are all gone."

His whole crew laughed, apart from Lotus Jane. Spartan noticed that she looked almost apologetic as her team leader insulted Techno and his friends.

"Maybe they designed the mixer that made these here mashed potatoes." He said and brazenly dipped his finger into Techno's gravy covered potatoes, glaring at the boy, defying him to protest the action with a sneering look.

Red splotchy anger was registering on the boy's face and neck as he fought to keep himself under control. Spartan could see that Techno was as red as a radish and was struggling to keep his temper in check. Normally the teen was pretty mild mannered but being embarrassed in front of his peers seemed to really be pushing his buttons. As Spartan watched, Techno lost the battle for self-control.

"You really are an asshole Cutter!" Techno declared. "A bully and a preppy faggot. Somebody's gonna put you in your place one day and I hope that I…"

Hearing Techno's verbal explosion, Spartan knew what was coming and moved to intervene, but he was not fast enough. Cutter's backhand fist flashed out and smashed into the bridge of Techno's nose. The boy flew backward, his tray full of meatloaf and potatoes catapulting through the air, before he landed on his back clutching his face in his hands. Two rows over, Spartan leapt up onto a bench and then onto the table before propelling himself through the air towards Echo team's malicious team leader. Sailing over several seated cadets, he slammed into the boy broadside, and they tumbled in a tangle of arms and legs over another dinner table spilling more trays of meat, green peas and brown gravy covered potatoes every which way and splashing open cartons of milk onto the floor all around them.

Orc moved to pull Spartan off of his team leader, but Freak grabbed the fang–toothed boy around the waist from behind and threw him backward in a suplex move that slammed him headfirst into the table that he, Jive and Taco had been talking at moments before. More food trays exploded outward, covering the cadets with meat and vegetable fragments as they exploded outward in a culinary bomb and the impacted table beneath smashed into a dozen wooden and metal pieces under the impact.

Deadeye was fighting his way through the crowd from the far side of the room when he saw a thin body that greatly resembled Skull from Echo team sailing through the air, only to vanish headfirst into the crowd that was circling the various fights. Then, he saw Freak roaring in unmitigated fury and towering above the crowd as he began shoving cadets out of the way to get to the human missile that he had just launched through the air, right after dumping the thick-skulled Orc onto his head. He also noticed that there appeared to be a silver dinner fork sticking out of the back of the giant's shoulder, with a small trickle of blood flowing down the dark blue jumpsuit. Doing a quick mental calculation, Deadeye concluded that Skull had come up behind Freak during the fight with Orc and had stabbed the powerful cadet from behind with the fork. This appeared to have a similar effect to slapping a bull with the willow branch in that the surface sting brought on by the wound brought the raging animal to life. Skull would be fortunate to survive the beating that Deadeye was certain to follow.

Cadets cheered as they slipped, tripped, and held each other up in an effort to maintain the fighting circle around the two battles that were raging amongst the milk and food products. Spartan and Cutter were trading blows back and forth, while Skull looked like a tomcat running from an enraged bull mastiff. Deadeye also saw Techno trying to get unsteadily to his feet with the lithe Dancer standing next to him for protection. Dividing her looks between Spartan and Freak while guarding Techno, she did not see Orc or Savage coming up behind them through the crowd. Trying to yell out a warning as he moved, Deadeye was drowned out by the raucously cheering crowd. Fighting through the crowd was taking too long, so Deadeye ducked down and scrabbled under the tables until he could see an alternative route to take along the fighting circle's edge. Racing low and fast, the boy crossed the room in seconds then reentered the crowd when he gauged that he was closer to Tech and Dancer. Like an avenging ghost, he emerged just behind the two Echo team cadets as Orc, who was less than an oratory genius, began to threaten Dancer. His speech was partially slurred from Freak's devastating wrestling move that had obviously scrambled his brain.

"You should'a never hurt me like that girly. Now I'm gonna hurt you. Gonna hurt you real bad, then when I'm done and you're all bleeding and shit, I might let you earn your forgiveness by kissin' what you kicked before until it's all better! Then I might just kill ya!"

The look of horrific revulsion on Dancer's face was enough to move the Native American into action. He swung a devastating sidekick into Savage's right kidney area from behind with his combat boot. The kick drove the boy into a sideways "V" and elicited a scream of pure agony as the nerves and pain receptors registered the debilitating injury. Deadeye followed the kick with a spinning leg sweep that took the staggered and shrieking boy to the ground. Orc looked down at the fallen Savage just as Deadeye applied an arm lock to the flattened boy, then over at the Alpha team cadet who was torquing the arm of his fallen partner.

"When I'm done wit' her runt, I will hurt you next!" He said almost impassively, like an afterthought.

Looking up from where he had Savage pinned to the floor, Deadeye smiled at the bigger cadet and then casually flipped him the bird.

"You tink dis is funny you little bastard?! I'm gonna hurt you bad!"

Deadeye's smile widened and he merely shrugged and then pointed with one hand behind the now distracted Orc. Turning with an almost cartoonish look on his pocked face, Orc found the once horrified Dancer now transformed into a whirling dervish of martial arts spins and flowing movements. "Urgh…" Was all the boy had time to say as Dancer's webbed hand strike struck him in the larynx and a lightning-fast snap kick drove straight into his solar plexus. Throwing his hands up to his injured throat, the boy was defenseless against the follow up sidekick into the boy's outer thigh. As the nerve strike overloaded the common peroneal nerve with pain, the teenager's thick leg folded and collapsed. Dancer immediately followed the teenager's body as it fell towards the ground, delivering several short, stinging right hands to the boy's face. Then, she seemed to swirl back into a new stance, preparing for the next series of moves.

Across the room, Freak pummeled Skull mercilessly with his meaty fists, blacking both of the skinny boy's eyes. The much smaller boy ran rabbit trying to find a way out of the circle only to be repeatedly turned back by the crowd of cadets that were howling for his beating like bloodthirsty Senators in ancient Rome watching dueling gladiators at the Coliseum. Out of desperation, Skull threw numerous trays of food, silverware and cartons of milk at the advancing giant and temporarily succeeded in blinding the big cadet just long enough to throw a punch that succeeded in splitting Freak's lower lip but did no other real damage. Skull then turned and ran for all he was worth, knifing through the resistant crowd in a frantic desperation to be away from the tower of muscle that was roaring like an enraged beast behind him. Breaking through the throng, Skull ran for the chow hall doors, bursting through them and never looking back just as an entire airborne table smashed into the doorframe behind him; leaving the rest of his team to fend for themselves.

Through an extended exchange of blows, Spartan and Cutter had managed to get back to their feet. Punches flew, blocks countered, and counter moves followed up strikes. Both cadets had scored significant hits, bloodying the other. A stinging jab from the Echo team leader caught Spartan on the chin. Cutter was fast and clearly a competent fighter. The jab was followed by a sidekick that Spartan smoothly blocked but left him open to an elbow that caught him in the temple, making the world explode into colors that blurred his vision and dropped him down onto a knee. As Cutter closed in, Spartan did his best to gauge the distance but struggled due to his blurred vision. Shaking his head rapidly side to side, he tried to clear out the cobwebs currently consuming his brain.

"Not so tough now are ya?" Cutter taunted. "Ya ain't got that mountain of muscle to back you up. I'm gonna show everybody that Echo team's leader is the toughest of all an' that the Alpha team's leader is nothin' but a bitch..."

Spartan used the boy's taunt to clear the haze and act as a focal point for his punch. Exploding upward he threw everything he had into an uppercut. The crunch of his fist as his knuckles met jawbone was emphasized as Cutter's jaw snapped shut with an audible clack, flipping the boy backward in an almost acrobatic flip. Still dazed, Spartan sank back down to one knee and continued to frantically try to clear his head. The elbow that Cutter had delivered to his temple was still affecting his vision, but the effects seemed to be lessoning with each passing moment. Starbursts waivered and blurred back and forth behind his pupils in a rousing Fourth of July style fireworks display that was set to the bass drum rhythm of his own heartbeat.

A gasp from the crowd and the snap of metal clicking and locking in place let Spartan know that not only was the fight not over, but Cutter had now armed himself with a knife of unknown proportions. Visually impaired as he was, Spartan knew that he was in very serious trouble. Rubbing his severely bruised jaw, the Echo team leader spoke to Spartan.

"Ya know what the problem with you Alpha team pricks is?" Cutter asked, his voice telegraphing his position as he moved closer and closer. "The problem is that you're all so self-righteous, so friendly, and yet so fake. That may have worked in the old world where words fought battles; but out here, since the world decided to use an undead phonebook and organize a party from Hell, well, words are a waste of time. So, I think I'm going to help you learn that lesson. And I think that you need to learn it the hard way. And since all this fight came from fat boy over there opening his mouth, I think I will cut out his tongue to prove my point."

The footsteps coming towards Spartan abruptly stopped and changed directions. In his distorted vision, Spartan could barely make out Cutter turning and advancing on Techno with the knife held out extended in his hand. The Asian boy held up a turquoise-colored plastic food tray in front of him like a shield, trying to ward off the slashing advances from the knife wielding team leader from Echo. It was no wonder Echo team had selected "Cutter's *Cutthroats*" for their team name. They all seemed to want to cause injury, death and mayhem to anyone and everyone around them.

Knowing that there was no way that Techno could defend himself against Cutter's superior fighting skills, Spartan moved out of desperation. Rising to his feet, he half ran, half dove at Cutter's legs from behind. So distracted was the Echo team leader with issuing his taunts towards Techno and the mayhem that he was going to cause that he did not hear Spartan running madly towards him. Like a blindside blitz in Spartan's long forgotten days of football, he smashed into Cutter's lower back from behind, wrapped his arms tightly around the boy's hips and used his leg strength to lift and drive the boy forward, up-ending him with a heavy crash. Cutter, caught fully unaware, could do nothing but flail at the air as he flew forward fully inverted and ultimately face planted on the cafeteria's blue painted concrete floor.

As Spartan's bodyweight crashed down on top of him, Cutter's air was driven from his lungs with a loud hissing gasp and the switchblade flew from his hands, skittering across the floor where it landed at Cadet Cowboy's feet. Casually the tough Texan picked up the blade, closed it, and then stuck the knife into the side of his combat boot.

Meanwhile Dancer's initially successful flurry of blows against Orc had subsided and the more powerful boy managed to get back to his feet and had delivered several bruising punches to the girl's face and ribs. Although she still scored successful hits against the pock faced cadet, the momentum of the battle had turned, and he was now shrugging off the majority of the shots no matter how much force that she put into them. She knew that if she did not end this fight quickly, she was in real danger of suffering a severe injury or worse at Orc's hands. Since aggressive strikes were not working, she began to work mentally through the brutal boy's attack pattern like her father had taught her. She looked for an opening to apply a joint lock or chokehold so that she could try to immobilize the much larger cadet. A surprisingly quick straight right hand from Orc struck her flush on the jaw, knocking her backward.

Allowing her momentum to drop her onto her back, Dancer absorbed the impact with the backs of her arms and feigned helplessness, attempting to draw the larger but much more stupid boy in. One of the earliest lessons in the mixed martial arts classes her father had insisted that she attend over the last ten years of her life had been that taking the fight to the ground offered the advantage to the superior grappler not the heavier striker because leverage was gone.

Orc stood over her guffawing and pointing down at his prey.

"Look!" He called to the crowd. "She can't wait for me to get between those legs!" Slowly he started walking forward, fists curled into heavy balls of bone and flesh the size of navel oranges. Dancer provided the expected response of curling her arms around her head to ward off the blows that both she and the crowd knew were coming. Falsely, she began to beg the boy to stop and not hurt her. That she'd had enough. Stepping past the girl's outstretched legs; Orc bent at the waist and reach down to grab Dancer's jumpsuit just below her collar. Wrapping his fingers into the navy-blue fabric above her right breast, he pulled her upward while simultaneously drawing back a meaty fist. As the big hand reached its apex, Dancer flashed into action. Her legs flipped up, one over the extended arm, and one bent at the knee behind the boy's head. As she locked in the triangle choke, applying devastating pressure to the arteries on the sides of the teenager's neck with her legs, she returned the boy's taunt.

"How do you like it between my legs now you fuckin' Tosser?!" She grunted, squeezing as hard as she could with her legs while keeping the boy's outstretched arm pinned down with her hand.

Orc flailed madly, punching her thigh and hip area with trivial effect. Seeing the Echo team cadet begin to stagger, and his eyes slowly roll up into his head, Dancer put all of her force into the application of the chokehold. The boy's trapped arm pinched against his neck and the blood flow was cut off to his brain. He fell over into unconsciousness without another sound. Seeing that he was no more of a threat, Dancer released the chokehold before permanent harm could be done and rolled away from the unconscious boy. *"Thank you, Daddy."* She thought silently, and then standing back up she kicked the unconscious boy several times in the ribs just to remind him that she was clearly not batting with a full wicket when he woke up. Perhaps the added pain would remind him not to fuck with her a third time.

Spartan and Cutter were both trying to struggle to their feet, each seeing through blurred vision and staggering side to side. Both cadets were battered and on the verge of collapse when the cafeteria door burst open with a bang and Drill Sergeants Hogg, Stone and Havoc entered the room. Almost as an afterthought, Lotus Jane slinked into the room behind the wall of drill sergeants and silently stood off to the side, willing herself to be invisible.

"Well, Hol-ee shit!" Drill sergeant Hogg called in a deep but loud bass voice. "What in the name of hell and hockey is fuckin' happening in my goddamn cafeteria! Do any of you goddamned peckerwoods want to tell me why all of this de-lic-ious meatloaf has been spilled across my clean goddamn floor!" Then, almost as an addendum to his thought; "and who the fuck wasted all of this Jell-O? It's a goddamn pity wasting lime Jell-O like that! Jell-O is like a food of the gods!"

Seeing the angered looks on the drill sergeants faces, every cadet in the cafeteria knew it was going to be a very, very, long night.

As they cleaned the floors, walls, and tables of the cafeteria, which turned out to be an all-new experience using toothbrushes, water and Pine-Sol, Spartan took the opportunity to keep his team together on the pretense of watching each other's back. It was not entirely an untrue idea since Cutter and the rest of his malcontents from Echo team seemed perfectly willing to attack individuals from behind or to try to intimidate small groups of people whenever and wherever possible. Now that Cutter had proven a willingness to pull out a knife against another cadet, that danger had been elevated to a new level. Although nobody had been cut, it was clear, as it actually had been ever since he and Freak had intervened in the restroom on the first day of the Academy that a special level of hatred rested in Cutter's heart for Spartan, Techno and probably Freak too. Orc was both in fear of and hated Dancer for her humiliating defeats of his psychopathic ways. The rest of Echo was just as bad. Social misfits and degenerates one and all.

Even so, Spartan could not bring himself to report Cutter's use of a knife during the fight to the drill sergeants. He knew without a shadow of a doubt, that the report would get the boy expelled from the Apocalypse Academy. That report would cause the boy to be forced to walk down Damnation Road and cross the Peoria Avenue Bridge to walk alone into the "Z" lands. No matter how bad a person was, even somebody as emotionally damaged as Cutter, he was still human. There were few enough of us left in the world since the HUNGER virus caused the dead to rise back up and begin eating the living. It just seemed wrong to sentence the boy to almost certain death without enough cause. To Spartan a threat with the knife was not enough. If someone had been cut or killed then yes, but fortunately it hadn't come to that.

Whispering softly to Techno, who was scrubbing chair legs to remove dried on chunks of mashed potatoes, red ketchup splashes and green Jell-O arcs that had splattered across them during the fight, Spartan asked about his disappearance from the range.

"So, what happened? Where'd you go when you left the range?"

Techno let out an embarrassed, soft chuckle and Spartan saw the boy's face flush it deep red color.

"Well, I tried to zero my weapon. You know, to find my sighting up to three hundred meters? I fired all ten sets of three rounds and walked down range with everyone else to get a look at my target so that I could adjust the sights if needed."

"Right, we all did that."

"Yeah, but after I got to the target, I could only find *two* holes. One in the head and one in the crotch."

"You completely missed the target twenty-eight times? How is that even possible?" Spartan said in disbelief. "It was only twenty-five meters away. Jesus Christ! You didn't even hit the paper?"

"No… I know it's horrible. I never grew up around firearms." Techno replied sheepishly. "I didn't know what to do so I raised my hand to request a drill sergeant to come assist me. Wouldn't you know the first sergeant to come over would be Sergeant Havoc. He took one look at my target and snatched it from me and then looked at the front side before turning it over and looking at the backside. Then he handed it back to me shaking his head."

"He didn't say anything? No advice or suggestions on how to improve your shooting?"

"Oh yeah, he said plenty without saying a lot at all. I believe his exact words were "*You're going to die when we go into a live "Z" environment, be sure to save at least one bullet for yourself.*" Then he walked away without another word."

No fucking wonder Sergeant Havoc was assigned to oversee Echo team. He certainly had their caring demeanor and demure charm.

"Anyway, I kept struggling until lunch. I shot, reloaded, and shot again but each time the results were similar. A couple of hits somewhere on the target and the majority flying off into God knows where."

Spartan just shook his head. It would definitely be a problem if his team went into the field and had to constantly cover themselves and Techno. Everyone had to pull their own weight, or the team; the Phalanx would fail.

"At lunch, when everyone else went to eat, I stayed on the range. Sergeant Boomer came over to talk with me. I explained my problems with hitting the target and he asked me to reload and fire another volley. So, I did."

"And?"

"Same results. I couldn't hit the broad side of a barn. So, I asked Sergeant Boomer if he could tell what I was doing wrong. He said my breathing was good and my trigger pull was smooth, so they were not an issue. He had me reload again but this time put his back to the target and kept his eyes directly on me. I fired all thirty rounds, but he didn't even bother to get the target. Sergeant Boomer told me to stand up and held his hand out for my weapon without another word. I thought I was done for. Out of the Academy, ya know?"

"What happened then?"

"Sergeant Boomer stood up and said something like "Son, if this were the Army, you'd be on a bus heading home. Your problem is those Coke bottles you're wearing over your eyes. Their bifocals, aren't they?"

"I had no idea how he knew that but he was right. I've had to wear bifocals since I was six because I am horribly farsighted. I thought he was going to take me to see the Colonel, you know for expulsion. We got into his jeep and drove. I wasn't paying much attention because I was feeling rather ill at the thought of walking Damnation Road. Instead, he stopped the Jeep in front of the Armory. Telling me to wait in the Jeep he took my rifle inside, I assumed so that I wouldn't lose it uselessly in the field. About fifteen minutes later, he came back out carrying an ugly squared off rifle and ammo can. Then we drove back to the range."

"After setting up a new target, he gave me a brief explanation of the weapon, showed me how to load it and told me to fire a few rounds just to get the feel of it. So, I did. The first round rocked the wooden frame of the target. The second cut the entire frame in half. I was horrified, but Sergeant Boomer was laughing hysterically. He motioned for me to put the weapon down and follow him down range. So, I did. He picked up the amputated target and frame, inspected it then showed it to me. The target was full of dozens of small holes from frame to frame. I had hit the target… A lot. I looked at him very confused."

"Holding up my weapon, he said *"this is a Benelli combat shotgun. It can hold twelve rounds of ammunition and of firing different types of shells either semi-automatic or in fully automatic mode. The types of shells that can be fired include: Buck shot, slugs, tear gas, and powdered zinc for breaching locks, beanbags and wooden batons. It is highly versatile and has a stock made up of polymer plastic as you can see. "It is a powerful weapon and if you didn't notice; is capable of delivering devastating damage…"* he said holding up my truncated target. *"And for the benefit of people like you that can't hit the south end of the northbound train, you don't have to be very accurate to kill with it."*

"He helped me shoot the rest of the day and helped me learn to clean the shotgun at the end of range time. By then we had several conversations about education and "Zs" and I told him how science and computers had fascinated me before the rising and how I had been moved into advanced placement in school. I explained that by eighth grade I could do advanced physics, calculus, robotics and advanced chemistry. Towards the end of the day, he kept me off the range and instead took me to meet with Drill Sergeant Surfer. I asked about earning my weapon proficiency and Sergeant Boomer just laughed saying that my firearm training was over and that I had mastered the art of "*spray and pray*.""

"When I met with Sergeant Surfer, it was in a chemistry lab. He immediately talked about chemicals and compounds, formulas, and slurries. Although I didn't recognize the formulas he was using, I did recognize the different chemicals. He began with mixes of simple pyrotechnics and over the course of the next few hours taught me to make everything from detonating cord to Composition Four. I learned to make homemade pipe bombs and how-to string Claymore mines. I built detonators and learned about slurries, liquids, gels and powdered explosives too. I even learned how to combine common elements that could be found in most pre -"Z" homes to create homemade explosive mixtures and even napalm in a pinch."

"By the time the day was over, I felt like I could have built an atomic bomb. I'll tell you this. I would never want to piss off Sergeant Surfer. He may seem like a laid-back dude, but the crap he knows is seriously creepy. I mean he talked about rigging surfboards with Claymore mines before he went surfing just in case the infection jumped species from mammals to fish and he was suddenly surrounded by "Z" sharks or killer dolphins or something. I really believe that he would hit the switch to blow up the world, and then ride the biggest wave that he could all the way to the end. Did you know that he holds the high score for the most confirmed "Z" pacifications achieved with a single explosive device not only here at the Academy but everywhere before the military collapsed? So far, he said his personal best was twenty-two for a school bus full of infected "Z" children and the driver who was a Reaper desperately searching for a way to open the locked, collapsible door at the front of the bus. He actually took the time to crawl under the bus, set a one-pound charge of C4 against the gas tank on a one-hour timer, then walked back fifty meters and opened up a lawn chair. Sitting down, he counted the various children's T-shirt designs with binoculars to get an accurate number of "Zs" on board the bus."

Techno shook his head up and down as Spartan said "Really?" in disbelief.

Techno then continued recounting the story. "He remembers the breakdown to this day: one uniform for the bus driver, six superhero shirts, four robots, five sports teams, two flowers, one puppy, two spangled hearts that he thought might have been twins and one fuzzy to the touch, white bunny rabbit. Supposedly as he sat in the chair, he opened an MRE, cooked it with the heater pack and then sat there eating Chicken à la King with a spork while the bus full of infected children exploded, splattering chunks of yellow metal and kindergarteners everywhere. Then he got up, grabbed his gear, folded up his lawn chair and then grabbed his surfboard and casually walked to the beach to catch a few waves for the rest of the day. Pretty sick huh?"

Spartan nodded. Although he did not necessarily approve of the tactic and the subsequent lunch, it was far kinder to vaporize those kids than to let them walk the earth as undead forever. He said as much to Techno.

As the last of the cleanup was completed, the cadets stood and stretched; elongating muscles that had become cramped from kneeling and scrubbing. It was well after midnight and they were all exhausted. As the cadets filed out of the entrance on the north side of the building, Spartan glanced back behind him. Standing near the south exit was the Echo team leader. Beside him stood the cronies from his squad. To a man, all of them were bruised and battered except Lotus Jane who had run off during the fight. Spartan hadn't thought much about it, thinking that the girl just didn't want to take the chance of being involved in the brawl and possibly re-breaking her arm. Then Spartan saw just how wrong he was. Lotus Jane had not run off in fear. She had run to get the person that was now standing to Cutter's right.

Making eye contact, Spartan felt a cold chill run down his back. Drill Sergeant Havoc glared menacingly at him. As Spartan began to turn away, he saw Cutter lift his right hand and slowly draw his extended thumb side-to-side across his throat simulating the blade style execution that people like

Cutter favored. Spartan turned and exited the room, a billion thoughts whirling in his head, not the least of which was that the quarrel with Echo team had now ramped up. They made no secret of their desire to injure, maim or kill any member of the Phalanx, especially Spartan. They would all need to be cautious, to watch each other's backs and if necessary, be ready to fight back against the members of Echo at a moment's notice.

Chapter Seventeen
Final PT Tests and the Sawdust Pit

If Alpha team felt that the final week of the Apocalypse Academy was going to be a cakewalk for the cadets, they were gravely mistaken. First on the agenda was the requirement to successfully pass the minimum standards physical training test. This would consist of a two and a half mile run in under Fourteen minutes, one hundred push-ups in two minutes, one hundred sit-ups in two minutes and a minimum of thirty pull-ups.

In the normal military, PT tests used to be prorated by gender and age. Essentially, if you were older or a female, the standards were significantly lower than they were for male cadets of the same age. Not so in the Apocalypse Academy. Each person had to be responsible for their own and their teammates lives because they may very well depend on the any cadet's strength and endurance in a fight or flight situation. So therefore, everybody had to meet the same standards or they would be removed from the team and be recycled into the next class of cadets, again forced to endure all of the training horrors again with a new team, or they would be expelled from the Apocalypse Academy to walk down Damnation Road and try to forge their own way in the undead world alone.

If you met the standards for the PT tests, you were far from in the clear. If you successfully tested in hand-to-hand combat, martial weapons proficiency and range qualifications for firearms, both side arms and long guns every cadet had to be entered into the *Lottery of the Damned.* In this wonderfully horrific practice, a cadet would be chosen at random to engage in unarmed, mortal combat with an equally random "Z". So, in theory the best or worst cadet could be forced to defend himself or herself from a Husk, a Romero or even a Reaper. The entire purpose for the spectacle was to determine through trial by combat if the Academy graduates had been successfully trained to survive in the post-Apocalyptic world and as such, were destined for greatness or if they were alternately destined to fail. To prove that the training had been insufficient to let them survive and thereby allow them to become a chew toy for the "Zs".

Every school had its traditions. Spartan could only hope that the lottery selection was neither he nor one of the Phalanx. He would gladly however volunteer any of the bastards from Echo team to participate. Spartan chuckled aloud to himself causing his team to look at him strangely. He was certain that if he explained the thought of Orc getting his skull gnawed on by a Romero, they would also see the humor. Seeing the question in her eyes, Spartan looked at Dancer and told her that they would talk later. For now, everyone needed to be completely focused on the PT test.

In all reality, the PT test should pose little problems for any member of Alpha team. The Phalanx had trained hard and was more than physically capable. Their weakest physical link was the once pudgy Techno. As the weeks of intensive physical fitness had gone on, the Twinkie fat of the boy that never left his computer workstation was replaced by lean muscle mass. His weight had dropped from a portly two hundred and ten pounds to a trim one hundred and seventy-five.

In addition, Tech had taken to training every morning with Dancer, learning the various karate katas, blocks and strikes associated with her style of martial arts. Push-ups, sit-ups and even pull-ups were no longer an issue for the boy. If there was any reason for concern at all it would be the endurance run. On average, Tech could make the run in about fourteen minutes and fifty seconds to fifteen minutes flat. However, there was always the "X" factor of his asthma. An attack in mid run could be disastrous, causing him to fail and be recycled or worse. Spartan needed to talk with Nurse Ortega before the run began. Perhaps she could offer some advice.

Seeing the nurse standing alone beside the camouflaged Humvee that bore the Red Cross on a white background, Spartan slowly approached her. For some reason he felt very intimidated by this mid-thirtyish woman. Perhaps it was her wealth of knowledge in the medical arts. She seemed to know everything about everything from bandages to first aid to surgery to field triage. It could also be because she had brutalized her infected husband in front of a group of cadets and then had stood by with little more than a scream of fury as Drill Sergeant Boomer had pacified the man where he lay strapped to the table during the week of first aid training.

"Ma'am?" Spartan called. "May I ask you a serious question?"

The nurse startled by the formality of the request; answered just as formally. "Yes corporal, do you have an injury?"

"No ma'am. It's actually about one of my team members; Cadet Techno. You see ma'am he has asthma, and while we're certain that he can complete the final PT run given ideal circumstances, we are concerned that the anxiety of this final week of testing may trigger an attack and cause him to fail. Is there anything that we can do to prevent this? Is there anything that he could take to keep it under control?"

Nurse Ortega smiled knowingly. "Wait here." She instructed and entered the rear of the Humvee. Five minutes later she reemerged with a crushable chemical ice pack and an ace bandage. In a conspiratorial voice she spoke very quietly to Spartan.

"Hold out your wrist. When I start to wrap it moan like it hurts. Under the ice bag is a syringe. Twenty minutes before the run, Techno gets all five cc's in the butt. No more, no less, and nowhere else. Now moan!"

"Aaugh!" Spartan moaned as instructed. To him it sounded like a hokey impression of a Romero.

"Don't be such a baby Spartan. It's just a sprain. Keep the ice on it until your PT test and you'll be fine."

Just then Sergeant Havoc walked by slowly. He glared daggers at Spartan, not even bothering to hide or conceal his contempt for the boy.

"Injured?" He snarled. "That's a shame. Slipped in the Jell-O did you?"

Spartan looked down trying to formulate a response. Before he could come up with an answer, Nurse Ortega spoke up.

"Perhaps if you were truly a good sergeant then you would have control over your private band of mercenaries. Instead, I'm stuck treating at least a sprain and possibly a green stick fracture because he blocked Cutter's steel toed boot with his wrist instead of his forearm. I hope you are fuckin' happy and proud of your team, because I know Julie would be so ashamed of them… and of you!"

The small Hispanic woman was nearly standing on her toes as her fury lashed out at the drill sergeant. The normally smug Sergeant Havoc reeled in shock at the verbal onslaught. Without another word he spun on his heels and marched away.

"Wow!" Spartan said.

"Sorry." The nurse replied sheepishly. "It's been building for a long time. Ever since he got his wife Julie killed. She was a good person, a friend of mine in fact and she never would've allowed him to act that way. Now, run along. Remember. Twenty minutes, in the butt."

"Yes ma'am." He turned and started to run back to where he had left his team. Then all of a sudden, he stopped and turned back to the nurse.

"Ma'am? Sergeant Havoc's wife; Julie. You said that she was your friend?"

The nurse looked at Spartan sadly. "She was not only my friend; she was my sister." As tears slowly rolled down her brown cheeks.

"I'm sorry." Spartan said again seeing a family tragedy on the kindly woman's face; then held up the ace bandaged icepack on his wrist. "And thank you."

Then he ran full speed back to his team. Arriving back at the barracks, he quickly assembled his team around him.

Rapidly he explained what Nurse Ortega had given him and they all agreed that it was in Techno's best interest to take the shot.

"But I don't need it!" Techno whined as his eyes traveled down to the hand were Spartan held the needle. "I've been training hard both at PT and with Dancer. I'm skinnier than I have ever been, and I haven't fallen out of a run since week six. I didn't even have an attack during the Dante course and that was really stressful."

"Are you willing to take that chance here Tech?" Spartan asked. "If you fail the test, there is no second attempt. You get recycled or you walk Damnation Road out to the bridge. I agree physically you're in much better shape than you were when you got here. Heck, we all are except maybe for Freak. But asthma can only be controlled to a certain point; then it becomes chance or luck. Hedge your bets. Take the shot." Spartan insisted.

Techno eyed the needle warily. It really wasn't the medicine that he was worried about. In fact, Spartan was probably right; it was in his best interest to be sure that he didn't have an attack while he ran. But the needle, if it could be called the needle, look to be at least three feet long and could probably be more properly categorized as a javelin, spear or even a harpoon. Just seeing the syringe in Spartan's hand was making his head spin and his heart race. Sweat was springing out on his forehead.

"I'm sorry Spartan. I can't! I know that you're just trying to help but I… well you see… it's not the medicine. It's… well… it's the… ah, shit!… It's the needle. I hate them. No – more correctly I am terrified of them and I cannot… will not voluntarily take part in using anything like that… that… demonic instrument from Hell!"

The last three sentences came out of Techno's mouth in a blur. Spartan was certain now that the boy had a phobia of needles. Fortunately, he had prepared for that eventuality. As Techno's voice rambled on, Deadeye and Freak quietly walked up behind the panicked boy.

"I understand and I'm sorry too Tech." Spartan said quietly, then looked over the Asian boy's shoulder and nodded once slightly.

As Freak and Deadeye each grabbed an arm, horror dawned on Techno's face. The boy struggled mightily, kicking his feet and swore everything up to and including his ancestors returning from the dead, traveling from Japan and eating the three boy's souls. None of it had any effect. Deadeye and Freak maneuvered the boy over to the table in the center the room where Spartan had calmly already walked to. To Techno's supreme horror, the syringe seemed to be growing exponentially in his team leader's hand with each step.

Spartan pointed to the table and Techno felt his feet leave the ground. His vision canted then inverted altogether as he found himself face down on the table. The next thing he knew, all two hundred and eighty pounds of Freak's bulk flattened across his back, crushing him against the table. His upper body pinned, he tried to kick his feet but found his legs similarly pinned by Deadeye.

"Noooo!" He screamed.

"Sorry Tech. This is for your own good." Spartan said. "Dancer; a little help please." The athletic girl entered the training room from around the doorway where she had been patiently waiting.

Techno's cry of terror changed to a plea for mercy, as he begged his teammate, his faithful morning training partner not to skewer him to death with the unholy instrument of torture. His pleas fell on deaf ears. Nodding to Spartan that she was ready, she took the syringe from her team leader and poised the needle over the struggling boy's buttocks.

"Remember what they taught us in first aid." She said with a smile. "When receiving a shot, clinching the muscles up makes it hurt far more. Try to relax."

Dancer had been the smoothest in the team for administering IVs and shots during the class. Although she was primarily the team sniper, she was also by far their best medic. Nodding that she was ready to her team leader, Spartan then grabbed Techno's sweatpants at the waist and yanked them downward, exposing the boy's bare buttocks.

"This may sting a little." Dancer said and Techno began to voice his last-second plea for amnesty but was cut off in midsentence as the syringe, now the size of a Tomahawk missile, rammed through his flesh and settled into his gluteus maximus muscle, delivering its payload. All the boy could do was emit a strangled cry of agony.

Then all the weight that had been pressing down on his body vanished and he was surrounded by his four teammates who were laughing so hard that tears were freely flowing from their eyes. Yanking his clothing up and re-tying his sweatpants and regaining his composure, Techno addressed his team, trying to find any modicum of dignity. "It's not funny. I hope you all had a nice laugh at my expense." And they laughed all over again. "Just remember paybacks are hell." Techno said and then smiled too. "Everybody's afraid of something."

As it turned out, the shot had side effects that while beneficial to Techno, were annoying to his teammates. A combination of bronchial dilator and antihistamine, Techno could hardly sit still and began to talk nonstop about ten minutes after the injection. Twenty minutes after the shot, he was like a little Asian super ball, bouncing all over the place.

As expected, push-ups were the first event. Freak made the test look ridiculously easy, knocking out one hundred push-ups within the first minute, before the drill sergeant told him to knock off the showboating. He then eased his pace to one push-up every two seconds for the remaining minute and stood up without looking even remotely tired. Competitively there were no physical specimens like Freak within the Academy. Not the cadets. Not the sergeants and other instructors. Freak was... Well just that; a freak.

Sit ups and pull ups came just as easily to Alpha team. After twelve hard weeks of physical fitness training, all the cadets were paragons of physical development. Muscles rippled and sweat dripped as the teams all vied for the coveted physical fitness supreme champion of the Apocalypse Academy championship belt. Gaudy and unwieldy, the idea had been pirated from the old pre-"Z" night wrestling shows. The Academy needed a champion. The fitness challenge was amazing to watch as were the variety of personas that arose, tied to their codenames. Cadets expended all of their physical prowess into earning the belt made of golden spray-painted plating over steel and fastened to a long strip of leather. Actually, the metal portion of the belt had been molded by taking a replica of an old-school championship belt, placing it against potter's clay to make a casting and then filling the casting mold with metal that had been smelted by Sergeant Boomer. The leather portion of the belt was an old-fashioned weightlifter's belt: wide in back but worn in reverse so the plate could be affixed to the front. As ugly as it was, the belt was a huge source of pride to all the cadets vying for it.

By the end of the pool of competition, it was obvious that Freak had a significant edge. Only four cadets were within range that they could theoretically catch the big man. They were Gator, Orc, Dragon and unbelievably… Techno. As the final competition lined up, Spartan could hardly believe his eyes and ears. Techno was in the running for the supreme physical champion of fitness at the Apocalypse Academy? What the hell had he injected the boy with? Liquid dynamite? Super serum? Whatever it was, it would sure as heck be handy to have about five extra vials in a med kit.

As the cadets prepared for the final event; the two-and-a-half-mile run, the top four contestants plus Freak lined up at the starting line in front of all the other cadets. Trash talking between teams was playfully flying back and forth as they all wanted a piece of defending the future supreme champion of fitness at the Apocalypse Academy for their team.

In the midst of the chaos, Freak saw Orc whispering to Cutter. Sensing the two were up to no good, the gigantic cadet nudged Techno and motioned with his head towards the conspiring teens.

"Watch yo' back brutha!" He said. "They are up to some cheatin' ass shit. Guarantee it."

Techno smiled and nodded "Thanks."

"Pass it on to Dragon, I'll tell Gator." And Techno did. By the time the race was ready to begin; all four cadets were staring holes into Orc's exposed back. When the fang toothed boy finally turned around, he took two steps backwards in surprise at the anger he saw displayed from the competitive cadets in front of him.

"Whatever you and that slimebag Cutter got planned, be warned. You cheat or you try to injure one of us and Dancer will feed the goats with your balls from a plate. By now they should be about as tender as mashed potatoes." Techno said calmly.

"Back home, we gots a sayin'" Gator added. "Don' start no shit an' dere won' be no shit. You fuck wit' us and I'm gonna gut you and sink yo' body in de quicksand. No body. No crime."

"In China," Dragon added. "If you are caught cheating in a race, they used to cut off your legs at the knees. That seems to fit here as well. Perhaps in your infinite wisdom you can figure out how to run from "Zs" on nubs. There is no honor in cheating."

Lastly, Freak stepped directly up to the boy. Orc was a big teenager. Almost 220 pounds of muscle of bad attitude. But next to Freak, he looked more like a middle schooler.

"You tell me now. You want to go South Side style? I'm game if you do. No rules, no crybabies. One winner and one dead man. So, if you got the balls; at least whatever the little lady didn't kick all the way to St. Louis, then speak up now. If not, you better just stay the fuck out of my way!"

Orc looked around desperately for support from his team leader but was surprised to find Cutter had stepped away at the first sign of conflict with the other teenagers and had subsequently missed all the threats of bodily harm.

"No" Orc gulped, his mouth suddenly bone dry. "Just runnin' that's all big man. No tricks, no plans. I really think that you're gonna win this race too big man." The boy said in a low tone, his eyes suddenly studying his shoes.

"Sure ya do Dawg. Just remember what we said. You fuck around wit' us; and you're gonna pay to us all."

Then Freak turned back around and took just long enough to grin covertly at Dragon, Gator and Techno. A few seconds later, the starter gun fired, and they all took off at a sprint. All of them except Orc, who was still standing it shocked fear at the starting line. When the boy finally realized that the race had begun, thanks partially in part to Drill Sergeant Havoc screaming that he was going to tear the boy's heart out and feed it to a "Z" for breakfast, Orc was already almost twenty full seconds behind the other racers. That is not much time when singing a song or building a house. In a race, twenty seconds is an eternity to make up.

Freak, Techno, Gator and Dragon ran for all they were worth. The race would run them lengthwise from the Apocalypse Academy steps, down the river road, beyond the Dante's fenced walls all the way to the Armory before reversing course and returning to ultimately finish back at the front steps of the Apocalypse Academy. Dragon took the early lead, setting a brisk, striding pace for the four contenders. Several of the more prominent cadets that were skilled at running also kept pace but at a respectful distance. Leading the quad of the cadets down river road, Dragon ran full out using the natural barrier of the Rock River to guide their course as it burbled merrily in the early morning sun. The flashes and sparkles of sunlight glistening off the water in the early morning daybreak brought a sense of calm to the urgency of the race and the boys settled into a comfortable pace. Cool morning river air caressed their brows, keeping the racing teenagers from overheating. Not surprisingly, they were unknowingly running in step with each other as they had been trained to do over the past weeks of intensive training at Apocalypse Academy.

Orc slowly made up ground, but to do so he had been forced to sprint almost all the way so far. As the cadets passed a grove of trees on the right side of the road, they were not surprised at all to see Drill Sergeant Stone standing next to a Humvee with a megaphone clenched in his fist.

"One half-mile mark. Three minutes, ten seconds. Keep it up!"

So, on the boys ran, the only sounds being their boots on the asphalt and the cadence of the river rolling by. Passing the entrance of the Dante, the cadets noted the permanent smell of decay and rot the came from within its fenced confines. Although the fences were chained and locked, the place was still a proving ground for death and their pace subconsciously quickened to get away from it and the horrors the course contained within.

Farther back, almost an eighth of a mile behind, Orc struggled to keep up his desperate run. Alone, whether by choice or by fear, the boy ran for all he was worth. Rounding a bend in the road he could see the Dante course's fences up ahead. Then, as if by magic he saw Drill Sergeant Havoc emerge from the tree line just before the obstacle course, waving frantically for him to alter his path from the road to the trees. Orc had nothing to lose and he was not about to disobey the pissed off drill sergeant. With one quick glance behind to ensure no one was looking, he darted into the tree-lined path behind his Sergeant. Without a word the drill sergeant turned and ran, and Orc followed.

Freak was starting to get a stitch in his side. The grueling pace set by Dragon was beginning to take its toll. By no means was he a distance runner. Sure, before "Z" night he had run track, but the longest distance he had run was the four forty or the two twenty which were sprinters events. Gator seemed to be having similar issues. Repeatedly putting a hand against his ribs, the boy's loping, awkward stride was shortening. Dragon and Techno showed no signs of fatigue at all. In fact, Techno seemed almost giddy.

Gritting his teeth, Freak began to call cadence to himself in the form of the Blues Brothers "*Sweet home Chicago.*" His mind distracted from the pain in his side, Freak passed the struggling Gator, who quickly began to lose more and more ground.

Upon reaching the Armory, the cadets were greeted by Sergeant Surfer. Standing on the hood of his Humvee in a wave catching pose like he was on a gigantic surfboard, the drill sergeant called out to them.

"Halfway dudes. Looking good at five minutes and thirty-six seconds. Gotta pick it up just a little. Touch the wall of the Armory, make a righteous turn back around and hang ten all the way back to the Academy." As each of the four cadets touched the wall, Sergeant Surfer popped flares, letting everyone know that the return run had begun.

Seeing the flares, Spartan hoped that his teammates were faring well. Although he probably could have been competitive throughout the physical fitness test, he had found himself severely distracted, thinking back to the hand gesture of Cadet Cutter in front of his team the previous week. No, the award wasn't important to him, so he had intentionally dogged the sit-up portion of the testing, claiming that he pulled a muscle in his stomach. Watching Cutter was. But if Freak or Tech won the race; and if Cutter decided to intervene or try to hurt one of his teammates, then he would be there to put an end to the threat. So, he ran along, exactly two paces behind the Echo team leader.

Passing back in front of the Dante, Freak could have sworn he heard movement in the trees to his left. Pausing in his cadence he continued to run but listened carefully. If a "Z" somehow got out of the Dante's fences now, they were all in deep shit since they were all unarmed. Hearing nothing else, he kept running but his song was lost, and so was his rhythm. He began to slowly fall farther and farther behind Techno and Dragon.

The two cadets raced on. Dragon used his martial arts mental toughness to drive his legs mechanically and Techno being propelled along by the Nurse's almost magical syringe of chemical super serum. This race would come down to the two of them. Chinese and Japanese heritage competed for dominance, as they had for centuries, before "Z" night.

Fifty yards behind the leaders, Freak saw Orc burst out of the tree line, sprinting for Techno and Dragon. The cheatin' bastard didn't even run the full course!

"Aww, hell no!" Freak said aloud to no one in particular, and then put everything he had into a sprint to catch Orc from behind. Freak decided then and there, that while he might not win the race, Orc would not stop Techno or Dragon from doing so, even if it meant breaking the boy's legs. Besides, he thought, he would probably enjoy breaking Orc's legs anyway.

Once again passing Drill Sergeant Stone, the time was called out through the megaphone.

"Ten minutes, fifty-three seconds!" He called out to Dragon and Techno as they passed as location. "Ten minutes, fifty-seven seconds" was Orc's time. "Eleven minutes!" was Freak's time. Three seconds behind the Echo team cadet. He poured on the speed. He had to catch him!

"C'mon!" Freak said to himself, pushing his body to the limits. *"Catch that fucker!"* Pumping his arms like pistons, the gigantic muscles responded, propelling him forward with renewed speed and began rapidly closing the gap between himself and Orc. Orc, in his single-mindedness to eliminate either Techno or Dragon, never heard Freak charging up behind him. A slim wooden rod about ten inches in length appeared in Orc's thick hand, from the rear of his waistband. Raising the weapon high above his head, he prepared to brain Techno from behind. Techno appeared to be singularly focused upon the race and did not see or hear the heavy-footed boy behind him. Perhaps sensing danger or a flicker of movement, Dragon glanced over and saw the Echo team thug preparing to strike the unaware Alpha team member

from behind with the wooden rod. Reacting from pure instinct or perhaps out of an ingrained leadership skill, Dragon threw himself sideways, striking Techno with a body block that took them both to the ground just as the primitive browed Orc swung his makeshift club with all of his might for the Asian boy's skull.

The blow missed as the boys tumbled to the ground with a grunt of pain from one and a "what the f…?" from the other. Orc's powerful momentum spun him in a half circle, stumbling sideways and disorienting him for a millisecond. Stopping to look at Dragon and Techno lying behind him on the trail, Orc was happily surprised to see neither one had stood up yet. Now he had time to teach these two chopsticks how to administer pain: The Orc way. Lumbering forward, Orc again raised the weapon over his head to strike Dragon as he was trying to rise back to his feet. Standing almost upon his tip toes, Orc pulled the weapon back and began to bring it downward in a vicious arcing blow that would've surely split the Bravo team leader's head open. Then, as fast as his swing began, it froze mid-motion, his hand trapped in the weapons thong. Looking up to see what the problem was, Orc came face-to-face with a very angry looking Freak who stood clutching the baton, holding it and the arm attached to it straight up in the air. The enormous cadet immobilized Orc's hand and without even straining, lifted up the stunned cadet. Orc dangled helplessly by one arm and watched helplessly as a fist the size of Connecticut drew back and flew forward, slamming into his unprotected face. The hand holding the baton dropped him effortlessly to the ground, where Orc laid clutching his smashed nose with both hands and trying to staunch the blood flow and hide both his tears and missing four front teeth.

Dragon took the initiative for a payback strike and drove a sidekick into Orc's already bruised solar plexus. Air and bubbled blood burst forward in a crimson mist as Orc sought to make his lungs work. Kneeling on all fours, the boy spluttered and begged for mercy in a lisping, miserable tone.

"Sure!" cried Techno, standing behind the boy. "Mercy it is. I won't kill you like you tried to do to us, but it is my belief there should always be payback for wrongdoing. So, here is yours!" As Tech kicked a field goal with the boy's testicles from behind. Squealing in pain the boy fell over; vomiting before his face hit the ground. His re-brutalized testes smashed for the final time, preventing the boy from ever needing to worry about having children and permanently changing the tone of his voice.

Freak looked over at Dragon and Techno. "You dudes ready to end this race?" He asked. Dragon replied. "May the best man win." All three boys nodded in agreement.

"On three we go. Ready? One, two, three!" And all three boys resumed racing for the finish line leaving the unmoving Orc lying face down by the roadside in a pool of his own puke.

In the end, whether it was the adrenaline of fighting with Orc or the personal challenge between the three boys, or just pure fortitude, all three cadets finished the run-in remarkable time despite the fight: just over eleven minutes and thirty seconds. Dragon beat out Freak and Techno in the final stretch by the length of his head, however in total points scored, Freak was untouchable. All the other cadets finished the course about a minute later including Orc who was literally drug by his arms as he clutched his battered balls across the end of the course by Savage and Skull. With almost a third more points than any of the other cadets, Freak beamed as he proudly accepted the Supreme Championship for Physical Fitness belt from the drill sergeants at an impromptu ceremony on the Apocalypse Academy steps. The remainders of the cadets were dismissed for chow. Many were congratulating Freak with cheers and back slaps or admiring his championship belt. Techno walked over to the Bravo team leader and offered his hand in friendship.

"Thank you for what you did out there in the race. You saved my ass."

Dragon shook Techno's hand. "Anything worth doing is worth doing with honor. If I won the race because you were attacked from behind and I did nothing, the race would've been meaningless."

Techno nodded, and then surprisingly both boys bowed to each other in the ancient tradition of respect. "Besides" Dragon said with a grin "I've been waiting to repay some of Echo team's kindness for weeks." Clapping Techno on the shoulder they both laughed.

Later that same afternoon, around 2 o'clock, the cadets were reassembled and marched to the sawdust pits for an exhibition dedicated to understanding the basics of hand-to-hand combat skills and close quarter battle. As with physical fitness, several cadets excelled here. One by one the least proficient cadets were eliminated until the last remaining combatants came down to Spartan and Dancer from Alpha team, Lightning from Bravo team, Deacon from Delta team and both Savage and Skull from Echo team.

To eliminate an opponent, the cadets had to either be rendered unconscious, submit to a joint lock or chokehold, or be tossed entirely from the sawdust pit. The final elimination battle would be an open combat so all six combatants would be in the pit at the same time. As Sergeant Hogg blew the whistle signaling the battle to begin, Spartan and Dancer immediately shifted to an instinctual back-to-back stance to prevent attacks from the flanks or the rear. Lightning darted in first throwing a sidekick towards Dancer. She blocked the kick easily enough but as he counter spun from the momentum; his spinning back fist grazed her chin, snapping her head back.

Spartan was similarly engaged by Deacon who was trying to use his greater reach to grapple with the Alpha team leader. Deacon, at almost 7 foot tall, was long and spindly. His arms were almost five inches longer than Spartan's, thus reach and leverage were at his command. Fainting a strike toward Spartan's head, Deacon shot in low to grab for purchase on Spartan's front leg. Spartan countered by locking in an over-the-top chokehold onto the gangly boy's long neck as he bent forward to grab Spartan's legs. Deacon immediately began to thrash, his arms shooting out, looking for purchase to pull Spartan's forearm from his windpipe. Watching Deacon to see if he tapped out, Spartan did not see Savage come up on his blind side until it was too late and all he could do was brace for impact as the boy's knuckles impacted on his exposed and unprotected jaw. Starbursts exploded behind his eyelids, but Spartan doggedly held on to the chokehold even as the momentum of Savage's punch drove him to the ground.

Savage did not hesitate in the least and began to rain stomps and kicks down upon both the defenseless Deacon and Spartan, not really caring who he hit, simply happy to be hurting *someone*. Deacon's helpless body suffered most of the booted impacts as he had landed on top of Spartan and was held in place by the choke hold. After the sixth successive kick to his unprotected ribs, the lanky black boy tapped out on Spartan's hip. Spartan immediately released the hold, rolling away from Savage's assault. Deacon fell limply to the ground, moaning in pain.

Dancer meanwhile was struggling with Cadet Lightning's continual flurry of blows. While his technique was not the prettiest, what he lacked in style he more than made up for in unbelievable speed. Dancer allowed her form to become more passive and began to redirect rather than block the boy's punches and kicks. Despite the tight defense, she was steadily being pummeled out of the sawdust pit, and there was little she could do about it. The lightning-fast boy seemed to have an endless supply of energy. If she lowered her guard to counterstrike at all, there would be at least two, possibly even three strikes waiting for her.

Then abruptly she felt more than saw the battering fury break off. Looking through her defenses, Dancer saw Cadet Lightning locked into a rear naked choke hold by Skull. Apparently seizing the momentum of Cadet Lightning's focused assault on the girl, Skull had come up behind the oblivious boy and slipped his forearm around his neck, clamping down on the carotid arteries. Shades of crimson darkened by the second under the boy's skin as his body struggled to pump the entrapped blood throughout his body. Momentary panic washed over Lightning's face and suddenly the teenager's arms fell limply to his sides as his eyes rolled up into his head. Even as the teen's body weight sagged into unconsciousness, Skull did not let go, instead grinning at Dancer and licking his lips as he applied increased pressure onto Lightning's neck.

"It's gonna be you next sweetie. Gonna pull you up close and personal like, feel your body against mine. Then, I'm gonna look into your eyes as you choke and squirm. Watch that light go out when you have no air. Maybe I let go, and maybe I don't. Mmmm-mm, maybe I put out your light for good."

Dancer's emotions raged between fear for Lightning who was now almost blue in the face and hanging limply in Skull's bony arms, to disgust at his callous suggestion that he was going to kill her. Her fighting rage took over as she stepped forward to engage Skull.

"Let him go!" She screamed. "You're killing him!"

"Yeah, that's the point. One less bloke to interfere between me and you. Why, when I'm done, I might even let you touch…"

He never finished the sentence. Dancer's side crescent kick flew like a laser over Lightning's bent forward head, over Skull's shoulder and smashed into his front teeth. Skull flew backwards, blood and teeth exploding between his lips as several shattered and broke away. Lightning dropped like a stone to the ground and Dancer paused long enough to ensure the boy was still breathing before she advanced on the prone Skull.

"You bloody, sick, sadistic piece of filth. You want to see pain? You get off on hurting people? Get ready. I'm coming to hurt you. I'm going to hit you, kick you, beat you until you bleed from a dozen bloody places you wanker! Then I'm going to pop your elbows and knees from their sockets like chicken legs from the thigh! When you are beaten, bloody and helpless, I'm going to do what you wanted. I'm gonna press my body tight against you, put you into a chokehold and slowly squeeze. You'll flail at first with your damaged arms and legs, but you won't be able to grab me. Then you will begin to fade into unconsciousness. But I promise, I will continue to tighten the hold and as you begin to slip into your final oblivion, your bowels will release from your broken body, and you will die twitching in your own shit and piss right here in front of everyone!"

The look in Dancer's eyes showed Skull that there was no bluff to her words. The British accent drove home the point as clearly as his broken teeth did. Skull did the only thing a sadistic coward like he could do. He crawled out of the sawdust pit, completely out of the ring and ran for his life amidst the laughter of the other cadets.

Dancer looked over to Spartan. Seeing her team leader on equal footing with Savage, she moved to check on Cadet Lightning. Spartan could hold his own against that boy. Lightning still had not moved from where he had fallen face down in the sawdust.

"Corpsman!" She hollered "Man Down!"

Spartan maneuvered himself so that he was between Dancer and Savage. Keeping the Echo team creep from his teammate and the injured cadet meant he was limiting his own maneuverability as well. Half circling, like a hungry predator, Savage paced back and forth looking for an opening in Spartan's defenses. A feral growl emerged from between the boy's lips, and Spartan suddenly had an epiphany as to why the boy had been given the codename Savage.

Two unknown Corpsman appeared through the doorway into the metal barn that held the sawdust pit. Trotting quickly around the circle, they entered closest to Dancer and began checking the boy's vital signs. Dancer's breath caught in her throat and Spartan instinctively knew that the results were not good. Thirty seconds later the cry of "Clear!" and the crackling electricity confirmed his fears as Dancer had begun to sob. Still the fight raged on. The drill sergeants showed no sign or inclination of stopping the battle because a cadet had fallen.

A red rage began to settle over Spartan, like a veil of crimson shadow that slowly tinted his vision and narrowed it until only he and Savage existed. His perception of his opponent changed from competitive to deadly serious in an instant. He could feel the blood rage pounding at his temples, the veins in his neck, arms and hands protruding as he flexed them back and forth. Gone in an instant was the kindhearted boy from Wisconsin. He had been replaced by a member of the world's most elite fighting caste, a Spartan warrior. Somewhere deep in his mind he remembered a lifetime of training to become one of the world's deadliest warriors. Heedless of the danger posed by the feral teenager in front of him, Spartan set his jaw into a snarl of his own and marched forward, intent on wreaking havoc and drawing blood.

Savage snapped off a quick front kick to Spartan's midsection, and followed it with a roundhouse right hand that sprayed blood in an arc across Spartan's face. The blood ran freely across his lips and teeth, giving the teenage warrior a demonic look to his visage. Though the punch snapped his head sideways and blood ran freely, Spartan showed no sign of pain, and no fear of injury. With the blood-flecked war cry of spittle and rage, Spartan lunged, grabbing the Echo team cadet by one ear and jerked his head forward. Forehead met forehead with an audible crack and Savage's eyes immediately began to roll up into his head, glazing over. Still holding the boy by the ear, Spartan delivered one, two, three, four devastating elbows to the captive cadet's facial areas. Cuts burst open above and below Savage's right eye as well as across the bridge of his nose.

Like Spartan, the cadet could not feel the pain of each successive thundering below as it was delivered. Unlike Spartan, it was because he was unconscious after the first head butt, dangling from one ear held in the teenaged warrior's fist. Holding the boy shoulder high and at arm's length, Spartan evaluated the blood and gore-soaked cadet. A faint moan seeped from the boy's mouth. Not enough to be a word but enough to be a catalyst for the warrior to act. Reaching up with his other hand to grasp the remaining ear, Spartan roared a battle cry and pulled the boys head viciously downward while driving his knee up to meet the descending cranium. The smash of bone meeting bone sounded like a gunshot and Savage flipped over, his legs slung over his head by the momentum of the blow, to land face down and spread-eagled on the hard ground outside of the sawdust pit.

Blood rage roaring in his veins, Spartan wheeled around and faced the only combatant left… Dancer. Seeing the berserker in front of her, Dancer was certain that no amount of physical punishment short of a killing blow was going to be sufficient to stop her team leader's assault if he came after her next. She was certain she wasn't willing to go that far just to obtain a trophy for being the best hand-to-hand combatant in her class at the Academy. Spartan was not only her team leader; he was her friend as well. Certainly, that was based on mutual need for watching each other's backs there was more to it than that. More feelings, more emotion had been built through their shared time at the Apocalypse Academy. There was an inherent goodness that he possessed. A willingness to be a defender; a knight in shining armor that stood out against the backdrop of the "Z" riddled world like a beacon in the night. There was the handsome build of his features and how a look from him made her heart race a hundred beats a minute. It would be so easy to fall in love… with… him. Then, like a bolt from the blue she knew how to win.

Watching his rage twisted face, she locked eyes with Spartan. Slowly she reached at hand up to her combat hair bun on the back of her head and began pulling the bobby pins free, one by one and dropping them to the sawdust. Her other hand she held up in a placating motion, palm extended waiting for Spartan to break the rage and mentally come back to reality. As her brown hair began to cascade downward over her shoulders, she saw the faintest softening of the anger in his eyes. Gently she took a tentative step forward and began to speak where only he could hear her, her eyes never leaving his.

"Spartan, it's me… It's Dancer." She said softly. "I know that you're angry, but I am not your enemy. I'm your friend, Spartan. D'you understand me mate?"

As she talked softly, Spartan's eyes lost their hard edge. The angry red tint that he was seeing through slowly eased back; being replaced by confusion. Dancer took another step forward now only an arm's length away from Spartan. If he attacked her now, she was doomed. He could easily overpower her. She knew that she could not, nor would not strike a killing blow against him. So, the battle for her would be over and so was her chance to win hand-to-hand supremacy. She would lose and maybe even suffer a serious injury because she was unwilling to fight this man at the level that she needed to in order to win. Instead, she trusted her instincts. Followed her heart. She kept talking to him softly; calmly. Soothing his rage with her voice. Forcing his will to override his anger through passive domination.

"I am here Spartan. It's over. You've won. I need you to come back to me now. You're all I have left in this world. My mum and dad are gone. So are my brothers and sisters. Dead or turned. Even my Gran, God rest her soul. You're all I have to hold onto. To make me feel like this life is worth living anymore, worth holding on for."

His face softened with each word. The angry red that had surged up his neck subsided completely. He gently reached up and took her extended hand in his own. "Dance?" He spoke. "What happ…?"

She cut him off with the shushing sound took the final stride forward into Spartan's reach. Her world zoomed in like a telescope to focus only on Spartan's face. She was close enough to hear his breathing. To see deep into the rich brown of his eyes; so dark that they were almost black. She pulled his hands to her waist, and placed her own around his neck, her eyes never leaving his. The auditory exclusion for them both eliminated all other sounds from the areas around the combat pit.

"I have something to tell you." She said in a voice barely above a whisper. "I guess I've known for a while but couldn't be sure. Now I am certain, but if you do not feel the same way then I will understand. I will even request to transfer to another team if need be, if what I have to say is too uncomfortable.

The thought of Alpha team's Phalanx without Dancer was almost impossible to fathom. She was their sniper, their medic, their flag bearer, and their friend. No, he would never let that happen.

"Say it." He said, his voice trembling with his nervousness.

"Okay, here goes." She said, gently rubbing the back of his neck with her fingertips. Licking her lips to find the moisture that fled with her nerves, she broke eye contact looking down at his broad chest and let it flow. "I know we should not care too deeply. In the world since "Z" night, when you allow yourself to care, people can die. But I cannot help it. I think about you and I become distracted. I look at you and I catch you staring at me and in my mind, I am exactly where I am now, in your arms. I love you." She looked back up into his eyes not really knowing what to expect. Acceptance, denial, rebuttal, or confusion. She just couldn't be sure. Instead, he leaned down and kissed her gently. "I love you too Dance." Then followed it up with "Let's get out of here." Together they walked out of the sawdust pit, certain to step out at exactly the same moment. Let the Drill sergeants figure out who the real "winner" was. In the eyes of Spartan and Dancer, what they had was better than any trophy.

The roar of the assembled crowd of cadets accompanied by applause, whistles and cat calls shattered the auditory lockout that had allowed them their personal moment of intimacy. They both flushed a deep crimson with embarrassment but continued to hold hands as they walked through the crowd only to have the parting of the cadets end at a severely pissed off looking, cigar chomping, bald Drill sergeant.

"What the hell do ya think you were doing?" He hollered "I ain't sure but I don't seem to recall givin' no commands or orders that say anything about you're supposed to be playing kissy face. This arena's for fightin' not lovin'. You want lovin', get a room!"

Spartan thought about his answer. He thought about the long talk he had had with Sergeant Hogg in the drill sergeants pre-"Z" night home. His answer came to his mind almost immediately.

"I thought we'd take the time to think about the future drill sergeant. Think about doing something today so that we do not regret anything if we never get to it tomorrow. It's a lesson I learned from a great man not that long ago. I call it the Catherine lesson."

Sergeant Hogg paused as anger smoked from the coal embers within the depths of his eyes, then he grinned around the stub of the cigar clenched within his teeth. "Get the fuck out of my goddamned face! Cadets dismissed!"

Chapter Eighteen
The Firing Range and the Lottery of the Damned

Qualification or "Qual Day" was really no major surprise. It would consist of basic handgun and rifle courses over distances from three feet or what was known as "danger close" to twenty-five meters for handguns and fifty to three hundred meters for rifles. Snipers were expected to shoot the handgun course then they would move to a much longer range, eliminating targets up to one mile distant.

Upon completion of the basic firing ranges, the cadets would be assembled in their full teams to be given the assault plans for the modified shoot house, a number of target "Zs" and information as to whether or not there were any living people to try to rescue. Determining success was simple. Survive unbitten, eliminate all of the "Zs" and rescue the living; if any, and your team was good to go. Get bitten, get dead or kill an innocent and you failed. Each team would additionally be issued three flash bang grenades for use in the mission.

Movement through the handgun course had become almost second nature after a full week of loading, firing, dropping magazines and reloading and then firing the weapons again before finally clearing them at the end of the run. Most of the cadets fired near-perfect scores with their strong hand and only pulled a shot or two off of the bull's-eye with their off hand. Some of the cadets were naturals, shooting with either hand without error or concern. Spartan had very little trouble with his Glock. The smooth trigger pull and lack of kickback or safety made the weapon easily transferable between hands. In fact, all the team leaders did extraordinarily well through the course.

Other cadets that stood out during the firing range were Bravo team's replacement Cadet Raven, Charlie team's Popcorn and Echo team's Cadet Skull. In the end, no one could draw faster or outshoot Charlie's team leader; Cowboy. Whether he drew from the thigh, hip or shoulder holster, his three fifty-seven just seemed to just materialize into his hand. His shots were groupings of less than one inch in diameter no matter what the distance, leaving the remainder of the target looking clean and pristine. Even reloading from the speed loader, he could fire off the required twelve rounds faster than the cadets with the semi-automatic pistols and with unerring accuracy to boot. In the end, no one was quicker, or more accurate than the friendly Texan. The shiny handgun trophy was his.

Rifle qualification was a different story. Most of the cadets who shot exceptionally well with a pistol had difficulties adjusting for windage, elevation, humidity and numerous other considerations with the long guns. A couple of cadets, specifically Princess from Charlie team and Pig from Bravo team had been required to do a period of remediation before being allowed to reshoot the qualification course after not quite making the grade the first time through. Both had passed on their second attempts. Interestingly, they had both had initially failed to qualify for opposing reasons. Princess had been unhappy about placing her immaculately clean armor down into a prone position in the dirt, so she kept squirming in an effort to stay clean, thus affecting her aim. Pig was just the opposite end of the spectrum stating that the continual squeaking of the plates attached to his armor were distracting him *"It's like a mouse continually squeaking in my ear."* After rolling around in the dust and the judicious application of lubricating spray, the boy had completed the course without further difficulties. Completely weird.

The long gun course also included a modified version for shotguns and the distance range for the snipers. Spartan initially thought Dancer would run away with the sniper trophy, however Gator and Skull were both excellent shots, and pushed the competition to the very last round. In the end, every target was hit by all five cadets. The Drill instructors, led by Sergeant Havoc, were forced to measure distance to the "X" ring bull's-eye to establish who had been the best of the best in the sniper school. The results were so close that they were measured twice.

"Cadet Lightning's total: 2.8 inches over thirty rounds." The Drill sergeant called out. Spartan was glad the boy had recovered from the previous week's choke out my Skull enough to keep pace even if he didn't win the competition. Spartan couldn't help but wonder how much the defibrillator may have affected Lightning's strength and ability to focus. The fact that the boy was completing the course at all was a testament to his personal toughness.

"Cadet Taco's total: 2.2 inches over thirty rounds." His team leader gave a loud "Ye – haw" and slapped the boy high five, apparently having earned his place in Cowboy's eyes as Roosters replacement. In a way, Spartan envied his counterparts continually positive outlook on life. It had to make getting through each day infinitely easier.

"Cadet Skull's total: 1.1 inches over thirty rounds." Spartan noted that there was no joviality from Echo team. In fact, they looked downright pissed off.

"That group is seriously dysfunctional." Spartan said to no one in particular as he read their angry body language.

"Dude, it took you this long to notice? Those dudes are like serious downers man. A real bummer." There was only one person that Spartan knew that talked like that, so he was not surprised at all to see Sergeant Surfer keep walking, without any further comment. What a paradox of personas that man contained; one part of laid-back beach bum, one part of demolition expert. Spartan wondered if he surfed to assuage the guilt of blowing people up or if he blew people up because he felt guilty over his passion for surfing? It was a paradox of personality traits. The last two scores for the Cajun-raised Gator and British-raised Dancer were about to be announced.

"Cadet Gator's total: .5 over 30 rounds. Excellent shooting. That is of a qualification level equal to what is required to participate in the Special Forces." Congratulatory backslapping and cheering came from his team as Gator beamed a wide smile.

Spartan held his breath. Dancer's scores were last. He hoped that that was an omen that her shooting had been enough to gain her the high score.

"Cadet Dancer's totals: .45 over 30 rounds. I present to you the long gun and Sniper champion: Cadet Dancer of Alpha team by .05 centimeters. Congratulations!"

"Yes!" Spartan said out loud and pumped his fist in celebration, then smiled as Dancer gave Gator and Lightning a quick hug out of sportsmanship. "I bet Skull would've never done that." He said elbowing Freak gently indicating the sportsmanship displayed by his teammate.

Upon completion of the target shooting competition, the cadets were all released to attend chow. They were given instructions to form back up at 1300 hours on the quarter deck and to be prepared for the shoot house challenge. Unlike most of the meals at the Academy, this one had an air of enthusiasm for the cadets. There was a good amount of backslapping and congratulatory remarks for the five contestants involved in the sniper challenge. As usual, Skull of the Echo team only snorted his derision through his broken teeth at coming in third rather than being in first place, complaining that the test was rigged and that he had shot better than anyone else on course. When someone, perhaps Cadet Popcorn, pointed out that Skull's own drill sergeant was one of the judges, the boy had nothing else to say.

After everyone had finished their meal, they were allowed time to clean their armor and perform a weapon check before forming up out on the quarter deck. Melee weapons were added to the cadet's armored attire and they were marched back to the area of the shoot house to prepare for the challenge that awaited them.

The shoot house challenge was similar in nature to the first-time Spartan, Deadeye and Freak had gone through it. The only difference was that now Techno had been incorporated into the assaulting third spot between Spartan and Freak. This allowed Freak to focus on performing his duties as the six man, covering the teams back while they moved. In addition, Dancer sat on the towered platform five hundred meters away, spotting for "Zs" through doors and windows through her sniper scope and looking for potential "Z" targets of opportunity.

Spartan gathered his armored entry team and directed a quick weapon check to ensure all the weapons were hot with a live round chambered. Then he ordered a "jump check". As he and his companions lightly bounced up and down, he heard a soft flapping noise coming from Techno's gear. Stopping Freak and Deadeye, he told Techno to jump again, listening carefully. The noise was coming from Techno's combat vest.

"What do you have in there Tech?" Spartan asked, pointing to the large cylindrical pouch on the right front side of the boy's chest.

"It's a study manual." He said sheepishly. "I was told by Sergeant Surfer to keep it with me at all times because it would become invaluable if I ever really needed it out in the field."

"A study manual? Like how to create homemade explosives, bombs and pyrotechnics? I guess it could have value in a pinch if we get pinned down and needed to improvise with scrounged items. Does it tell…"

Techno cut them off. "That's not exactly it." He said. "I know how to do all of that stuff. It's really not hard at all."

"Oh, well what is it then? What could you need out the field with the study manual? Let me see it." Spartan said, and held out his hand expectantly.

Techno hesitated.

Giving an audible sigh, Techno reached in and pulled out the small spiral ring binder. Four inches across and six inches in length, the booklet had a creased and worn yellow cover.

Opening the first page, Spartan skimmed the title and the table of contents. When he finished, he lifted his visor viewpoint until he was looking directly at Techno.

"You're serious?"

"Dead serious."

"Yo Dawg, what's up? What you readin' dude? Come on give a brotha a break?!" Freak called out.

Techno stood immobile and said nothing at all. Spartan read the title allowed over his team's helmet communications.

"Riding the Wave: Searching for tranquility on a sea of undead. The Zen lessons in peace of mind as recorded in the memoirs of Sergeant Surfer."

"Holy shit." Freak said softly. "We're gonna learn to surf?" Then he got loud. "Dude that's freakin' awesome! You can be like the kung fu surfer, and I can be the Blues surfer. Hell, the Apache can be the scalping surf dude too! Of course, Spartan and Dancer will have to have a special board for *couples surfing* if you know what I mean bro!"

Both Dancer and Spartan keyed their mikes simultaneously in response. "Fuck you Freak!" They both said in unison. Then Spartan added, "There's not even a board big enough for your ass!"

"You finished?" Techno asked in a serious tone, holding out his hand for his book.

"Yeah, sorry Tech. Just having a little bit of fun. We're done. Just secure it so there's no battle rattle to give us away. Okay?"

Techno nodded and took the notebook back, securing it under his armor. Looking up, he saw the individual light blinking on his internal visor screen indicating that someone was attempting a private communication. Techno keyed the switch expecting more ribbing. He was surprised to hear Deadeye's voice.

"Yeah" he said.

"I wanted to take a moment to commend you on your search for inner peace. My people believe in much the same concepts as your Zen. Peace, harmony and tranquility are all values to be aspired to. The power of nature, whether it's in my forests or in your oceans can provide this peace. That's all I wanted to say." And he clicked off the comm line without waiting for a response.

Techno had known that the teasing would come one day when his team found out about his Buddhist beliefs, but he had not expected Deadeye of all people to be the one to speak up in the positive. There was a deeper person inside of the Native American cadet and one day perhaps he could share the philosophy of the wave with Deadeye and compare it to the philosophy of the forest that the Apache believe in.

"All right people, we're up next." Spartan's voice came across the communications on Alpha team's helmets. "Remember we have "live" "Zs" and possibly live human beings as well. Be certain of your targets. Deadeye: you are on point. Let's be silent if we can, to prevent attracting all of the "Zs" into one area where we could be overpowered.

Dancer: I want you always looking one room ahead of us. Any movement: friendly or "Z" let us know. Freak: nothing comes up from behind us. Techno: you've got the 'bangs and powdered zinc rounds for your shotgun in case we run into any locked doors inside or if we need a distraction. Are we ready?"

"Yeah, I'm good." Techno said. The rest of the team acknowledged they were ready as well.

"Okay. Flash bangs only if called for, or if we are in deep shit. Any last questions or comments before we enter this hellhole? No? Then let's lineup. One last note: Dancer…"

"Go ahead."

"After the first shot has been fired, you are cleared to engage any hostile's ahead of us."

"Copy That." Was all she replied. The girl's voice sounded serious as if she was completely and totally focused on the mission at hand.

Just then Sergeant Hogg walked up. He addressed the whole team through a boom mike that lowered from beneath the brim of his round brown hat.

"Those sum'bitches from Echo team just put up the top score at one minute, fifty-five seconds. Four "Z's" were pacified. They also had one civilian that was terminated which cost them a thirty-second penalty. So, it two minutes and twenty-five seconds in total. Even with the penalty time, they were still well ahead by almost a full minute over Bravo, Charlie and Delta teams. To tell you the truth, I think they shot the civilian on purpose. Twisted little bastards."

The drill sergeant paused to pull the well chewed end of the cigar out of his mouth and spit a wayward piece of tobacco out onto the ground before re-addressing his team.

"Don't you dare let those masochistic, psychologically inbred, genetically deficient pieces of trailer park trash beat you in this course! You are the Phalanx. An unstoppable wall of armor and weapons! Get in there and stomp a muddy hole in those undead asses and walked them dry all the way to victory!"

As one Alpha team cheered. Turning away, the drill sergeant strode purposefully into the shoot house. Spartan saw the private link flashing on his helmets view screen. Executing the command to open the link, he could suddenly hear the drill sergeant's voice again.

"Spartan, can you hear me?"

"Yes, drill sergeant!"

"Good. Listen close these are your mission parameters. There are four "Zs" inside the building. Two are adults and two are children. They are to be pacified. No options. There's also one civilian, live, trapped inside as well. Do you understand?"

"Yes, drill sergeant!"

"Repeat orders!"

"Neutralize four "Zs". Two adult, two children. One living civilian to be rescued. Maximum time for operation: two minutes twenty-four seconds."

"Good." Then the drill sergeant spoke up again. "And Spartan; don't fuck this up. I am your civilian to be rescued. If you or one of your men shoot me by accident or let a "Z" take a bite out of my ass, I am going to be seriously pissed off at you!"

The communications link clicked off. Spartan quickly relayed the mission intelligence to his team. Two minutes and some change was very little time to complete the operation as assigned without having any casualties. He needed to change the tactics.

Mission parameters did not prevent observations of the exterior of the building prior to the mission beginning. "Dancer can you see any "Zs" from your vantage point up high?"

"Ten – four, it looks like mama "Z" is in the kitchen. The window is open and there is movement inside. There's a window in the first room as well but there are heavy curtains hanging so I can't tell if this is just the wind blowing the curtains, our civilian or if there's a pus bag inside. Be cautious."

"Confirm the following orders. Once we stack, we will breach when you neutralize mama "Z". That would drop our targets inside by one. After that you are cleared to acquire targets of opportunity. Just ensure that it's not one of us or the civilian."

"Copy, Alpha team breaching on my shot. Acquiring target now. Free fire to engage any hostile's after that."

The team lined up to the left side of the door except for Freak who held the battering ram on the right as he had the during the last mission. Techno, then Spartan tapped up the line to Deadeye. Deadeye then gave Freak a thumbs-up gesture and upon receiving the confirmation from the giant, gave the verbal go-ahead to Dancer who was eagerly waiting up high.

"Phalanx is green... Repeat Phalanx is green."

A second passed. Then two. Suddenly like a clap of thunder, a single shot rang out.

"Go! Go! Go!" Spartan cried out and Freak simultaneously breached the door. Wood splintered and flew apart is the door, frame and all, disengaged from the wall and flew into the center of the room. A quiet call came over the communication system.

"Mama "Z" confirmed pacified."

"Copy... Keep looking." Spartan replied. Deadeye had gone right entering the breach and Spartan pivoted left following the contour of the wall. Techno and Freak followed the same pattern. Seeing nothing of interest in the first room they moved to the door on the opposite side, leading into the living room.

"Negative contact: moving."

Deadeye got to the door first. Reaching up he gently turn the knob; it was unlocked. Just then a low moan came from behind the closed door. It was a moan that spoke of misery, of hunger, and of a tortured soul. It was a moan of the undead. "Contact." Deadeye said in a whisper, then motioned for Freak to come forward. Flashing hand signals, he indicated that Freak should pull the door open and then he would engage the "Z". Letting his M4 fall to his side on its three-point sling, the Apache pulled his combat tomahawk from his belt. Ready for close quarters combat, he nodded at Freak. As the door was pulled open, Deadeye moved directly to the contact. Spartan and Techno each peeled right and left respectively and flew along the walls as Freak covered the rear to ensure that they missed nothing.

The Apache cadet dropped low and flung the Tomahawk as hard as he could at the adult male "Z" that shuffled across the floor towards him. It was obviously a Romero from the way it moved. Fifteen inches of razor-sharp steel flew forward in a twirling blur. The black blade reappeared as it embedded itself into the "Zs" forehead, splitting the skull like a ripe melon. The creature fell to the ground; its body leaned awkwardly against the dining room table leg.

"Papa "Z" engaged and neutralized. Time hack?" Spartan called.

"Thirty-five seconds…" Came Dancer's reply. "No movement in room three, offside of the house is still unknown."

"Copy" Deadeye said, as he ripped the Tomahawk loose from the skull of the Romero in a single snatching motion while he moved; never slowing down. The team moved forward quickly. The third room was the kitchen where Mama "Z" had been pacified. Her brains and blood splattered across the stove like some bizarre form of gray spaghetti. Avoiding the bloody mess, the team moved ahead towards the bedrooms.

"Three rooms to go. Two bedrooms and a bathroom. Tech …bang them all. Remember there's a civilian in here somewhere. Mark your shots. Tech with me on bedroom one, Freak and Deadeye on number two. If there is no contact, then we rally in the hall and deal with the bathroom last."

Techno passed the flash bang to Freak. It was about to get very loud inside this building while he modulated the ZAP armor's helmet visual and audio sensors to modulate the noise and reduce the impact on his own vision.

"Time's ticking people" Spartan said. "Let's make it count. Standby, standby, go!"

The two two-man teams breached the closed bedroom doors simultaneously, each throwing flash bangs into the room and waiting for the dynamic sound and light explosion that followed before entering. Seconds later came calls from Freak and Techno over the communication system.

"Contact civilian! On the ground, Mother Fucker, on the ground! Are you bitten!?" Spartan couldn't help but chuckle to himself as he knew that Freak had just put the big drill sergeant onto the ground forcibly and with a loud thump and was currently zip tying his hands together.

"Copy contact. Secure and hold onto him until you get out into the hall Freak. Then turn him over to Techno for extraction. Our room is clear. Negative contact. Deadeye and I will clear the last two rooms. Once extraction has been completed, flow up the hall and meet up with us at the end."

Five seconds later, as Freak and Techno combined their efforts and evacuated the Drill sergeant, Deadeye called out the "clear" to Dancer as he and Spartan reentered the hallway from the bedroom. That left only the bathroom in the two missing "Z" children. The problem was if the bathroom was as small as they remembered from the previous training mission, then only one person would fit in there. Spartan made a command decision.

"Freak, Techno: evac back with the civilian! Deadeye hold the hall. I'm taking the bathroom."

"Copy." Came Freak's reply. "Be careful."

"But…" Techno started to say but was immediately silenced by Spartan.

"No time for arguing Techno. Follow orders! Dancer…Time?!"

"One minute forty-four seconds!" Came the reply.

Spartan turned and kicked in the bathroom door without another word. Immediately, he heard the sound of splashing water. Sweeping his tactical light on his M4 across the room he sighted past the sink, the toilet and finally across to the closed shower curtain. The splashing sound was coming from behind the brown and tan checkered piece of plastic.

Reaching out a single hand, Spartan ripped back the curtain. What he saw was so repulsive he almost ran from the room. Two toddlers sat in waist deep water, surrounded by fluffy white bubbles and wearing chains around their necks. Each one had suffered multiple bites before they died and then rose again as one of the undead. One was bitten on the cheek, its off-white teeth showing through the torn flesh of the cheek. The other had been bitten on its belly; its intestines partially hanging out of the wound like a sick, perverted gray snake. Neither of them could have been more than two years old. A deep sadness settled onto Spartan as he looked at the children. The red dot from his site was focused squarely on the first one's forehead.

"One minute forty-five seconds, Spartan! Let's go!"

Spartan did not respond.

"Spartan! Are you okay?" Came Deadeye's call over his helmet communications.

"Yeah." He said softly and depressed the trigger of his M-4 twice, pacifying each child with a single round to the skull. The last thing he saw as he left the room was a small body sinking slowly beneath the bubbles.

"Clear" he called; thankful no one would ever see the tears that fell behind his visor.

"One minute fifty seconds!" Came Dancer's call.

"Deadeye, go!" And together they ran down the hall backtracking pass the bedrooms, the kitchen, the dining room and living room.

"One fifty-one, one fifty-two, one fifty-three…"

Deadeye and Spartan burst out of the shoot house door. "One fifty-four!" They had beat Echo team's time by a full thirty seconds.

The celebratory atmosphere upon completion of the shoot house was short-lived. The remainder of the day and night was uneventful for most of the cadets. Weapons were cleaned, stripped down and cleaned again. Throughout the entire process, the majority of the cadets engaged in jovial conversation, laughing and joking back and forth; remembering various events from week one when they had all been traumatized orphans until today when they had become established in new "families" within their teams and the Apocalypse Academy as a whole.

Two specific groups did not participate in the festivities and laughter. One, as usual, was Echo team. Although they had to draw cleaning supplies at the Armory just like everyone else, they quickly exited, with no talk and no smiles. The only hint that any of them were even part of the overall team was a look of longing that flashed briefly across Lotus Jane's face as she caught sight of Techno. The curve of her lips vanished just as quickly when she caught Dancer watching her. With a swirl of red and black hair, she vanished.

"What the hell was that about?" Dancer asked Raven who was seated next to her. They had been deeply involved in a conversation about pre"Z" night hair care products before Echo team's arrival.

"I don't know. Maybe she wishes she wasn't part of that pack of strays." She said, flipping her two-foot-long braid over her shoulder.

"I don't know. I don't trust her. I think she might be looking for a new victim to stick a knife in. If I had to guess, it would probably be from the back!" Dancer replied snidely. She made a silent vow then to keep an eye on the girl. Techno was the proverbial low esteem, fat kid. If that blinkin' tart thought she was going to pull his heart strings and dance over his grave too, then she was sadly mistaken. She would have to go through Dancer first and that nasty assed skank wouldn't have a chance in hell.

Looking around, she saw Spartan sitting off by himself. His back was facing the crowd while he field stripped and cleaned his M-4 for the third time. He hadn't spoken to anyone since the shoot house. There was no joviality in the victory, no orders to follow, no suggestions to debate and no conversation to engage with. If someone asked him a question, he answered with a grunt or in some other noncommittal way. He had not even acknowledged Alpha team's victory in the shoot house competition.

Leaning back, she elbowed Freak in the kidney to get his attention, and then spoke quietly to him so that no one else could hear.

"What the bloody hell is wrong with Spartan? With only two days until graduation, he is more down in the dumps than I remember him being even at the initial in-briefing. Did one of the Drills jump his ass for something or what?"

"I dunno. Dude hasn't said a word since we cleared the shoot house. It's almost like he's not even really home upstairs. Just constantly lost in his own thoughts." Freak said pointing at his temple. "Like his body is moving on muscle memory and reflex but his brain has taken a subway ride down into hell. I hope he snaps out of it. The lottery is tomorrow. If he should happen to be the number one draft pick like this, then he's going to be in deep shit."

"Do you think I should try to talk to him?" Dancer asked.

"Nah. Not right now at least. Too many people around and if talking takes him into a bad place like it did at the sawdust pit, then it'll be better if no one else sees it. Besides, Spartan's my boy. He'll be okay. He just needs time to work through whatever's eatin' at his guts. I've seen it before; usually after a drive-by shootin'. One of the kids gets capped and family and friends fall apart. A few days later, they get it together and usually go looking for revenge. He'll be okay. You'll see."

Dancer wasn't so sure. Over the course of training, she had come to trust Spartan. Even to love him. His self-control and sureness of action were some of his most endearing traits. Whatever happened in the shoot house, she had not been able to see through her sniper scope. She had watched the teams every movement, room by room. Had seen the pacification of Papa "Z" after she had done the same to Mama "Z" long range. That had left… the children. She had not been able to see the pacification of the children, but that was the only missing piece left to the puzzle. The only unknown. Maybe there was a tie to his past…Something that had popped up in his clouded memories; to a time before when the Apocalypse Academy staff had found Spartan. She had to talk to him and help him if she could."

"Thanks Freak."

"You bet." He replied.

Dancer turned back to Raven and found the girl talking to a very quiet boy code named: Skunk. Rumor had it that the boy, who had come into Delta team after the death of Cadet Knight on the Dante course, had been so scared by whatever circumstances he faced during "Z" night that his black hair had actually drained itself of color right down the center of his head. Whether or not this was true or just an urban legend; Dancer didn't know but "Z" night had changed a lot of people; emotionally, psychologically and maybe even physiologically. There were stranger stories out there.

Dancer listened quietly while Raven regaled the striped haired boy with stories of her lost dog, Cuddles, her love of ice cream, which unfortunately had also disappeared during the days following "Z" night, and the fact that she owned at least thirty-six separate pairs of shoes. Dancer quietly wondered if she had ever been that shallow before the "Zs" had risen to take a bite out of the arse of the world. Thinking back on her own past, she remembered taking shopping trips to London and Paris with her mum. The dozens of bags of useless stuff they had bought. Shoes, fancy dresses, perfume, art. In the long run, it was all a waste of resources and time compared to the martial arts teachings and demand for physical fitness that her father had held her to.

She vividly remembered her Mum and Dad arguing about how the years of her youth should be spent. The two opposing skill sets, shopping and survival, had not matched up in the post "Z" night world. The need for the frivolous, had become replaced by a need for the practical. High heels had become combat boots. Makeup had become camouflage. Credit cards and wallets full of money had transformed into guns full of bullets and scabbards for blades. She supposed there was still a fondness in her memories of the old days shopping with her Mum or talking on the phone to her friends, Bailey and Marissa, about boys. A benign longing for the carefree giggling of her youth; laying on her fluffy pillow topped bed, cuddling with Mister Snuggles, her favorite teddy bear. But she had also been trained since her youth to survive; to be physically and mentally tough enough to adapt if the world went to hell. It was almost as if her Father had been precognizant during her childhood. So, in her eyes, the Apocalypse Academy was no better and no worse than shipping off to another boarding school; it was just a different type of curriculum.

After two hours, most of the cadets had gone off to bed or moved on to other concerns. Spartan sat alone at his workbench, the sword of Leonidas leaning beside him in its sheath, as he began to field strip his assault rifle for the seventh or eighth time. Other than the movement required to disassemble the weapon, the Alpha team leader had not varied in his spot or general position for more than three hours.

"Ahem!" Came a soft call from behind him. His body tensed visibly but he did not turn around. The large empty room echoed with the sound of a pair of combat boots approaching across the tiled floor.

"Do you mind if I sit down?" A feminine voice asked. It was Dancer.

Spartan grunted in a noncommittal reply.

Dancer walked over and sat down beside Spartan, gently sliding the gun cleaning kits to the side. She looked down at the pile of cleaning squares lying in a pile on the floor at Spartan's feet. The average cadet used five to six squares per cleaning. Maybe as many as ten if the weapon was really filthy or had been fired hundreds of times. Spartan had more than a hundred squares at his feet. The gun looked immaculate; probably better than it had straight out of the shipping crate, yet still he cleaned it, oiled it and cleaned it again. Gently she reached over and placed her hand over his hand, stopping the repetitive cleaning motion.

"Spartan, whatever it is, you know that you can talk to me. Right? The team and I are very worried about you. You haven't said three words to anyone since we left the range."

"Nothin' to talk about." He replied quietly, his head still looking down at the floor.

"Nothing? If you don't want to talk about the range and the shoot house, fine, but at least talk to me about what happened at the sawdust pit. It seems like we should at least discuss that or was that just a spur of the moment comment. An offhand remark that you said, and maybe even didn't mean and now regret."

The room was quiet in response. Dancer's heart began to beat faster, her teenage fear of being rejected pushing her heart rate up. She opened her fingers to let go of his hand, giving him the freedom to pull away if that was what he wanted to do. But instead, he held fast to her delicate fingers. When he spoke, it was barely above a whisper.

"No. It was not a mistake. I do love you Dance." He turned his head to look at her. She almost gasped out loud. His eyes were so red that they had passed crimson and now were on their way to almost a shade of violet. Large purple rings pouched his eyes making them look swollen. If she had not known that there was no way that he could have become infected, she would've sworn that he contracted the Hunger virus. The only indicator that he had been merely emotionally suffering rather than being in the first stages of turning, were the twin tear trails that had eroded the grime and dirt off his face.

Dancer tried to speak; to say something to ease her team leader's pain. To calm the suffering of her friend or to comfort the heartache of the man that she had come to love during their time together at the Apocalypse Academy. Her brain grasped for fleeting words, but her thoughts could not wrap around the pain that the man was feeling. She knew there were words that she was supposed to say to bring comfort. She had been brought up in the church and taught that certain words make you feel better in a time of need. But as her jaw moved to match those words that she had been taught, somehow her mouth prevented the thought from coming out. In the end she looked very much like a fish out of water, mouth gaping open and then closed, and feeling very foolish.

"It's okay." Spartan said. "You don't have to say or do anything. I'll be ok. I appreciate the thought." After pausing to take a deep breath that ended in a shallow mournful sigh, the Alpha team leader began to confide in his teammate. Slowly at first his sorrow leaked out, then increasing in volume and content until the pain flowed outward, surging out of him like a roadside creek filled by the summer rains.

"It was the kids." He said in a hoarse voice. "The shoot house scenario "Z" family." He added when Dancer did not seem to understand what he meant.

"Pacifying the mother and father was no issue. They were "Z's" through and through. Putting an end to their miserable affliction before they spread the infection had seemed… proper, I guess. Maybe even merciful. In the end, it's what we have been trained to do. To save that little remaining piece of humanity and to prevent them from sharing the eternal undeath that their kith and kin had already suffered. To grant them a sort of final peace."

"When I rounded the corner into the bathroom of the shoot house, I had been expecting children, maybe nine or ten years old. Old enough to have been a threat. To run, to bite. Instead, I found two toddlers. Both were no older than two years of age, sitting calmly in a bubble bath, chained around the neck and completely transfixed by the soapy bubbles. They were not concerned with me in the least. They did not moan or reach out to grab me. They did not gnash their teeth or try to crawl out of the bathtub or make any type of effort to pass on their infection. They just looked up at me as if to say *"See, we are just like other kids."*

Spartan paused as a fresh round of tears spilled out silently, gouging new pathways down his grime-streaked face. Dancer sat across from him; her hand held loosely over her mouth; a look of horror in her eyes. Tears fell freely from her eyes as well, accompanied by black streaks of mascara.

"I pacified them both as mercifully as I could. I do not know why, but the whole scene felt like an instant replay. Like I had lived through it already and my heart knew what type of pain to expect. Maybe it's a subconscious memory of something that has already happened in my past or maybe it's just a repressed fear of the future. I don't know because I don't know who I am or what I have done before, except for the few details that Sergeant Hogg has told me. All I know is that both times that I pulled the trigger to pacify those children; my head was telling me that I was doing the right thing; that I was showing them mercy and helping to save humanity. But at the same time my heart called me a murderer. A baby killer. A monster of a sort far worse than any "Z"."

"I'm so sorry Spartan." Dancer said, now holding his hand with both of her own. "For what it's worth, and I realized that this is not much of a concession, I could not have done it. Even if I had the perfect shot through the bathroom window, I could not have pacified them. But that's why you were selected to be our team leader. You, of all of us, alone have the strength of character to make the hard decisions. To do what's best for the team and if it came down to it; to even pacify one of us. Not everyone has that mental toughness to make the right choice no matter how painful it may be to us personally. You have done it twice now; first with Rooster, then today with those poor children. We have all been trained to be warriors. To fight… to kill. But only a select few of us can truly be leaders. That's what you are. That special combination of field command ability and controlled compassion is what makes you the best of all of us all to lead Alpha team."

"She's right." Came a voice from across the room. Dancer and Spartan both looked up and saw the rest of Alpha team standing there.

"They're getting ready for the lottery and want us all to assemble on the quarter deck at 2100 hrs. When we couldn't find you in the barracks, we decided to come look for you just in case Cutter or one of his flunkies tried to take advantage of your vulnerability." Freak said. "Besides, I always sleep better if I can open a can of grandmamma's whoop ass 'fore I go to bed. Too bad them A-holes ain't around to say good night to." Freak said with a grin, his white teeth glinting in the armory's light.

"By the way Dawg, Deadeye told us what happened. None of us could've taken the shots and done what needed to be done. It sucks to be sure, but you've got to remember that they ain't kids no more. They might look like 'em. But the HUNGER virus took out their souls. They're just meat puppets now man. Shells shaped like people. And I expect that the whole scenario was set up just to see who was tough enough to lead. To see who had the guts to do what needed to be done." Freak said.

"Shit Dawg. You lead the Phalanx. Together there ain't nobody, "Z" or otherwise is bad ass enough to get in our way and our leader is the toughest-assed S.O.B. of 'em all."

Deadeye added on to Freak's conversation in a tone that was exactly opposite of the giant's boisterous wording.

"In my tribe, many of the young braves aspire to be Chief. They go out and kill many deer for the meat and create intricate carvings from the antlers as tributes to the ancient spirits of their elders and forefathers. But when the age of adulthood comes, they fail their tests. Not because of a lack of bravery, or determination of spirit. These they all possess. They fail because they do not understand that to be a leader of men; you must possess the wisdom of the forest to accompany the trophies of the living. To the white man this is confusing. But to the Apache, it means that each and every life is sacred in its value. That the value of the passive turtle's spirit is just as important as the soaring spirits of the hawk in the sky or the mighty bear in its den or the sly fox creeping through the night. To be a Chief or in our case, to be a leader, you must be able to be all of these at once or none at all, depending on the needs of the moment. You must be able to separate yourself in time of need to provide the leadership that is needed based on the situation. Most braves only find a single totem spirit and are limited to that group or class. Thus, they fail to ever become Chiefs. You, my friend, possess many totem spirits and will lead us for a long time to come."

"You are our leader. Our Chief as it were. You possess the bravery of the grizzly, the majesty of the eagle, the tactics of the wolf and the protectiveness of the wolverine along with the wisdom of the owl. Do not be ashamed of these attributes; be proud of them because very few are the man that can have them all."

"Ya, it's kind of like memory chips on a motherboard." Techno added. "The chips are useless without the motherboard to guide the pathways and programs. You're our motherboard."

All four cadets looked at Techno in unison, and then began to laugh hysterically.

"What?" Techno asked not seeing the humor in his statement. "What did I say that was so funny?" Which made Spartan and the rest of Alpha team laugh even harder.

"I guess you really are a "*mother*" now Spartan." Freak said.

"We hope you don't get "*bored*" with us!" Deadeye added.

"Oh, that will only happen if he is "*programmed*" that way." Dancer chimed in.

After a few more moments the laughter died back down, everyone wiping tears away from their eyes except Techno, who still didn't get the joke.

"Thank you all." Spartan said. "You will always be able to count on me, for as long as you want me as the leader of the

Phalanx." Looking at his watch they had only five minutes to be on the quarter deck and in formation at twenty-one hundred hours. Shoving all the contents of the cleaning kit back into the green waterproof bag, they took off at a full sprint, Spartan leading the way.

***

The formation was guided along the route by Colonel Slade. All five drill sergeants led their respective teams, marching in unison to the Colonel's cadence. Marching past the Armory and Nurse Ortega's residence, the cadets silently wondered what was to come with the lottery. Who would be chosen, and would that person survive the battle still to come?

Finally, the formation was called to a halt. Spartan noted that they were in front of the open field where Techno had so long ago almost gotten them all killed by the motorcycle riding Lords of Death. The Colonel walked around to the front of the formation and addressed the cadets and Drill sergeants together for the first time as a unit in the field.

"Today I have the unique privilege and dubious honor of selecting the first Apocalypse Academy lottery participant. Before I make that selection however, I want to talk to you all about the education and training that you have been entrusted with and that you will hopefully continue to build upon. In the days, weeks, months and even years to come your lives will depend on the skills and training that you have learned here at the Academy. In addition, the lives of your teammates and those of numerous civilians may depend upon you making the right choices in any given opportunity. When and how to fight, when to run, when to take the time to provide pacification and when to let the undead wander away are all just some examples of these choices that you will be forced to make in the coming days."

"For all of you the training has been the same. The expectations have been the same for each one of you since your arrival at the Apocalypse Academy as orphans. Without this training, most if not all of you, would have surely perished in your cities, towns or farmhouses where we found you. It is our sincerest hope and desire to continue that tradition. As you and your teams are sent into the field, you will come across orphans that will need shelter, training and reestablished structure to their lives. In finding and bringing these children to the Apocalypse Academy's doors, you will be helping to provide hope for humanity's continued survival and in essence, paying for all of the long hours of training that you have already received."

"Toward the ultimate end of training to further humanity's survival, we've established this final test. A randomly selected cadet whose name shall be pulled from an old bingo game letter generator, essentially written on a ping-pong ball, will be responsible for defending all of you, your Drill sergeants and me from being infected by an equally randomly generated "Z". The selected cadet will have no weapons and no armor when they fight this battle. They will be required to depend solely on their training, their wits and perhaps a modicum of luck to persevere. If the cadet fails, he or she will become infected and potentially infect any number of their fellow cadets and Instructors. In the end, this final test comes down to skill, strength, speed and agility as well as the will to survive and to protect themselves and their teammates from becoming one of the walking dead."

“We are almost ready to begin. Do any of you have any questions? Yes, Echo team leader, I believe your name is Cutter, you have a question?”

“Sir, yes Sir!” He hollered then added “…well actually more of a comment Sir!”

“Proceed.”

“I just wanted to say that any member of Echo team is ready, willing and able to volunteer for the selection in the lottery and to demonstrate how efficiently we are capable of removing a “Z” from the field of play with our bare hands.”

Spartan thought the wide-eyed look of surprise on Lotus Jane’s face did not echo her team leader’s readiness to volunteer her into the face of possible infection or death. It was just another example of how dysfunctional Echo team was.

“Thank you, cadet. I am sure your enthusiasm is appreciated and well backed by your drill sergeant as well. Anyone else?”

“Yes… Corporal Cowboy isn’t it? Charlie team leader?”

“Sir, yes Sir.” Cowboy southern Texas twang made it sound more like “Suh, yes Suh!”.

“I was wonderin’ if the cadet was selected and all with this here lottery and someone, say maybe a team leader or somethin’ was willin’ and able to take their place and all, could we do that? I mean, no disrespect intended to the ladies, but no slip of a girl should be going out there to take on no "Z" barehanded. That's man's work and all. You know, protect the family type thing. That's all Sir."

Spartan could hear Dancer grumbling down the line, venting to either Deadeye or Techno on either side of her. The "man's work" comment had surely pissed off the female cadet. Everyone that had seen Dancer fight over the last twelve weeks knew that she was more than capable of defending herself. Spartan only hoped that she held back the raging volcano of emotions long enough to realize that not all of her female peers at the Apocalypse Academy had received the benefit of hundreds of hours of martial arts and weapons training from a military father. For many, combat training before "Z" night had consisted of preparing to power shop at three am on the day after Thanksgiving in an effort to deprive another sale paper scavenger of a two-dollar savings on some kid's Christmas present. Although cart ramming, hand slapping, and teeth gnashing antics were in many ways reminiscent of the current "Z" filled world, they were far less deadly on the Black Friday's of old.

"From some of the looks in the crowd of cadets, I would say that your sexist comment was not generally shared. However, if someone was willing or felt compelled to volunteer and if the original lottery selectee was willing to step aside, then an alternate combatant could be utilized." The Colonel replied.

"Anyone else? No? Then let me close out my speech with this: by surviving, both at your homes near and far and through the trials here at the Academy, you have all demonstrated that you are all true warriors born and bred. That you all have the metal to see comrades in arms fall before the undead horde, yet you will continue to strive to survive; to become a beacon of hope for humanity and with a little bit of luck, to one day take back our world from the undead. Whatever happens here today, I am proud of you all and I can honestly say for the first time since "Z" night that I feel, what I hope and pray to be the first of many feelings of hope and confidence. I am certain that we are on the path to setting the scales between life and death right."

"Drill sergeants post!" Came the call from Sergeant Stone. Sergeants Hogg, Havoc, Boomer and Surfer all broke away from the ranks of their formation and created a square fifty yards apart centered on the Colonel. Sergeant Stone walked over to the Colonel, saluted and removed a small folding table, more like a TV tray from before "Z" night from where it was strapped to his rucksack. Setting it down onto its four legs, the drill sergeant removed his rucksack and pulled two round wire balls out of his bag's main compartment. Each wire ball contained a set of white ping-pong balls, a small wooden or plastic pedestal and an old-fashioned hand crank. The drill sergeant sat both of the wire balls on the table in front of the Colonel. After saluting again, Sergeant Stone moved to stand behind the Colonel.

Pointing to the wire ball on his right, the Colonel spoke. "This basket contains thirty-one ping-pong balls. There is one for each of you cadets, one for each Drill sergeant, and one for me. You may wonder why the Drills and I were included; the answer is simple. We are all part of the same team. The dangers that you face; I should also face as should the men that have trained you. We should be no less willing to brave danger than any of you."

"This basket..." He said indicating the one to his left, "contains thirty-one ping-pong balls as well. In it are ten Husk "Z's", ten Romero "Z's" and ten Reaper "Z's" each with their own ball. The selected "Z" will be the opponent. Questions?"

"Sir?" Spartan heard the Bravo team leader Dragon speak directly behind him. "You stated that there were thirty-one selections for the "Z's", but sir you only gave the numeric breakdown for thirty of them. Is that correct Sir?"

"Yes cadet, that is correct. The thirty-first ball is the ultimate test of a cadet's skill and endurance. That ball represents the need to combat one "Z" from all three categories at the same time. In other words, the chosen cadet will face a Reaper, a Romero and a Husk all while being unarmed and unarmored. The chances for a fatal infection to the cadet or one of his or her fellow teammates are much higher, and the chance of failure is much greater."

A buzzing murmur shot through the assembled cadets. Three "Z's" at once! If that ball was drawn then the cadet was doomed and so too were potentially the rest of them! There were very few instructors that could handle those types of overwhelming odds much less cadets.

The Colonel held up his hand for silence. "You must trust in your training. In the field you may find yourself in far worse odds than 3 to 1. When we found many of you, the "Z" to human ratio was 100 to 1 or greater. Twelve weeks ago, none of you were truly skilled combatants. Some of you were brawlers or possibly had received some exposure to knives or guns in your youth. Now you have all ranked as proficient at all these tasks. You have newfound skill sets and have honed them to a fine point. You have survived exposure to actual "Z's" in the field not once but twice. The first time being in the Dante obstacle course and the second time occurring in the shoot houses as you graduated from your firearms training."

"Have faith in yourselves. Have faith in your teammates. Whoever is selected, whether it is the biggest, toughest, calmest, meanest son of a bitch or the quietest, meekest, kindest mouse of all of you, remember that you all have received the same training to survive this final test."

"I found many years ago on the field of battle that anticipation is one of the worst enemies one person could face. Let's get on with this shall we?" He said and began to turn the crank on the wire cage on the right. Ping-pong balls tumbled, rolling over each other in a sudden wave of white plastic. Their sight and sound reminded Spartan of a popcorn popper that he had had as a child. Interesting. Another memory returned in the face of potential danger. He would have to remember to ask Sergeant Hogg about it, provided they all survived the day.

Spartan tried to see the cadet names that were written on the white ping-pong balls as they spun and tumbled by, but they turned and twisted so quickly that he could not make out the words. Then just as quickly, the rattling wire ball stopped and the Colonel reached into a small door, grasping a ball without looking. The ball with the cadet's name on it was handed over to Drill Sergeant Stone as the Colonel closed the door with an audible click.

Sergeant Stone read the ball and spoke clearly. "The name of the cadet that will represent the Apocalypse Academy in trial by combat…" the Sergeant paused, holding his fist up in front of him to shoulder level.

"Is…"

The drill sergeant opened his fist and rolled the ball around so that he could read the name. Showing the name to the Colonel, he then turned the ball back around to face the assembled Cadets as he made the announcement.

"… Cadet Princess!"

An immediate and sudden verbal outburst erupted from the ranks as relief at not being selected overlapped concerns for the girl's safety and doubt for the entire group's overall survivability.

Freak voiced his opinion to Spartan through a simple "Awww fuck!" but whether that was due to concerns for the delicate girl's safety or they were due to the disappointment at not being able to take on the "Z" himself, Spartan did not know.

What could he do? He watched as the cadet exited the ranks and marched determinedly towards the Colonel, her long blonde ponytail bobbing behind her beret like a horse's tail. Even after twelve weeks of combat training, the girl still walked like she was heading down a pageant runway rather than into the mouth of danger. Spartan watched as the cadet walked up to the Colonel, saluted smartly then was instructed to stand beside the Academy's Senior Officer. The girl did not smile. She did not look at the other cadets or at anything else. She merely stood rigid at attention, her eyes front, her hands down at her sides resting lightly on her jumpsuit seams.

The assembled cadets immediately quieted as the crank for the wire bingo ball on the left began to turn in the Colonel's hand. Around and around the crank turned; churning the potentially deadly balls that would determine Cadet Princess's opponent. Would she be fortunate enough to face a nearly immobile Husk with its contaminated dust, or maybe a Romero with its slow but steady pace but deadly, tearing teeth and decaying body? The worst-case scenario would be for her to have to fight a Reaper. One of the freshly risen, a Reaper "Z" was as fast as a man, immune to pain and ravenously hungry, plus it could spew out infection laden vomit. Spartan hoped for Princess's sake that it was not one of the latter. He doubted she would ever survive against a Reaper.

As the wire cage stopped turning, Cadet Princess repeated the Colonel's previous process of selecting a ball without looking and handing it in a closed fist to Sergeant Stone. In essence, the girl was selecting her own fate. Turning the ball inward, the drill sergeant began to frown; his jaw muscles clenched tightly. After a brief inquisitive glance at the Colonel who conferred with the Sergeant on the selection, Sergeant Stone cleared his voice to address the cadets.

"She must've gotten a Reaper! Look at the look on Stone's face." Someone behind Spartan said in a whisper.

"She is so screwed." Said another voice.

"Man, are you kiddin'? Dat girl don' kill it good, we all gonna be in de boilin' pot!" Came the Cajun accented response that Spartan knew to be uniquely Gator's. "She gon' have to be quick and smart to take out de Reaper all by her lonesome."

Drill Sergeant Stone turned the white plastic ball around in his palm to face the assembled cadets as he done previously. No name was displayed on the ball. Instead, number thirty-one had been written in black permanent marker. Cadet Princess had drawn the ultimate danger in the inaugural Lottery of the Damned at the Apocalypse Academy. She would be fighting all three "Zs" at once; alone and unarmed.

If there were any emotions from Cadet Princess, they were secured where no one could see them. She stood there stoically, staring straight ahead as if resigned to her fate. Although Spartan knew that they all had been trained for combat, it felt wrong to allow this fragile girl to face danger while he stood off to the side. The first hints of the red rage began to bend inward from his peripheral vision. Before he had time to consider his actions, Spartan took a full pace forward, out of ranks and called out to Colonel Slade.

"Sir, permission to speak, Sir!" Spartan yelled, his adrenaline beginning to kick in.

"Sir, it's this cadet's opinion that he would be better suited for combat with three "Zs" simultaneously than Cadet Princess. This cadet would like to replace the chosen cadet in the trial by combat, Sir!"

"Come forward Corporal."

Spartan took two full paces forward, executed a sharp left turn by pivoting on his right foot and marched to the Colonel's position. Arriving in front of the Senior Officer, he executed a crisp salute. The Colonel returned the salute and indicated that Spartan should stand beside him facing the assembled team members.

"Corporal Spartan. Please explain your rationale. Why do you think you would be a better selection for this honor than

Cadet Princess? Is there a justifiable reason, or is this merely hubris or ego?"

"Sir, this cadet understands the nature of this trial to be a demonstration of the combat skills that had been honed during the training cycle at the Apocalypse Academy. Skills, while equitable to all, should be displayed by leaders and emulated by his or her subordinates. I am the leader of Alpha team. It is my duty and my responsibility to lead by example; to be competent in every aspect of training and to be fearless during a time of decision-making. To allow anything less would be a dereliction of my duty and a betrayal of my team's trust."

"Are those the only reasons for volunteering?" The Colonel asked. "Is there anything more personal that you might have as a motive?"

Spartan felt the initial insinuation like a slap from the superior officer. He had never been interested in the girl from relationship standpoint, considering her much to froufrou for his taste. But then the more he thought about it, Spartan considered the Colonel's question. There was in fact another reason that he was willing to volunteer.

"Sir, yes Sir there is an additional reason which I hold at a personal level Sir!"

"Continue."

"Sir," Spartan said, his eyes leveling down to meet Dancer's. "This cadet has recently discovered what it means to love someone. Cadet Princess recently suffered a system shock when Cadet Knight, with whom she was romantically involved, died in the Dante obstacle course. I believe that although Cadet Princess has successfully completed all the assigned requirements of the Apocalypse Academy that are needed to graduate, Cadet Princess may still be suffering emotionally from the loss of the cadet that she loved. This in turn can cause her to hesitate or to make an irrational rather than clinical decision in combat that could not only result in her potential infection and death, as she would be required to fight all three "Z's" and that infection could mean the death of us all." Spartan concluded, and then quietly added "I'm sorry Princess, but it's true."

"Cadet Princess, you've heard the volunteer for replacing you in this challenge. It is your right to accept his offer, to refute his claim as to your fitness for battle or to refuse his offer as you otherwise see fit." The Colonel explained.

"Sir," Cadet Princess replied. "May I address Cadet Spartan directly?"

"Absolutely." The Colonel replied taking a step back to allow the two cadets to face each other at the front of the formation.

"Thank you." She began "but if you understand love, and you understand what Cadet Knight truly meant to me, then you will not interfere in this challenge. I owe a debt of honor to Knight's memory. He was brave beyond compare and was everything that I had ever dreamed of in a man. I will not sully his memory by wavering in the face of this challenge. I will stand fast and stand tall as he did upon the log bridge and I will emerge victorious by carrying the memory of us as a couple with me."

Pausing, she reached into her pocket and pulled out a plastic identification bracelet. Slipping it over her fingers, she grasped the band in her palm. The name was emblazoned across the plastic in bold letters and lay flat across her knuckles. It read "Knight."

"Besides," she said holding up the dead cadet's identification band. "As you can see, I am not alone."

Spartan could only nod.

Turning away from Spartan, Cadet Princess addressed the cadets in formation.

"I want you all to know a few things before this challenge begins. I feel that it's important to say these things now before a situation comes along where I may not get that chance ever again. I missed that opportunity once. I do not want to do so again."

Princess paused to look down at the bracelet. When she looked back up, silvery tears underscored her eyes, threatening to fall but held back by the determined girl's sheer force of will.

"It is an honor to know you all. Yes, even you mutants in Echo team."

This brought a great giggle from the crowd.

"It is an honor because… we are all human. We think, we feel, we decide what is right and what is wrong. Each day we make a thousand decisions that the walking dead will never be capable of making again. By their very nature they are basic creatures, animated primal shells. They cannot speak, they are guided only by urges to rot and to eat and to infect others. A stagnated existence to be sure and one that if we as human beings strive and dare to live and to love and to care about each other, can ultimately overcome."

"So, no matter what happens today, whether I live or die, believe as my beloved Knight believed, and I still believe. If we put the needs of our kingdom; living human beings, before our personal wants and desires, then the existence of our humanity cannot, no, will not, be extinguished."

Princess took a deep breath and held up her fist, with ID bracelet prominently displayed upon it.

"He believed in all of this, as do I and so should all of you! Long live humanity!"

The crowd erupted with applause and cheers. Even the normally sarcastic Echo team displayed appreciation for Cadet Princess's emotion filled speech. All the drill sergeants applauded heartily as did Colonel Slade. It seemed that humanity was the one thing that they could all agree upon. Then, Princess stepped away from Colonel Slade and walked up to Dancer. Taking her by the shoulders, she gently hugged her. Quietly she spoke in the girl's ear where no one else could hear her.

"You are a very lucky woman. Be proud of your love with Corporal Spartan. Be there to protect each other always." Then she turned and walked purposefully to the middle of the field and prepared to fight the three undead to the death.

The cadets were assembled by team with the ten-yard intervals stretching between each member around the open field. Combined the cadets created a square of personnel with the drill sergeants pillorying at each of the four corners. Colonel Slade stepped into the ranks of Charlie team, filling the gap left by Cadet Princess's selection. Echo team, unsurprisingly, volunteered for cage duty and would be responsible for setting the "Zs" loose that would try to eat Cadet Princess and potentially the rest of them as well.

At the far end of the field sat three Humvees. Each camouflaged vehicle pulled a trailer behind it. Atop each trailer sat a single cage, similar in most respects to a shark cage used by pre-"Z" night scuba divers. Inside each cage sat one of the three "Z's" in various stages of decaying animation. The cage on the trailer farthest to the right contained the desiccated and nearly immobile corpse of a husk. It was so dried out that the cadets could not tell if the corpse was even a male or a female. This was good and bad for Cadet Princess. Good in that the "Z" would be so slow-moving that the Cadet could literally walk around it all day and it would not be able to catch up. It was bad in that since she would be obligated to pacify the creature, the undead's body was going to be extremely brittle and contain that much more powdered HUNGER virus.

The second cage, the one in the middle, contained a Romero well into its degenerative stage of rot. Thick black slime spilled from one corner of its mouth hanging in an ebon rope of mucus and rotten blood dangling halfway down to its waste. The creature appeared to be a male, perhaps six feet tall, that had suffered a grisly wound to his face and neck which left teeth, gums and muscles exposed. Cadet Princess should still be able to outmaneuver the corpse, however it was probably stronger than she was and completely immune to pain, so if it got its hands on her or she slipped and fell, things could go bad very quickly. A low moan of undead longing for flesh rolled over the field from the creature's mouth. Its eyes roamed from cadet to cadet before finally focusing on the nearby Princess. Stretching out its rotten arm, the animated corpse reached through the steel bars, straining against the barrier to get to the cadet.

The last cage on a trailer farthest to the left contained a teenage girl roughly the same age as Dancer or Princess. The girl was clad in a pink jogging suit and matching pink sneakers. Around her right upper arm appeared to be a black plastic band with wires leading up to smaller earphones that curled around each ear in the shape of a "C". The only visible sign that this girl was one of the walking dead and not a cadet was a small open bite mark on the outer edge of her left hand. The wound was so small that Spartan was certain that it had to have been made by a small child, probably no more than five years of age. Red rimmed eyes and a savage snarl completed the image, confirming that this girl was in fact wholly a "Z". The creature crouched like an animal at the rear of its cage, hunched with its muscles tensed as if ready to explode into action at any moment.

Cutter looked to Sergeant Havoc from beside the cages. "There's no way she's gonna hold up against three of these. I think the Reaper is going to be too much for Little Miss Dainty all by herself. All it has to do is keep her busy until the Romero gets there to join in and then they will tear her apart."

"Are you an idiot?" Sergeant Havoc asked calmly, looking directly into the boy's blue eyes. Cutter swallowed hard. Looking into Sergeant Havoc's eyes was like having a staring contest with a cobra. "Providing your assumption goes as you have stated and the cadet standing out there gets her tits torn off, who do you suppose the remaining "Z's" will come after next, hmm?"

"Oh" was all Cutter could say, embarrassed at having been chastised by his drill sergeant.

"Yes, well, obviously *you* thought this all out. I really must congratulate you on a plan fully worthy of someone with say… Orc's level of intelligence. Well done." Sarcasm and disdain dripped from the drill sergeant's voice like snake venom.

"Thanks drill sergeant!" Orc said, oblivious to the intent of the demeaning comment. Sergeant Havoc rolled his eyes and ignored the stupid cadet altogether, not even bothering to acknowledge that the moron had spoken at all. Turning back to Cutter, the drill sergeant gave him explicit instructions.

"You will set loose the "Zs" one at a time at two-minute increments. You will begin with the fastest, the Reaper and end with the Husk. If the cadet has not dispatched the "Z" within the two minutes, you are to feign difficulty with the lock and stall, giving her up to another full minute. Do you understand?" The drill sergeant hissed.

"Yes, drill sergeant." Cutter gulped.

"Don't fuck this up boy, or I will feed you to the undead at the first possible moment when we begin patrolling for "Zs" outside of the Academy walls." He said and turned, stalking back to his post at the corner of the square. Cutter felt the sweat run down his temple as he considered the drill sergeant's words. He had no doubt that the man would take a great deal of pride in ending his existence at the teeth of the undead. He had read it in the man's eyes. His drill sergeant carried with him a malicious air that was no doubt well-earned and deserved.

"Cadet, are you ready?" Came the call from the Colonel over megaphone from his location between Bravo and Charlie teams.

Princess nodded, her fists doubling, and her right foot drop back into a defensive martial arts stance, dropping her body weight low to center her gravity.

"May victory come to you upon wings of gold!" The Colonel said. "Keepers loose the "Zs"!"

Hearing the Colonel's command, Cutter pulled down hard on the chain that held the cage door closed for the Reaper. Initially the undead did not seem to realize that it was free. Then, as a savage understanding emerged, the jogger burst free, leaping from the trailer, and racing towards Princess who stood alone and completely unprotected in the middle of the open field. The Reaper practically flew across the ground, focused on its efforts to get to the defenseless girl. In life, this undead girl was probably an accomplished athlete, perhaps a jogger or an aerobics instructor. In death she was a deadly foe, yet Princess stood confident and serene in the meadow, poised and ready for the confrontation, arms hanging loosely at her side.

The undead's black ponytail flew out behind the charging Reaper in stark contrast to the neon pink jogging outfit that she wore, waving like a battle pennant in the breeze during a medieval joust. She closed quickly on the Cadet. Fifty yards… Forty… Thirty… Twenty… Still Princess remained motionless, her hands lightly clenching and unclenching in preparation for the imminent life and death battle.

Ten…

Dancer screamed for Princess to move, terrified that the girl was going to commit suicide by allowing the "Z" to take her as the other undead had taken her beloved Knight on the Dante course.

Five...

Four yards...

Three... Two yards...

The cadet burst into action. Dropping to a squat and canting her body sideways, Princess snapped off a side thrust kick. The Kevlar plated sole of her combat boot connected with the Reaper's knee as it was extended forward in full stride. Bone shattered backward as the savage undead's leg reversed directions, fully inverting the creature's knee, creating a compound fracture of its leg. Rendering the leg utterly useless.

Black and blonde ponytails swirled through space, looking like a bizarre paradox of good vs. evil unicorns battling in the field. Princess tumbled away as the "Z" face planted into the dirt, smothering its scream of rage with a mouthful of soil and grass. Leaping to her feet, Princess raced over to the crippled creature and placed her boot firmly in the center of its back, pinning it to the ground. Reaching down with both hands she wrapped her fingers in the girl's black ponytail and began to pull backwards with all of her might while pressing down on the creature's spine with her boot. The jogger's pink earbuds popped loose, spilling faint music across the battlefield as Princess strained, pulling the muscles, tendons, and bones of the girl's neck backward as hard as she could.

Pre-apocalyptic metal rock music screamed "*Highway to Hell*" as the undead's vertebrae snapped, cutting the spinal cord, Immediately, ceasing the creatures' movements. Slowly, Princess looked over her shoulder. Seeing no imminent threat from the other "Zs", she un-velcroed the plastic band from around the Reaper's arm and placed it onto her own. Wiping the earbuds clean on her uniform, she inserted them into her own ears. Looking down at the iPod held within the plastic and Velcro arm wrap, she pressed the menu button and immediately began to shuffle the available songs. She was met with an old tune that she remembered her father playing on records, he had outright refused to update his collection to CDs. A band called Blue Oyster Cult began to sing *"Don't Fear The Reaper"* into her brain. *"How appropriate,"* Princess thought and readied herself for the remaining two undead that she knew were still to come. *"Well at least now I can rock out."*

Spartan glanced over at Dancer. The girl shrugged as if answering the team leader's unspoken question with a question mark of her own. Princess had been the epitome of the prissy little pansy at the start of the Academy. She had been far more concerned with chipping a nail or not having fashionable clothing than she had been worried about learning fighting styles and combat techniques.

Somewhere in the span of a few weeks, that Spartan suspected began with the death of Cadet Knight and ended today, the girl had become a serious warrior capable of kicking mega –"Z"–ass. Spartan knew the girl had been through a lot emotionally but based on what he was seeing out in the field, the tinfoil girl who had come to the Academy toting a bag full of makeup and a roll of sweet tarts had vanished and in her place was a transformed, battle hardened she-wolf capable of rendering undead bone and rotting sinew as well as any other cadet there. He was even more amazed by her calm demeanor. The old Princess shrieked at the sight of a mouse or a cockroach or even something as innocuous as an earthworm. While this new girl waited calmly, peacefully even for certain danger to come to her, like she had entered a form of Zen.

The clanking of metal chain being drawn up and the low, wailing moan of eternal hunger announced the release and approach of the next undead. The Romero shambled closer to Princess, its black blooded rope of mucus swaying with each tottering step. The red tinge around its eyes made the creature appear almost remorseful, perhaps even within the depths of its rotten brain, sorrowful as it moved incessantly forward. Despite its sad appearance, every cadet surrounding the field knew that it was moving with the sole purpose of tearing off Cadet Princess's face and eating her liver. A steady, low noise escaped from its lips; a sound that had brought terror to many people who had survived the onslaught of the undead during "Z" night. The same fear that paralyzed their limbs and prevented many of the formerly living people from fleeing the undead until it was far too late now reverberated across the field.

Princess held no such fear in her heart, for she had not heard the moan. The slow movement of the Romero had allowed Blue Oyster Cult to finish its song only to be replaced with the wailing guitars and heavy drumbeats of the Scorpions as they began to sing "*Rock You Like A Hurricane.*" The Romero trudged on, becoming more frantic in its reaching arm movements the closer he got to Princess.

When it was ten yards away, Princess dashed forward, closing the gap quickly in a headlong charge directly at the undead's grasping arms. At the last moment, the cadet tumbled to the left, rolling to the "Zs" flank before he could react and used her momentum to spring back to her feet. Her left foot flew forward in a scintillatingly crisp crescent kick directly into the creature's exposed lower back. Ribs and kidney exploded as the steel toe of Princess's boot drove through rotten flesh and diseased bone deep into its back. Though the creature did not feel the pain of the blow, the lack of bones to one side of his torso canted its body to the right, causing the undead to look hunchbacked and awkward.

As the "Z", now leaned over at a thirty-degree angle, turned to face its attacker, it reached a clawed hand out for the cadet. Princess blocked the grasping hand by crossing her hand over the dead man's forearm, grasping the wrist and spinning the "Z" one hundred and eighty degrees so that its back was once again towards her and the diseased arm was fully extended immobilized in an Aikido lock. Using the heel of her boot, she stomped down on the back of the undead's exposed calf as hard as she could and smiled grimly as both bones in the lower leg snapped with an audible crunch. The "Z" fell to the ground, still feeling no pain, but unable structurally to support its own body weight on the destroyed limb. Lying on his side, another moan of misery and death dragged out of its mouth; sound gurgling through the rotten blood pooling in its throat. Princess took four quick steps backward and paused, looking up long enough to see that the Husk had not yet been released while she fought the other two "Zs".

Cutter watched impatiently from where he stood next to the Romero's now empty cage. There was something fascinating to him about the deadly attacks of the undead creatures and the cadet's vicious counter attacks. He had always found Princess to be an annoying and whiny little bitch, but suddenly he was feeling more excited by the prospect of either watching her die a violent death or becoming infected. Perhaps he could convince Sergeant Havoc to let him pacify her like Spartan had done for that kid Rooster. He could just imagine the flesh slide open as he would drive the pacification spike up into her brain and silence her lovesick whining forever. Now that was an image worth holding on to. Unfortunately, the girl had neutralized the Reaper and was holding her own against the Romero. Still, one could hope…

Another flurry of movement and a second gurgling moan drew her attention back to the Romero that lay crumpled on the ground before her. Even critically injured as it was with wounds that would never heal; the creature instinctually rolled onto its back and reached out a clawed hand to grab and eat her. Contempt and disdain filled the cadet's thoughts. This creature was an abomination to all that she believed in. It and all its' undead kindred had deprived her of all that was good and happy in her life. Makeup, pedicures, shopping at Macy's and most of all her love, Cadet Knight.

With a scream of rage that boiled up from within the depths of her soul, Princess charged forward and delivered a savage kick to the creature's skull, shattering its forehead and sinking the steel toe of her combat boot three inches into the "Z's" rotten brain matter. Blood, brain and bone splattered outward in an arc as Princess's booted foot penetrated, then exited the hideous skull. Rage filled her soul, while adrenaline filled her muscles. She raced across the field, screaming her anger to the heavens for all the cadets, the instructors, the Husk and any God that was listening to hear. Van Halen's "*Running with the Devil*" ringing in her ears.

Five yards from the barely mobile creature, Princess launched herself into a flying kick. The soul of her booted foot smashed into the just released creature's chest, knocking it fiercely to the ground. Every cadet, drill sergeant and even the Colonel, held their breath waiting for the expected puff of infected air to emerge from the creature. None came. Fortunately, it seemed that the rain that had gone on for so many days had soaked the corpse with water enough that the infection remained contained. Nonetheless, the move was reckless but lucky, and effective.

Landing lightly, Princess used the back of her hand to wipe the spittle from the corner of her mouth where it had flown during her primal rage. Turning back to the creature, she walked slowly up to it and placed her boot on the "Z's" throat. Slowly but inexorably, the cadet began to ground her boot downward, crushing cartilage and tissue carefully but unceasingly. She stared hard into the "Z's" dead eyes as she crushed its spinal cord and its feeble struggles slowed then stopped altogether; paralysis of a severed spinal cord rendering it completely immobile and effectively "dead".

Carefully she readjusted a couple of wayward hairs that had flown loose from her ponytail and smoothed out her rumpled jumpsuit as she calmly walked back to the lottery table and stood before Colonel Slade. Snapping a sharp salute, she spoke.

"Mission accomplished Sir!" Princess said, removing the earbuds.

"Well done Cadet Princess! Your battle prowess and the tactical sense that you have displayed have done your Academy class proud. In recognition of this accomplishment, you have earned a weapon or piece of equipment of your choice to go along with the gear that you have already been issued." The Commandant of the Apocalypse Academy commented.

"Thank you, Sir!" Princess said quietly, "but I would rather have a separate reward if I may request it."

"Continue."

"When I arrived at the Apocalypse Academy, I did not understand what the world was becoming. I was naïve and shallow, worried only with my own well-being. Now, after all that has happened, that spoiled little "Princess" who thought the world owed her a clear path because of her looks and her money has finally died."

Slowly, she reached up a hand and grasped the plastic armband that she had worn since her arrival at the Academy. Straining against the microfilaments inside the band, she snapped it and handed the identification band to the Colonel.

"As my reward, in recognition of who I have become after seeing all that I have loved die and finally recognizing all of the evil in the world, I would like a new codename."

The Colonel raised his eyebrow in surprise. It was highly unorthodox for anyone to request a new codename in any branch of the military service much less after the Apocalypse.

"From now on I would like to be called "War Queen!"

The Colonel thought for a moment on the request; then looked over at the assembled drill sergeants. Seeing them nod in agreement, he made an announcement in a loud and powerful voice to the assembled cadets.

"The Princess is dead! Long live her new life as the Apocalypse Academy's War Queen!" The resounding roar from the cadets told the girl formerly known as Princess that they had all approved of her choice.

Chapter Nineteen
One More Time

Alpha team sat quietly chatting in the rec room, reminiscing about their experiences at the Apocalypse Academy and guessing what challenges the future might bring. They all agreed that it would be odd to not have the barking instructions of the drill sergeants following them around. As strange as it sounded, the drill sergeants had become something like surrogate parents to the cadets, since all of their own families had died either during "Z" night or shortly thereafter, leaving them all orphans. Although over the course of the last twelve weeks they had become skilled warriors, trained in the arts of combat, first aid and land navigation, in many ways, hidden deep inside themselves, they were all still children wanting the approval and guidance of their parents.

"Do you suppose they are going to keep our team together?" Techno asked aloud. "Or do you think they will send us off to specialized groups?"

"Huh?" Came Freak's reply. "C'mon Dawg, they can't split us up. We're family."

"I don't see it happening." Said Spartan. "We've spent weeks learning to move and act as a team. We've learned each other strengths and weaknesses and adjusted our approach to our strategies based on that. Why would they split us up after teaching us how to perform together?"

"Well, eventually I would think that we would go to some sort of advanced training, kind of like an Apocalypse Academy part two. There must be so much more that we can learn. That's what the military does. Schools like linguistics or explosives or Ranger school and stuff like that. The really cool jobs are getting to fly aircraft or pilot submersibles or drones. That would be so cool."

"Like what?" Deadeye asked the Asian boy. "Are you planning on flying around in a helicopter or maybe becoming the captain of your own ship on a sea of the dead? We seem to be a little short on those vehicles right now..."

Freak snorted, and then added. "No man, does he look like a pilot or a boat captain to you? My man here is gonna be an astronaut. Keep the "Zs" from invading outer space!" The giant started laughing as he clapped Techno on the shoulder. "So far he's just been a Space Cadet!"

"Maybe he can one day become a Jedi?" Dancer added, jumping on the bandwagon at Techno's expense. "But he's going to have to add a lot more juice to that stun baton of his if he's going to upgrade it to light saber status." She said with a smile changing her voice to mimic Yoda, the little green Jedi Master who so valued the positive characteristics of personal development and honor. "The force is... Well... Almost better than average with this one! Yes it is..."

"Oh great," Techno thought. *"How'd you discover my secret passion for Star Wars? Now that he'd shed most of his fat and built a little self-confidence and self-esteem, here comes the next round of annoyances as they classify me as a nerd or Star Wars geek."*

"Ease off the Star Wars references guys…" Spartan said out of the blue. "Some people may consider them geek entertainment but in my eyes; they are the best movies ever made. I mean look at how our own group compares to their original heroes. We have our own Wookie..." He said pointing it Freak. "…and a brave, scoundrel warrior and a sassy Princess from another land." He said pointing to himself and Dancer. "Heck we even have a guy from the wilderness with his own mystical powers." He said pointing over at Deadeye.

"What about me? Who am I?" Techno asked, completely engaged into the conversation and not sensing the inherent danger of his words.

"Well," said Spartan drawing out the suspense. "When you got here, I would've said you were either one of the green skinned, pig-faced guards based solely on your size and shape, but now…" Spartan looked up to see the look of horror on Techno's face and trying desperately to hold in his laughter. "You're definitely more of the droid type. Computer skills, technical expertise, logical calculating capabilities, how could there be any other choice?"

Together they all laughed, even Techno. The answer to that question could have definitely been worse like being called a Jawa or as fat as he had been, Jabba the Hutt.

"Awww, how sweet." Came a call at the rec room door. Alpha team turned around and saw Cutter standing there, spinning his knife back and forth across his knuckles. "Losers talking about nerd fandom. Not very original… But quaint just the same."

"What you want Cutter? Can't you find a puppy to kick?" Techno said, doubling up his fists.

"Well, since I don't fit into your little imaginary world, I suppose I did come here with a purpose."

"You mean besides stinking up the place?" Dancer asked quickly, then added "Bloody wanker!" in a disgusted tone under her breath.

Cutter shot the girl a "*go to hell*" look then focused on Spartan.

"I actually came by here specifically to talk to you Spartan." Cutter said pointing at the Alpha team leader with the needle-sharp tip of his knife. "I wanted to let you know that just because were graduating tomorrow, it doesn't mean that the issues are closed between us. Sooner or later…" he said pausing to draw the knife across his throat. "We're going to meet up again. When we do, you won't walk away, and neither will any of the rest of these losers that you call your team. Just watch the shadows, because very soon, my boys and I will be in one of them. We haven't forgotten that we still owe you for getting' into our business on that very first day here. I never forget the things that have happened in the past; at least not until I get my revenge."

Spartan leapt to his feet, pulling the sword of Leonidas from its scabbard. Twenty-four inches of shining steel glistened in the light as the rasp of metal on metal rang throughout the room.

"We don't have to wait you slimy little piece of shit!" Spartan said with a chilling edge to his voice. "We can do this right now!" He said as the beginnings of his rage sparked adrenaline along his nerves and muscles.

"What? You want me to kill you right here in front of your nutso Limey girlfriend and then what? I have to take on your pet gorilla, your wannabe fugitive from the jungle book and a fan boy of a space opera? That's too much, even for me to stomach. It would be like eliminating the entire cast of the children's television show in one fell swoop. What a bunch of losers!"

"You didn't say anything about fighting me?" Dancer said. "Maybe you don't have a plan for dealing with me." Dancer added in a tone that was clearly meant to be intimidating.

"Oh, don't you go worrying your pretty little head about that." Cutter replied. "The boys and I have a *special* plan in mind for you. It just doesn't involve a fight or my blade. We talk about it all the time. It's something a little more… up close and personal." He said with a wink.

Then as if reconsidering his last statement, Cutter added "Well, then again, I suppose it could theoretically involve some fight since you are something of a hellcat but either way, the end result would still be the same. You might even enjoy it. You seem like the type."

The blood rage surged even harder in Spartan's veins and he longed to take his sword and ram it straight up Cutter's pompous ass. His muscles flexed as anger expanded his veins, pumping blood faster and faster, increasing the flow of oxygen to his lungs and heart as he geared up for combat. Dancer gently placed a hand over his forearm halting the rise of the blade in his hand. Instantly, as if the switch had been flipped, Spartan's blood rage subsided, and his thoughts were again clear.

"Don't." She said quietly. "If you kill him, you'll be expelled from the Apocalypse Academy. It's not worth it. You'll just hurt our chances to survive. Trust me, I know his type. He's all mouth. He doesn't have the stones to mess with us." She glared at Cutter, and then spoke through her teeth. "But just in case you should get the itch to try, I want you to understand this. If you or any of your pet guard dogs try to hurt me, rape me or whatever, I will hunt you all down to the ends of this earth and cut that off…" she said pointing at his crotch "and let you watch as I feed it to a "Z" while it is still warm."

"Ooohhh, ain't you just a tough little twat?" Cutter mocked. "You've got me scared now."

"That's it! I don' care about getting 'xpelled none. It's time to deal some pain out to this fool!" Freak growled, pulling out one of the Blues Brothers and in one smooth motion, slung it overhand at the Echo team leader.

Seeing the bat come out of its holster on the giant's back, Cutter ducked back around the doorframe and into the hall just as the meaty end of the bat sunk six inches into the sheet rock where his head had been just seconds before. Had the bat hit him in the face, it would've crushed his skull for sure. Instead, the Echo team leader looked back around the corner at the metal bat and tapped it repeatedly with the blade of his knife. "Nice throw." He said genuinely. "Too bad your too muscle brained to know that knives are made for throwing and bats are made for swinging. I'll show you the difference soon enough though. Still, it was pretty impressive. Well, I'll be seeing you all soon." Then he turned and walked off casually down the hall.

What the hell had that been about? Spartan wondered. Certainly, there was no love lost between Alpha and Echo teams, but this was the second time that the Echo team leader had threatened them. Soon, they would be out in the "Z" lands, running operations at the behest of the Colonel. They would have to be certain to watch for not only the "Zs" and the undead worshiping biker gangs but Echo team as well. He needed to talk to Hogg or maybe even Sergeant Stone and let the sergeants know what was happening. Maybe Cutter was dropping over the deep end? Or maybe it was all bluff and bluster. Either way, it was beginning to really piss him off. Hearing Techno clear his throat, Spartan looked back at the boy.

"What are we going to do?" He asked seriously. "Are we going to have to dodge them for the rest of our lives? I had to do enough of that stuff in elementary school."

"I say we just go find them and whoop their asses and set the standard now!" Freak said. "You don't come into my house and insult or threaten my family Dawg!"

Spartan nodded. He understood exactly how the giant felt. "I could get into their dorm. Kill them all in their sleep. They would never feel a thing. No one would ever be able to prove that I was there." Deadeye said in a voice lacking any sort of emotion. Spartan shook his head. The result would still be the same. They would all be suspected and then expelled; forced to walk Damnation Road in shame, forgoing all weapons and armor. Their chances of survival in the "Z" world would be slim to none.

"If they are for real, then they'll come to us soon enough." Spartan said. "We just need to be ready for them when they do. Just watch your backs."

Dancer nodded her agreement. "The rest is just words. Lip service like talking trash to make themselves feel important. At heart they are all cowards. They may never even try to take us out. And if so, we know we can take them."

"I sure the fuck hope they do!" Said Freak, as he ripped his bat out of the sheet rock where it was embedded, casting dust and debris down to the ground. "'Cause the Brothers and I are going to play a whole muthafuckin' concert for their asses when they do!" Then he looked over sheepishly at Dancer and said, "Pardon my language."

The girl nodded and smiled at the big black teen. She knew exactly how he felt.

"Well, one thing is for certain." Tech said, drawing everyone's attention.

"Oh yeah, what's that?" Spartan replied.

Techno smiled. "At least now we know who the Sith Lord at the Academy is! It's Cutter!" He said, with a huge grin. The effect was instantaneous as everyone in the room groaned, then as one they burst out laughing.

Chapter Twenty
Graduation

The thought of beginning a new chapter in their lives, much like the imagined possibility of a reoccurrence of "Z" night, could not have brought as much anxiety as graduation morning did. Boots were polished, and then re-polished until they gleamed like mirrors. Uniforms were starched and pressed, with awards and ribbons carefully placed for those cadets that had either won individual events or been part of team trophies.

It was also the last time the drill sergeants could formally screw with the cadets' minds and bodies. After the ceremony was over, the cadets would be warriors in name as well as their personas, so the drill sergeants were getting their last licks in. Cadets were dropped to do dozens of exercises for the smallest of offenses. Push-ups, boot beaters, Burpees and the ever popular but really painful, "dying cockroach" all got utilized in an effort to make the last hours as a recruited cadet…memorable, much to the entertainment of the cadre.

Everything had to be perfect. Not only for themselves, but all the cadets wanted to make the ceremony a memorial of sorts for those cadets that were no longer with them. Conversations commonly reflected on those same cadets, especially Rooster, as well as the common hardships that they had all endured to reach this point. A sense of pride permeated their words as many of the cadets realized, perhaps for the first time, that they were no longer untrained youth seeking a way to survive minute by minute in this new cruel world. Now, they were trained warriors. They were soldiers of a new breed that were designed to be specifically adaptable and mentally prepared for whatever the

HUNGER diseased future was to bring their way. After graduation, they would be moved into permanent quarters within the facility to still allow for team deployments but with a little more individual privacy. All their gear was packed and stowed for transport. The students were expected to secure their weapons and armor in packing crates, to provide maximum recognition of the dress uniforms and the attention to detail that they had all taken in preparation for graduation.

Spartan was just finishing up securing his armor and the sword of Leonidas in its black plastic transport case when he heard a knock at the barracks door. Looking up he saw Dancer standing there, a look of concern creasing her brow.

"Got a minute?" She asked, hoping Spartan would not turn her away.

"Sure Dance. What's up?" Spartan said as he sat on the metal foot rail of his bunk.

The girl chewed on her lower lip obviously struggling with the decision to talk to him or not. Sighing deeply, she began to speak while walking across the room to lean against the built-in desktop opposite of where Spartan currently sat.

"When we got here, at the start of the Academy, we had all barely survived "Z" night and the return of the dead. We had all seen our lives hopelessly destroyed one by one, as each of our families and friends were either eaten or infected; eventually dying and leaving us all as orphans. That pain for most of us was devastating. Some of the cadets, were either fortunate enough not to see their love ones eaten or, as in your case, found a way to put up a mental barrier to block it all out. Never having to remember the horrors of "Z" night or what we each had to do to survive."

Although Dancer could not possibly know it, he hardly considered himself lucky. Sure "Z" night was blocked by his amnesia but so was every other memory of his family. Who they were and how they died would be a mystery to him as long as his mind refused to deal with the stress of the moment of their deaths; possibly forever.

Dancer continued.

"In being here, I have what I thought I would never have again in a world gone mad; a world that is been filled with the living dead. I have friends again. I have a "family" of sorts from the Colonel, to the drill sergeants and all the way down to the Deltas but of course, discounting the dysfunctional and probably psychopathic Echoes. After today, that will again all be gone. Not as permanently as "Z" night had done but gone just the same. Alpha team will have each other to be sure, but the others; the drill sergeants and the other cadets will all move on to either perform missions on their own or be in charge of instructing new classes of orphans that I'm certain will continue to come to the Apocalypse Academy. Some will even die without us ever knowing it. It's sad."

Tears slowly rolled down the girl's smooth tanned cheek, her hidden pain evident in her watery eyes.

"When the HUNGER virus began, my father knew it was bloody bad. He was involved in military intelligence, as was Mum and as the infection began to spread, they knew, maybe instinctively or maybe from an inside source, that there would be no stopping it. In fact, I remember that he even made the comment to me that there may be no stopping the virus ever. I don't know if he was predicting the future, or just talking out loud at the time. Despite our being British nationals, my father used his connections inside of the government to evacuate my mum and I to New York City where the virus had not yet been reported. From there we were supposed to be transported to somewhere in the Canadian wilderness, far from the infection until the HUNGER virus "ran its course". My father handed me a satellite phone, gave me calling instructions and kissed my Mum and I goodbye at Heathrow airport just before we were hustled onto a big white private jet. The last time I saw him was as a man in a British military uniform approached him. The man said something that I could not hear, and then my father turned and left without another word or so much as a wave good-bye. I didn't cry. I had seen the news of the infection spreading on the telly and I knew that he was doing whatever he could to try to save us, even though it would likely mean sacrificing his own life. I also knew that it meant I would likely never see him again."

Tears began to flow more freely as the girl spoke of her father.

"When we arrived in New York ten hours later, we found out that his information had been wrong. The HUNGER infection had already reached the United States and much of New York City and Manhattan had already been lost. The National Guard had been fully deployed and was losing the battle to keep the infection in check. Our pilot deviated from his assigned flight plan, abandoning JFK airport and took us further north up to Syracuse. He hoped that we were going to outrun the infection and thought that by seeking out a smaller airport we were improving our odds of dodging the chaos that was spreading so rapidly. He was wrong. Radioing ahead, a military vehicle was dispatched to meet us on the runway and then to takeover transporting us to the location of safety in Canada."

"When we landed, we may as well have landed in a sea of undead. Living people begged, pleaded, bartered, bribed and negotiated for our jet. The pilot, Mister Hanover, calmly explained that the aircraft was the property of the British government and as such he had no authority to release it at any price, as much as he would like to help. The military men were hustling my Mum and I into the waiting black SUV when the first shot rang out. Looking back, I saw Mister Hanover lying in a spreading pool of blood with a wide-eyed look of shock still on his face. The crowd went insane, surging for our jet. Shots were being fired repeatedly by both the panicked crowd and the military men surrounding our SUV. The screams of the dying were horrible to hear. I will never forget it."

"A young military man shoved my Mum and me into the SUV, with no luggage, no food, no water and no further explanation. The remaining military men turned back to the crowd, apparently intent on restoring order. The windows of the SUV were locked closed and tinted dark black so I could see very little past the automatic muzzle flashes from the military's rifle fire as they blew apart the uninfected but berserk civilians. I can't help but wonder if there was even a pilot in the crowd that could've flown a jet after they so stupidly killed Mister Hanover or if in their panic to escape the infection, the thought never even occurred to the crazed mob."

Spartan wanted to say something; anything to make her feel better. He just didn't have a clue as to what that something should be. Maybe he should just try to hold her hand or hug her.

"Dance…" He started but was cut off as she held up a hand, pulling away from his touch.

"Please let me finish, I don't know if I'll ever be able to let this out again, so I need you to hear this, to decide if I should still be part of the Alpha team."

Confused, Spartan shut his mouth and just nodded, allowing Dancer to continue.

"The SUV was driven by a young man not much older than me. As he drove wildly up the highway, he tried to chit chat; kind of flirting with me and on several occasions over the next three hours of driving I caught him staring at me in the rear-view mirror. I don't know if he was driving as fast as he was out of fear of the virus or if he was truly trying to impress me, but if he not been doing either then the bloody git would have seen the pickup truck that ran the yield sign from the merge ramp onto the interstate and collided broadside with our SUV. Fortunately for me, my Mum had always been a stickler for using seatbelts. Had I not had one on when the SUV began to roll over, I probably would've been seriously hurt or maybe even killed. As it was, I got a lump on the side of my head the size of a crumpet and found myself hanging upside down from the shoulder harness. It was then that I heard my Mum frantically whispering to me.

"Honey, wake up baby, please wake up!"

"I could feel her hand grabbing for me and I took it without opening my eyes. My head hurt so bad that I couldn't think straight.

"You've got to get out of here baby. Undo your seatbelt. They're coming." She whispered; a terrifying urgency apparent in her voice. I did what she said, still completely disoriented from the knock on my head. Clicking the release on the seatbelt, I dropped to the roof of the upside-down SUV with a thud.

"Mum, why…? Who's coming?"

"Shhhhh" she said urgently. "You're in danger darling. You got to run. Get out of the car now and run for all your worth!"

"Confused, I looked around at the vehicle's interior. The young soldier that had been staring at me so intently when we crashed was clearly dead, his head hung off to the side at an angle that was impossible to achieve without a broken neck. His vacant eyes now stared at the upside-down floorboard. My backpack lay at my feet and appeared to be accessible. Grabbing the pack, I looked over at my Mum for the first time and what I saw made me gasp."

The pickup truck had impacted the SUV right on the rear passengers' door, crumpling it inward over the seat and on top of my Mum's legs. The blood that seeped out from her hip line over the ragged metal edges of the bent door frame told me that there was another injury besides being pinned down by the twisted metal. Remembering the first aid courses my father had insisted on my learning, I looked for something to staunch the bleeding. My mother only smiled a weak sad smile, grabbing me by the arm to get my attention.

"Look Sweet Pea." She said quietly using her pet name for me that she hadn't used since I was a tot. With a weak nod she indicated that I should look out of the broken window as people approached to either offer assistance or to rubberneck at the accident until the police showed up to run them off. I was wrong on both counts. Realization set in as my Mum squeezed my arm hard and again told me to get out of the car; to get away. To run."

"Grab your backpack baby and take that bottle of water next to it too so that you can refill it when you find water later." I complied almost robotically, trying to talk back only to hear a tone of voice that I had heard only a few times in my life from my Mum; it was a voice that brooked no arguments.

"Don't sass me young lady. You must do this. You need to be safe. Now get your bum in gear!" She said sternly. "Take the driver's gun out of his holster and any extra ammunition if you can see it and can reach it easily. If not, leave it. Now go!"

"But Mum…" I said suddenly very afraid. "I can get you loose! We've got time, we will go together! Please!" Tears fell from my face in hot little rivers as I tugged on her seatbelt and pushed against the bent metal door with all of my meager strength; all the while knowing deep down in my heart that it was hopeless."

"I felt her let go of my arm and place her hand on the side of my face. Despite her obvious pain she was so calm. "No sweetie. My legs are both broken. I can't feel them, and I think my back is too. Keep yourself safe for me. Remember that I will love you always okay? Remember everything that your Dad taught you and you'll be ok."

"All I could do was nod."

"Mum, I'm scared. Please don't make me go alone. Please." I pleaded.

"Glancing up, I saw the approaching infected barely scant yards away. I know now that they were Romero's. If there had been Reapers in the crowd, I would have been doomed as well as my Mum. I looked back to my Mum and slowly nodded. Leaning over, I kissed her softly on the cheek."

"I need you to be strong sweetheart. Now go on, run and no matter what you hear, don't look back." She said with a gentle shove to my shoulder. "I will delay them as long as I can." She said pulling out a snub-nosed thirty-eight revolver that she carried in her purse for self-defense."

"Pushing open my door with a screech of bending metal, I scrambled around to the driver's door and pulled it open, spilling the gawking soldier's remains to the ground. He wore a Beretta in a hip holster at his waist. I ripped the belt from him and looked one last time at my Mum as the first of the "Zs" reached the mangled passenger side of the SUV. Then I ran as fast and as far as I could. No matter how fast I ran, I could still hear her screaming as they tore her apart. She fired five rounds, screaming curses at the undead that tore at the SUV trying to pull her out. After several long seconds the sixth and final round fired, and her screaming stopped abruptly."

Spartan didn't say a word. He didn't have to.

"Don't you see? I knew deep down that I couldn't save her, but it never occurred to me to pacify her. To keep her from becoming one of them. Instead, I ran. Ran like a frightened little child and never stopped to think of the consequences, for my Mum … or for myself. It wasn't until we were at the funeral after the Dante course that I considered all the possibilities. I mean… All this time I assumed that the "Zs" had eaten her. But what if I mean… It's possible that she could have been infected. She could be pinned in that SUV, turned into the walking dead and left to rot in every type of season and weather. I… I… should have at least… made sure… she… she…" Dancer's facade of being in control shattered as she disintegrated emotionally in front of Spartan. The Alpha team leader stood up and stepped across the small gap between them and took Dancer into his arms; letting her cry out the emotions that have been held in check for far too long.

After several long minutes, the shuddering sobs subsided. Spartan held his teammate at arm's length and looked directly into her soft brown eyes.

"Either way, there was nothing you could've done; the "Zs" had compromised the vehicle. If you had taken the time to pacify her, you would have at least been infected and at worst been killed. Your mother knew what she was doing. She knew what was coming. She chose your safety over her own life. How could you do anything less than fulfill your mother and father's last wishes? They wanted you to live. In the end she saw to her own pacification." Spartan said, as he gently brushed away the last of her tears.

"I just need you to believe that if… if the same scenario happened now, to you or to Freak or Deadeye or to Techno, that I wouldn't run until I made sure that I did not repeat my mistake that I made with my Mum. You are all my family now and I will not let any of you down."

"I've never doubted you for an instant." He said with a smile. "You have to remember that even though it was only a few months ago, we are not the same people now that we were then." Then he added, "Well at least I don't think I am, but since I can't remember my past beyond an occasional feeling of déjà vu, I suppose that it could be entirely possible that I am the only person here at the Academy that was born and raised to kill undead monsters. I mean that it's almost like a manifest destiny or something."

Dancer rolled her eyes as she listened to Spartan theorize how ironic it would be, to be named *"King of the Undead World."*

"If you are quite through," she said sternly "perhaps your Highness would like to get ready for our graduation ceremony."

"Last question" he said with a smirk. "What would be the most appropriate way to pacify an infected King?"

She paused then looked him directly into the eyes and said, "With a Dragonov sniper rifle at six hundred meters. No pain, no sound. Just one quick impact. Then boom and you're gone."

"See", he said. "That's why I love you. Efficiency." Dancer jumped off the countertop and kissed Spartan lightly on the cheek. "I know." She said, and then started to walk away. Reaching the doorway, she turned back and offered a small smirk. "Thanks for the confidence and understanding. I will never let you or the team down." Then she turned and walked out of the dorm room. Of all their individual crosses they each bore from the actions that they had been forced to take during the days following "Z" night, hers was perhaps one of the heaviest. Then he refocused himself to finish packing. He wanted to be ready for graduation when the Sergeants came to get them.

At 1000 hours, all five drill sergeants arrived at the quarter deck to lead their individual teams to graduation. Any of the cadets that thought the spit and polish job they had done on their combat boots was of a superior quality could only gawk in wonder at the sergeant's uniforms. Creases so sharp they looked like they could slice apples ran down the center of their sleeves or pant legs. Metallic taps had been added to their boots to provide a uniform announcement of their march. The steady click, click, click of their boots led the formation down to the parade grounds in front of the long-abandoned amphitheater that at one time had hosted the Drum and Bugle Corps competitions for the Midwestern region of the United States.

Standing on the platform of the band shell, impeccably dressed as usual, stood Colonel Slade. Ribbons and medals covered his chest, reading like a list of achievements categorizing his many military years. He waited to speak until the cadets were placed into "open ranks" formation allowing each team to offset from the one ahead of it, with every other line parallel. This allowed for greater visibility of the individual cadets. This would also facilitate the walk-through process of delivering the blood patches to the cadets that would signify their graduation.

The drill sergeants posted in a single rank down the left-hand stairwell to the bandstand. Silver handled sabers hung from their sides, decorating each of their dress uniforms.

Anticipation was clearly evident on the faces of the cadets. The last twelve weeks had been grueling, and in several instances; deadly and death-defying. They had lived and trained as part of a larger team, but for the members of Alpha team at least, they had become as close as family. Dancer and Freak had both referred to them that way and Techno seemed fully in the same line of thinking. The only potential question mark was how Deadeye felt beyond his obvious commitment to the team. There was no doubting his loyalty to be sure, but the boy was so reserved and quiet that determining his underlying feelings about anything was often very difficult to read.

The Colonel cleared his throat and spoke in a voice that rang of both confidence in himself and of his vast pride in the graduating class of cadets.

"Today is the first day of humanity's long journey towards reclaiming our civilization and our lives from the grasp of the undead scum that have seized our world in their viral decaying fists. We have all watched as our love ones, our families, our friends and acquaintances fell like wheat before the scythe… in an onslaught of teeth and claws; the likes of which our planet has never seen before. No one was immune, no class of people exempt; no race, creed or religion protected by their God's hand. Even the animal kingdom has suffered under this plague, turning many of the gentle creatures that we treasured as lifelong companions into deadly carriers of the HUNGER virus. Turning them on their owners and destroying millennia old bonds between animal and master."

"Our once great cities have burned and been obliterated; as have our homes, our forests and in some cases our very souls as the HUNGER virus swept from continent to continent. Governments were wiped out; militaries fell, and empires were destroyed when wave after wave of the living dead marched upon their lands. Unlike a conventional army whose ranks would dwindle through the natural attrition of battle, instead, the dead tore through the bone and sinew of every country in the world and their numbers grew. Those poor souls of the recently fallen rose back up to join the ranks of their undead brothers and sisters in battle against their former comrades. In truth, they seemed unstoppable."

"When desperation became the word of the day, world leaders agreed to forfeit their claims on many metropolitan areas throughout the globe. Nuclear weapons were deployed across a large majority of major metropolitan hubs, where people… or those beings that had formally been people, were believed to be the thickest. The hope was that the nuclear firestorms would provide a form of firebreak; that the initial blasts would destroy the walking dead with a massive number of casualties and then the remaining undead could be mopped up by local militia and the other remaining military forces. The world would soon discover that they were very, very wrong."

"Just in the United States alone, nuclear weapons with a minimum of five hundred kiloton yield were deployed in twenty major cities within the first wave of the bombs. New York, Washington DC, Philadelphia, Chicago, Cleveland, Detroit, St. Louis, Miami, Atlanta, New Orleans, Orlando, Dallas, Denver, Los Angeles, Seattle, Phoenix, San Francisco, Salt Lake City, Albuquerque and Memphis all blinked out of existence amidst fiery explosions and devastating concussive force at midnight on October 31; Halloween. The resulting electromagnetic pulses destroyed every non-hardened electrical grid across the country, plunging the northern hemisphere into a darkness of our own design. Nothing mechanical moved. Then as the dust began to settle and the air cleared allowing for visibility, rubble was cast aside and many of the undead that were not fully incinerated simply stood back up. Broken, torn, burned and just as deadly as they had ever been. The few fortunate or perhaps unfortunate depending upon your point of view, pockets of survivors that managed to survive both the initial blast impacts and the resulting firestorms were wiped from the earth as millions of radioactive undead resumed their search for fresh meat. What the world was not prepared for was the resulting amplification of danger, that had been magnified tenfold when the "Zs" that were not at Ground Zero, absorbed massive amounts of radiation and then began to walk away from their former cities. The scientists and theorists who had convinced the President to provide the devastating nuclear option to his own country, had been so convinced that the "Zs" could not survive the initial blast effects, that they never considered the "*what if*" element if a nuclear attack actually failed. Now millions of radiologically and biologically infected undead stalked the countryside. We quite simply made matters worse through our own panic and ignorance."

"Intelligence began to filter in of refugees fleeing attacks from "Zs" in the suburbs of large cities only to fall deathly ill from radiation poisoning. Reports began to flow in of "Zs" that had absorbed so much radiation that their skin had lost all signs of pigmentation, leaving only a glowing, walking skeletal apparition behind. There were tales of the living dead whose touch allegedly burned and whose bite tore and seared the flesh of any living survivors that they found. The United States had gone from bad to worse within forty-eight hours after dropping the twenty megaton bombs across its heartland and the surrounding major cities."

"Worse still, many of the major cities around the world were simply wiped off the map by nuclear strikes of proportions that dwarfed Nagasaki or Hiroshima; all in an effort to staunch the growing tide of undead in those nations. London, Paris, Rome, Tokyo, Buenos Aires, Cairo, Berlin and Moscow were all sanitized by their own militaries. Humans died, "Zs" transformed and could now kill with their radioactive bites, their claws and even just their proximity. We have been extraordinarily fortunate to have not encountered any of these creatures yet here at the Apocalypse Academy."

"As time passed, the survivors of "Z" night formed small pockets of life. Resistance's if you will; to the army of the dead. The children of these survivors often found themselves orphaned shortly after. Abandoned by fate or chance or maybe through that fickle hand of fate they have found new life here at the Apocalypse Academy. Some of those former "*children*" are all of you. The once hapless, hopeless and helpless offspring of deceased parents are now trained to be warriors, tacticians and operational specialists. I am damn proud of you. As you will learn in time, each of you is very, very special. The remaining fragments of government around the globe activated a Special Operations plan that has literally been centuries in preparation. It was called Project: Orphan. I will not bore you with the details of a classified briefing but suffice it to say that there is a specific reason as to why you are here now and more specifically why you have all received the type of training that you have."

"It is my sincerest hope that through not only the combative training that you have received but also through continuing your education, teaching you to conduct a tactical analysis of the undead and by studying the evolutions they portray in their various lifecycles, that we can begin to forge a new life for humanity. To rise from the ashes like the legendary Phoenix to see mankind reborn as masters of the world once again. I ask you all to never forget the destruction that you all saw firsthand on "Z" night and the sacrifices that you have all made to survive and persevere here at the Apocalypse Academy since then."

The Colonel paused long enough to take a long swig of water from a bottle that had been concealed behind the podium where he stood. Replacing the bottle, he continued.

"Make no mistake. The training that you have all received, although invaluable in nature, does not make you invulnerable. Be proud of what you have achieved with your successful graduation from the Apocalypse Academy in its inaugural phase. Wear your patch with honor in memory of those that have died or that were turned and then pacified. Remember, that it was their sacrifice that allowed you to be here today. Be loyal to your team as your lives will continue to depend upon each other. Lastly, never forget all that you've been taught and share that knowledge with the survivors that you come across in the field. For it will only be through the sharing of knowledge that we will help this great nation rebuild itself once again."

"In recognition of this first class, I commissioned a seamstress years ago to create a unique patch for your uniforms. No longer will you wear the blue jumpsuit of the cadet, but the black battle dress uniform of a Special Operations soldier. The handcrafted patch is to be worn on the left breast above the pocket over your heart. It consists of a single red teardrop, crossed from behind by a sword and rifle. In the center of the tear sits a single skull emblazoned with the offset "AA" of the Apocalypse Academy upon its forehead. This patch is symbolic on several levels. The teardrop is for our fallen brothers and sisters. The red is for the blood that was spilt in the rising of "Z" night and in every pacification that we have had to endure since that time. The white of the skull represents our healing from death. The skull's top five teeth are a symbol of the drill sergeants who have taught you to survive in this inaugural class. The five teeth on bottom represent the five squads of warriors that have been trained to fight and to thrive in our apocalyptic world. The "AA" upon the skull's brow serves as a reminder to us all, that this is where we were reborn. Lastly, the crossed sword and rifle behind the skull show us the tools that we will use to take back our world from the grasp of the dead."

"Just as many of you are from different cities, and in some cases different countries, so too are the tactics of your individual squads different. Do not be judgmental of each other and the future stories you will hear as we move forward with the plan to begin a new life for humanity. We will begin here in the United States of America, forging warriors and destroying the dead. Though we have no communications with any other continent, it is our hope to eventually build sister academies in Europe, Asia and South America. Your jobs as we send our teams out into this desperate world are fourfold."

1. Survive.
2. Destroy any undead that you come across, as long as it is safe to do so.
3. Gather intelligence as you move from place to place and share the knowledge of survival that you have garnered here at the Apocalypse Academy.

4. Protect any orphans that you may encounter returning them to the Academy for training as you were all trained.

"After graduation, you will all be granted seven days leave to allow you to relax and unwind. During that time, the team leaders will be approached and advised of your first mission's briefing dates and times. While on leave and prior to receiving your operational briefing, each of you will have a choice to make. Now that your training is complete, you must choose whether you will remain with your team, receiving the protection and supplies of the Apocalypse Academy in return for fulfilling various missions or if you will take on a more individualistic approach and select a career as a Paladin. Paladins answer to no one, choosing to walk the earth alone with the sole intent of destroying the undead. Any cadet voluntarily choosing to become a Paladin will be furnished with a full suit of "ZAP" armor, a long gun and a handgun of choice, two hundred rounds of ammunition divided equally between weapons and a hand-held melee weapon of their choice as well. Paladins are welcome back to the Academy at any time, although the odds of individual survival are significantly lower. Supplies and ammunition can be bought or bartered for, but as a graduate of the Academy the cost will be minimal compared to the black markets of the various survivor groups that you will be forced to do business with out in the "Z" filled world."

"Let us be clear on one point. There is no stigma attached to becoming a Paladin, no-fault and no negativity. There is only a personal desire or maybe an individual need to walk alone. Each one of you will have different reasons for selecting such a path as none of us are clones nor have we experienced the same challenges in life. If you wish to select this route, please advise your drill sergeant before the seven days of R&R is complete so that we may provide a proper ceremony of farewell to those brave and individualistic souls as they walk out of the Academy grounds on Damnation Road."

"I will close on this note. Whether you believe in fate or karma or just plain old luck, each of you has survived the rising of the dead for a specific purpose. You have all been given the knowledge, skills and training to survive and bring pacification to our world. In the ancient world it was called the Agoge. It was an ancient Greek training system that taught children from a very young age to become the world's most fearsome warriors. We, here at the Apocalypse Academy have adopted that principle and have passed that knowledge onto all of you. Use it wisely. If the time comes when you have been infected or you find yourself facing insurmountable odds, do not sell your soul cheaply. Fight until the last round has been chambered and delivered in a lead hailstorm of death to the walking dead and then find your own peace through the pacification of yourself, or at the hand of a friend or teammate rather than allowing yourself to become an abomination to life and a carrier of the HUNGER virus."

"Again, I am proud of you all. To face all that you have faced individually, as untrained civilians, was staggering and in many cases almost unbelievable. To be willing to place your personal losses and fears aside in order to learn to survive in this time of hell on earth is a feat worthy of the epics that have been written about the greatest warriors of history such as Hercules, Odysseus, Perseus, Sinbad and many others. Time will tell if the deeds of your lives will be annotated in writing as theirs were. The drill sergeants and I congratulate you. Well done!"

The Colonel quietly folded his notes and returned them to his jacket's interior pocket. A single person, somewhere within the ranks of the cadets, began to clap. This was almost immediately followed by several more sets of hands every second or so. Thirty seconds later the entire cadet class as well as the drill sergeants were all avidly applauding for their senior leader. A man who, through his vision of preparation, had been prepared to offer the people subordinate to him, both soldier and cadet; opportunities to survive in the New World.

Sergeant Stone left his position at the top of the stairs and came to stand beside the Colonel, still applauding as he walked. Arriving at the Colonel's side, the drill sergeant held up a single hand motioning for quiet and the applause immediately died away. The drill sergeant spoke loudly and clearly. His voice echoed against the band shell and was projected by the structure's natural acoustics.

"In nineteen eighty-six, the then President of the United States; Ronald Reagan, commissioned the redesign and supplemental structural creation of both the high school and National Guard armory in his former hometown of Dixon, Illinois in an effort to ensure that the structure could withstand the severe weather that occasionally comes to the Midwestern United States. Structures were reinforced on the interior with steel girders and concrete joisting to withstand winds in excess of three hundred miles per hour and impact resistant enough to stay standing in the event of anything short of a direct nuclear blast. This reconstruction is well documented within the city's downtown archives."

"What is also well documented but little-known to the general public is that the President also signed a classified

Presidential Order selecting a Special Operations veteran by the name of Second Lieutenant Armbruster Slade and assigning him as Commandant of the National Guard Armory and these emergency facilities. For more than forty years, that order has stood and Second Lieutenant Slade quietly became First Lieutenant Slade, then Captain Slade, then Major Slade, light Colonel Slade and eventually Colonel Slade. So many of you will ask how a man, assigned to a seemingly mundane duty could progress in rank at all, much less as quickly as this man did. To be promoted within the first round of eligibility every time and *willingly* renew his obligation to watch over an armory and what was perceived to be a simple high school bomb shelter out in the middle of corn country, rather than being deployed around the globe in glorious pursuit of evils to purge, terrorists to hunt and dictators to overthrow."

"The answer was simple. In nineteen eighty-four, then President Reagan received an intelligence report from the Department of Defense. Within that report, was a vivid description of an experimental medical process that was progressing towards the successful reanimation of dead tissues by application of viral bonding with an experimental prion based organic material. The organic material was a type of congealed jelly-like substance that had come into being as a byproduct of the massive Hadron Collider experiments in Europe. Funding, although primarily sought through the Department of Defense, was also requested through the Center for Disease Control or CDC as it was known through its acronym."

"Initial testing yielded mild successes. Soldiers suffering from gangrenous wounds voluntarily submitted to become test subjects, with the hope that the experimental processes would be successful in saving their ravaged limbs.

Approximately 12 percent of that population was considered a success with mobility and usage being re-attained by the afflicted soldiers, although certain modifications or mutations were noted by the scientists. These structural changes were studied and considered benign with the benefits of the serum far outweighing any potential hazard that could be observed by some book worm in a laboratory. The program was met with high regard at an international level and coveted by almost every military in every government around the globe. Conversations about the application of the virus on a grand scale such as a battlefield cure for trauma began to occur at levels even beyond the President's knowledge. Being able to return twelve percent of your fighting men to the field of battle would be a huge boon to any country's defenses. Funding was provided through overt and covert sources as every major scientific community sought to replicate the viral serum without placing the necessary safeguards in place. Then came the secondary analysis results and our world began its self-destructive spiral."

"Of the six hundred seventy test subjects in America, Europe and China, a large majority fell ill within weeks of inoculation with intense flulike symptoms. Coughing, fever, chest congestion and burning of the eyes and throat struck virtually every candidate. Symptomatically, the viral attack was similar in nature to Marburg Hemorrhagic Fever which directly attacks the volunteer's nervous systems. Crushing spasms wracked the individual infected bodies and seizures followed as everything from the tear ducts to the small muscle groups began to collapse into chaos."

"The only relief for the infected came through the ingestion of red meat. Meat, but not meat products seemed to retard the devastating infection. These victims ate usually rare and sometimes even raw meat which seemed to be processed in a separate area within the stomach, pancreas and intestines for the virus to attack rather than the carrier's own musculature. When red meat could not be obtained in sufficient quantities or if the wait was more than the infected individual could tolerate, they began to look for new meat sources. Domestic animals disappeared first, and concerns about wild animal attacks filled the headlines. Then the infected found one food source that was both bountiful and by the majority, quite helpless. They began to attack humans. With a singular, dedicated mindset and pain receptors blocked by a need to feed on the red blood cells and tissues of their fellow man, these poor souls, all six hundred seventy of them, became our first "Reapers". The first of the "Z" plague that would destroy the world."

"Drill sergeant!" Techno called out. "Are you telling us that we unleashed the HUNGER virus on purpose, number one and that the Reapers are not really "Zs" at all because they're not really dead, just infected?"

Sergeant Stone ignored the improprieties of how the questions were asked, preferring to focus on the answers instead. He had expected at least a moderate amount of concern to be voiced by the cadets when he gave them his speech.

"Yes cadet… to both questions but only partially so. I will continue and perhaps you will all understand."

Techno nodded and said nothing else.

"If you recall, I said that the virus was injected to affect *dead* tissue. Although the subsequent side effects of blood rage and hunger for red meat were notable, the study was for the regeneration or perhaps more accurately rejuvenation of dead flesh. That is why the initial project and viral strain were coded as "Prometheus" after the Greek Titan who had an eagle eat his liver each day only to regenerate it on the following morning. He was also a figure who represented human striving, particularly for scientific knowledge and the risk of overreaching our intended consequences."

"The infected do not become "Zs" of either the Reaper, Romero or Husk typing without several conditions being initially met. First and foremost, the individual must die. Denied red meat the individuals became savage. Scientists worked continuously to find a cure, but in the end they failed. After several lab attacks on scientists where the creatures burst their restraints and killed the staff, the decision was made to pull the plug on the program and destroy the test subjects. Every one of the individuals were executed in the most humane way possible and the bodies were shipped off to Bethesda for study, vivisection and dissection. In every case, the neural pathways and synapses had ceased functioning and the bodies began to degenerate. As you know, muscles, depending on the extent of the wounds the victim suffered at the time of death will become rigid, accepting the various stages of mortise. We also know that minimal electrical impulses carry on within the body for a time after death and can be observed through the growth of nails and hair after a person's demise. To the best of our scientists' knowledge, it is at this stage when the HUNGER virus becomes the dominant factor within the host as the virus replicates within the dying nervous system. For an unknown reason, the virus attaches directly to what are called "Z particles" A name that believe it or not existed before the dead walked the earth. A "Z" particle is a nanoparticle that acts upon all known subatomic particles in a person's body."

"Z" particles specifically are theorized to be linked to a body's rate of decay. They were originally found to exist during the nineteen eighty-three higher energy proton – antiproton collision experiments at the European Organization for Nuclear Research. Though the leading scientists were awarded the Nobel Prize for physics the following year, perhaps a more in-depth study of their nanoparticle would have been commissioned if they had known of its future impact in the destruction of humanity."

"All six hundred and seventy first generation Reapers had been systematically destroyed and President Reagan ordered all files on Project Prometheus sealed and locked away, deeming them to be a threat to all of mankind. Media coverage of the attacks was squashed or spun to include dozens of different storylines. In short, the President felt that this would, if released, be an extinction level event for the entire planet. It was officially labeled a war crime to be engaging in further development of the Prometheus virus with sanctions against the whole country if even one scientist delved into this forbidden lore. Fear and good judgment ruled, and all of the files stayed sealed."

"Fast-forwarding twenty-eight years to two thousand and twelve. The current President was up for reelection after a mediocre first term in office in which many of his opponents claimed he was elected for his race rather than his political skills. Seeking a catalyst to act as the figurehead for his National Health Insurance Plan which was key for him in his efforts of reelection, the President ordered every file to be reopened and re-examined by the scientific brain trust in an effort to spark interest and support. "Z" particles again came into the news, as the media puppets espoused the "*miracle of the modern age.*" Every security lesson from the previous generations that had studied Project: Prometheus were swept away in a media campaign that sold the "Z" particle therapy through pharmaceutical companies as a cure for everything from the common cold to cancer, to Aids, to old age and even ulcers. Numerous "Z" particle products began to surface on the open market without the approval of the FDA. Medical cures entered the market to be sold as the miracle drug to end all drugs and of course the President of the United States of America had taken full credit for the wonder drugs' research, development and testing; claiming that it was all a byproduct of his National healthcare program to make America stronger..."

"Through political censorship and strong-arm tactics with the FDA, the drug was sanctioned and immediately available only through participation in the national health plan initiative. The initial outcry of support, driven solely by the availability of the regenerate care from the drug in the presence of the National Health Plan was similar to the expressions of love that crack whores and junkies often had for their pimps. The President marched along his campaign trail, handily crushing the Republican and independent opponents at every rally. Debates were almost pointless as very few people were willing to face the political juggernaut that was in motion thanks to the National Health Plan and its association with the now officially labeled drug; Prometheum Z40. By October first, the primaries for the presidential campaign had been completed and the expectation was that in another two months, the incumbent President of the United States would be reelected to a second term of office in a landslide victory."

"On October fifteenth, less than six months after the first dosage of Prometheum Z40 was provided to supporters of the national health plan, the virus mutated bonding at the

"Z" particle level to the brains and nervous systems of the people that had taken the miracle drug. Hunger driven Reapers by the thousands raged through the streets, ripping and tearing and eating anyone that they came in contact with. The National Guard was called upon to quell what was originally thought to be civil unrest; they were slaughtered. On October Twenty-fifth, the President went on television and declared an official state of emergency for the United States. He went on to say that communications with several countries had ceased and that the American people should take caution when and if they were confronted by one of these diseased individuals. The people were reassured that the CDC and the World Health Organization were both investigating the outbreak of this unknown disease and that all would be well as long as the American people stayed strong in this hour of darkness. Two days later, the president's wife, several members of his cabinet as well as the senior scientist from the CDC were slaughtered on board Air Force One as it flew above the Atlantic Ocean enroute from Washington DC to the CDC headquarters in Atlanta Georgia. As best as could be ascertained from the frantic calls for help by the pilot and copilot; at least two Secret Service agents had been infected, either through personal use of the Prometheum Z40 drug or by bites from infected individuals while defending the First Lady in route to Air Force One. The pilot's final call for help ended in a bloody gurgle as one of the agents tore his throat out, his hand spasming on the microphone key. Two minutes later, the wife of the POTUS, several of the Joint Chiefs of Staff and the scientist of the CDC perished, regardless of the state of infection, as the enormous aircraft crashed into the ocean and disintegrated into a million fiery pieces."

"So, when the "Z" particle or prion that had been used to create Prometheum Z40 bonded at a molecular level with the mutated strains of hemorrhagic fever that would eventually become the HUNGER virus, the scientists' did not even know where to look for a cure. The living dead existed only in science fiction and horror movies. There was no precedent for such a creature in modern science. Humanity died by the thousands in the first day, millions by the end of the first week. Militaries were called to arms and martial law was declared in every town across every nation. But those actions were for human beings and laws meant little to the infected who rose back up and sought only to eat the flesh of the living. Reapers were killed by the millions, in every country around the world. Blood soaked with the "Z" particle-based Hunger virus sank into the ground, dripped into waterways and ran by the gallons into drains and sluice ways. The first Romero's rose two days later, as if Hell had reached its rental capacity for souls and it was spilling its excess dead back out into the gutters of the world. Death, decayed muscle and a lack of motor coordination did nothing to stanch the hunger that the creatures felt as a Romero. As such, the low agonized moan of eternal damnation and everlasting pain became the battle cry of the risen dead."

"The Romero's were far worse than the Reapers in that you can put a Reaper down temporarily with a heart shot or a broken back; long enough to deliver the coup de grace to the undead creature's brain. Although their nerve conductors and pain receptors were dulled, they were still freshly dead flesh and as such could be destroyed much more similarly to the living. Romero's had no such restrictions. Wounds that would maim or kill a living person, as you all learned in class, held no damage for the decayed, walking corpses. So, humanity was again taken by surprise as the waves of Romero's washed over the survivors, slowly devouring everything and everyone in their path. Millions more survivors fell before the raging onslaught of the animated corpses as they methodically plodded forward; never stopping, never fearing retaliation from the living."

"Religious men of all dominations gathered their flocks to their churches proclaiming the "End of Days" and the coming of the prophesized rapture and revelations from the Bible, Torah and Koran. Truth to be told, perhaps they were right. Perhaps the world is ending, one bloody bite at a time. However, assembling hundreds of weeping and praying people without any firepower to protect them was like ringing the dinner bell for the undead. The slaughter was merciless. Blood and torn flesh splattered pews, crucifixes and altars as if pagan rituals had been performed on the once holy grounds. To this day the undead thrive heavily in the religious structures around the country and around the world and are to be avoided at all costs."

"Interestingly, it was in these church slaughters that we first saw the appearance of the separate two types of Husks. Many churches had adjoining graveyards. One type of Husks is now believed to be the reanimated corpses of the more distant dead. Dried out, desiccated; the Husks clawed their way painstakingly out of the rotting coffins, graves and tombs as the HUNGER virus permeated the soil. Advanced rot had destroyed their bodies and eliminated all bodily fluids thus making them brittle and extremely slow-moving. The second type of Husk is believed to be originally a Reaper or a Romero that has had no exposure to fresh flesh and blood and has subsequently dried up like their grave rising cousins. So brittle were these corpses that a single bullet, regardless of caliber, maybe even a BB gun, would generally cause them to burst in a puff of brownish yellow dust. This initially was cause for celebration amongst the survivors. Husks were easy to kill. Just walk up and punch one. What no one realized was that the puff of yellowish–brown dust was the HUNGER virus becoming airborne. So now the infected had three distinct cycles: fast-moving carriers in the Reapers, relentless animated walkers in the Romero's and immobile, undead dried-up corpses that carried the airborne virus in the Husks. Humanity as we once knew it seemed doomed."

"Through it all, Colonel Slade followed the official orders that he had been given directly by the President of the United States thirty years prior. The Armory was stockpiled with every type of weapon and ammunition as instructed in his briefing. The building of the high school had been transformed and refitted with roll down, locking metal storm shutters under the financial support and guidance of the Federal Emergency Management Agency stating the need to protect the children from natural disasters such as tornadoes and river flooding when classes were in session. Food stores were filled to capacity deep underground, stockpiling and securing thousands of canned goods, MREs and bottles of drinking water. Electric and manual pumps were driven into deep wells under the school grounds to provide secondary water sources and uniforms began to arrive by the truckload. The supplies were never delivered in a military vehicle though. They always arrived in either a nondescript moving truck or a local department store delivery van."

"Thanks to his devotion to duty, your survival and your training were able to be precipitated here at the Apocalypse Academy over the last twelve weeks. Without the Colonel, we would all probably be dead or maybe worse. Furthermore, it was his vision to seek out the children in accordance with Project: Orphan and to bring them here for shelter. It was his hope to give all of you a chance to learn how to survive in this new horrific world and to prepare you all to fight back when the time came. We all owe him a great debt of gratitude and loyalty for his unswerving devotion to our survival. So, as you receive your blood patch today, never forget the lessons of the Apocalypse Academy and its Commandant. Know your enemy, be devoted to the cause of survival, be faithful to your team and be dedicated to finding the orphans of the world so that they may get the same benefit from the Academy that you all have!"

An impromptu cheer erupted from the transfixed formation of former cadets. Even those individuals that were normally somewhat shy and reserved like Dancer were roaring madly like a Celtic war party getting ready to charge into battle. For the first time since his arrival at the Apocalypse Academy, Spartan saw the camaraderie that could only be exhibited by the living. Cadets cheered and celebrated both the Commandant and the drill sergeant's rousing speeches. High fives were exchanged as the now former cadets acknowledged their Commander's years of personal sacrifice.

From beside Spartan a formal command was barked. "Alpha team: attention!"

With a quickness that spoke of reflex rather than thought, the team complied instantly silencing the jovial mood. Sergeant Hogg stood beside Spartan, grinning like a madman in his immaculate uniform and smelling of booze. Probably rum if Spartan had to guess.

"File by column to the Colonel, present arms, and receive your blood patch!"

Spartan executed a textbook sharp right face maneuver and began to march towards the side of the bandstand, opposite of where the remaining drill sergeants stood. Moving briskly but formally across the stage, Spartan stopped directly in front of the Colonel, executed another right face so that he stood face-to-face with the Apocalypse Academy's Commanding Officer and brought up a crisp salute. The tip of his middle finger barely touched the bottom rim of his beret that sat upon his brow. He waited for the Colonel to return salute.

Returning the gesture, the Colonel lowered his salute and extended his right hand to Spartan. "You would've made a good soldier even without "Zs" to fight Spartan. Congratulations."

Spartan shook the pro-offered hand. The grip was strong and sure. "Thank you, Sir."

"You're welcome," the Colonel replied handing Spartan his crimson teardrop shaped patch. "Lead them well."

"I will, Sir."

Spartan saluted again and walked to the end of the stage waiting for the rest of his team. Freak led the way followed by Dancer, Techno and finally Deadeye. As one they walked past the drill sergeants, shaking congratulatory hands as they walked. Sergeant Havoc was last in line, but never moved to shake Spartan's hand, instead glaring at him with contempt and barely concealed hatred.

"Is there a problem Sergeant?" The slightly slurred familiar voice of Sergeant Hogg asked. "You did hear the Colonel's words 'bout being one big happy family, right? So why don't you just man up, grow a set of balls and shake the boy's hand… for old times' sake. Never know when sumthin' evils gonna jump up and take a bite outta your ass. Then you might not even get a chance to tell the sum'bitch goodbye."

Despite being slightly drunk, there was an underlying tone of malice in the burly drill sergeant's voice. A unique timbre that hinted less than subtly of mayhem, violence and smiley face stickers. Whatever it was, Sergeant Havoc seemed to recognize it and wanted no part of it. Reaching out, he grasped Spartan's hand.

"Yes, you just never know what evil will find you, do you boy?" The Echo team's drill sergeant said his voice just above a whisper. "You should watch your back out there." Then let go of the corporal's hand.

Spartan felt as though he'd just let go of boa constrictor's tail. Cold, clammy and calculating. The look that the sergeant wore on his face matched the grip of his hand. Almost reptilian with no emotion or expression. Spartan withdrew his hand and led his team, patches in hand, back to their assigned spots at the front of the formation. So, it went, cadet by cadet until each and every one of them had stood before the Colonel and received their Apocalypse Academy's badge of honor.

Looking out at the assembled squads with obvious pride, Slade spoke again. "Lastly, we have two final honors to bestow. Drill Sergeant of the Cycle and Cadet of the Cycle. What makes these awards worthwhile apart from the obvious prestige associated with them; is the right of the recipients to request any one item from the Academy storeroom or if unavailable there, from the future scavenging trip to what was once Chicago."

"So, without further ado, the selections as nominated by their peers are as follows."

A long pause ensued as the Colonel remove the white envelope from his jacket and began to open it. Nervous shifting could be heard as several of the former cadets eagerly anticipated the award like it was an Oscar or something. Spartan wondered to himself if Cutter was delusional enough to think he actually had a chance at receiving such a prestigious honor.

"The Drill Sergeant of the Cycle… is… Sergeant Hogg! Congratulations Sergeant Hogg, do you have a request at this time?"

"Sir, actually I have one statement and then one request if that is acceptable Sir."

"Of course, Sergeant, make your statement and follow it with your request."

"Number one, what candy-assed, mamby-pamby, rainbow wearing, horse loving, son of a turd biscuit put me in for this award? I hope they ain't expectin' no kisses fer it. Number two… where do you keep the rum?"

The entire crowd laughed. Everyone knew how much stress and strain Sergeant Hogg had been under since the death of Band-Aid. It was good to see him lighten up a little. The Colonel cleared his throat and the laughter and clamor quieted down. The Cadet of the Cycle was a big deal. Everyone wanted to be recognized as the best Cadet of not only the inaugural class but also of the entire Apocalypse Academy. From the back of the room Spartan could hear Cutter say something to the tune that "this was going to be his award." The thought made Spartan snort under his breath. As if they would allow a preppy psychopath like that to win the most prestigious award at the Academy.

"And the Cadet of the Cycle… goes to… Cadet Spartan! Alpha team leader! Corporal Spartan you have a request at this time?"

Amidst all the clamor and congratulatory backslapping, Spartan managed to reply. "Yes, sir I do. However, it's not so much a thing but a what."

"I see that your drill sergeant's manner of speaking has worn off on you. Continue."

"I would like to be allowed to select the first mission from the Apocalypse Academy for both my team and the Academy at large."

The Colonel looked sharply at Corporal Spartan. "Granted and congratulations."

"The boy made a good choice." Spartan heard Sergeant Hogg grunt off to the side of the platform. "But I ain't sharing my rum with him …

SERGEANT STONE'S CADENCE:

Momma, momma can't you see,
What the Academy's done to me.

They gave me a new ID,
Now I'm known by that only.

Momma, momma can't you see,
What the Academy's done to me.

They took away my favorite shoes,
Now I wear Academy blue.

Momma, momma can't you see,
What the Academy's done to me.

I used to date beauty queens,
Now I'm hunting Z's with my M-16.

Momma, momma can't you see,
What the Academy's done to me.

Reapers, Romeros and a Husk,
I hunt the Zs from dawn to dusk.

Momma, momma can't you see,
What the Academy's done to me.

EPILOGUE
WRATH OF A DEMON KING

Xerxes grabbed a lesser horned demon by the throat and hoisted it effortlessly in a single clawed hand. Grasping the black scaled creature by the thigh he effortlessly tore the demon in half, casting its remains behind him into the molten lava in a fit of rage. There, the halves of the beast sizzled and melted as the damned soul was obliterated into nothingness.

Why had there been no report from the Baron? Why had the Academy not yet fallen beneath the horde of the undead? His spies had revealed that the soldiers of this "*Apocalypse Academy*" were gaining in both numbers and in strength. This could not be allowed. They must be wiped out before they could deliver a hope of deliverance to the masses. They must be utterly destroyed before they could display a human spirit filled with determination to survive and a willingness to fight against his demonic forces.

With a savage growl that terrified the lesser horned demon vassals that surrounded him and caused them to skitter away in abject terror, Xerxes ordered a flame portal to be opened so that he could speak to his general. Red scaled demons wove sorcerer spells of communication that breached space through the lava pools, flaring them up into a nigh living curtain of raging flames. Within moments the combined sorcery of the red demons had opened the flame portal and they now continually fed the flames the damned souls of humans to maintain the unholy connection. Through a shimmering haze of heat, the Red Baron's kneeling visage came into the Demon King's view.

"My great and all-powerful Lord, how may I serve you?"

The Red Baron kept his head bowed low in subservience, not daring to look upon the Demon King. Whatever reason Xerxes had for calling out to him from Hell, it was best not to risk his wrath.

"You have not done as I commanded. The Apocalypse Academy still stands! Why have you failed me?" The Demon King's voice drove through the Red Baron's mind as surely as if it had been an arrow fired from a composite bow. An unabated scream of agony shrieked from the Baron's mouth and blood began to flow freely from his eyes, nose and ears.

"Oh, Greatest of Kings!" The Red Baron forced the words from between his clenched teeth. The pain was beyond exquisite. "We… are marshalling to the north… of the academy even now. We have… amassed a vast army of both the living…and the dead! Soon… we shall…destroy the humans…utterly and completely…as is your will!"

The Baron crumbled to the ground, his bloody face and body prostrated in the dirt, curling like a scorpion being touched by a flame.

"Do not fail me General! The penalty for your failure would be so much more than your pitiful mortal shell. I shall shred your very demonic essence into scraps that the hounds of Hell shall feast upon for a thousand years!"

The Red Baron was nearly incapable of speech. His body quaked beneath the psychic assault of the Demon King's speech. It was a noise that no human ears were ever meant to hear. The Demon King's power held no peer in the realms of Hell and was only ruled by the Lord of Death directly.

The Baron gasped for breath, snot and blood bubbling from his nose. The information he possessed may have one of two possible responses when he shared it with the Demon King. He would either be granted reprieve or he would be destroyed. Summoning all of his will, he slowly rose back to both knees.

"Milord…Our spies have revealed from a competent source that every member of the Apocalypse Academy all share a common ancestry…"

The Baron paused. There was no other way to impart the intelligence other than just to say it. Steeling himself for the Demon King's wrath, he clenched his teeth and continued.

"…The Apocalypse Academy are all blood descendants of the original three hundred Spartan warriors who stood against you at the Hot Gates of ancient Greece. They are the descendants of the men of King Leonidas of Sparta!"

Psychic energy blew outward as the Demon King roared in anger. Rage filled Hell fires blew upward from the magma pools causing the very walls to tremble and demons and damned human souls alike were cast out into the flames by the psychic lashing. Xerxes' own Demon Lord essence protruded from his hate filled face. Great horns of bone ripped the flesh of his brow and scales of red and black tainted his skin. A dozen fangs the size of daggers tore through his gums and muscle rippled and expanded across his body, destroying the ornate golden chains and bracelets that had hung from his brow, neck, and wrists. In anger he dug a clawed hand into the black basalt wall, tearing loose a massive chunk and casting them into the lava. His now reptilian eyes savagely bore into the Red Baron though his eyes were still closed, filling his soul with hopelessness and despair.

Acidic saliva dripped from the elongated tongue that lashed about outside of Xerxes' mouth, hissing on the hardened lava beneath the clawed feet. A thick reptilian tail lashed outward, striking an obsidian pillar with such force that the black rock shattered into shards.

For a long moment the Baron feared that the Demon King would strike him down in his uncontrolled rage. Dozens of lesser demons had been destroyed in the earliest moments of the King's unbridled fury.

"I want their heads! All of them! Destroy every brick! Rend every stone! Tear them all to pieces! But bring me their heads! We will feast once and for all upon their life essences and completely eliminate the threat of Sparta once and for all! When you are through, I want there to be no trace nor record of the Apocalypse Academy having ever existed!"

Without another word the connection to the pit of Hell was severed and the Red Baron was left in silence. Wiping his bloodied mouth and nose upon his sleeve, he rose unsteadily up to his feet. He had his orders. The Apocalypse Academy would fall in the bloodiest way possible.

About the Author

Anthony C. Kallas II has always been lived his life as a life of action. Out of high school he was recruited as a multi-sport athlete. He has also been a soldier and a Counterintelligence agent for the United States Army. In addition to spending numerous years in Law Enforcement which included being a nationally certified SWAT instructor, he finally ended his career with the Department of Homeland Security as the Assistant Federal Security Director.

He is an avid weightlifter, staunch supporter of Law Enforcement and have a sincere love of Role-Playing Games. Dark Origins is the first book The Apocalypse Academy trilogy. This is the author's first book.

The Apocalypse Academy will return in Book 2:

For Duty and Humanity

Made in the USA
Coppell, TX
23 June 2021